RAVES FOR
JAMES PATTERSON

The
Horsewoman

For a complete list of books, visit
JamesPatterson.com.

The
Horsewoman

————— *A Novel* —————

James Patterson
& Mike Lupica

GRAND CENTRAL

New York Boston

Grand Central Publishing
Hachette Book Group
1290 Avenue of the Americas, New York, NY 10104
grandcentralpublishing.com
twitter.com/grandcentralpub

Originally published in hardcover and ebook by Little, Brown & Company in January 2022
First oversize mass market edition: September 2023

Grand Central Publishing is a division of Hachette Book Group, Inc. The Grand Central Publishing name and logo is a trademark of Hachette Book Group, Inc.

The publisher is not responsible for websites (or their content) that are not owned by the publisher.

The Hachette Speakers Bureau provides a wide range of authors for speaking events. To find out more, go to hachettespeakersbureau.com or email HachetteSpeakers@hbgusa.com.

Grand Central Publishing books may be purchased in bulk for business, educational, or promotional use. For information, please contact your local bookseller or the Hachette Book Group Special Markets Department at special.markets@hbgusa.com.

ISBNs: 9781538752944 (oversize mass market), 9780316499781 (ebook)

Printed in the United States of America

OPM

10 9 8 7 6 5 4 3 2 1

*This book could not have been written
without Taylor and Hannah Lupica,
mother and daughter, whose love for
show jumping, and for each other,
informs every page of our book.*

—M. L.

The
Horsewoman

"Little (Horse) Woman"
YouTube.com
1.5 million views
Originally posted: January 15, 2012

THE VIDEO SHOWS a little girl alone in her bedroom. Maybe she is ten years old, maybe a bit older than that. As we watch her, she carefully places a small stool in front of her full-length mirror. The camera pans to shelves filled with trophies and walls papered with brightly colored ribbons, almost all imprinted with the image of a horse.

As she turns slightly, we see that one of the ribbons is hanging from a string around her neck. She squares herself in front of the plastic stool, as if about to step onto a medal stand, then pauses to reach down and press a button on her phone.

We hear our national anthem begin to play. Now the girl, her long hair in a ponytail, beautiful face solemn, places a hand over her heart, and stands at attention.

That girl was me once.

Then I grew up.

It's like one of my trainers would tell me, much later:

Shit happens.

ONE

EVEN IN A HORSE FAMILY, I was the black sheep.

I was late getting to the barn the morning everything changed, for me and for all of us. Even the horses.

It was said at Atwood Farm that I was operating on Becky Standard Time. BST. Whenever I made excuses for being late, my trainer, Daniel, shortened it to BS.

New Year's Eve was still a few days away, but today my reason was simple enough: I'd been out way too late the night before and ended up crashing at a friend's house, where I'd blown through two alarms on my phone.

Sunday night was party night for the horse people in Wellington, a Florida town built around the horse business—the Winter Equestrian Festival, the dressage show across Southshore Boulevard, and the Masters Series for jumpers at Deeridge Farm.

There were no events at the WEF on Monday or Tuesday, so I headed out with riders and trainers and grooms and owners, even the polo players who'd spent the weekend competing at the International Polo Club. I was one of those college kids who liked to party.

I hadn't learned anything about riding last night.

But I had woken up with the Monday-morning lesson that drinking tequila with polo players makes me feel as if one of them had taken a mallet and hit me in the head.

My name is Becky McCabe. Short for Rebecca. Just Rebecca of Sunnybrook Farm—one of the stories my mom used to read to me when I was little—but Rebecca of Atwood Farm, owned by my grandmother, Caroline Atwood.

She'd never been a Granny or Gran or some other nickname. That wasn't her. She was just "Grandmother." Or "Caroline." Nothing more cuddly than that. "The grandmother," like it was her official position, was another way I thought of her, maybe the way that described her best.

"Your mother's on her way to the Olympics," Grandmother had said the night before. "And you're on your way to the bar."

I'd grown up watching her stop horses in the ring with just the snap of her voice, like she was cracking a whip. I once told her during an argument that she was a lot like those horses—only they were nicer.

"I'm not Mom," I said.

"Not exactly breaking news at this point," Grandmother said.

"You keep forgetting I'm twenty-one, Grandmother," I said.

"And proud of it," she said.

She was seventy-two, proud that she still owned the barn that she and her late husband, Clint, a legendary horseman, my grandfather, had built together. She was still a great beauty, even in an Atwood Farm navy windbreaker, jeans, and boots, her steel-gray hair pulled into a ponytail. I could see Mom in her. And myself.

Now I was pulling into the driveway at nine thirty—no one at Atwood Farm's definition of an early start time—having just blown through a couple of lights on Southshore Boulevard, hoping this might be the one morning of the whole year—or of her whole life—when my mom, Maggie, had gotten a late start on her trail ride.

No chance.

Noticing again how run-down our barn looked from the outside, I ran for the tack room, where I kept spare riding clothes in a locker. One of our grooms, Emilio, was leaning against the wall where the bridles were hung, arms crossed in front of him and sadly shaking his head.

"You got left behind, *chiquita,*" Emilio said.

"How long ago did she leave?"

He pulled out his phone and squinted at it.

"Thirty-one minutes," he said. "And counting."

"How pissed was she?" I said.

"Not any more than usual," he said.

"You think I should try to catch up with her?"

"Was me, *chiquita?*" Emilio said, grinning at me now. "I would saddle up on Sky and start riding south and maybe not be stopping until I got to the Florida Keys."

Sky was my horse. My baby. Technically she was a gray, even dark gray as a foal. But more white now. A Dutch warmblood. Riding horse bred to be a jumper. Smaller than Mom's horse, Coronado, by a lot. We'd found out about her from a trainer moving back to Ireland. When I saw her, I'd fallen in love with her after riding her just one time. All it took.

Mom and Dad were divorced by then, and we couldn't afford to buy another horse. But when I told

Dad about Sky, he bought her for me. Called it an early birthday present. Now the little horse was my best friend in the world.

Sky seemed to love me just the way I was. I loved her even more fiercely back. She didn't want me to work harder, or win more, or party less. Or wake up earlier. It didn't matter to her that Maggie Atwood had been a champion from the time she'd been the age I was now.

She was Atwood, by the way, and I was McCabe because she'd given up my dad's name after the divorce. I'd kept it. People sometimes wondered if we were even related.

Oh, Sky and I had won our share of jumping events over the years. At our best, we were a perfect, fearless match. Even after Sky had knocked down a rail or two and taken us out of the running for a ribbon, I'd come out of the ring and see that our time was five seconds faster than anybody else's. And as hard as I tried, I couldn't feel sad about that.

It was why my trainer, Daniel, had taken to calling me Maverick, after the character Tom Cruise played in *Top Gun*.

"You have the need," he'd said, "for speed."

"I'm not still in pony camp," I'd said. "I just don't know what I want to be when I grow up."

"When?" he'd said. "Or if?"

Where I pushed boundaries, Mom was precise. We were all sure she'd be riding Coronado in the Olympics in Paris late next summer. She was one of the best riders in the country. Trying to prove she was one of the best in the world.

Mom only went as fast as she needed to when she was in the ring. Even when one of her horses refused a jump at the last second, I had never seen her fall off.

Other riders, sure. It had happened to me plenty of times. Her? Never.

In every area of life, she stayed in her lane, and excelled there. She wasn't reckless. Didn't take chances. Even when she and Coronado got a bad start in the ring, I'd watch her figure things out in the next half minute. Sometimes sooner. Like she'd hit a reset button.

We didn't need a handyman at Atwood Farm as long as Mom was around. If something broke, she put it back together. A saddle. A bridle. A spur.

Wonder Woman, the horsewoman.

Don't get me wrong: We loved each other. A lot. We were just different.

A lot.

It's why Mom and Grandmother—and Daniel— believed that Sky and I weren't at our best often enough, that I wasn't the champion they needed me to be.

One of the beauties of our sport is that men and women compete against each other, from the time they're teenagers until some of them are past sixty.

Maggie Atwood didn't only aspire to being an Olympic equestrian, she was a serious gym rat. She was on the clock with an exercise class, followed by a session at the gym, and a massage booked for after that. She couldn't afford to waste precious minutes waiting for me.

Another time fault for Becky McCabe.

Emilio said he'd throw a saddle on Sky. In the bathroom next to the tack room, I got into my riding pants and boots and helmet, came out and took the reins from Emilio and started walking Sky toward the schooling ring. It was then that I heard shouting, saw Daniel and Emilio running toward the main road.

Then I saw why.

Mom's horse, Coronado, her ride to the Olympics, was coming straight for them, at full gallop, as if he were the one feeling the need for speed.

Daniel took charge, motioning for Emilio to fan out from the out-of-control horse, protect themselves from being trampled.

No shouting from them now. They had their arms out in front of them, trying to calm Coronado, slow him down.

Usually that would have been the rider's job.

Mom's job.

But Coronado's saddle was empty.

TWO

"HE KNEW ENOUGH to come home," Daniel said to me.

Home meant the barn.

One firm barn rule was that nobody went out on a trail ride alone. Mom had just done it — her idea of being a maverick. Now I had to break that same rule if I had any chance of saving her.

In my heart I knew that if the situation were reversed, Mom would jump on Sky and ride all the way to the Florida turnpike and back if that's what it took to find me.

Now I jumped off Sky, handed her reins to George, one of the other grooms, and moved closer to Daniel and Emilio, keeping my distance, not wanting Coronado to spook more than he already had.

Then Daniel slowly reached for the horse's bridle, talking softly to him in Spanish now. As he did, I came in behind them and put a foot in the stirrup closest to me.

"Let me go find her," Daniel said.

"No," I said.

He put his hand on my arm. I looked down, glaring his hand away.

"My mom," I said. "Her horse."

We had a brief stare-down, until he nodded and let go of the bridle.

Emilio gave me a leg up into the saddle. Mom's saddle. Her horse. They were connected in the same way I was connected to Sky.

When I was on Sky and trying to get the distance between jumps exactly right, I was never really sure how much of it was me and how much of it was a combination of her breeding and training and instinct and even muscle memory. In those moments of trust between horse and rider, it was as if we were sharing one brain.

There was always a mystery, even some magic, to what horses knew. And didn't.

Now I wanted Coronado to know where Mom was, and take me to her.

THREE

I'D RIDDEN CORONADO plenty, worked him out when Mom and Caroline traveled to look at horses for the barn, even jumped him one time when Mom was down with the flu.

This time I was just along for the ride, headed back out the trail along the Palm Beach Point canal, past the Nason barn next to the huge new barn being built by Wellington newcomers, a Kentucky family with money to burn.

Usually I loved being out here, loved the solitude of it and the quiet and the open space. Mom said she did, too, though sometimes I got more enjoyment when Mom wasn't with me.

Not now. All I could think of was the question she'd once asked me about people who don't ride. "How can they really feel alive?"

Please let her ask me again.

If her horse came back to the barn alone and she was somewhere out here, it had to be bad.

Coronado and I weren't going fast. It's one of the myths of our sport that a horse has to be going fast to throw its rider.

We were out into one of the last undeveloped parts

of Wellington. Someday there would be barns out here, too.

Where was she? Was she badly injured? I could feel the panic building inside me. If somebody hadn't found her by now, put her in a golf cart, or an ambulance, I was going to be the one. There had to be a damn good reason why she had ended up off her horse.

My eyes kept searching the narrow canal as we moved north, not wanting to see her down a glorified ditch.

If I hadn't been late this morning, none of this would have happened.

I saw her then.

Saw her and felt the air coming out of me all at once, as if I'd been the one who'd gotten thrown. She was maybe fifty yards ahead, between the trail and the canal, on her side.

Motionless.

Except that her body seemed to be going in two different directions at once. The boots I'd ordered special from New York City, for her birthday a few weeks ago, were pointing toward the water, and her upper body was pointing toward the trail.

I was afraid my mother might have broken her neck. I'd seen it happen once before, in person, a Grand Prix event. A horse had refused a jump and threw his rider, who'd gone down and had stayed down until the ambulance was in the ring. He recovered from the injury to walk again, eventually. But he never rode again.

I walked Coronado to her, knelt down. Her eyes were closed, but I could see that she was breathing. She was still wearing her helmet, caked with dirt, like the rest of her.

I knew enough not to move her. I just leaned close. "Mom," I said. "I got you."

Then I took the phone out of my back pocket and dialed 911 thinking, *Yeah, Becky, you got her*.

A half hour too late.

FOUR

AWAKE, IF NOT ALERT, Mom was telling us about the fox that had appeared out of nowhere.

She had come through the surgery to repair the small fracture in her pelvis and the torn medial collateral ligament in her left knee. She had narrowly missed puncturing a lung, but there was no treatment but the passage of time to heal the two broken ribs.

They had been going slowly, she said, but suddenly Coronado had reared up on his hind legs, making an unfamiliar, guttural sound. He threw her off to the side, then fell on her before she had the chance to roll away. She said she felt as if she were drowning. She tried to breathe, but couldn't, as if she were underwater, not underneath her horse. The last thing she remembered was the day going completely dark.

"You're lucky to be alive," Grandmother said, barely hiding the fear beneath her anger.

Daniel liked to say that Caroline Atwood wasn't just any tough old bird, she was the toughest of them all. Not tonight.

"I don't feel lucky," Mom said, her words dying in the air a few inches from her mouth.

"Well, you are," her mother said.

"People talk all the time about being strong in the broken places," Mom said. She paused, wincing as she took in a breath. "Except I feel like all my places are broken places right now."

She reached out. I took her hand, gently, afraid of squeezing hard enough to break it.

"Finally found something I can't fix myself," she said. "Me."

She managed a small smile then, though it appeared to take all the energy she had in her. I'd never seen her strength at such a low point.

I'd been lucky in my life, luckier than a lot of other riders I'd visited in the hospital when they had gotten hurt. Even with my share of spills, I'd never broken anything.

I remembered the first time I fell off a horse. Grandmother had been in the practice ring that day. She hadn't even made a move in my direction. When I'd finally cleaned myself off and walked over to her, she'd seen my red eyes and said, "If you want to cry, go watch a sad movie."

We'd always been big on tough love in our family, but now the injured rider was Mom.

"How's my horse?" Mom said now.

Now I felt myself smiling, for the first time since I'd found her.

"Pissed," I said. "He couldn't understand why he didn't get to come to the hospital, too."

"Don't make me laugh," she said, "or they'll be wheeling me back into surgery."

"I'll try," I said, gently squeezing her hand again. "But you know how hard it is for me to hold back the funny."

"None of this is funny!" my grandmother said.

She was on the other side of Mom's bed. In a gallant attempt at affording us privacy, Daniel stood in the corner.

"You'll ride him for me tomorrow?" Mom said to me.

"Don't worry about that right now, Maggie," Grandmother said.

"You worry about me," Mom said. "I'll worry about Coronado."

"I got you," I said.

"Could we stop worrying about the goddamn horse for one minute?" Grandmother snapped. "Good God, Maggie. He threw you. He fell on you. It wasn't the other way around."

"But then he led me right to her," I said.

Grandmother made a snorting sound, not unlike one of her own horses.

"Great," she said. "Million-dollar rescue animal. Just what we needed to bet the farm on."

"Mom," Maggie said, "that's a little dramatic."

"Maybe," Grandmother said. "But if not now, you tell me when?"

My mom closed her eyes now. For a moment, I thought she'd gone right to sleep with the rest of us still in the room.

"She needs rest," Grandmother said.

My mom opened her eyes.

"I need to get better," Mom said. "I asked Dr. Garry about the recovery time."

"Probably asked before the anesthesia wore off," Grandmother said.

"I asked how many weeks," Mom said. "Doc gave me one of those patronizing doctor smiles and said, 'You mean months.'"

She squeezed my hand now, hard enough to surprise me.

"I told him I don't have months," she said.

My whole life, I had been watching Mom in and

out of the ring. I'd seen her compete from here to
Calgary and back. Seen her take on the most famous
riders in the world and beat them, men and women.
I knew how much pride she took in not showing her
emotions, win or lose, especially after she lost. She
was every bit as tough as her mother, even though she
didn't feel the need to broadcast that.

But I thought she might cry now.

"This was the one," she said.

I didn't have the words to make her feel better, or
hurt less. Maybe no one did right now. I stood there
holding her hand and wished it had been me who'd
gotten thrown and not her. Wished that for once in
my stupid life I'd been on time.

"Doctors can be wrong about the speed of athletes'
recovery time," I said.

That was all I had.

She looked up at me and said, "Told you before.
Don't make me laugh, kiddo."

Then she closed her eyes again. A few minutes later
she was asleep. Grandmother led Daniel and me out
of the room.

Once Daniel had gently shut the door behind us,
Grandmother said, "I hate this sport."

I looked at her.

"You know you don't mean that," I said.

"Don't tell me what I mean," she said.

"Sorry," I said.

"You want to be sorry about something?" Grandmother snapped. "Be sorry you weren't there."

Then she walked away.

FIVE

Maggie

HAPPY NEW YEAR to me, Maggie Atwood thought bitterly.

No one in the room had spoken of the multiple Olympic qualifiers over the next several months that would decide which four riders—one an alternate—would represent the United States in jumping in Paris. Nobody had even spoken the word *Olympics*. But it was the thousand-pound horse in the room. Like her dream horse had tried to crush her whole world.

She'd gone out for a trail ride, an equestrian walk in the park, and ended up here.

Broken.

She'd been bred to her sport the way horses were bred to it. She aced the fractional calculations that made the difference between winning and losing— the split seconds of timing, the measure of an inside turn, the pressure of a horse's back leg on a rail that stayed in place versus one that fell, the numbers that measured the distance between first place and fifth. When she made mistakes in the ring, she owned them. Somebody else won. You lost.

And sometimes being the better rider was less important than riding the better horse. The more expensive horse. Simple, basic economics.

Then Coronado came along, and she was the one

with a top-tier horse, one that really did change everything, for all of them. He was a Belgian warmblood, sired by a famous stallion named Chacco-Blue, who had been an FEI champion—International Equestrian Federation—in his career. The mare was a Belgian warmblood who had one of those fancy show names that Maggie loved: Hypnose Van Paemel. She had won a half dozen FEI events in her career.

Atwood Farm had a solid enough reputation. Caroline Atwood liked to tell Maggie that she never imagined herself getting rich in the horse business. But now they were just getting by, struggling, even. Her mother once told her that she'd retire the morning a groom or trainer found her facedown in a stall, because she planned to work until she died. In the past they'd travel with the horses to all the best shows— now it was only some of them.

"You know how they call equestrianism the sport of the rich and the poor rich?" Caroline asked Maggie, then answered her own question. "Sometimes I feel like we're just poor."

"I can do something else," Maggie said.

"No," her mother said, "you can't. And neither can I."

They couldn't afford a horse like Coronado on their own, no matter which way Caroline and the accountants ran the numbers.

A friend of a friend had told Caroline about the horse. A barn owner in Lexington had run out of money and decided to cash out. He was banking on Coronado, his best horse, to bring top dollar. Caroline and Maggie had worked Coronado out, fell in love with him the way they had his bloodline. Found a deep-pockets partner in Steve Gorton, a New York hedge-fund guy with a place in Palm Beach who'd followed his Florida friends into horses.

Caroline Atwood had explained to Gorton that she thought the horse had a chance to be special, and proposed a fifty-fifty split, even knowing that it would be a scramble to come up with her end, going into her savings, still needing help from the bank, feeling no different than a desperate bettor at the racetrack.

"You're the expert," Gorton had said, then asked, "And what exactly do I get for my half?"

"Half the profits," Caroline had said.

Most people, Maggie had observed, were intimidated by her mother. Not this guy.

He had laughed suddenly. The sound reminded Maggie of glass breaking.

"I was born at night, Caroline," Gorton had said. "But not last night."

"I'm not sure I understand," she'd said.

The joke on Wall Street, he'd said, was that nothing was more limited than being a limited partner of Steve Gorton. Take it or leave it: he'd take care of 60 percent of the asking price, and she could take care of the horse, and decide who rode him.

When Caroline resisted, Gorton had simplified the terms. If she didn't like the deal, she could find somebody else to write her a million-dollar check.

Maggie had watched them debate, but knowing the finances of Atwood Farm as well as her mother did, this particular movie had only one ending. Caroline and Gorton had finally shaken hands.

Gorton, Maggie knew, had no love for horses, only for money. When she started winning right away on Coronado, Steve Gorton happily envisioned the pot of gold the sale of the horse would bring him.

Maggie thought only of a gold medal. The one

she'd been dreaming about her whole life. That and a dream horse. She'd never thought she was owed a ride like Coronado. She knew sports didn't work that way. Her sport certainly didn't.

She had never been much of a party girl in high school, or college at Florida Atlantic, just up the road from Wellington. She liked boys well enough, had never had much of a problem keeping a boyfriend, at least until she'd lose interest and move on to the next one.

That was until Jack McCabe came along. Jack, the funny, smart, cool young New York lawyer. Different from the riders she'd dated. They'd fallen in love and gotten married too soon. Then she'd gotten pregnant.

But all she really wanted to do was ride.

Jack had even taken a year off from his father's law firm in New York to travel the circuit with her, content to play Mr. Mom while she was competing, in Kentucky or North Carolina or Canada or DC or in the Hamptons. But as with many couples driven to be the best in their chosen professions, they drifted apart.

She was riding in the Hampton Classic, out on eastern Long Island, when they took a walk on the beach as a way of trying to clear the air. But suddenly they were standing in the dunes toe to toe, as if fighting for the title.

He finally told her he was leaving in the morning. Becky was three at the time, back in Florida with the nanny. Jack said he'd explain to her what was happening as best he could when he flew down to pack up his things.

"You're not even going to stay for the Grand Prix?" she'd said.

It had been the big event to cap off the week. Even then, her mind had gone right back to the ring.

"You'll be fine without me," he'd said, before adding, "But then you always were."

She'd won the next day, one of her biggest career victories to that point.

She'd nearly made it to the Olympics in London with Lord Stanley, until the horse came up lame in the spring of 2012. She'd accumulated enough average points the previous year to have already made the short list of ten elite riders trying to qualify for the US Olympic team. That list would eventually be shortened to four, three rider–horse combinations and a reserve after they'd competed the next year at a certain number of what were called "observation events."

After what happened to Lord Stanley, Maggie feared that her best shot at the Olympics had come and gone. But she'd kept at it, teaching Becky along the way that the right combination of hard work and talent would bring good results. Maybe even great ones.

She had always believed that. Until now.

The nurse poked her head in. "How are we doing?" she said.

We, Maggie thought. Like they were a team. Like Maggie and her horse.

"Fine," Maggie said.

"Are you sure you don't want something for the pain?"

"No, thank you," she said.

She'd seen it happen too often with other injured riders who would have taken anything except engine fuel to get back up on their horses.

The nurse closed the door. Maggie closed her eyes and listened to the night sounds of the hospital.

But then she was seeing the fox again, and could feel Coronado rising up underneath her, out of her control. Then she was in the air again, landing hard on her shoulder, right before the horse was on top of her, as if she were collapsing into herself.

Some riders said they went numb when their horses fell on them. Some said they could feel bones inside them snapping like twigs. She hadn't felt any immediate pain, just the terror of being unable to take in oxygen, even as she felt Coronado try to get his legs underneath him.

That was the last thing she remembered. She had no memory of them lifting her into the ambulance until she awoke on the way to the hospital and saw Becky sitting beside her.

"How's my horse?" Maggie had asked.

First words out of her mouth.

Becky had told her Coronado was fine, and how the horse had brought her to the spot where Maggie was lying near the canal.

"Such a good boy," Maggie'd said, and then passed out again and didn't wake up until she was out of surgery.

Now she had nothing but time to think, and all she could think about was time.

"The Olympics start at the end of July," she'd told Dr. Garry, "which means I'd have to start qualifying no later than the spring."

"If you don't qualify this year," he said, "then you can shoot for next year."

"You don't understand," she said. "The Olympics happen every *four* years."

When the doctor left, she checked her phone. Only nine o'clock. She felt as if the longest night of her life was just beginning.

SIX

Caroline

CAROLINE WAS ABOUT to fix herself a cup of tea when her doorbell rang. She moved stiffly to answer the door.

She had been a rider herself when she was younger, though she hardly rode at all these days. But her own career, because of the daredevil way she rode—more like her granddaughter than she'd ever admit—had been littered with falls, and injuries to her knees, shoulders, neck, and back that showed themselves with stiffness and a lingering limp. She sometimes thought she had an easier time managing her diabetes than she did all her aches and pains.

"Sorry I didn't call first," Steve Gorton said.

Caroline managed a thin smile before answering, "No, you're not," then waved him in.

He was maybe six one or six two, and had been an unmemorable college football player at Penn back in the early nineties. She'd looked it up, along with his age—past fifty now. He wore his hair piled too high on top, probably colored it, and shaved it too close on the sides in a way that accentuated his jowls. Even in Florida, he sprayed on his tan. Forever young, or trying like hell to look that way, in T-shirt and jeans and sneakers.

She asked if he wanted a drink. He said Scotch if

she had it. She went into the kitchen and poured him a glass of Dewar's and brought it out to him.

"How's she doing?" he said.

"Considering a horse landed on her," Caroline said, "about as well as can be expected."

Gorton nodded. "We need to talk about my horse, Caroline."

"Our horse," she said.

Now he smiled.

"Sure," he said. "Go with that."

They both understood the terms of their partnership. It was an arranged marriage, the kind they'd called shotgun marriages when she was young. A horse like Coronado, what they were sure was their Olympic horse at last, was as much Caroline's dream as it was Maggie's. She'd eventually mortgaged the barn for the final time, gambling away what little financial stability they had left.

Maybe more.

"I've been talking to some of my friends in the business," Gorton said. "About potential riders for Coronado."

You have friends? Caroline thought, but held her fire.

"You gave me rider approval in the contract," she said. "And for now, that rider is still my daughter."

"All due respect," Gorton said, "but Maggie is lucky if she can ride a wheelchair right now."

"The accident just happened," Caroline said. "There's still nearly seven months to the Olympics. Her results from the end of last year roll into this one. Even if she doesn't start competing again until the spring, there are still enough qualifiers for her to make the team."

Gorton sipped his drink, placed his glass on the

coffee table, ignoring the coaster she'd placed in front of him.

"Never bullshit a bullshitter," he said.

"We don't need to go shopping for another rider when she's barely out of surgery," Caroline said.

He sighed.

Maybe it was part of the Wharton curriculum, but Caroline interpreted his every gesture, every sound, as dismissive.

"I may be new to this sport," he said, "but I can read a calendar as well as the next guy. Maggie's first event of the year was supposed to be the Grand Prix, the date for which is coming up soon. Now she's not going to be in the ring. But let me explain something to you: Coronado sure as hell is."

Caroline started to speak, but Gorton raised his hand and continued.

"I got into this sport to win," he said. "When I win, somebody else loses."

"A beautiful thing," she said. "Truly."

"Isn't sarcasm supposed to be a weapon of the weak?" he asked.

"Trust me, Steve," she said. "If I ever pull a weapon on you, it won't be that."

He picked up his drink and toasted her with it.

"You want to know an inconvenient truth, Caroline?" he said. "We're more alike than you'll ever admit. Because you want to win just as badly as I do."

"Do you ever listen?" she said. "This isn't about me. This is about my daughter."

"Until she couldn't manage to stay on our million-dollar horse," he said.

Caroline felt the sudden urge to cross the room and slap him. But she didn't. It didn't matter what language was in the contract. They both knew that the architect of one of the largest hedge funds in the country, maybe the world, could make the owner of a small family barn in Florida go away if he wanted to, with another dismissive wave of his hand. Bottom line, Coronado was his horse.

He stood now.

"Thanks for the drink," he said.

"Good talk," Caroline said.

He either missed the sarcasm this time or simply ignored it.

"You know the other top riders better than I do," he said. "Either you figure it out, or I will. Something else you don't want to admit? This is what's best for the horse. And what's best for the horse is best for the two of us."

He turned then and walked out the front door.

"Bastard," Caroline Atwood said after he'd shut the door behind him.

Only because she knew the bastard was right.

SEVEN

I LOOKED OUT the barn window and saw Mr. Gorton, Grandmother's latest ATM, blow past me and down the driveway, driving his Porsche like a getaway car.

We'd needed more money, and more horses, around Atwood Farm for as long as I could remember. The barn needed renovating, the fencing in the schooling ring needed replacing. Every season, Grandmother would say she planned to spend money on improvements, but every time I'd walk into her bedroom and find her seated at the desk, she'd only say that she was "trying to pay bills."

As far as I was concerned, Steve Gorton and my grandmother deserved each other.

She didn't want to blame the horse. She certainly wasn't going to blame Mom.

Be sorry you weren't there, she'd said.

The words had stung like a slap. She was putting it on me, for letting her down. Letting everybody down. Again.

Grandmother had offered to drive me home from the hospital. I told her I'd take an Uber and request no conversation with the driver.

"You're saying you don't want to talk to me?" she'd said.

"I don't want to listen to you," I'd said.

When I got to the barn, I'd stopped at Coronado's stall first. Coronado could have been injured, and badly. But our vet, Doc Howser, had checked him out as thoroughly as he would have vetted him for a sale, and pronounced him completely fine.

Dr. Richard Howser wasn't just a great vet and trusted family friend, he was a really good guy who cared about horses the way everybody in the family did, even though Maggie would occasionally call him Dr. Doom when he delivered bad news.

Coronado was on his side, asleep. Most horses slept standing up, but, according to studies, some horses preferred to sleep lying down, that they got a deeper sleep that way.

I liked watching horses sleep. *You don't love it enough,* Grandmother would say when we argued about my riding. I'd tell her that I loved being around horses just fine, but humans kept getting in the way.

I moved quietly through the row of stalls, past the bridles hung on the wall, and the saddle racks, past the tack room.

"Hey, girl," I said when I got to Sky's stall near the end.

She leaned her head out and gave me a pointed look.

"I can't believe you're even asking if I brought treats," I said, then reached into the front pocket of my jeans and palmed a red-and-white mint. With a minimum of slobber, she quickly made it disappear from my outstretched hand.

Then she snorted.

"You're welcome," I said.

She was ten now, but still my baby girl. I retrieved a folding chair from the tack room and placed it so that with Sky's head extending from the stall, it felt as if she were resting it on my shoulder, or maybe looking out for me.

I looked up at her.

"What are we going to do, girlfriend?" I said. "This is so not fair."

I sat near Sky for a few minutes. And then I was up and out of the chair and into the tack room, grabbing my helmet, finding Sky's CWD-brand saddle that Mom bought me when I graduated high school.

Saddles were heavy as hell. With no grooms around, I managed to put two saddle pads on her, then the saddle itself, the girth that held it in place, the bridle last. I opened the double doors, threw the switch for the floodlights, and the two of us walked toward the schooling ring.

I wanted to ride. To move. I leaned down and said to Sky, "You get extra treats later."

Then we were circling the ring, past where the jumps were lined up and stacked, slowly picking up speed. I wouldn't have jumped Sky, not at night, even with the ring lighting enhanced tonight by a full moon.

Just me, alone in the ring with Sky and her horse sounds, Sky's breathing and her hooves. Not going against the clock. Not trying to calculate distances and clear jumps and beat the other horses.

Or Atwoods. Even with Mom down, I could still hear her and Grandmother telling me I wasn't the rider I was supposed to be, or that I didn't love it enough or want it enough, or that I'd never be the rider Mom was. That I wasn't enough of an Atwood, as if somebody had slipped me the wrong DNA.

Just remembering what I always loved about this

sport, what I still loved when people would just leave me the hell alone.

"Slow down!"

I knew Daniel's voice instantly.

"Leave me alone," I said, heading back to the far end of the ring. When Sky and I finally did come back around, as if we'd turned for home, he'd walked out and was standing in the middle of the ring.

I thought about doing one more lap. But I just slowed Sky down instead, brought her to a walk and finally to a stop, patting her head the way I did when we'd finished a good round.

"I was not going too fast," I said.

"Yes, you were."

"I'm not an idiot," I said.

"No comment," he said. "Now please take your horse back to the barn."

"Don't tell me what to do," I said.

"I said please, didn't I, *chiquita*?"

"Emilio gets to call me that," I said. "You don't."

"Yes, *jefa*."

Boss lady.

"Don't call me that, either."

Daniel Ortega was a few years older than I was but acted much older and more mature than that. He had only been my trainer for the past couple of years. He was Mexican by birth, having been brought to America, then raised here, by undocumented immigrant parents. But he spoke perfect English, even if his use of words sometimes sounded overly formal to me. Almost mannered. He worked his words as precisely as he did his horses.

And I knew this about Daniel Ortega: He lived in constant fear of being deported because of the changed reality and polarizing politics of immigration in America. A couple of months ago, he'd requested a few days off with no explanation. When I'd asked him about it later, just once, he'd shaken his head and said, "I was raised to believe that being a Dreamer is a good thing." And left it at that.

Since then he'd become increasingly impatient with my riding and my attitude. When, out of frustration, I'd given him the finger, he'd said, "No, Miss Becky, you're not number one."

He was a great trainer, both gifted with horses and passionate about them. I considered him a good friend, but neither one of us ever forgot that he worked for Atwood Farm. As an Atwood, technically he worked for me, too.

"I thought you'd be happy that I'm riding," I said, "and not out drinking with my friends."

"It's too late for you to be in the ring," he said.

He reached for Sky's bridle, but I gently moved her a couple of steps away from him.

"Your mom would never have Coronado out at this time of night," he said.

"Can we please not start talking again about how I'm not her," I said. "As if I need to be reminded."

"I never said I wanted you to be her," he said.

"Are you serious?" I said. "Everybody does."

"I just want you to be the rider I know you can be, whether you're here or at college."

The season was starting in a few weeks, and since the last one had been the worst of my life, I'd be competing here instead of on campus. No more coming up from Miami on Thursday night, riding on Friday, Saturday, and Sunday before heading back to school on Sunday night. I'd gotten into a slump early and kept finding ways to lose. I'd give Sky a bad distance. Or start out too fast and then pull up and confuse her into refusing a jump and we'd circle and get disqualified. Or we'd have a clean round going and then I'd get her too close to the last jump, and we'd get a rail, or crash right through the jump.

Mom even convinced me to see her sports psychologist, who'd told me that when athletes in any sport started waiting for bad things to happen, they almost always did.

Not Sky's fault. Mine. Totally my bad. Bad Becky. I either had to have my saddle monogrammed that way or put college on hold.

I'd ended up having a slightly better summer, not feeling as much pressure as I had in the spring, telling myself that next year would be better, that maybe Sky and I just needed to get out of Wellington. Then Coronado came along and I decided to make Mom my main focus.

Only the focus had shifted now—from getting her to the Olympics to getting her better.

"What happened to your mother wasn't your fault," Daniel said, now in the ring.

I had climbed off Sky and was walking her back inside. Daniel was walking with us.

"Try telling Grandmother that," I said.

Just then, from the open doors to the barn, I heard Grandmother say, "Tell her what?"

"Just that we're done for the night," I said.

"What the hell were you doing down there?" she said.

"Doing what you're always telling me to do," I said. "Trying to get better."

"Well, you picked a hell of an odd time to start," she said. "Now get up to the house. I need to talk to both of you."

Then, for the second time tonight, she walked away from me.

I walked Sky back inside her stall, gave her the treat I'd promised her, and wished I could spend the rest of the night with her.

EIGHT

GRANDMOTHER'S LIMP LOOKED more pronounced than usual as she paced the living room, back arched, head high, fists clenched, as if she were challenging the world to a fistfight.

"Why the hell did I ever go into business with that hideous man?" she said.

"You know why," I said. "To get Coronado."

"If there was a better way," Daniel said, "you would have found it, *jefa.*"

She liked it when he called her that.

"I should have looked harder," she said.

She sat down in the antique rocking chair positioned in that exact spot for as long as I could remember. Like Grandmother, it was rickety, but built to last. She grimaced slightly, then stretched her left leg out in front of her.

Next to her was one of her favorite photographs, Mom and me in our riding clothes, looking more like sisters than mother and daughter. She was taller. Even though my blond hair had darkened considerably since I was a little girl, hers was still darker. I thought she was prettier, and when I'd tell her so, she'd laugh and say, "Tell me another one."

"He wants to find another rider for Coronado," she

said. "Any rider will do, as long as he—or she—rides him all the way to Paris."

"He can't give up on Mom this quickly," I said.

"Oh, really?" she said. "Because his heart suddenly grew a few sizes? That's if he's actually got a god-damn heart."

"What if the doctors are wrong about Mom," I said. "What if she gets better?"

In the soft light of the standing brass reading lamp, I took a closer look at the woman who kept herself around horses. Since I'd found Mom near the canal, she appeared to have aged ten years.

"This was our dream, Maggie and me," she said, as if talking to herself, as if Daniel and I had disappeared.

Not *Mom's* dream. Theirs.

"Any other rider on Coronado," she said, "will make him Gorton's horse and not ours."

"Does he know which rider he wants?" Daniel said.

"Knowing that bastard? He started calling around before Maggie was out of surgery and has already made his selection, like some fantasy football draft."

"Grandmother," I said, choosing my next words carefully, "wouldn't having an Olympic horse help the barn, even if Mom doesn't get better in time to ride him?"

"Oh, now you get practical?" she said.

She rocked slowly back and forth in her chair.

"Horses are more than a business for Atwood Farm," she said. "You know that."

"People in outer space know that," I said.

"That man is nothing like us," she said.

Daniel smiled at her now.

"Except you both care for the winning," he said.

Her head whipped in his direction and she snapped her eyes like a whip.

"That's exactly what he said," Grandmother said. "The sonofabitch."

"Let me help you with this, *jefa*," he said. "I have a rider in mind."

"Who?" Grandmother asked. Her voice may have stopped horses, but not Daniel.

"Becky," he said.

NINE

Daniel

AS SOON AS he'd heard about the accident, Daniel had decided that Becky had to be the one to ride Coronado.

A trainer, he knew, dealt with what he had, not what he did not. He had learned that from old Buck Starr, a trainer in North Carolina. When the barn's star rider, Wiley, had broken a leg before a big show at the Tryon International Equestrian Center, Starr had looked at Daniel and said, "Who's Wiley?"

If they were going to get Becky up on Coronado, they couldn't afford to wait. So he told them.

Mrs. Atwood was staring at him with that look she expected to scare not only the staff but the horses. Daniel was convinced that if you took away her bluster, she would merely be old.

"You're serious," she said.

"Always," he said, "when the subject is your horses."

Always her horses, never his.

Horses were so much more than just Daniel Ortega's job, no matter who owned them. One day horses would give him the good lives they'd already given the Atwood women—if it wasn't too late for people with stories like his own.

"My granddaughter rides Coronado over my dead body," Caroline Atwood said.

"Took the words right out of my mouth," Becky said.

Daniel couldn't repress the smile from his face. Never mind the wrath of the old lady of the house. "The two of you hardly ever agree about anything," he said. "Until now."

Mrs. Atwood stood from her rocking chair then, nearly knocking it over as she took her first straight-backed, stiff-legged steps over to the trophy case. Maggie Atwood had won enough trophies to fill two cases, one here in the living room and a second in the den, along with two walls covered with ribbons. Becky's awards were in a television room on the second floor. Mrs. Atwood studied Maggie's trophies for a moment.

"She can't win often enough on her own horse," she said.

"She can," Daniel said. "Just not lately."

"I'm here," Becky said from the sofa. "I can hear you two."

Standing directly behind Becky, Daniel gently put a hand on her shoulder. He hoped she understood that the less she spoke right now, the better it would be.

"Both of you hear *me* out," he said. "Please."

As aware as Mrs. Atwood was of her place with Mr. Gorton, Daniel was even more aware of his place with her. And her daughter. And even her granddaughter.

"I'm listening," Mrs. Atwood said.

"Same," Becky said.

He breathed deeply, feeling his shoulders rise and then drop as he slowly let the air out.

"I know Coronado," he said. "And I do not believe just anybody can ride him."

"Steve Gorton isn't talking about just anybody

riding the horse," Mrs. Atwood said. "He'll shop around and buy his top pick."

"But that is not necessarily what is best for the horse," Daniel said.

"Mom's horse," Becky said.

"Not now," Daniel said. "And not for a long time. And maybe, though none of us wants to speak of it, not ever again. But you can ride Coronado. I've seen you on him. You fit this horse better than you know."

"The horse could fit her like a pair of damn riding gloves," Mrs. Atwood said, spitting out the words the way a horse spits a bit. "Even if I agreed to this, Gorton never will. See all the trophies in that case? This horse is his trophy. And he's going to want a trophy rider."

Ahi esta, Daniel thought.

There it is.

"But he does not get to pick the rider," Daniel said. "You do. It is in the contract."

"And how do you know that?" Mrs. Atwood said.

"Because you asked me to look at it before you signed it," Daniel said. "He agreed because we all thought Miss Maggie was going to ride him, all the way to Paris. She was going to be his trophy rider. He knew enough to know she was a star."

Daniel was right. So was Mrs. Atwood, who had once told him that even people who gave an inch were giving too much.

But the old woman's voice softened now.

"This horse has greatness in him," she said. "He can carry the weight riding on him, I know it."

"So can Becky," Daniel said.

"I'm still right here," Becky said.

She stood and walked over to the picture window, facing both of them.

"You can do this," Daniel said to Becky, then turned to her grandmother and said, "She can do this."

"You mean finally think of somebody other than herself?" Mrs. Atwood said.

"Taking a semester off from college to help Mom doesn't qualify?" Becky said.

"This isn't some side ring on a Saturday morning," her grandmother said.

"So you're saying I'd be out of my league?" Becky said.

"This is good," Daniel said. "You're getting to it now."

Daniel watched as Becky put her hands on her hips and looked more like the old woman than ever.

"I don't want you to let your mother down," Mrs. Atwood said.

"Don't you mean let *you* down? Again?" Becky said. "It's not Gorton who doesn't want me on Coronado. It's you."

"This isn't your call, Daniel," Mrs. Atwood said, the snap back in her voice. "And it's not my granddaughter's. It's mine. You honestly believe that she can do this?"

"Yes."

"You're willing to bet your job on that belief? Knowing how much an Olympic champion horse could mean to this family?"

"Yes," he said.

And she had still not said no. Neither had Becky.

Daniel had never known a family like this, in all the horse business, where most of them were *alocado*. Cracked.

Becky headed for the front door now.

"Where are you going?"

"Out," Becky said.

"You think that's going to help get me on your side?" Mrs. Atwood said.

Her granddaughter turned at the door.

"I don't even know which side that is anymore," she said.

TEN

I DID THINK about calling my friend Madison, another rider from our barn, and telling her to meet me at the Trophy Room for a drink. We were both twenty-one now. After years of using fake IDs to drink illegally, it seemed almost against the law not to go to bars now.

But I didn't. I drove to Wellington Medical, even knowing it was past visiting hours. No way Mom was going to be asleep, unless she'd given in and allowed them to slip her the kind of happy pill she said she was going to resist.

No, she'd be lying there in her bed, her brain working a million miles an hour.

When I got to the hospital I bluffed my way past the nursing station on her floor, showing the night nurse the backpack I'd brought with me and saying I'd brought some toiletries my mom had requested, even though my backpack held only my cell phone, lip balm, hairbrush, and a bottle of water.

"If she's asleep," I told the nurse, "I'll just leave the stuff inside the door."

"Promise?" the nurse said.

"Yes, ma'am!" I said. "Thank you *so* much."

My dad had told me once that nobody faked sincerity better than I did when I put my mind to it.

Truly, no matter what Grandmother decided, I wanted to know what Mom thought.

My whole life I'd wanted her to respect me as a rider but at the same time hated being compared to her, mostly because I'd convinced myself early on that I'd never measure up, not just to what she was, but what she and her own mother had decided I was supposed to be. Somewhere along the line, they'd decided that I didn't care enough.

But I did. Just in my own stubborn way. When I was eight or nine, Mom had caught me in some dumb lie and grounded me. I told them I didn't want to live here, packed my little pink Hello Kitty suitcase, and walked out the door, good-bye.

Made it all the way to the end of the driveway before I turned around and came back.

I was still here, and I still cared. Except now Daniel wanted me to be Mom, on her horse.

Shit happened.

I poked my head into her room and said, "You awake?"

"So awake," she said. "Just please don't ask me how I'm doing, or I'm getting out of this bed and challenging you to a fistfight."

"I was afraid of this," I said. "You're not acting like my mom. You're acting like yours."

What sounded like a laugh came out of her before it quickly turned into a coughing fit. Not a pretty sound.

"Sorry, Mom," I said.

"Lost my ride," she said. "But apparently not my sense of humor."

I pulled a chair over to the side of the bed.

"Aren't visiting hours over?" she said.

"I might have lied my way in," I said.

"Bad Becky strikes again."

But she was smiling. She looked tired as hell. No makeup. Probably not eating. Still beautiful.

"You look like something's on your mind."

"Oh, baby," I said.

Then I told my mother about her mother's conversation with Mr. Gorton, and the one she'd just had with Daniel and me. She listened, no change in her expression, until I finished.

"Crazytown, right?" I said.

"They're both right," Mom said. "Mom and Daniel."

She motioned for the water cup with the straw in it on the bedside table. I handed it to her. She drank deeply and handed it back. Even now, she didn't miss a chance to hydrate like a triathlete.

"It's not just another rider," she said. "If Gorton goes out and gets some hotshot rider, that guy is going to want his own trainer. So then not only would I be gone, so would Daniel. And with another rider and another trainer, what's left for Mom? Silent partner? Good luck to the lawyers trying to enforce that."

I stood up now, needing to move, even if it was just to the other side of the bed.

"The important thing is that Daniel thinks you can do this and so do I."

"Are you sure you're not on drugs?" I said. "I know I'm a good rider. And since I know you and Daniel don't lie about horses, I'm not going to, either. As much as I'd love to show Grandmother she's wrong about me, I would be out of my league here."

"Bullshit," Mom said.

"Now you do sound just like her."

"Just because we both call BS when we see it," she said.

"So you're telling me that after the worst year I ever

had in riding I can start training with Daniel now and still be ready to ride Coronado in the Grand Prix in a few weeks?"

She tried to sit up straighter in the bed now. The pain flashed across her face like some sudden flash of lightning in the darkened room.

"Let me ask you a question," she said when she had control of her breathing. "What do you have to lose?"

"Your shot at the Olympics," I said.

"Our shot."

"Either way," I said, "you're telling me I should do this?"

She closed her eyes and smiled.

"Hell, no," she said. "*I* want to be doing this. I want to be in my own bed and asleep already so I can get up early in the morning and ride the living shit out of my horse."

"Your mind is made up, just like that?" I said.

"I am not going to lie to you," Mom said. "The day I'm out of here and see somebody else up on that horse, it's going to hurt even more than I'm hurting right now. But it will hurt a hell of a lot less if it's you."

She told me that if I really wanted her advice, it was for me to ride the horse every day for a week, ride him as hard as I could, ride him in the ring and on trail rides, and see if I had a feel for him and he had a feel for me, because it always came back to that.

"Then you can decide whether you're in or out," she said. "I'm not sure you've been all in since we put you up on Frenchy."

My first pony.

"You always said that the biggest mystery is how

much of it is the horse and how much of it is the rider," I said.

"Well, kiddo," Mom said, "we might be about to find out."

Then she said to leave her alone, maybe by some minor miracle she might get some sleep tonight.

ELEVEN

THE NEXT MORNING Grandmother sat at the kitchen table eating her usual breakfast of nuts and berries and oatmeal. I was having coffee and toast.

"Your mother said you went to see her," she said.

"She wants me to ride Coronado," I said.

"So I heard," she said.

She sipped tea. I sipped my coffee, happy that I'd only taken a few bedtime hits of tequila, sleep having come to me more easily than I'd expected on one of the longest days of my life.

"If you don't want me to ride Coronado, go find another rider."

"It wouldn't be difficult."

"So what's stopping you?"

"Your mother is stopping me!" She spoke even more loudly than usual now. "She wants the horse to stay in the family and she actually believes you can pull this off."

"So does Daniel," I said, taking a self-consciously defensive stance.

"Stop taking a goddamn poll about whether you want to do this!" she said, as if trying to out-shout me. "However you got here, you're being given a chance to ride a goddamn Olympic horse all the way to the Olympics in Paris goddamn France."

She was leaning forward now. I'd done the same without realizing it. "You want to ride this horse or not?" she said.

"Yes," I said.

She looked at her watch. She said she needed an hour to meet with Doc Howser over at WEF about another horse of ours he'd just vetted for sale.

"And when I get back," Grandmother said, "I want you to get your skinny ass up on that horse and act as if you belong there."

TWELVE

DANIEL HAD SET up the course for ten jumps, not the sixteen I'd encounter if Coronado and I did make it to the International Arena for the Grand Prix, the Sunday after next.

Once he set the course, we walked it, just as if we were showing for real, pacing off the distance between the jumps, six or seven strides for the horse, except for the triple Daniel had set up in the middle. He'd also thrown in a couple of tough rollback turns, where the trick was to come out of one jump already making a sharp turn into the next, a simultaneous challenge of speed and distance.

When we finished the walk, I turned and looked back at the course, picturing the order of the jumps in my head, waving my right hand in the air in front of me, as if I were conducting an equestrian orchestra.

"You know how to get a horse around," Daniel said.

"Yeah, but the horse is Sky," I said.

"Horses for courses," he said. "And only one course matters in the next few minutes, and one horse."

"This shit is about to get real," I said.

"En el nombre del padre y el hijo y el Espíritu Santo," he said as he made the sign of the cross.

"Do I need divine intervention today?"

He smiled and said, "I want the good Lord on our side even if your grandmother is not," he said.

"She probably thinks she could take God in a fair fight," I said.

"Attitude," Daniel said.

"Grandmother thinks it's a bad thing."

"Maybe not so much today."

We walked back to where Emilio was standing with Coronado, just inside the gate. Grandmother was back and hanging over the fence at the far end of the ring—the schooling ring at our barn.

"Let's do this, Maverick," he said.

Baby steps, I told myself, on an animal whose normal stride was about ten feet long. Maybe more on a horse as big as Coronado, so significantly bigger than Sky.

I got into the saddle, patted the side of Coronado's head, and leaned over and said, "Just you and me today, big boy."

The worst thing I could do was transfer my nervous energy to the horse. He'd been Mom's horse the way Sky was mine. Today I had to start making him my own.

It was just Coronado and me and Grandmother and Daniel and the grooms who'd come out of the barn to watch. And a video camera. Mom had called from the hospital and told Daniel to have somebody video my session on Coronado. But as I began to walk Coronado around the ring, I heard the slam of a car door.

I stopped Coronado and watched Mr. Gorton get out of his Porsche and stand in front of it, leaning on the hood. He'd parked so close to the barn I wondered if Grandmother had promised him a preferred parking spot inside. I was sure he was looking at me.

He wanted me to know he was here, riding what he called his horse.

Owners didn't belong at the in-gate. At WEF, some of them stood there for everybody to see—and to put more pressure on the riders. Maybe that's what he wanted to do now. No way Caroline Atwood had just up and told Mr. Gorton, in time for him to blow over here from Palm Beach, that I was riding Coronado this morning. Maybe she had, or maybe it was someone else at our barn. And maybe he'd just shown up, unannounced, to see his horse.

Blinders, I told myself.

So I didn't acknowledge his presence, not even with a nod, just turned Coronado back toward the course, stopped to show him a couple of the jumps. The next time around, still warming him up, I let him out a little so that he could get his legs underneath him while I made sure I remembered the course that Daniel had set up for us.

I made one last stop where Daniel was standing with the grooms.

"Do not focus on the one your grandmother calls a horse's ass," he said, lifting his chin toward Gorton. "Just your horse."

Just get around the first time clean.

Then I was into the first jump and then the second, taking it slow. When Sky and I were in the jump-offs that would determine the champion horse among those with clean first rounds, when we were really busting for speed, when we had it all going on, when I felt in perfect sync with my legs and hands, keeping her on her hind end, I would take out strides on our lines between the jumps, knowing that even a half second could make all the difference.

But I wasn't doing that today on Coronado.

Show that man you can get around clean.

Show everybody.

Trust the horse and have the horse trust you and screw all the rest of it, including Steve Gorton.

We got around clean. No rails. On the second-to-last jump, I gave Coronado a bad distance, got him too close, and he clipped it with one of his hind legs. But he adjusted. Then we cleared the last one with ease.

I patted his head again and said, "Such a good boy," trying to channel Mom. Holy crap, I thought, maybe we really could do this, and my deep exhale broke into a smile.

I turned the horse so I could see Daniel's reaction. He was standing near the last jump now, arms crossed in front of him, shaking his head.

He was not smiling.

"What?" I said, walking Coronado over to him.

"If you're going to ride the horse scared, maybe we do need to find another rider," he said, making certain Mr. Gorton could hear.

Before I could respond I heard the door to the Porsche slam and Steve Gorton put the car in reverse, spraying gravel as he turned it around, and was gone.

THIRTEEN

Daniel

"I DIDN'T KNOW I was on the clock," Becky said. "And thanks for calling me out in front of that guy. He must be so proud that I'm part of the team."

"We are *all* on the clock," Daniel said to her. "And today is not about the owner. It is about the rider."

Becky was still on Coronado, and she turned the horse to walk him out after his round. When she finished, Mrs. Atwood had joined Daniel in the ring.

Now she got off and handed the reins to Emilio.

"Did you tell Mr. Gorton that I was riding?" Becky said to her grandmother.

"Why in the world would I do that?" she said. "I try to be in that man's company as little as possible."

"Whatever," Becky said, then turned to Daniel and said, "I wasn't going to push him, no matter who was watching me ride."

"No one asked you to push him," Daniel said. "But why ride this horse as if the two of you were pulling a carriage?"

"It was a solid first ride and you know it," she said. "You *both* know it."

"It was a careful ride," he said. "That's not you."

"Agree to disagree," she said.

"Shut up and listen to the man," Mrs. Atwood said to Becky.

"*Please* listen," Daniel said to Becky, "even though that is not always your greatest skill as a horsewoman."

"You added strides three different times," Mrs. Atwood said to Becky now. "If this were a real event, you would have lost."

"*I just wanted to go clean!*" Becky yelled.

"So we could give you a pat on *your* head when you were done?" her grandmother said.

"Please listen," he said again, "because we are all on the same team. And we are trying to help you."

Daniel was expecting her to walk away. But she did not. Good. He wanted to use her anger in this moment.

"This horse is the one who has the need for speed," he said. "You must allow him to be himself, even here, with only a handful of people watching him. He only understands one way."

Becky started to say something. Daniel patiently held up both hands.

"Let me finish," he said. "There is a reason I wanted you on this horse after your mother fell. I believe the way you ride and the way he can run and jump means you, even more than your mother, are made for him." He gestured toward the ring now.

"Just not riding him like that," he said.

"I could have gone faster if I wanted to," Becky said.

"What was stopping you?" Daniel said.

"I wanted him to get to know me," she said.

"Then let him get to know you as the rider you are," Daniel said. "This horse runs one way. You ride one way. Now let's get him out of the barn and do it again, all right?"

They both knew he wasn't asking.

Becky turned to her grandmother and said, "Anything you'd like to add?"

"Hell, no," she said. "I'm an old woman, but I could have ridden that horse up better than you just did."

Then Mrs. Atwood was yelling at Emilio to bring the damn horse back out, and to be quick about it.

When Coronado was back in the ring, Mrs. Atwood said to Becky, "Now ride the damn horse without your foot on the damn brake."

Becky said, "Screw all of you."

She looked at Emilio and said, "Give me the reins and all of you get the *hell* out of my way."

Then Daniel watched as Becky rode the horse the way he wanted her to ride him, rode him hard, flying around the ring, not coming close to a rail, holding back nothing. Same horse. Different rider.

When Becky finished the course, she came back around with Coronado, took off her helmet and the hairnet she wore underneath it, shook her hair loose. Full of challenge, she looked down from the big horse and said, "Was *that* good enough for you?"

"Better," he said.

He went inside the barn and placed a call.

"Maybe my plan wasn't so crazy after all," he said.

"She can't do this without you, Daniel," Maggie Atwood said.

"Deja que ese sea nuestro secreto," he said.

"I only recognize the last word," she said. "Secret."

"Let that be our secret," Daniel said to her.

But not the only secret, Daniel knew.

FOURTEEN

Caroline

THREE NIGHTS LATER, Caroline Atwood requested the table in the far corner of the back room at Oli's, a favorite restaurant among Wellington horse people. Gorton arrived a half hour late.

"We took off late from Teterboro," he said.

The regional airport was no Andrews Air Force Base, but Caroline knew it was where he kept his personal Air Force One when it wasn't flying him into Palm Beach International.

She thought about saying *How awful for you,* but didn't, remembering Becky's directive that she needed a charm offensive tonight.

"What in the world is that?" Caroline had said to her granddaughter, who had been heading out to dinner with friends.

"Heavy on the charm and light on the offensive," Becky had said.

"Got it."

"Basically," Becky'd said, "try to be good."

"I thought that was my line," she'd said.

She hadn't spoken to him in days, since he'd told her to get a new rider on Coronado. He hadn't said "or else," but the threat was clearly implied.

Oscar, her favorite waiter, brought Gorton a vodka martini and Caroline an iced tea. "We'll wait to order food," she told him. She thought, *If we ever get that far.*

Gorton raised his glass and clinked it against hers.

"*Cin,*" he said.

Sweet Jesus, she thought.

He drank down half his drink, smacked his lips, and said, "First of the day. Nothing like it—except making some of the boys and girls in the fund enough money to buy the Bahamas."

Caroline took a deep breath and remembered what Becky had said.

Try to be good.

"So," he said, "have you given much thought to our problem?"

"Maybe finding the right rider to replace my daughter is not a problem at all," she said. "Maybe it could turn out to be an opportunity."

"I'm listening," he said.

"I think we've found someone. Well, me and our trainer."

"The Mexican kid," Gorton said.

"Daniel," she said.

"Sure," he said. "So what's this rider's name?"

"Becky McCabe."

Gorton laughed. "Your granddaughter? You're shitting me. I saw how badly you and the Mexican kid reacted when she rode the horse the other day." Caroline didn't bother to correct him again. Sometimes Daniel called him *bastardo.* More often he called him *el cabron.* An ass. Actually worse. "She's gotten better since then."

"I don't care," he said. "She's not riding the horse."

He barked out another laugh.

"Despite what you saw," Caroline said, "she happens to be perfect for this particular horse."

"My ass," he said.

"Let's talk this through," she said.

"What's there to talk about?" Gorton said. "The granddaughter you say has never applied herself to riding? The one I hear you bitching about, and the trainer bitched at the other day? *That* grand-daughter?"

"She gets better on him every day," Caroline said.

"She's got a horse of her own, right?"

"She does," Caroline said.

"Good," Gorton said. "She can ride her horse, not mine."

"I'm telling you," Caroline said. "She's the best rider for this particular horse."

"Then why did you buy him for her mother and not her?"

She answered his question with one of her own. "How did you happen to show up at my barn the other day?"

"Got lucky with the timing," he said. He shrugged. "It happens that way a lot. It's another reason why I'm richer than shit."

She looked around and saw some of WEF's biggest riders and trainers, a lot of them still in their riding clothes. She imagined herself yelling out, *Who wants to ride Coronado?* and seeing hands immediately shoot into the air all over the back room.

"I'm acting in Coronado's best interest," Caroline said.

Gorton had finished his drink. He yelled *"Hey!"* at Oscar and then pointed at his glass.

"Not to push too fine a point," Gorton said, "but that's not your call, Caroline."

She looked discreetly at her watch.

Hang in there.

"Becky can win on Coronado," she said. "They both like to go fast."

"What? The other top guys want to go slow?"

"She's watched her mother win on this horse," Caroline said. "She knows how to do it."

Gorton leaned forward now.

"I asked you to take care of this," he said. "Maybe I don't just need a new rider. Maybe I need a new partner, too."

She could no longer contain herself.

"Good luck with that," she said.

"What does that mean?"

"Our contract gives me the right to choose the rider," she said.

"The hell it does."

She knew right away that he didn't know. And probably hadn't cared when he signed the contract because he never assumed anybody except Maggie Atwood would ride the horse. Caroline had checked what was boilerplate language in most standard partnership agreements involving horses. Even though Daniel actually trained the horse, Caroline was listed as the trainer of record in the contract. Her lawyer had done his best to bury it. But the language *was* in there — she'd checked after talking to Daniel. Caroline was sure Gorton's eyes had gone right past it, or his lawyer's did.

"That's the way you want to play this?" he said. "Seriously?"

"I want us to be on the same page," she said.

"Well, that's not going to happen, is it?" he said. "You don't need to saddle up, Caroline. You need to lawyer up. Not that it will matter, because my lawyers are better."

Not with this contract, she thought, and checked her watch again.

Come on.

"Do you really want to be that guy, Steve?" she said.

"And what guy is that?"

"The new guy who wants to take a horse away from a rider who just ended up in a wheelchair," she said. "At the end of the day, this is a small community. Word gets around."

"And what would happen then? People would stop thinking I'm a nice guy? News bulletin. I'm *not* a nice guy."

"But you're a dealmaker," she said. "So let me offer you one."

"You're in no position to make a deal," he said, "whatever you say the contract says."

Now Caroline leaned forward, elbows on the table, chin resting on her hands.

"Give Becky one month," she said. "If she falls on her ass, literally or figuratively or both, you can pick whatever rider you want and I won't fight you."

"You're not listening to me," he said. "This fight is over already."

Oscar showed up with Gorton's second martini just as Caroline heard the sound of applause in the back room. He saw some of the riders in the room standing as Caroline couldn't help doing the same.

It was all because Daniel Ortega was wheeling Maggie Atwood through the crowd toward their table.

"Sorry I'm late," Maggie said. "Did I miss anything?"

FIFTEEN

Maggie

MAGGIE HAD BEEN discharged from the hospital that morning.

"Knowing this guy," Caroline had said to her daughter before leaving the house for Oli's, "I may need you to be the cavalry."

Now Maggie, with an assist from Daniel, was making her entrance at Oli's. Hoping she was riding to the rescue.

Gorton tried to act casual, sliding his chair to the right and making room for hers. Daniel quickly excused himself to the bar.

"Two of you, one of me," Gorton said. "So the sides are even."

"Nice to see you, too, Steve," Maggie said, flashing her biggest smile.

She was watching his face for signs of anger or annoyance, but he seemed mildly amused at the guest who'd unexpectedly shown up at the party.

"How are you feeling?" he said.

"Like a horse fell on me," she said. "But thanks for asking."

"You're welcome," he said. "But no chance that you showing up here is going to get me to change my mind about your daughter."

Oscar appeared, shook her hand, and welcomed her back, and asked what she'd like.

"A new pelvis?" Maggie said, then told him a glass of sparkling water would be fine. When he was gone, Caroline's recap of the conversation was thoroughly unsurprising.

"Would you like to know what I think?" Maggie said to Gorton.

"Do I have a choice?" he said.

"Listen, none of us wanted to be in this situation," Maggie said. "Certainly not me. But here we are, anyway, all in this situation. Together. And you need to know that Daniel and Mom have been watching Becky jump the horse the past few days. They're convinced she can ride him in competition, and win. And now that I'm out of the hospital, I can help train them, too."

"This isn't the same as buying her first goddamn pony," Gorton said. "Wait." He held up a hand. "Let me amend that. It's not like *me* buying her a goddamn pony."

Maggie watched her mother now, who looked as if she might turn the table over. But she just sat there, gripping the arms of her chair as if she wanted to squeeze them into dust.

"Steve," Maggie said gently, "from the start, we all agreed that there had to be an element of trust in this partnership, or it was never going to work, whatever the financials were. All Mom and I are asking you to do is trust us."

"After she throws the contract in my face?" he said.

"To get this horse," Maggie said, "we would have done this deal on a handshake."

Okay, she thought, *I am officially lying my ass off, just as Becky always said I could.*

"Good thing you didn't," Gorton said. "Or I'd be back on the island already."

He never called it Palm Beach, Maggie knew by now. Always "the island," in keeping with the rich men and women in their world. She and her mother had done business with a lot of them—and none of them ever wanted to hear the word *no*.

She reminded herself to remain as still as possible in the wheelchair. Just about any quick movement these days lit the pain fuse. Explosive jolts would come at any time, from everywhere.

She turned her head slightly and said to her mom, "You asked Steve for a month, correct?"

"Correct," Caroline said.

Maggie turned her head to face Gorton.

"So give us the Grand Prix, it's right around the corner," she said. "Then the Longines two weeks after that. If my daughter hasn't proved she can do the job, you won't have to take her off the horse. *I* will."

"Worst case," he said, "we've lost a month. To quote Caroline, 'A month can feel like a lifetime in this sport.'"

Caroline winced, but Maggie pushed forward.

"It's not even February. A new rider would still have five months on Coronado to qualify for Paris."

"Say I go along," Gorton said. "What's in it for me?"

Always looking for an angle, Maggie thought. *For an edge.*

Her mother jumped in now.

"If we're wrong," she said, "that means you're right, Steve. If we lose, you win."

Gorton briefly checked his phone, ate an olive, patted the table a couple of times. But then smiled.

"Deal," he said. "You get a month. Either way, I really do win. Best kind of deal there is."

He pushed his chair away, stood up, and left.

"I get broken in half," Maggie said, watching Gorton go, "and the money man sticks us with the check."

Maggie angled her wheelchair to have a better look at the room. Three men and a woman were sitting together at a four-top. The familiar faces of her fiercest competitors had softened with pity. She waved. They all waved back.

She turned back to Caroline and said, "Some things never change. I'm still on the clock."

SIXTEEN

Gorton

STEVE GORTON WALKED past the kitchen, past the bar where he saw the Mexican kid nursing a beer and talking to a smoking-hot bartender. It was still early. Maybe, Gorton thought, he'd take the car home and get a driver, head over to Honor Bar and see if anybody who wore a tank top and jeans as well as this bartender did was looking to have some fun.

He thought briefly about grabbing their waiter and offering to pick up the check for drinks, or even dinner for his partners from Atwood Farm.

But what the hell for?

They'd already gotten everything they wanted.

Or thought they had.

For now.

What a waste that he had driven the Ferrari. After two adult beverages, he'd have to stay under the speed limit.

Inside the car, Gorton placed a call. "Where the hell are you?"

"This place called Oli's," said the man who answered.

"Seriously?" Gorton said. "I just walked out of there."

"I saw you," the man said. "But I didn't think it

was a good idea for the whole town to see us talking to each other."

"Well, I'll talk now," Gorton said. As he pulled out onto Forest Hills Boulevard, he quickly related his conversation with Caroline Atwood.

"I don't want this kid to win," he said. "I'm sick of the Atwoods calling the shots. You want the horse?"

"You know I do."

"Then figure something out," Gorton said.

He ended the call, took a right on Southern, then put on some Sinatra and continued his slow ride to the island.

Trust us, she'd said.

What kind of schmuck did they think they were dealing with?

SEVENTEEN

"YOU'RE SURE YOU'RE ready?" Mom said.

Two days after Mr. Gorton had given us his dead-line, we met in the schooling ring and laid out our competition schedule. I'd show next weekend on both Sky and Coronado at a height that was just under four feet eight inches, listed in programs as "1.45." The following week would come WEF's Saturday Night Lights, where Coronado and I would compete in the International Arena at the Olympic height, the height of the jumps would be just under five feet three inches. It would be like jumping a horse over *me*.

"Can I be ready but not *sure* I'm ready at the same time?" I said.

"Whatever gets you around clean," Mom said.

"And fastest," I said.

"You don't need to win first time out of the gate," she said. "I'll take any kind of ribbon."

"Did you used to think that way?" I said.

"Well," she said, "you got me there."

She was already out of her wheelchair. Classic Mom.

"No, thanks," she had said, when Dr. Garry suggested that she stay in it a few more days. "Not my kind of ride."

She'd leaned her crutches against the fence and draped her long, lean arms over the top rail. My mom had an awesome figure. Anyone approaching her from behind, in her breeches and a T-shirt, would mistake her for a college girl. But the riding pants, which usually looked as if they'd been spray-painted on her, same as mine did, looked loose today, signaling how much weight she'd lost since her fall.

"Coronado is ready," I said, "to jump the big-boy height right now—"

"You're not," Grandmother said.

"Let's get through the first event," Daniel said.

"Keep reminding yourself you've never ridden a horse this big or strong in competition," Grandmother said. "You're a career prop-plane pilot who's taken control of a jet."

"Keep your voice down," I said, grinning at her. "Sky's in the barn, waiting for me to ride her. She'll hear you."

I was still on Coronado, the only horse in the ring right now. "Coronado doesn't much like being close to other horses, even in warm-ups," I said. "I'll need to watch out next weekend, when the schooling ring at WEF will look like rush-hour traffic on Southern Boulevard."

"Doesn't play well with others," Mom said, feigning confusion with an exaggerated scratch to her head. "Now who does that remind me of?"

"May I answer that one?" Daniel said.

"I'll try to be good," I said to both of them.

"We're looking for great," he said.

"On it," I said.

Mom said she'd stay and watch me trot Coronado, and then look at the video she'd taken of our round. Grandmother headed for the house, Daniel for the barn. As I watched Daniel walk away, I said to Mom, "Ask you something?"

"Ask away."

"Do you think he likes me?" I said. "Like in a way he might like me if he wasn't my trainer and didn't work here?"

"Now that, kiddo," she said, "is something only he knows, and you need to find out, at least if you want to."

"Don't you think it would be weird?" I said. "Sometimes I get the feeling he knows me better than I know myself."

"He might," she said. "But I've got news for you. They're *all* weird."

I put Coronado back in motion, easing him into a trot toward the far end of the ring. Mom was still hanging over the fence, clearly happy to be outside, happy to be back in this world, even on the sidelines. Her next stop, I knew, was the gym.

Coronado and I were rounding the far end of the ring when I brought him to a stop.

"He's limping!" I yelled.

EIGHTEEN

Maggie

IN A BLINK, Daniel and Emilio both came running, Maggie Atwood trailing behind on her crutches, feeling as slow as a plow horse. Emilio got to Coronado first, helping Becky down.

"Which leg?" Daniel said.

"Hind left, pretty sure," Becky said.

The horse could not be hurt, Maggie repeated to herself. *Could. Not. Be.*

"What did I do to get the horse gods pissing on me this way?" she said to Becky, borrowing an expression from Caroline.

Daniel had taken the reins and was walking Coronado, noticeably limping now, slowly back to the barn. Emilio ran up to the house to get Caroline Atwood.

When they had Coronado in his stall, Emilio took off his saddle and Daniel carefully removed the horse's boots from his lower legs. All Maggie and Becky could do was stand and watch helplessly.

"Somebody should call Dr. Howser," Maggie said.

"I already did," Daniel said without looking up.

Maggie hadn't even noticed him on his phone. She had been too focused on her horse.

Maggie heard Becky say, in a voice that wasn't much louder than a whisper, "Please don't let it be bad."

"Back at you," Maggie said.

"I wish we could ask Coronado," Becky said.

"You always want to ask," Maggie said. "But they never talk."

Then they both heard Daniel say, "Maybe here."

He was in a crouch next to Coronado's hind left leg, the boot from the lower leg still in his hand. He pointed to an angry-looking red spot, the size of a show ribbon, some dirt caked on it. To Maggie, a former high school soccer player, it looked like turf burn.

Emilio carried a bowl, sponge, and clean white towel from the tack room. Daniel gently went to work soaping the cut, already looking hot and painful and swollen, while Emilio patted Coronado's head and spoke softly to him in Spanish.

"Did I do something wrong?" Becky said to her mom. "You can tell me if I did."

Maggie put her hand on her daughter's shoulder.

"You rode your horse," she said.

Maggie took in some air, felt the pain she still felt in her ribs when she didn't regulate her breathing properly, and let it out.

"I'm just worried it might be cellulitis," she said then. "Not like I haven't seen that before."

Daniel turned to look at Maggie and said, "Please, let's not go there."

"Try and stop me," Maggie said.

Lord Stanley had been stricken with the bad bacterial infection the last time she was on the Olympic short list, the first time she felt as if the gods had pissed on her, royally.

Maggie had been around vets her whole life and had educated herself as best she could about what could go wrong with horses. She called it her advanced barn degree in veterinary medicine.

Cellulitis attacked the tissue below a horse's skin and could affect any part of a horse's body. And could cause the kind of swelling they were all looking at right now with Coronado. It was most common in the hind legs and could cause lameness so severe that eventually the horse was unable to bear weight on the affected leg.

That was where the infection attacked Lord Stanley, Maggie's dream horse before Coronado became her dream horse. They had treated him with antibiotics, but then the cellulitis came back, worse than before, and more lameness along with it. The antibiotics had worked better the second time around. The horse eventually stopped limping, but he never jumped again. He was now living at a farm in North Carolina owned by a rich woman who took in injured horses the way shelters took in stray dogs.

"What happened?" Maggie heard her mother say now as Caroline Atwood marched into the stall.

Maggie told her, keeping her voice down, her eyes locked on Daniel and Coronado.

"Shit," her mother said. "Shit shit shit."

"Happens," Becky said.

How fragile a thousand-pound animal, even one fast and strong and amazing in the ring, can be, Maggie thought. *How fragile the whole damn sport can be.* She'd just found out herself, the hard way, on what was supposed to be a simple trail ride.

"Where's our goddamn vet?" her mother said.

"On his way," Daniel said.

A few minutes later Dr. Richard Howser walked into the barn.

Steve Gorton was right behind him.

"Just what we need," Maggie whispered to Becky.

"Somebody needs to tell me what the *hell* is going

on here!" Gorton said, as if addressing all of them, and maybe the horse, too.

"He was limping when he left the ring," Maggie said in a quiet voice. "We found a cut, and called Richard, Dr. Howser, and now here we all are."

Gorton turned and looked at Becky.

"Did you do something?" he said.

For once, Maggie watched her daughter hold her tongue.

"I rode the horse, Mr. Gorton," Becky said.

"Why don't we let Richard do his work," Maggie said, "and then we can all talk about it."

The verbal fire that burned in Caroline and Becky had skipped a generation with her. Maggie's anxiety ebbed a bit as she watched Dr. Howser at work. He was as calm as anybody Maggie knew, with the possible exception of her ex-husband.

The vet methodically examined all of Coronado's legs, then took some blood, promising he would fast-track it at the lab.

"So what is it?" Gorton said, with the authority that signaled this stall was now his office.

"I wouldn't even speculate at this point," Howser said, then reached into his medical bag for bandages he began to apply to Coronado's left hind leg.

When he'd finished, they all stepped outside. Steve Gorton said, "All due respect, I need to get a second opinion here."

Maggie fought back a smile at hearing "all due respect"—blunt-force code for bad news.

"With all due respect to *you,* Mr. Gorton," the vet said, "any second opinion would be the same as mine. We just have to wait and see. And not jump to any conclusions."

Gorton looked at Maggie now and said, "He's aware that he works for me, too, right?"

"Richard is the best there is," Maggie said, attempting to avert a scene. "Coronado is in good hands."

Gorton turned back to Becky.

"You're sure you didn't notice something on your ride, and the Atwood Farm family isn't just covering for some mistake you made in the ring?" he said.

"I can answer that, Steve," Maggie said, "because I watched the round and watched the video of it afterward. It was a perfect ride."

"No shit?" he said. "If it was such a perfect ride why'd the doctor have to make a damn house call once it was over?"

Dr. Howser held up the vial of blood he'd taken and said, "I need to get this to the lab. As soon as I get the results, I'll call."

"I want to be in the loop on this," Gorton said.

"You will be," Maggie said.

"Just so we're clear," he said.

Maggie thought, *We couldn't be more clear if you'd hired a skywriter.*

"By the way, Steve?" she said. "How is it that you happened to show up right behind Dr. Howser?"

She saw him hesitate, just slightly.

"I was meeting a friend at the tent," he said. "Thought I'd pop in, maybe get to see her ride him. Good that I did. I don't like to get this shit secondhand."

He started walking toward the driveway, as if he'd just adjourned a meeting. Over his shoulder he said, "Happy New Year, by the way."

He was in his Porsche again today, Maggie saw. He got behind the wheel, slammed the door shut, gunned the sleek car into reverse. As they watched the speeding car disappear up Stable Way, Maggie said, "Should *new* acquaintances be forgot."

She wasn't entirely sure why she thought he was lying about meeting someone at the tent, and just happening by the barn. But she was pretty sure. It reminded her of something Jack McCabe had said once about a lawyer he knew who made frequent appearances on cable news.

"The guy lies to stay in practice," Jack had said.

But if him showing up at the barn *hadn't* been a coincidence, who'd called him?

She steadied herself on her crutches and went slowly back inside to be with her horse.

Shit shit shit.

NINETEEN

DANIEL AND I were in a back booth at La Fogata. Bad Mexican food was better than none, Daniel always said.

After we'd ordered dinner, a plate of nachos and Dos Equis on draft, he said, "We have to believe that the horse is going to be all right."

"And on what do you base that belief, Dr. Ortega?"

He smiled.

"Because he *has* to be all right," he said.

"What a long day," I said. "About to become an even longer night."

"Amen," he said.

"Speaking of freaks," I said. "How about Steve Gorton? That you agree he's a world-class jerk is written all over your face whenever you're around him."

"I need to do a better job of hiding it," he said.

"He dishes out crap to people as if it's ice cream," I said. "But I'm onto his act, and I'm not taking it from him anymore."

Daniel did not hesitate.

"Yes," he said, his voice barely carrying over the din of the place, "you *are* going to take it. We are all going to take it. And *keep* taking it."

He somehow made his eyes seem as quiet as his

voice, and in that centered space I tried to sort through my feelings for him. I'd be lying to myself if I didn't admit that I did wonder if we could ever be more than friends.

And every time I *was* with him away from the barn and the horses, on the other side of a table or seated next to him at the bar, I always had the feeling that he was studying me as much as I was studying him. His life away from the barn was such a mystery to me that I thought of it as his secret life. It was difficult for me to accept that he probably did know me better than I knew him. Every time I tried to get to know him better, he would smile and hold me off, keeping me as much at arm's length as he did the rest of the world.

"Anyway," I said, "Screw Steve Gorton and the Porsche he rode in on."

I raised my glass in a toast. Daniel raised his.

"Very funny, the part about the Porsche," Daniel said. "Remember, though, an attitude like that could cost us this horse."

"But you keep telling me I'm riding him now the way you want me to ride him," I said.

"It doesn't matter to him," he said.

"It's all that's supposed to matter!" I said, suddenly slapping my palm on the table and rattling the dishes and glassware. "This guy doesn't know a bridle from a bridesmaid. Why should I listen to him about anything having to do with Coronado?"

"Because he is looking for a reason to fire you," Daniel said.

The restaurant kept getting louder and more crowded. Daniel leaned forward, as if protecting our conversation. He seemed to go through life worried that somebody might be listening to him. Or watching him. Or both.

Now he said, "A man as rich as Gorton takes control, even in an area, like our sport, about which he is almost completely ignorant. In his mind, he only made a deal for your mother to ride Coronado. He feels that this deal is now…" He stopped, as if searching for the right word. *"Vacio,"* he said finally. "Void."

I started to answer, but he put a finger to his lips and continued.

"He wants to go over to the horse show, look at the standings on the leaderboard, pick a name, and get him to come ride the horse," Daniel said. "It is really as simple as that."

"Wait," I said, "I know he doesn't like me. But you're telling me he wants me to *lose*?"

"Without any doubt," he said.

"In his mind he wins if I lose, just like Grandmother says."

Daniel nodded now. "He does not like the way your grandmother talks to him. She has no respect for him and he wants to be rid of her."

I noticed Eric Glynn, an Irish rider and good guy who was even better company, waving at us from the bar, margarita in hand like a trophy. Normally I would have waved back and asked him to join us, but tonight I just gave him a quick shake of the head. He nodded his understanding, turned back toward a couple of other riders.

"Eric's here," I said to Daniel. "But we haven't finished our conversation."

"Mr. Gorton gave us a month," Daniel said. "So he only wants the horse to lose for this one month, and *then* have a reason to get another rider, many months before the Olympics."

"Is that why you wanted us to have dinner tonight?" I said. "To make sure I understand all this?

Because if that's what you were looking for, mission accomplished. I get it."

He hesitated then. I studied his face now the way he always seemed to be studying mine, and felt he was trying to make up his mind about something.

"No," he said finally. "There is more."

"Please don't give me any more bad news," I said. "Not sure I can handle any tonight, especially if we might be looking at more in the morning with Coronado."

Neither one of us had eaten much. He'd only finished half his beer. I watched him now as he pushed tortilla chips around his plate, as if buying himself some time.

"Don't make me order you a margarita to get you to talk," I said. "What are you not telling me?"

"That neither one of us might make it to the Olympics with this horse, even if we find that his leg is sound," Daniel said.

"What does that even mean?" I said.

"That I am afraid I might get deported before we ever get near Paris," he said.

TWENTY

Daniel

FROM THE TIME they had arrived at the restaurant, every time he felt the words starting to form, he pulled them back. But then he had been doing that for weeks.

Becky had asked him once if he liked talking about anything other than horses and he had said, "What else is there?"

So much else.

There was so much about himself he kept from everyone, including those with whom he worked most closely, and cared about the most. Becky was the one to whom he felt closest of all even as he tried to hide that from her.

But Daniel had finally decided to share something with her he had not even shared with his parents, both of whom were back in Mexico now, working for the rich owner of the Hipódromo de las Américas, the thoroughbred track in Mexico City. Every time he spoke with them by phone, they made sure to tell him that whenever he wanted it there was a job waiting for him as a trainer.

"Ven aqui antes de que venga por ti alli," his father had said just a couple of days before.

Come here before they come for you there.

"They are not coming for me," Daniel had said.

"Liar," his father had said.

He had not been lying to Becky, except perhaps through omission. But he had still decided to tell her the truth.

"Tell me everything," she said now at La Fogata.

"Not here," he said. "We need to talk in private."

"Then let's get the hell out of Dodge," she said. "And right now."

He called for the check, determined to beat Becky to it for once. When the waiter came with it, Becky tried to take it out of his hand, but Daniel was quicker and paid in cash.

Daniel gave the Uber driver the address of the small ranch house Mrs. Atwood had rented for him on Pierson Road, a short walk from the horse show. But as they were approaching the entrance, Daniel suddenly told the driver to stop.

"We can have all the privacy we want right here," he said.

"You didn't want to talk at the restaurant, or in front of the driver," Becky said to him as they walked up the hill toward the main entrance. "I've waited long enough."

He took in a deep breath and let it out. "I like to come here at night sometimes, walk the place like it's a small, empty city."

They passed the place called Hunter Island, where the youngest riders competed on lower jumps, judged for style and not speed, the grace of the horses sometimes more important than the skill of the riders.

"I believe they are watching me," Daniel said now. "Me and all the other undocumenteds who work at this show."

"Define 'they,'" Becky said.

"The *federales*," he said.

"They sound like bad guys in a movie," she said.

"They are much worse," he said, "and not just putting people in danger here, but at Deeridge, and at Global right across the street."

Global was the annual dressage festival, an event that Daniel had always classified as horse dancing. Daniel had always preferred show jumping. Nothing was subjective. Clock and course. Get around fast, no rails down. He wished the world were as simple and as clear cut.

"I'm an idiot," Becky said now, "but I thought Dreamers like you were safe."

"So did we, once," Daniel said. "But now it is as if the government keeps making up the laws as it goes along. And even though I have spent most of my life in America, I am still as undocumented as my parents were when they came here. We have to renew our DACA status every couple years, and mine is due. I just have to find the time."

Becky had told him once that she had studied the Deferred Action for Childhood Arrivals policy, known as DACA, in her political science class, and knew the bare bones of it, that it was intended to provide protections to people in the United States without immigration status, children brought to the country when they were young by undocumented immigrant parents.

"Gotta admit," Becky said, "I don't think I could pass a test on the policy now."

"I'm not sure the politicians fighting about Dreamers could pass one, either," Daniel said.

By now they had walked through the archway of the International Arena, past the old-fashioned carousel, and were passing all the tents that sold saddlery and jewelry and clothing and leather goods and even paintings.

"Do you have a lawyer?" Becky said.

"I have spoken to an immigration lawyer in Fort Lauderdale, yes," he said. "He told me what to do and what to say if the *federales* from ICE ever come looking for me at the barn or the show or even at my house with what they call their administrative warrants. You know ICE, right?"

"I know what they do, just forget what it stands for," Becky said.

"Immigration and Customs Enforcement," he said. "All undocumenteds live in constant fear of them. Now more than ever before."

He felt as if he were giving her a different kind of training now, about a subject that did have him living in constant fear, especially as ICE raids became more and more aggressive, and so often violent. He had spoken to Becky tonight about losing the horse, when he feared losing everything.

"How can I help?" Becky said.

The only sound they could hear now, other than their own voices, was an occasional security golf cart patrolling the barn area.

"You can't help," he said. "Too much else has changed with the government and the courts since my parents brought me here. It is why they finally gave up and went back. My father said it would be his choice, not theirs."

Daniel looked around at the halo of lights shining over the International, the horse show that reminded him of a theme park after hours.

"So what can *you* do?" Becky said.

"The same thing I have been doing," he said.

"Watch and wait. And pray that the blue vests do not come and try to arrest me one day."

"Arrest you for what?" Becky said, her voice suddenly angry. "For being a good person?"

He smiled.

"For not being American enough," he said. "Then they send me back to the other side of the wall."

"Grandmother has lawyers, too," Becky said.

"Mine told me that sometimes trying to stop the deportations feels to him like shouting at the ocean," Daniel said.

"Let me at least ask Grandmother, or Mom, to help," Becky said.

"*No,*" he said.

It came out much sharper than he intended.

"You have to promise me that you will keep this secret for me," he said. "The fewer people talking about this and knowing about this the better."

He turned to look at her.

"Promise," he said.

"I promise," she said.

They had made their way past some of the outdoor restaurants, over the bridge between the International Arena and its schooling ring, finally down a short stairway through some of the luxury boxes down to the in-gate. The jumps were stacked against the wall. The gazebo where the public address announcer sat was empty. Lit from overhead, the rings stood as quiet, Daniel thought, as a cathedral.

They stood and stared silently at the ring where in a couple of weeks Becky and Coronado would ride, with so much at stake, for all of them.

"I can't do this without you," Becky said. "I can't lose you."

He turned to her now, the expanse of the arena

behind them. Wanting to comfort Becky, Daniel moved into a moment he had often imagined. He put his arms around her, neither one of them moving. Daniel did not know if anyone might be watching them, nor did he care.

Becky smiled and turned her face toward his as if to speak.

"Callate," he said softly, knowing she knew what the word meant in his language.

Shut up.

And then before he had time to think, Daniel was pulling Becky close to him and she was letting him and then his arms were around her, and they were kissing.

TWENTY-ONE

DANIEL HAD NEGLECTED to yell "Incoming!" before he dropped two bombs tonight, one after the other.

Dinner at La Fogata hadn't started out as a date. But it had sure ended up as one. Dinner with a friend—or the friend who was your trainer—didn't end with a kiss.

It ended with two, actually.

We didn't talk about the first one as we walked to meet my Uber on Pierson Road.

When the car showed up about ten minutes later, Daniel opened the back door for me. But before I got in, I was putting my arms back around him and initiating a good night kiss, one that lasted even longer than the first, neither of us caring that the driver was sitting right there. Certainly not me.

"We'll get through this," was all I could think of to say when we finally pulled back from each other.

"Who ever said any of this was going to be easy? For now, let's hope for good news tomorrow about the horse." Then he smiled at me and said, "Those were very pleasant kisses, by the way."

"Pleasant?" I said. "That's all you got?" I shook my head, then said, *"Callate."*

The car dropped me home, and it took me a long time to get to sleep. I was way too jazzed, as I kept reviewing the whole day and night, start to finish, like I had them on a continuous loop: The injury to Coronado. The scene with Steve Gorton. The first bomb Daniel had dropped, the big one, about the possibility of deportation.

Then the kisses, especially the first one, the one that transported me back to teenage me and Joey Wolfe making out for the first time in the back seat of a car.

I would have been lying if I told myself I'd never wondered what it might be like, Daniel holding me and me holding him right back. But the last thing I needed right now was another complication in my life. Or a boyfriend. Especially as bombs kept dropping, not just by Daniel Ortega, all around me.

Morning came and Doc Howser didn't call. He might be treating another horse, or in surgery. I came downstairs for coffee and found a note from Mom on the kitchen table.

Might as well do some real sweating while we sweat this out. Should be at the Wanderers Club awhile if you want to join me.

When I got to the gym, I saw Mom before she saw me. She was seated at one of the machines, under the watchful eyes of Todd, who was as much her physical therapist as her trainer.

Right after Mom's fall, I'd done some reading about pelvic injuries, and learned that the recovery time varied from person to person, depending on how long after surgery it took for the fracture to heal enough to safely sustain weight-bearing exercises.

She was doing arm pulls. Even using the lightest possible weight, her face was red with strain and she was sweating through her workout gear.

"We can stop anytime," I heard Todd saying to her.

"No," Mom said through clenched teeth.

"This isn't a competition," he said.

"To me it is," she said.

Todd shrugged. "Okay, then," he said. "Five more."

"I *know* how many reps in a set," she said.

It was when she finished the five that she saw me standing just inside the door.

"Any word?" she said.

Coronado.

I shook my head. "Not yet."

"You have your phone with you? I left mine in my locker."

I produced my phone from my back pocket.

"Can you keep it with you while you work out in case he calls?"

"That's the plan," I said.

"I keep telling myself that no news doesn't mean bad news," she said, as if trying to convince herself. Then she added, "On a more pleasant note, how'd dinner with Daniel go?"

I paused and then said, "Interesting is the word I'd use."

"Good interesting or bad?"

"Little bit of both," I said. "Tell you about it later."

"That sounds mysterious," she said.

"No shit, Sherlock," I said.

She tried to stand, rose halfway, sat back down hard. Todd extended a hand to her. She waved it off. Then got to her feet the second time and without her crutches limped toward the next machine. Over her shoulder she said, "Wanna arm wrestle?"

"I'd need to work up my strength," I said, heading to the exercise bike.

"Ha," she said.

She and Todd went over to one of the leg-press machines, which she worked with her left leg until she'd done three sets of fifteen reps each. I kept sneaking looks at her, seeing the same fierceness on her face that I always saw in the close-up photographs Grandmother paid to have taken of her up on her horse.

No, I thought. This was another level up from that, a look that bordered on obsession. I couldn't lose, or lose this horse, because of what losing would do to her, forget about the rest of us.

Every couple of minutes I'd look at Mom and then look at my phone.

Still nothing from Doc Howser.

After doing a couple of miles on the bike I began my usual weight circuit, alternating upper body and legs, three sets at each machine, feeling a little obsessive myself, feeling pissed off at Steve Gorton all over again, angry that even if I did win on Coronado, he won, too.

I was finishing my last set with free weights when I saw Mom, a towel around her neck, taking a rest on one of the benches.

"Still nothing?" she said.

"I'm fixing to call him myself," I said.

"No," she said. "When he knows something, he'll call."

"How can you be so calm about this?"

"It's just a cruel deception," she said. Then she grinned. "I've been watching you," she continued. "You look like you're in the ring already."

"Sometimes I wish it were a boxing ring," I said.

"Fight fight fight," she said.

I grinned back at her.

"You sound like a cheerleader."

"About all I can handle these days," she said.

Just then I saw the double glass doors to the fitness center open, and Dr. Richard Howser walked through them, looking around until he spotted Mom and me.

He walked over to us, his face, as usual, showing nothing. He also never screwed around, even when he was Dr. Doom, about to deliver some particularly shitty news.

Please don't let it be bad.

Then he smiled.

"The horse is fine," he said.

Now he was the one I wanted to kiss.

TWENTY-TWO

"A MILD INFECTION," Doc Howser said, "caused by dirt getting inside the cut. You could probably get away with giving him just one day off."

We decided on two. Back in the ring, not doing any real jumps, using ground poles for distances, Coronado was perfect.

Now it was Saturday afternoon, our first competition together, the $10,000 Jumper in the International Arena.

My class was scheduled to start at one o'clock. I had been awake since five in the morning, the hour I'd sometimes get in after a party night. Now I was wide awake. Tried to go back to sleep. Couldn't. Daniel and I would head over to the show about eleven and since I was going thirtieth in the order, I wouldn't be in the International Ring with Coronado until after two.

He was probably still sleeping.

My brain was running hot.

Trying to step lightly so as not to wake Mom or Grandmother, I got out of bed, walked to the window that looked down at the barn. The wall was hung on both sides with ribbons I'd won on Sky, a handful of times beating out Mom and some of the other top riders.

I'd trade every single ribbon on this wall, I thought, *to win just one today.*

What had Mom always said?

One chance to make a good first impression.

I snuck downstairs now and made myself my first cup of coffee, brought it back upstairs. Waited for the sun to come up.

I knew when it finally did the day would move like that television commercial. Life would come at me fast.

Just not yet.

I looked at the clock on the nightstand.

Still just five fifteen.

Only my heart was going fast. Running as hot as my brain. How was I going to handle these feelings when they maxed out in the ring? When it was showtime?

Get a grip, bitch.

Yeah, right.

I put on jeans and a T-shirt, went downstairs, fixed myself another cup of coffee, silently let myself out the back door. I walked down the hill to the barn, only to be near the horses. Let them sleep, even if I couldn't.

I stood at the fence near the in-gate, placed my cup on top of one of the posts, and thought back to when I was six years old, getting up on Frenchy for my first ride around the ring. Loved my first pony then the way I loved Sky now.

I'd only walked Frenchy before that day.

But that day I was going to ride her. *Really* ride her. Mom hadn't thought I was ready. Grandmother had insisted that I was. I'd screwed up my six-year-old courage and got around on jumps as low as Grandmother and Mom could make them.

I had been as scared then as I was now.

You're not a little girl anymore.

I stayed long enough down at the barn to watch the sunrise. Then I walked back up to the house. Longest morning of my life still stretching out ahead of me.

TWENTY-THREE

DANIEL AND I were walking the course with the rest of the riders and trainers, pacing off the distances between jumps.

Half hour until the round started. It felt by now as if I'd been awake for about a month.

"Well," I said, "this shit is about to get real."

He grinned.

"Were you always this much of a poet?" he said.

"Goddamn right," I said.

"Relax," he said.

"I am relaxed."

"You are about as good a liar as you are a poet," Daniel said.

We reached the middle of the course then, staring down the double combination before the last jump. What Daniel called the main event. Six strides leading into the first jump, then room enough for just one stride before the second one. In that moment flying and landing in a small space, then flying again. After that it was something right out of the movies. Fast and furious to the finish.

I knew I didn't need to win today. But I couldn't look like a total loser, either. I wanted to get around clean and pick up some points on what was known

as the Average Ranking List, which was about results, but consistency, too. By the time summer rolled
around, the top three American riders on that list
would be chosen to represent the US in Paris.

Fifty horses entered, almost all of the top riders,
men and women, riders as old as sixty and as
young as sixteen. I really did love this distinctive
quality that separated our sport from all others. Men
against women. Teenagers against grandparents. All
that mattered was being good enough, having enough
horse underneath you.

I, along with all the other riders, was using this
event as a warm-up for the Grand Prix happening in
two weeks, in this same big-ass arena.

Matthew Killeen, number one in Ireland, just
ahead of his best friend, Eric Glynn, was walking with
his trainer about two jumps ahead of us. He wasn't
just a great rider. He was a good guy. At one point
he'd turned around and yelled at me, "Slow down,
McCabe, you're already making me nervous."

I'd grinned and given him the finger.

"Always the lady," he said.

"My way of saying you're number one, Killeen," I
yelled back.

Matthew was good-looking, too, if a little old for
me at thirty-five. It hadn't stopped me from having
a major teenage crush on him when he'd started
competing more regularly at WEF.

Behind us was Tyler Cullen, always near the top
of the American rankings, but currently number two
behind Tess McGill, whose father was lead singer for
the rock group Snap. I'd waved at Tyler when I'd first
gotten on the course. He ignored me, even though I
knew he'd seen me. Daniel saw what I saw, and just
shook his head.

"If Mr. Steve Gorton were a rider," Daniel had said to me, "he'd be Tyler Cullen."

"Oh, hell, no," I said. "Even Gorton isn't that much of a prick."

When we finished the course, we stopped briefly at the in-gate, where we made out like high school kids. Amazing how sometimes everything could still feel like high school. Daniel hadn't mentioned the kiss since that night. I hadn't, either. Maybe next week I could pass him a note after chem class.

Focus, I told myself, but not, *Relax.*

I'd always felt nerves, what Mom liked to call the good nerves that came with competition.

Never like this.

I was happy to be going thirtieth in the order. I'd have a chance to watch how the preceding riders and horses handled the course—where in the second half to pick up speed, where others had taken chances and they'd played it safe.

Today's event might have been titled "Power and Speed." The course seemed to break at the eighth jump. That's when the clock started. That's when a rider who could manage to keep the last eight striped poles off the ground had the chance to post a score.

As nervous as I was, I was stupidly excited at the same time. This was the biggest jumping event of my whole stupid life.

Focus.

Up in the tent, Mom and Grandmother were at their table. They'd decided to watch from there, even though Grandmother said she couldn't curse freely without scaring the decent people. Daniel would shout any instructions from the in-gate, though he was convinced that if he'd done his job during the week, I'd be fine out there on my own.

"What do you want to do until Emilio brings up Coronado from the barn?" Daniel said.

He meant the small Atwood Farm barn at the show. The way it worked, Emilio would bring Coronado to the schooling ring about twenty minutes before my spot in the order, and we'd start jumping in there until my name was called.

Mr. Gorton would be here eventually. Knowing him, he'd demand a private viewing stand next to the central announcer's gazebo.

"I just want to be alone for a few minutes," I said. "You okay with that?"

"Yes," he said.

"Relax," he said again, smiling at me.

"Callate," I said.

I found a place high up in the bleachers, on the opposite side of the ring from where Mom and Grandmother were. Matthew Killeen went out early and posted 30.19, a banging time that put him right into first place. Tyler Cullen, going twentieth, posted a time of 30.58. When he finished the round, he turned to look at the clock and I could see how pissed off he was. He'd come so close to Matthew's time, and he hated to lose to anybody, Matthew most of all.

Ten out now.

I heard my phone beep with a message, pulled it out of the back pocket of my breeches and saw:

he's here.

From Daniel.

He meant Coronado.

I made my way down through the bleachers and over to the schooling ring, to where Daniel and Emilio stood with our big horse. Just without Mom in the saddle this time. Emilio helped me up. Daniel handed me my gloves, then walked over to the middle of the ring. I put Coronado in motion, a couple of slow laps around the ring, then over one of the jumps. Then another lap, and over the other jump.

More nervous than ever.

Still stupidly excited.

I heard the in-gate announcer say, *"Frankie next, then Adam, then Georgina."*

Georgina Bloomberg. Her father had been mayor of New York City once. Later on, he'd spent enough money to buy our whole sport running for president.

What the hell was I doing here?

"Becky four," the announcer said.

The next few minutes were a blur, until I heard the announcer say, *"Becky next."*

I slow-walked Coronado over to where Daniel was already waiting for us in the gate. He looked up at me, smiled, nodded, put out his fist so I could lean down and bump it. I looked around now, taking in the whole scene: the course, the tent to my right, stands that were mostly full, one of the biggest rings in the whole sport. I was about to take my place at the grown-up table.

My heart thumped like the palpable bass of a rap song playing from the next car at a stoplight.

I heard the announcer naming me as the rider of Coronado, owned by Steve Gorton of New York City and Caroline Atwood, Atwood Farm of Wellington, Florida.

The horse that had gone before me walked past us. I gave Coronado a little kick to get him going.

Then I heard, "Is this where I wish you good luck?" from the other side of the in-gate from where Daniel was standing.

Steve Gorton.

No owners ever came down here. There he was, anyway.

Don't look back, I told myself as Coronado walked out into the International.

Showtime.

TWENTY-FOUR

DON'T THINK ABOUT Gorton.

Think about the sixteen jumps out here.

Eight before the speed round.

Let's go.

No need to push Coronado in the first half. Get through the first eight clean. After that, let the big guy run.

Just like that, we were over the first jump. Six strides in the line between the first and the second. Then we were over that one. No big turns in this part of the course. No surprises. It would be the second half that felt like Daytona.

Don't get ahead of yourself.

The next two jumps were along the wall in front of the members' tent. Cleared both, then went right into a slight turn, quickly squaring him up, counting strides inside my head as I did.

Four.

Five.

Six.

Cleared it with ease.

Come on.

It was as if somebody had hit a mute button inside the ring. I couldn't hear the crowd, couldn't hear the sound of the PA announcer's voice. All I could hear was my horse, his breath, the sound of his hooves.

The next line was a stride longer.

Five.

Six.

Seven.

Another one clean.

We made a wide turn at the opposite end of the ring from the in-gate, approaching the big screen in the corner down there. There was a clock in the corner of the screen.

Don't look at the time.

Three more jumps to clear before the speed round.

Damn, this horse felt good.

Then it was one more jump before the speed round, and we were over that, room to spare.

Come on.

Ten seconds from the finish.

Or less.

Eight jumps.

Cleared the first. Cleared the second. Handled a tight rollback with ease, not cutting it too close, not wanting to take a chance there.

Nailed the jump. What was the term in gymnastics? Stuck the landing.

Came around and was facing the big screen again. The horse flying now.

Don't look at the clock.

Listen to Daniel's words. All that ever mattered was the next jump.

Handled the next two with ease, perfect distances both times. I wasn't one of those riders who'd tell you afterward they had a clock inside their head.

But we were getting after it.

Now I was yelling "Come on!" at Coronado.

Tough rollback coming up, tightest on the course. But Daniel had said that if I was going to steal some time, this was the place, if I was sure I could make an inside turn at one of the decorative flower beds. But only if I was sure I could get Coronado squared up in time.

I went inside.

Knew we had picked up time once I did.

Maybe that half second could make all the difference.

The stands were flying past us now, Coronado passing the announcer's gazebo, then around close to the tent.

Yeah, I thought.

Hell, yeah.

Look at us. We can fly.

The double combination was dead ahead of us now. Then one last jump. I could feel him pick up speed without me asking, as if he knew exactly where he was, what he needed to do, how much course we had left.

Three jumps.

Ten seconds, tops.

Six strides to the first jump in the combination.

I was counting again.

Four.

Five.

Six.

No.

Shit shit shit.

I was too far away. Our first bad distance. I tried to add an extra stride and hoped it wasn't too late.

It was.

We were too close.

Coronado tried. Tried his ass off. But we *were* too

close when we went into the jump. His front legs crashed into the top rail, propelling it into the air in front of him.

The horse landed one stride distant from the second jump and when he saw the rail drop in front of him, came to a dead stop.

He refused the jump like he was slamming on the brakes.

I felt the horse duck and spook, as I flew forward toward an airborne state. That left only one strategy.

I bailed.

That's what riders called it.

I bailed, and let go of the reins, and slid down the side of Coronado and landed on my butt.

TWENTY-FIVE

I'D NEVER RIDDEN any horse in competition and ended up on the ground. Had come close a few times, once hanging on for dear life in Kentucky. But I'd never found myself in the dirt when I was going for a ribbon until now. Definitely not here.

At least Coronado didn't bolt. Horses often did when a rider came off them, started galloping around the ring at full speed. Daniel and Emilio had gotten him under control the day he came back from the trail ride without Mom. Sometimes in a ring as big as this one it would take a half dozen or more people.

Coronado just stayed where he was between the two jumps, as if waiting for me to tell him what to do and where to go.

Three more jumps.

I got to my feet, did a quick physical inventory, realized I wasn't hurt. Apart from my pride.

Emilio was now taking control of Coronado, walking him around the second jump and slowly back to the in-gate. Daniel was still there. I'd waved him off, signaling him that I'd take what I'd always considered a rider's walk of shame alone.

"It was all my fault," I said when I got to him.

"At least nobody was hurt," he said.

"He's all right?" I said.

"He seems to be fine," Daniel said.

"Makes one of us," I said.

We exited the in-gate so that the next horse could enter, then headed for the schooling ring. I could feel the eyes of the spectators up there in the expensive seats, looking down on me.

Yeah, I thought.

Looking down on me in every way.

I just needed to get around clean, whatever my time was, whether I ribboned or not. Show everybody I belonged. Then we were into it, Coronado and me, feeling it, and the speed round was nearly over, and I thought we really *could* win.

But the only thing I could absolutely not do, one hundred percent could not do, was have my horse leave the ring without me on it.

Bad Becky.

I looked down at my jacket and breeches and saw they were covered in the dirt I hadn't stopped to clean off in my push to get out of the ring. Screw it, I thought. I'll clean up later. How long since Daniel and I had walked the course? Ninety minutes? Two hours?

Now this kind of walk.

"You want to talk about it?"

"There's nothing to talk *about*," I said. "I know exactly what happened and why it happened and what I did."

"It was a mistake," he said. "A mis*step*. Not the end of the world."

Before I could answer I heard Steve Gorton shouting. He was standing with Mom and Grandmother outside the schooling ring, his voice loud enough that riders had stopped their horses to watch.

Daniel and I stopped, too. When Grandmother tried to speak, Gorton started shaking his head like a horse shooing away flies.

For once, I thought, Grandmother didn't have the loudest voice in the room.

"No!" Gorton shouted. *"I'm not here to listen to you. You're here to listen to me."*

I started to move in their direction then, but Daniel gently put a hand on my arm.

"No," he said.

"Why not? They weren't riding the horse. I was."

"Trust me," Daniel said. "In this moment you cannot help them. Or yourself."

Then everybody near the schooling ring and maybe all over the grounds heard Gorton say, *"I want her gone now."*

Mom tried to argue, but he waved her off.

"What I'd really like to do?" Gorton said. *"Fire her right now and then call her in a hour and fire her again."*

He turned to walk away from them and saw Daniel and me standing in the ring. Gorton, big as he was, managed to squeeze himself through the fence, only to risk getting kicked by the horses around him.

His chest was heaving, his face clenched as tight as a fist and the color of a stop sign.

"Did you hear what I just told them?" he said.

"Everybody heard," I said quietly.

"You know who could have ridden that horse better than you did today?" he said, spitting out the words. *"Anybody."*

Then he turned to Daniel.

"Remind me again why this girl was the one to ride this horse now that her mother can't?" he said.

Before Daniel could answer, Gorton walked past us unscathed by the horses. We both turned and watched him go.

"He is a bad man," Daniel said.

"Yeah," I said, "he is. But when he's right, he's right."

TWENTY-SIX

Maggie

RIGHT AFTER STEVE GORTON walked out of the schooling ring, Becky disappeared for a few hours. She didn't answer any of Maggie's calls or texts. She'd finally taken a call from Daniel, who told her that Caroline was convening a family meeting at the house, at eight.

Becky came through the front door on time, still in her dirty riding clothes.

"Are you okay?" Maggie said to Becky.

"Fine," Becky said in that contrary way she'd had since she was a little girl.

"Honey," Maggie said. "You've lost before."

"Not like that, I haven't," Becky said.

"We all lose more in this sport than we win," Maggie said. "Matthew Killeen. Tyler Cullen. Rich Grayson. Georgina Bloomberg. Tess McGill. *Me.*"

"Mom," Becky said, "I love you to death. But the last thing I need right now is a pep talk."

"It's the truth," Maggie said.

"My whole life you've talked about people's truths," Becky said. "Trust me, tonight yours isn't close to being mine."

Little did she know.

They heard Caroline coming down the steps then.

She had changed out of the riding clothes she always wore to the show, as if still a competitor herself.

"Well, well," she said. "The gang's all here."

In jeans and sneakers, she crossed the room, rolling up the sleeves on her Atwood Farm sweatshirt before sitting down in her rocking chair. Daniel was standing near the front window. Becky stood next to him. Maggie had taken the couch. She'd been on her feet enough today. Her bad knee felt as if someone had stuck a needle in it.

She was all talked out by now. Or shouted out. This was her mother's show.

"Before you say anything," Becky said to her grandmother, "if this is about the way I rode, I *know*, okay? I *know*. I thought I could get him to make up the distance. All of us saw what happened after that."

"Everybody makes mistakes, kid," Caroline Atwood said.

Didn't see that one coming, Maggie thought.

"I couldn't afford to make one like that today," Becky said.

"Like we say all the time around here," Caroline said, "shit happens. And today, all of us stepped in it."

Maggie watched as her mother rose painfully to her feet. Like mother, like daughter.

"Not the kind of night I was hoping for," she said.

"None of us were," Maggie said.

"It is like I told Becky," Daniel said. "It was a mistake, not the end of the world."

"Thank you," Becky said. "I mean that. But nobody's talking me down tonight." She grimaced. "Or back up. All I can say is I'm sorry."

"I didn't ask you here to get an apology out of you," Caroline said. "I've told you since you were a little girl. Sorry doesn't fix the lamp."

"Can I say what I've been thinking about since I walked out of the ring, Grandmother?" Becky said. "If you and Mr. Gorton want to find another rider, I'm totally down with that. I did this to myself."

"No," Caroline said.

Maggie was watching her daughter now, seeing the surprise on her face. Or maybe relief.

Knowing it wasn't going to last long. All afternoon Maggie had been arguing Caroline's decision, but her mother insisted it was final.

"No," Becky said, "meaning…"

"*No* meaning I've decided to cash out," Caroline Atwood said.

"Cash out?" Becky said, as if she hadn't heard correctly.

"Sell our share of the horse."

TWENTY-SEVEN

AFTER ALL THE bombs I'd had dropped on me lately, this was the big one.

"You're joking," I said to Grandmother.

"Do I sound as if I'm joking?"

I gave Daniel a quick sideways look. If he'd known this was coming, he was a better actor than DiCaprio. Then I looked over at Mom, frozen in place on the couch.

Her reaction was no reaction at all.

She knew, I thought.

"Gorton and I had a long talk on the phone after he got back to Palm Beach," Grandmother said now. "He admitted that he'd given us a month, but after what he saw today, if Becky rode Coronado in the Grand Prix, any possible outcome was bad. We'd lose time that we really don't have. Or the horse could get hurt, at which point he'd be worth a bucket of spit. And if *that* happened, I might as well have burned the money we put up for him."

"And you agreed with him," I said.

My dear grandmother sighed.

"I told him I couldn't *dis*agree," she said. "I'm the one who's sorry, I guess."

"You don't have to apologize, either," I said.

"Like you say," she said. "It is what it is."

"But it doesn't have to be!" I said. "It was a crap ride. But it was one crap ride. I thought I had a month, not one damn day."

"I haven't told you all of it," she said.

"We're all listening," I said.

"He offered a million dollars, right now, to buy me out," she said. "Buy us out and give him what he wants, which is full control of the horse."

I heard a sharp intake of breath from Daniel.

"I'm going to accept," she said.

I looked over at Mom now.

"Jump in anytime," I said.

"There's more to this," Maggie said. "Mom showed me the books today. She's afraid that we're going to lose the barn. She gambled when we bought Coronado that once I started winning on him, that would attract new riders and new families to the barn. But it hasn't happened. And now I *can't* ride Coronado."

Grandmother said, "Listen, I know that the value of the horse could go sky high if he does make it to the Olympics, whether we end up with a gold medal or not. But I did gamble everything once. I can't afford to do it again. None of us can. Not with an offer like this in hand."

Daniel took a step forward.

"We only had a week to get ready," he said. "You know this world as well as anyone, *jefa*. A week is not enough time to make a serious decision."

He paused and said, "I promise things will be different in the Grand Prix."

"You can't make a promise like that," Grandmother said. "And neither can my granddaughter."

"Things will be better," Daniel said.

"Or much, *much* worse," she said.

"I know you have a deal with that slug," I said. "But forget about that. *We* had a deal, Grandmother. You and me."

"Deals get broken all the time in this business," she said. "The days when my late husband operated on a handshake are long gone."

"Holy...*holy,*" I said. "You'll be giving him exactly what he wants, before we get anywhere near the Grand Prix. We lose. He wins."

"And gives us a parting gift of a million dollars," she said. She steepled her hands together, almost like she was praying.

"I met with Andy yesterday," she said.

Her accountant.

"And Andy told me that we'll be lucky to make it to the end of the year if we continue trying to live on the margins," she said.

"What's the word you always use to describe Steve Gorton?" I said. "Transactional? You sound as transactional as he does."

"Becky, that's not fair," Mom said.

"Yes," Grandmother said, "it is."

"We're just asking for a little more time," Daniel said.

"He told me to take the offer or leave it," Grandmother said. "If there's another disaster at the Grand Prix, we're out a million, and he takes complete control of the horse. It will be as if we lost Coronado twice."

It wasn't a fair fight, from either side. Grandmother looked beaten down already.

So I turned to Mom.

"How much is first place in the Grand Prix worth?" I said.

"Honey, you know I love *you* to death," Mom said.

"But you can't think we're going from what happened today to first place."

"I can tell you," Grandmother said. "It's a five-star event. First prize is two hundred and fifty thousand dollars. Our cut would be more than a hundred."

"Let's say I do shock everybody and win on a horse we all know is good enough to win," I said. "Wouldn't our finances get better in the short run?"

"You're being silly," Grandmother said.

"Just asking," I said to her.

"In that scenario," she said, "yes, an infusion of cash like that would feel as if we'd won the lottery."

I was just pulling stuff out of my butt now.

"And in that moment, at least hypothetically, the value of the horse would be as high as ever, correct?" I said.

"Hypothetically, yes," Mom said.

"Without the one mistake," Daniel said in a voice even quieter than normal, "they would have won today."

"If the queen had balls, she'd be king," Grandmother said. "And I can't bet a million dollars on what almost happened today. Like an old friend of mine used to say, what could've happened *did*."

She sighed again.

"The answer is still no," she said.

"There must be something I can say to change your mind," I said.

"Not when it's made up," she said. "You should know that as well as anyone."

TWENTY-EIGHT

ATWOOD FARM WASN'T close to business as usual when Mom went to the gym in the morning.

The only glimmer of good news was that she was getting better. Starting to get her appetite back, if not regaining much weight. She'd already tossed the knee brace and only a slight limp remained as an indicator of what had happened to her, how badly she'd been injured.

Grandmother had a nine o'clock appointment with Andy, the accountant. Before she left, I'd said to her one last time, "Are you sure?"

"I'd better be," she said.

By nine thirty Steve Gorton was due to arrive at the house to close his deal with Grandmother. She'd decided he could talk to me instead.

"You can handle him," she said.

"Yeah," I said, "the way I would a python."

I'd never really been alone with Steve Gorton, but riding Coronado had made him more mine than anybody else's, so I should be the one giving Gorton the official word.

As I sat at the kitchen table with a fresh cup of coffee, I wondered if he'd be on time for once. Hoping he would be, so I could quickly get this over with, go down the hill, and ride my horse.

When I heard his car in the driveway, I checked my phone. Nine forty-five. Not bad for him. Gorton's version of Becky Standard Time.

I walked into the living room and parted the drapes enough to see that today he was in the red Porsche, looking shiny and showroom-new, the sun reflecting off the windshield, like the car was giving off a beam of light.

He walked toward the house nodding his head at a caller on the phone he carried in one hand, a legal-size envelope in the other. A descriptive line about a mouse who'd grown up to be a rat surfaced from one of my writing classes.

Get it over with.

When I answered the front door he said, "Where's your grandmother?"

"Not here," I said.

"Where is she?"

"She had an appointment," I said.

"What the hell?" he said. "Her appointment was with me."

"Would you care to come inside?"

"I have to be somewhere."

"Same," I said. "But my family has decided that whatever you needed to say, you can say to me."

I showed him into the front room, asked if he wanted coffee, at least making a pass at sounding polite.

"No coffee. No screwing around," he said. "You know why I'm here."

"I do," I said, taking the rocking chair.

He sat down on the couch, tossed the envelope on the coffee table, pointed at it.

"I'll leave this agreement for her," he said. "I've already signed it. As soon as she countersigns, I'll transfer the money into her account." He made a snorting noise. "I can't believe I wasted a trip."

"Sorry," I said, as if feeling him.

"Are you?"

"Time is money," I said.

"Is that supposed to be some kind of smart remark?"

"Not if you have to ask," I said.

"I know I'm supposed to be the bad guy here," he said.

"Actually, in this case, you're not."

"But none of this is my fault," Gorton said. "You had your chance and you blew it. We need to stop jacking around with the notion that you should be riding this horse. Or ever should have been riding this horse."

"You made that pretty clear yesterday," I said.

"The guy who tells people what they want to hear?" he said. "I'm not that guy."

I grinned.

"So I've heard."

"I'll send somebody to pick up the signed papers," he said.

"You can actually take them with you," I said.

"She needs to sign them first," he said.

"Well, see, here's the thing," I said. "She's not signing. And we're not selling."

"We had a goddamn deal," he said.

"And now we don't."

"That's it?" he said. "Care to explain?"

"You wouldn't get it."

I got out of the rocking chair and walked across the living room and opened the front door for him. He walked past me, close enough for me to smell his cologne, turned when he got to the driveway.

"You're telling me that she's walking away from a million dollars now, even though you all know I get control of the horse in a couple of weeks?" Gorton said.

"Crazy, right?"

"You really don't care to tell me why?"

"She changed her mind," I said.

I shrugged.

"If it's any consolation to you, Mr. Gorton?"

"What?" he snapped.

"Shocked the hell out of me, too."

TWENTY-NINE

The night before.

I THREW EVERYTHING I had at Grandmother, queen of the manor, if you could call Atwood Farm a manor.

I reminded her that I'd been told my whole life that we weren't in the horse business for the money. That if it were only about the money, she wouldn't have basically mortgaged her whole life to have enough money to get a share of Coronado. She'd done it because she loved Mom enough to give her this chance. And this horse.

No go.

"We keep talking and talking but arriving back at the same damn place," she said. "And that means *this* place. Your grandfather and I built it up from nothing. It's been the last fifty years of my life. First with him, then with you and your mom. You know how much I hate to do this. But there will be other horses."

"Not like this one."

"Maybe not," she said. "Maybe not. But your mother was on her way to the Olympics with Lord Stanley before he went lame."

By then I only had one bullet left.

"Then sell *my* horse," I said.

"Sell Sky?" Mom said. "You don't mean that."

"Yeah, Mom," I said. "I do."

She knew how much I loved the horse. So did Mom and Grandmother. We'd all known it from that first day I'd ridden her. And even though I hadn't done nearly enough with her last year, nobody was blaming the horse. We all knew that every year when WEF would start up again, there was an Irish trainer named Dermot Morgan who'd try to buy her. I'd always give the same answer. She wasn't for sale.

"I'd never let you sell that horse," Grandmother said.

Like we were back on the same side all of a sudden.

"It's my horse," I said. "And even though she won't command nearly what Coronado would, I know what Dermot has offered in the past."

"You're coming off your worst year," Mom said.

"Wasn't Sky's fault," I said.

"You're willing to place that kind of bet on yourself?" Grandmother said.

At least I had her attention. Still had her talking. Even I wasn't sure whether I was bluffing.

"Damn straight," I said. "Dermot writes me a check, I hand it over to you, and we all get ready for the Grand Prix."

"Have you spoken to your father about this?" Mom said.

"He says it's my horse and I can do what I want with her," I said.

I actually hadn't spoken to him since the night after Mom had been thrown.

Grandmother was staring at me.

"You'd seriously be willing to do this to get one more chance on Coronado?" she said.

"One hundred percent," I said. "Daniel's right. I can win on this horse. I should have won today."

The living room windows were open to let in the

night air. One of the horses in the barn gave a loud whinny, but no one spoke.

It was Mom who finally did.

"Becky's right," she said. "It was never about the money with you, any more than it was with Dad."

She gave her mother a long look and said, "What would Dad say if he were around?"

"Now who's not being fair?" Grandmother said.

"Me," Maggie Atwood said. "Because we both know the answer."

"Clint Atwood would have poured himself another whiskey and then said we were going to let it ride," Grandmother said.

She slowly and deeply breathed in, let it out even more slowly.

"God forgive a fool like me," she said now, then looked directly at me. But she was smiling.

"We let it ride," she said.

THIRTY

Gorton

"WHAT DO YOU mean the old bat changed her mind?" Gorton heard now on speakerphone.

He was driving east on Southern Boulevard, on his way to the bridge that took him from mainland to island and finally his home on Ocean Boulevard. What he and his friends jokingly called "the hood."

"That's what the little wiseass just informed me," Gorton said.

"Our Becky," the man said. "You're telling me that they passed up the money?"

"That's right."

He thought he was going to make the light before the bridge, didn't, saw it go to red and the drawbridge begin its slow rise toward the sky.

Perfect, he thought. *Just perfect.*

My morning just keeps getting better.

"So what are you going to do?" the man said.

"I know what you're going to do," Gorton said. "You're going to win the goddamn Grand Prix."

"If it's not me, it'll be somebody else, but never her," the man said. "That was a total choke job yesterday. As easy a distance as there was on the course. It would have been like Secretariat's jockey finding a way to lose."

"Long shots have hit before," Gorton said. "Not just horses. Even my Jets won a Super Bowl once."

A silence settled between the two men. Bridge was still up.

"You saved yourself some money today," the man said. "You take complete control of the horse in two weeks, correct?"

"But that little punk talked to me—to my face— like I was one of her grooms," Gorton said, then paused. "Remember that movie with Tom Cruise and Jack Nicholson where Nicholson lost his shit in the courtroom?"

"A Few Good Men."

"Those people screwed with the wrong Marine today," Gorton said.

He sat there drumming his fingers on the steering wheel as the bridge finally started to come down. Still seeing the look on Becky's face. The one who'd landed on her ass the day before acted like she won something today. Now every member of that family had treated him like some sort of schmuck.

"Like I said, you just need to stay cool."

"You know what makes me lose my cool?" Gorton said. "People telling me to stay cool."

"Hey, I'm on your side," the man said.

"Then call me back with something I can use against them," Gorton said, "just in case I need to."

He was about to end the call when the man said, "Wait, I just thought of something."

"What?"

THIRTY-ONE

IT WAS SUNDAY morning, less than a week to go until the Grand Prix qualifier, Daniel and I in the tack room, Emilio outside putting a saddle on Coronado.

Daniel wouldn't have Sky and me jump at all when we were close to showing. He'd only had me jump Coronado at Atwood Farm after Mom got hurt to give me a chance to know the horse.

"I keep thinking that if I win, I win more than a hundred thousand," I said. "If I lose, we all lose a million bucks."

"Ve con dodo," he said.

"That one I don't know."

"Let it ride," he said.

I didn't have to win on Thursday. Just needed to go clean and be in the top forty riders and make it to Saturday.

I went around the long course clean now, then waited on Coronado while Daniel set up the kind of jump-off course we'd encounter next week in the International Arena. Get around clean on the long course, in the time allowed, and you qualified for the jump-off. Half as long and twice as tricky, like riding full speed through a maze.

I nearly made a mistake today on the second-to-last jump, when I didn't support Coronado enough, and felt his hind legs clip a rail. But the rail stayed up. It was all Coronado. In moments like that, you were supposed to imagine you were riding with your arms, helping to carry the horse over the jump.

This time I pictured myself nearly dropping him.

But didn't.

"You relaxed," Daniel said.

"I'm about as relaxed these days as a hummingbird," I said.

"Then you lost concentration," he said.

"Now *that* I can do," I said.

"A boxer drops his guard and gets knocked out," he said.

"Boxing is dumb," I said.

"Losing concentration on this horse is much dumber," he said.

"Your motivational speaking needs some work, have I ever mentioned that?" I said.

I trotted Coronado then. Emilio helped me down and walked the horse back to the barn. Daniel and I watched the video he'd taken of both rounds on his phone. He pointed out a couple of other technical mistakes, especially a rollback early in the jump-off where I'd taken the safe route and not made as much of an inside turn as I could have.

"A half second," he said, "could make all the difference between qualifying and not qualifying."

"At least I went clean," I said.

"Barely," he said.

"Come on," I said. "You know I did good today."

He smiled. "How about I reward you by buying you a burger later?" he said.

"Sure," I said, hoping I didn't answer too quickly and sound too eager. "But no drinking. I'm in training."

"In that case, you drive," he said. "Pick me up around seven."

"Deal."

Well, I thought, *look at him. Asking me out on a real date.* I'd said yes before really thinking about it. He could make the next move, if there was ever going to be a next move.

I wasn't even sure I *wanted* there to be a next move.

Then why are you even going?

I knew that answer, too. Because I was curious to see if he *would* bring up that night.

Daniel was good and good-looking. And kind. Definitely kind. But still my trainer. It was probably inevitable that if some kind of romantic relationship did start, any awkward twist would mess up my relationship with him *as* my trainer.

And given my short odds with long-term boy-friends, it *would* get messed up. Maybe that's what I ought to tell him if he brought up the kisses we'd shared.

If he *didn't* bring it up, well, then screw it and screw him.

Not that I was on edge.

I didn't need Daniel telling me to relax right now, like I was going into the ring. Needed to do it myself.

You're going out for a burger, not looking to make things official.

I was about five minutes late arriving at the small ranch house on Pierson. Becky Standard Time. I'd thought about getting my hair done but had decided I didn't want to look like I was trying too hard, going all girly-girl on him.

Yup, I thought.

Your move, Daniel.

But when I pulled into the driveway, his used Kia, which he liked to say had a million miles on it, wasn't there.

Maybe for once he was running even later than me. Or he'd loaned his car to one of his carless friends from the other barns.

I checked my phone to see if I had missed a text. Nothing. Got out of the car and went and rang the doorbell.

Waited.

Nothing.

Pulled out my phone and texted him.

where the heck are u?

No response. I called his number and was sent straight to voicemail.

I went back to the car and sat there waiting.

Seven thirty.

Now I was worried, not about him standing me up, but that something might have happened with what he called the *federales*.

Texted him again.

No response.

Called again.

Voicemail.

I waited until eight o'clock and drove home. The other two Atwood women were out to dinner. I cooked up some pasta, ate it. Texted and called again.

Nothing from Daniel.

Around eleven o'clock I couldn't take it, got back into the car and drove back over to his house. No car in the driveway. No lights.

The next morning, he didn't show up at the barn.

THIRTY-TWO

DANIEL USUALLY BEAT the grooms to the barn. I didn't hear from him on Monday. He didn't show up for work on Tuesday morning, either.

"We need to call the police," Mom said. "Something has obviously happened to him."

"We can't," I said.

"What do you mean, we can't?" Grandmother said.

"Daniel is more afraid of the government than ever," I said.

I didn't feel as though I'd betrayed his confidence.

"So what are we supposed to do?" Grandmother said.

"Wait," I said.

"Not my strong suit," she said.

"You know it's not mine," I said.

Mom watched me in the ring with Coronado both days that Daniel had been gone. She said that as concerned as we were about Daniel, we all had to be practical. Coronado and I were competing in the International Arena on Thursday afternoon. With or without Daniel. As long as Mom and I stayed inside the ring, things still felt normal.

After I fed Coronado a carrot, Emilio took him back inside the barn. Grandmother had left for a doctor's appointment, saying she wanted her blood pressure checked, "for obvious reasons."

Where was he?

Why hadn't he even called?

"Don't you have that Find My Friends app on your phone?" Mom said.

"He won't let me use it with his phone," I said.

"Why not?"

"Because he's Daniel," I said.

"Say he is in trouble with the government, even being detained somewhere, wouldn't he have called us for help?" she said.

"He doesn't ever ask anybody for help," I said.

"What can we do, besides wait?"

"Try to find him," I said.

I'd waited as long as I could. But we were moving up on forty-eight hours since I'd heard from him last. Emilio had already sworn to me that he hadn't heard from Daniel and didn't know where he might have gone.

At the horse show I had met Daniel's trainer and groom friends from the other barns. Most but not all of them were immigrants. So they had their secrets, too. But maybe one of them knew Daniel's secrets, where he'd gone, when he might be coming back, and if he was safe.

If.

By the midafternoon, Emilio and I'd made a tour of eight barns in our general area. We spoke to trainers and grooms and some riders, giving them my cell phone number but trying not to sound any alarms. Trying not to let them see that I was worried out of my skull.

But nobody we spoke to had seen him. Nobody had heard from him.

Totally off the grid for two days now.

Where was he?

I told Emilio, who was as afraid of the government as Daniel was, that my own worst fear was that he was at some detention center and they hadn't even allowed him a phone call.

"He will explain when he returns," Emilio said.

"If he returns," I said.

I kept calling Daniel's phone. Kept texting. We took one last swing by Daniel's house. Nobody home. He knew how much the qualifier on Thursday meant to all of us. Something bad *had* to have happened.

Please don't let it be bad.

We were back to that.

By five o'clock we returned to Atwood Farm, exhausted.

Mom and Grandmother invited me to dinner. I told them I'd be terrible company.

"You're going to sit at home and worry yourself sick," Mom said.

"Sounds like a plan," I said.

They didn't leave until a little after eight, later than I preferred to eat. I was up in my room by then, anxiously texting and calling Daniel again and again. I went downstairs, poured myself a glass of white wine, brought it back up to the room. Tried and failed to follow a book and then a Netflix movie. Realized I hadn't touched my wine. Picked up the glass, put it down hard enough that I spilled some.

Screw it.

I was going to take one last drive over to his house. Picturing myself pulling off Pierson and seeing the house lit up and the Kia parked in his driveway. Picturing myself ripping into him for disappearing this way.

I stuffed my phone into my back pocket, grabbed my car keys, took the stairs two at a time.

When I opened our front door, there he was.

THIRTY-THREE

Daniel

HE HAD BEEN rehearsing on the long ride back to Wellington what he was going to say to Becky, provided she did not slam the door right in his face. But when he saw her right there in front of him, it was as if all the words drained from his head.

It was not the first time with Becky that he had lost his words, though never in the ring. He would never completely understand her, no matter how long they were together. But by now he knew her, sometimes better than she knew herself, as annoyed as she would get when he would say that to her.

He had never told her of so many times when he felt...what was the expression?

Lengua atada.

Tongue-tied.

She spoke first.

"Nice of you to stop by," Becky said.

But she was smiling.

It was a good sign.

He nodded at the car keys in her left hand.

"Were you about to go out?" he said.

"Where the hell have you been?"

"You have a right to ask that," he said. "And you have a right to be angry with me."

"I'm not angry, Daniel, swear to God I'm not,"

she said. "If I was, believe me, you'd know it. Maybe the neighbors, too, and the horses down in the barn. But I knew it had to be serious for you to be gone this long."

"It was important," he said. "On that you must trust me."

"Now I'm just relieved that you're back," she said. "Just please tell me where you've been, okay?"

"No," he said.

THIRTY-FOUR

Maggie

"AND THAT'S THE way you two left it?" Maggie Atwood said to her daughter the next morning over coffee at the kitchen table. "He just said 'no'?"

"Yes."

"And you're okay with that?"

"For now," Becky said. "Like I tell you and Grandmother all the time: he's Daniel."

Caroline Atwood was already out for her "power walk." She still got her three miles in most mornings, to Southshore Boulevard and back, but as Maggie saw—and sometimes heard—there wasn't much grace or power left in her mother's stride.

"At some point you and Daniel are going to have a lot to talk about," Maggie said.

"Tell me about it," Becky said. "But for now, my dear mother, I'm going down the hill and get on our horse and work with our trainer and try to act as if everything's normal."

"Nothing has been normal around here for a while," Maggie said.

"You going to work out this morning?" Becky said to her mother.

Maggie didn't go to the gym every morning. She'd occasionally give herself a day off. But never more than once a week.

"I am," she said. "Soon as I change."

And she *was* going to work out.

Just not at the gym.

She hadn't technically told her daughter a lie, even if Becky thought she meant the gym. But she wasn't telling the truth, either. Maggie was on her way to Gus Bennett's small horse farm, at the other end of Palm Beach Point.

She was going there to ride.

She hadn't mentioned it to her mother. She didn't want Becky to know, either. She'd sworn Gus to secrecy, and exacted the same promise from his small staff, telling them that if people in Wellington were talking about Maggie Atwood riding horses again, he'd find out who couldn't keep their mouth shut and fire their ass.

Dr. Garry had told her she was still a long way from riding. If that. Maggie'd finally decided that she couldn't wait that long to get up on a horse again.

Gus Bennett hadn't even blinked when Maggie floated the idea. But Gus was no ordinary trainer and knew more than Maggie ever would about the damage a riding accident could do. He had once been a world-class rider, on his way to the 2008 Olympics when he had been thrown at a qualifying event in Rome and suffered a "low C-level injury" to his spinal cord that had paralyzed him from the waist down and put him in a wheelchair for life.

But in all the years Maggie had known him, she had never heard Gus complain about his accident, or even discuss it. Ever since, he had acted as if it was the rest of the world that was disabled, not him. There had been worse riding injuries. Another great rider, Kevin Babington, was now paralyzed from the shoulders down, but had continued his own career in the sport as a trainer.

Gus wasn't just a trainer now, he was one of the most sought-after in the country.

But he worked only with a select few riders. "We call it the *no a-hole* policy at this barn," he said. "If I think you are one, you don't ever make it into the ring."

"Does that apply to the trainer?" Maggie had joked to him one time.

"No," he'd said. "Lucky for him he's the a-hole who gets to make the rules."

She needed to be up on a horse to start feeling whole again. Was never going to do that with free weights or on a treadmill or a sit-up board. She had to be up on a horse. Today was finally the day. She didn't think she'd been feeling sorry for herself. But knew she never could in Gus Bennett's ring.

Not looking to ride fast. Probably not doing much more than a walk. Not jumping. She was realistic enough to know that she was nowhere near that. But she brought her boots and helmet and breeches with her, changed in Gus's tack room. One of his grooms, Seamus, walked out the horse Gus had chosen for her to ride, one he called an "oldie but goodie" named Paladin.

"Oldie but goodie sounds a lot like me," Maggie said.

"Stop complaining," Gus said.

He was in his Zinger, the all-terrain electric wheelchair he used to get around at his barn. Not because he needed electric. By now, from using manual wheelchairs, he had Popeye arms. When he was working, and wanted to get somewhere, he wanted to get there fast.

"You're sweet."

"Like hell," Gus said.

Seamus helped her up into the saddle. She took a deep breath, gave the horse a quick pat, started Paladin off at a walk, and a slow one at that, one time around the ring. The next time around she jogged.

Suddenly she felt her heart pounding and she struggled to catch her breath. She pulled on the reins and brought the horse to a stop.

"Did I tell you to stop?" Gus yelled.

"Just lost concentration for a second there," she said, willing her breathing back to normal. "More out of practice than I thought."

"Get over it," Gus said.

Maggie looked down at her hands on the reins and saw them shaking.

"This isn't the pony ring," Gus said. "Are you ready to do this?"

"I'm ready," she said.

"Show me," he said.

She managed to grin. "A-hole," she said.

Already she could feel the strain in the muscles in her back. She went around the ring again. Could already feel the ache in her bad knee, because she was squeezing the horse too hard with her legs. But she wasn't stopping.

You came here to ride.

She did that now, still jogging him, feeling the slight morning breeze in her face as she made a turn at the far end of the ring. Feeling more alive than at any moment since the accident.

Like the person she used to be.

Smiling.

She was a few strides past Gus, about to make another turn, when she felt her right foot slip out of its stirrup. It could happen on any ride, could even happen in competition.

Now it was happening to Maggie.

Afraid—make that scared to death—that she was about to fall off, Maggie felt herself leaning hard to her right, starting to slide down the horse, her boot trying to find its way back into the stirrup but flailing in the air.

A shout escaped her that sounded like it came from a little girl using grown-up language.

"Shit!"

She could see Gus putting the wheelchair in motion, not that he was going to be able to do much to help her.

Her boot found its way back to the stirrup and she jammed it in there, hard. The rough motion shot searing pain from her bad knee up her leg and nearly to her rib cage. She ignored it as best she could and managed to straighten herself in the saddle. A minute later she had brought Paladin to a walk. She handed the reins to Seamus, but when the groom reached to help Maggie down, Gus yelled at him to stop.

"I thought we were done," Maggie said.

He spun the wheelchair around, spraying the horse with dirt.

"We're just getting started," Gus said.

Maggie called after him, "Catch me up: are you working for me or am I working for you?"

Gus didn't even turn around.

He just threw back his head and laughed.

THIRTY-FIVE

I WAS SCHEDULED to go dead last today, sixtieth out of sixty horses. And was totally fine with that. By the time Coronado and I were on the course, I'd know exactly how the field had performed, what kind of time I needed, if I could get away with four faults—one rail—or eight. Or even more.

For this one day, as crazy competitive as I usually was, as much as I wanted to prove that my flawed ride was a one-off, the reality was that, like an Olympic sprinter in a qualifying heat, I only needed to be fast enough to make it to the finals. I didn't need to break any records, not today.

Daniel and I watched together from my perch up in the bleachers. Today I wanted his company, to not only see what was happening on the course through my eyes, but his as well. I even had a pen and the order sheet, checking off names and marking down scores. Halfway through the round, only six riders had gone clean. Matthew Killeen was one of them, with the best time so far, 70 seconds flat, well under the allotted time of 74. He was in the jump-off, so was Tess McGill. So was Tyler Cullen. And Rich Grayson, who'd been making a big move up the rankings for months.

"Just because you don't need to be perfect doesn't mean you can get away with even one sloppy line," he said.

"So, perfect-ish?" I said.

When it was time, I followed him down through the bleachers, and finally to the schooling ring, where Emilio was waiting with Coronado. Daniel was a few paces ahead of me when I heard him say *"Mierda"* under his breath.

I knew that one without a translation, because I'd heard it from him often enough.

Shit.

Steve Gorton was leaning against the fence, about ten yards away from Coronado, champagne flute in his hand. It was only four o'clock, but he'd clearly decided it was the cocktail hour. I knew he wasn't here to toast me.

Daniel quietly said to me, "Please do not engage."

But as soon as Emilio had me up in the saddle, Gorton came walking over. Everybody in this ring knew the protocols of our sport, everybody except him, apparently. The only people a rider wanted to talk to before going into the ring were his trainer and sometimes his groom. No one else.

The last person I wanted to talk to right now was this guy, finishing the last of his champagne, walking across the ring as if he owned the place, and all the horses and jockeys in it.

"Let's try to stay on today," he said when he got to me.

Seriously?

If Gorton heard Daniel exhale loudly, he didn't show it.

"Let's try to stay on today," he said.

"That's the plan," I said, my voice even.

"You actually look pretty relaxed for someone who rode him the way you did last time."

Well, I thought, *maybe I can engage him just a little.*

"I mean, what the hell, right?" I said. "The worst thing that could ever happen to me on this horse already happened."

I tried to make myself look busy fussing with Coronado's reins, and checking the stirrups, even knowing they were already perfect. Hoping he would take the hint that our conversation needed to be over now.

"I'd wish you good luck," he said, "but you'd know I didn't really mean it."

"You know what, Mr. Gorton?" I said, smiling down at him, thinking he looked even smaller from up here. "Kind of thinking that luck's not going to have anything to do with it."

Then I turned Coronado so quickly that he nearly knocked Steve Gorton on his ass.

"Oops," I said.

THIRTY-SIX

MOM AND GRANDMOTHER were in the tent, but I knew Mom was keeping score herself up there, checking off the riders one by one. As always, Daniel was holding my phone for me. I heard it ping as we got to the in-gate.

He looked down and checked it, put it away.

"Under nine faults and we're in," he said.

I could get away with two rails, then. But nothing more than that. If I did get two rails, it meant I had to be under 74 seconds. If I wasn't, it would mean nine faults, and good-bye.

"You are in control now," Daniel said, and put out his fist.

"About time," I said.

There were no easy parts of today's course. But the second half was harder, no doubt. It almost always worked that way. And the jump-off course, if we made it, would be like one of those crazy car-chase scenes in the movies.

Coronado had a perfect distance on the first jump. Perfect distance. Perfect timing. And the second one. And third.

Okay, I thought.

Okay.

I was still nervous as hell, but I wasn't in panic mode. I wasn't riding scared.

Just riding my horse.

Made the turn and came around past the hated big screen. It was there so the fans had full view of every jump, especially the ones in the corner. But I always ignored it. It made me feel as self-conscious as if I were looking at myself in a mirror.

Coronado was riding easy. Cruise control. I knew I had more horse than he was showing. But for now, I was keeping him under the speed limit, even if it went against who he was and who I was.

Two more jumps clear, on the far side of the ring from the tent. They could have raised the top rail on the last two jumps and we could have cleared them both with room to spare.

Quick combination now.

Nailed the sucker.

Halfway home, just like that.

Straightforward jump coming up to start the second half. Good distance again. Still riding easy. Made sure to ease him into the jump, not feel as if I had gotten ahead of my horse.

Another perfect distance.

Didn't matter.

I felt him clip the rail with one of his hind legs. Heard it go down. To a rider, it sounded as loud as a window breaking.

Still I didn't panic.

We were out of the jump-off, but I didn't care about the jump-off. Just finish clean. Or with only one more knockdown.

Just no more than that.

The toughest rollback in the round was coming up, followed by a quick combination. I cut the turn perfectly, squared the horse up, gave him the exact right distance.

Five.

Six.

Cleared the first jump.

And then, damn damn damn, clipped another rail on the next one.

Heard it go down. Sometimes you clipped them like that, or even rattled them, and they stayed up. Not this time.

The drop on this one sounded to me like a bomb going off.

Now there was no margin for error. Eight faults still got me to Saturday. Another rail—or a time fault—and we were out.

I had to be under 74 seconds. If I went over by a tenth of a second, I got a time fault and some other horse would be the last qualifier for the Grand Prix.

We had just passed the big screen. This time I would have looked at my time on the way by. Too late for that now.

Maybe too late for us, period.

I didn't know where I was against the clock.

But Daniel did.

"*Go!*" I heard from the in-gate, as loud as I'd ever heard him with me, or Mom, or anybody.

"*Go…go…go!*"

Then I was the one shouting "*Go!*" at Coronado.

Let it ride.

We were both running hot now.

One last combination.

One jump after that.

But the horse was flying now.

Nailed the combination.

"*Come on!*" I yelled, as much at myself as my horse.

In other sports, the players could see the clock when they were trying to beat it at the end of a game.

Not me, and not now.

Seven strides to the last jump.

Coronado took them so fast it felt like one.

Cleared it with ease.

Big screen was behind us, far end. I jerked my head around, saw our time up in the corner:

73.9.

Tenth of a second under the number.

Boom.

THIRTY-SEVEN

DANIEL ORTEGA, WHO never liked to let his guard down, who never wanted you to know what he was really feeling, looked as happy as I felt.

He walked up and took Coronado's reins, smiling broadly, and planted a big kiss on the side of Coronado's head.

"Oh, sure," I said. "*He* gets a damn kiss."

Then Daniel reached up for a high-five and I slapped him one as hard as I could.

"Holy mother of God," I said.

"I may have said a prayer myself," he said. "In two languages. I watched just about every horse out there today. And I knew their times going into the last three jumps. You and Coronado beat them all by two seconds."

"Thanks for the heads-up, by the way."

"I might have scared people on the side rings." He grinned and said, "Other than that, we had it all the way."

"Yeah," I said. "Piece of cake."

Results were posted on the monitor next to the in-gate. While Daniel went to check them, I turned Coronado back around, walked him a few yards back into the ring. Daniel always told me that a deeper understanding of the course comes from looking back at it when the round was over.

One tenth of a second.

We'd made it to Saturday night by that much.

When I turned Coronado back around again, I saw Steve Gorton standing with Daniel, nodding as Daniel pointed at the ring, Gorton's face looking slightly flushed, another glass of champagne in his hand.

Daniel extended his hand to Gorton then. Gorton either didn't see it, or simply ignored it.

"I got it, okay?" I could hear him saying to Daniel. "I don't need a tutorial on the scoring."

Then Daniel said something that I couldn't hear.

"I told you, *I...get...it,*" Gorton said.

Then he was walking out on the course as Coronado and I walked toward him. I actually thought he might be smiling. The round hadn't gone the way I would have drawn it up. But that didn't matter now.

"So what did you think?" I said.

"Not good enough," he said.

THIRTY-EIGHT

DANIEL AND EMILIO walked Coronado back to our barn. I told Daniel I'd see him down there later, then went looking for my mom and Grandmother in the tent. No one was going to be celebrating, or as Grandmother liked to say, spiking the ball. We'd live to fight another day. Still a good day for us. We'd had enough bad ones lately.

They were still at their table when I got there.

"Well," Grandmother said, "that was certainly fun for the whole family."

"And certainly not dull," Mom said.

"From the time he landed until I turned around and saw the time," I said, "I'm pretty sure my heart stopped beating." I grinned. "But only for a tenth of a second."

"You rode great, honey," Mom said. "Neither of those rails were your fault. You know I'd tell you if I thought they were."

"It wouldn't have mattered whose fault they were if we hadn't picked it up the way we did at the end," I said.

"But you did pick it up, that's all that *does* matter now," Mom said.

"Great jockeys talk about asking their horse in the

stretch," I said. "Not sure I ever really understood until today."

"Asked and answered," Mom said.

"Great horses have an extra gear," Grandmother said, waving at a waiter and telling him she needed a damn drink, and she needed it right now.

"Top riders, too," Mom said, patting me on the arm. "Your old mom is thinking that maybe you answered some questions about yourself today."

Mom moved her chair close to mine then, picked up her phone, hit Play, and showed me the video of the round, breaking it down. For as long as I had been riding, she'd never been close to an easy grader. She was almost as tough on me as she was on herself. And her standard was to jump even higher than everybody else in the field. Mom's score on any round I rode secretly mattered more to me than any judge's, whether or not I won a ribbon.

I could see how fired up she was today, the excitement in her voice and in her eyes, pausing the round a few times, showing me places where I'd picked up time, even when I wasn't pushing the horse, especially on what she called one ballsy turn where I went inside the flowers and not out.

"That," she said, "was riding."

"Good thing," I said. "Or we finish out of the money. Pretty much in all ways."

"There's a great old sporting line," Mom said. "What could have happened *did*."

Then she was the one giving me five. As she did, we heard a loud explosion of laughter. About ten tables down from us, Steve Gorton was sitting with Tyler Cullen.

We watched as Gorton leaned across the table, said something to Tyler, who laughed his ass off until the two of them clinked glasses, finished their drinks, and stood up. As Tyler came around the table, Gorton clapped him on the back, then put an arm around his shoulder, like they were heading back to the frat house together.

Mom and Grandmother were staring at them the same as I was. "Well, pardon my French," Grandmother said, "but there's a couple of pricks who deserve each other."

"Gee," I said, "and we were all having such a nice day."

"We're still having a nice day," Mom said. "And they do kind of make a cute couple, don't you think?"

I was barely listening as I watched Steve Gorton and Tyler Cullen head down the ramp. As they disappeared through the tent door, I said, "At least we know who Gorton wants the next man up on Coronado to be."

THIRTY-NINE

GRAND PRIX SATURDAY.

With a 7 p.m. start time, I didn't do much to shorten my day by waking up—not that I'd slept much to begin with—at six in the morning. No point in trying to roll over and go back to sleep. *That* wasn't happening. So I threw on some sweatpants and quietly went down to the kitchen and put on coffee. Drank two cups, went back to my room, got into my workout clothes and drove over to the gym at the club. Made myself promise not to look at the clock until I'd done my weight circuit, three sets on each machine, and at least twenty minutes on the treadmill.

Finished on the treadmill, toweled off, drank a bottle of water. *Then* looked at the clock.

Still just nine o'clock.

But three hours down.

I went to the barn and rode Sky, who was still riding like a dream, every damn day. If I *could* win tonight—because that's what I was thinking, even if I wasn't saying it aloud to Daniel or Mom or Grandmother or anybody—maybe I could start showing Sky again, even against Coronado.

Just not tonight.

Tonight, it was Coronado and me against the world.

I had to keep busy, or I was going to have an

hours-long panic attack lasting until it was time to leave for the show grounds. My idle mind kept turning to the money, the million dollars Grandmother had passed up. Life-changing money for all of us.

In the end, she had placed a seven-figure bet on me.

Longest day of my life, I thought, and it wasn't even noon yet.

After Sky was back in her stall, I took another shower—by the time seven o'clock rolled around I was going to be the cleanest rider in Wellington, Florida—and drove over to my favorite beach in Manalapan, just south of Palm Beach. I didn't often go to the beach, even though in light traffic the drive took only a half hour. The ocean was there when I needed it.

I needed it today. Spread out a blanket and walked for about an hour. Came back and sat and stared at the water and then walked across the street to my favorite ice cream place on the planet, the Ice Cream Club, bought a pint of coffee and a pint of chocolate, then drove back to Atwood Farm.

By six o'clock Daniel and I were ready to walk the course. Tyler Cullen and his trainer were right behind us. He tried to ignore me. Wasn't happening this time.

"Didn't know that you and Steve Gorton were boys, Tyler," I said, trying to sound casual.

"I like being around money," Tyler said. "You should know that by now."

"Your horse isn't enough for you?" I said. "Now you're trying to poach mine?"

Tyler shrugged. "Can't have enough money," he said. "And can't have enough prize horses."

He winked at me.

"Long as you can hold on to them, of course," he said.

I smiled now.

"I better get movin', Tyler," I said. "If I stand here like this much longer, people might start to think I'm the bitch."

As Daniel and I took off, Daniel leaned down and said, "Never heard that one before."

"Been saving it for the right occasion," I said.

Forty horses tonight. One of the richest purses of the year. Probably the biggest crowd of the season. Atwood Farm needed that first-prize money as much as I wanted to win it. But the stakes were way bigger:

Ride my horse well enough to keep it.

Once we got away from Tyler, Daniel did all the talking. He had taken a series of pictures of the course on his phone, as if he were walking it inside his head before I even arrived.

Then we were pacing it off for real. He showed me the four different places where I could pick up speed. Then we were analyzing the jump-off course—Daniel kept saying *when* I made the jump-off, not if I made it—and showed me the spots where he said I would have no choice but to take chances if I wanted to win tonight.

"In it to win it," I said.

"Yes, Maverick," he said.

"You know what they say about second place?" I said. "Just means you're the first loser."

I looked around and saw the stands beginning to fill up. There was always a band and a singer on Saturday nights. I could hear the singer now, a woman, ease into her first song, a really bad version of Taylor Swift's "You Need to Calm Down."

Yeah, right, I thought.

I was going twentieth in the order tonight. Matthew was set to go right after me. Tess was going after him. Tyler was last.

Not at the kids' table anymore.

We stood off to the side now as the other riders and trainers finished their walks. There were even spectators out there. WEF enhanced the fan experience by allowing them to walk the course if they wanted to. It's why the International looked like a sea of people, men and women, grown-ups and kids. It meant the ring looked exactly like the sport.

"You ride the whole course tonight the way you finished on Thursday," Daniel said.

"Yeah, but Gorton was right about one thing," I said. "Just good enough *won't* be enough tonight."

I checked my phone. Six thirty. Just a little more waiting. I couldn't tell the difference between good nerves and bad nerves right now. I was *all* nerves. I tried to lean back casually against the sidewall, fighting a wave of dizziness thinking about what was going to play out over the next couple of hours. What was on the line.

Get a grip.

If you're like this now, are you going to be in control when you're up on your horse?

Daniel headed down to the barn so that he could walk back here with Emilio and Coronado when it was time.

I took one more look around the course and then headed to retrieve my backpack from the schooling ring. I was passing beneath the stands when I heard a familiar voice calling my name.

When I looked up, I saw him hanging over the railing, getting ready to take a picture of me on his phone.

"Smile," he said.

"Hey, Dad," I said.

FORTY

I BOLTED UP the steps to where he was standing and hugged him. Right after I jumped into his arms and nearly knocked him over.

"You're still full of surprises," I said. "And it's not even my birthday."

"It's not?" he said.

He looked exactly like, well, Dad. Maybe a little extra gray in the hair and beard since I'd seen him at Thanksgiving in New York. Despite the heat, he was wearing a blue blazer over a white button-down shirt and jeans, and looked nothing like the legal heavy hitter he'd become.

In New York he was known as Black Jack McCabe, now head of the firm he'd taken over when my grandfather had died suddenly of a heart attack. To me, he was just Dad, and I didn't mind telling him that even though he wasn't in a business suit, he was still overdressed.

"I heard there was some snob horse race down here tonight," he said, "and thought I'd stop in and check it out."

"You know they don't call them races," I said. "And you're the one who sounds like a snob calling everybody else one."

"Force of habit," he said. "The only time I ever really like this sport is when you're in it."

"What about Mom?"

"The feeling passed eventually," he said.

He grinned then.

"So how we lookin'?" he said.

"Not much on the line tonight," I said. "Just Mom's horse, is all. And maybe the barn."

"And this used to be such a quiet little town," he said. "Now it sounds like a reality series."

"Lot going on, no doubt," I said.

"How soon before you go?" he said.

I told him where I was in the order, so I had some time before I'd be up on my horse.

"I never liked bothering you once you had your game face on," he said.

"Just because you've watched me ride so often," I said.

He shook his head.

"That's my girl," he said. "Don't give an inch."

"You never do," I said. "And by the way? Can't you see I have my game face on already?"

"I thought that was your normal RBF," he said.

We both knew he meant *resting bitch face*.

"And people wonder where I get my smart mouth," I said. Then I grabbed him by both shoulders and shook him and said, "Holy crap, Dad, I can't believe you showed up!"

"You know me," he said. "Always would have dressed up like a rodeo clown to get a smile out of my kid."

We took an empty table at one of the outdoor cafés on Vendor Row.

"Your mom told me you pulled one out in the qualifier like my Yankees in the bottom of the ninth," he said.

"Not gonna lie," I said. "That one didn't suck."

I asked him how much he knew of the whole story with Coronado. He said that Mom had pretty much caught him up before he swore her to secrecy on his plan to be here tonight. Then I asked how much he knew about Steve Gorton.

"The only thing that amazes me is that this guy isn't a lawyer," he said.

"Wait," I said, "*you're* a lawyer."

He put a finger to his lips.

"Don't let that get around," he said.

As nervous as I was, I laughed. It felt good. He was never around, my dad, at least not enough to suit me. I didn't get to New York as much as I'd like to. But he was here now. All that mattered.

We were both silent then. I looked down at my phone to check the time.

"So how are you doing, really?" he said.

"Other than being scared out of my mind right now?"

"Yeah."

"I actually like my chances tonight, crazy as that sounds," I said.

"Doesn't sound crazy to me," he said. "I've seen you ride."

"It's mostly because of the way we finished on Thursday," I said. "I honestly think I've got more horse than anybody."

When the PA announcer welcomed everybody to the $500,000 Longines Grand Prix, I said, "*Now* it's time for me to put my game face on."

The two of us walked down Vendor Row and were about to head into the tent when one of the golf carts that shuttled guests from the VIP parking lot pulled up and Steve Gorton got out with a blonde almost as tall as he was who looked about my age.

Not now, I thought.

Dad and I felt obligated to walk over to him. He introduced his date as Blaine. I introduced both of them to Jack McCabe.

"Heard a lot about you," Dad said to Gorton.

Gorton looked at him, then at me, then back at him. Grinning. "Well that can't possibly be good for me," he said. "Don't believe everything she says about me. No matter what she told you, I never slashed the tires of her car."

I said I had to meet Daniel at the ring and get up on my horse. Dad kissed me on the cheek and wished me luck. For once Steve Gorton didn't have much choice but to do the same.

I was about to make the turn toward the pedestrian bridge when I stopped and turned around. Blaine must have already gone inside.

Just my dad and Steve Gorton now.

Then I saw Dad lean close to Gorton and say something into his ear and pat him on the shoulder before leaving him there, Gorton staring at Dad's back until he disappeared into the tent.

FORTY-ONE

THURSDAY HAD BEEN all about getting to the Grand Prix. Tonight's first order of business was to get to the jump-off.

"How do you feel?" Daniel said after Coronado and I had done some light jumping in the ring.

"Like I want to throw up," I said.

"I'm being serious," he said, as if Daniel Ortega were ever anything but.

"So am I," I said.

"Matthew next, followed by Andrew Welles," the starter said. *"Then Rich."*

Rich Grayson. Appropriate first name. His father was the fourth or fifth wealthiest guy in the country.

He'll be fine wherever he finishes tonight, I thought. *Or doesn't finish.*

He'll be pissed. He's as competitive as I am. But his life won't change at all.

"Then Tyler four," the starter said, *"Eric five. Becky six."*

"Just a little more jumping, please," Daniel said. "Don't forget to use your legs as well as your hands."

If I wasn't calm, he was. It made me feel better. The way seeing Dad had made me feel better. *The two men in my life,* I thought. *Only one of them official.*

Maybe Daniel and I would never be official. But I

was glad he was here. He was smart. He was good. He only wanted the best for me. And even though I hated to admit it, he probably did know me better than I knew myself.

After Daniel signaled me to stop, I walked Coronado over to the fence.

"At least I haven't seen Gorton down here," I said.

"He is not even worth thinking about right now," Daniel said. "He does not matter. The course matters. It is difficult, but it is fair."

"Yeah," I said. "But the jump-off was designed by some sick, twisted monster."

"What jump-off?" he said.

Daniel being Daniel. He was telling me that all that mattered in the world right now were the next sixteen jumps.

"Eric next," the starter said. *"Then Becky."*

Time coming at me fast now.

"Breathe," Daniel said.

"Easy for you to say," I said.

I heard a cheer from inside the International, then a groan, then heard the PA announcer saying that Eric Glynn had gone clean until the last jump.

The in-gate now for Coronado and me. Daniel next to us. I heard the announcer say Coronado was next in the ring, and then we walked out there and went into a trot around the outside of the course. Then I slowed him down to a walk and took one last look at the course, using a finger to map it out in the air in front of me.

We headed for the first jump. When we were six strides out, I heard the buzzer, which meant I'd passed the sensor and the clock was starting.

Cleared the first one.

Then the second.

We were into it now.

Sometimes a rider knew how much horse was under saddle on a given night. And sometimes it was a charade leading up to a big, hot mess.

Tonight I knew.

I *knew.*

The first combination came up on us now, right in the middle of the course. About the same place where I'd given Coronado a crap distance and he'd plowed through the jump and stopped and sent me flying.

Not tonight.

Takeoff. Landing. Takeoff. Landing.

Perfect.

Yeah, I thought. *Yeah.*

Now you're riding.

Two jumps on the tent side of the course. Gave him the right distance on both. Felt him clip the second jump. Closest I'd come yet to putting a rail on the ground. The rail stayed up. Into the far corner now, underneath the big screen, going into the second half of the course. Running easy. But running hot, too.

First tough rollback for us. Cut the turn as sharply as I could. Knife through butter. Squared him up. Cleared the jump with plenty of room to spare.

Two more jumps before the most dangerous double. Got over them clean. Now the double, the two jumps so close to each other riders thought of them as one piece. Like 15A and 15B.

I was talking to Coronado now.

"Hey…hey…HEY!"

Landed the first jump clean.

"Up!"

Nailed the second.

No thinking now. Just reacting to what was left.

Just looking at the last jump. Focusing on the line. Seven strides in it.

Focus.

Five.

Six.

Seven.

Into the air one last time. Over the jump. Feeling a slight chip on the rail, but knowing he hadn't hit it hard enough to knock this one down, either.

Still not done. Knowing there were a couple of strides left after the jump to where the timer was, before the round was officially over.

Finish the round, Daniel always told me.

I rode Coronado as hard those last few strides as I had anywhere else on the course. We finished the round strong. He did. I did. I hadn't heard the crowd the whole way around. I'd only been hearing the sound of my horse. But now I heard an explosion of noise from the stands and the announcer saying our time was 79.2 seconds. The great Matthew Killeen went next and was a full second slower. I was in first place, at least for now. It wouldn't matter in the jump-off, when all the horses who made it would start even. A whole different competition.

Slowed Coronado down to a walk, then brought him over to where Daniel was standing. Daniel's face was totally blank. No reaction from him at all.

"You got nothing?" I said. "I've got the best time so far."

"Night's not over," he said, and headed back to the schooling ring to wait for the jump-off.

FORTY-TWO

Daniel

DANIEL WAS GOOD at waiting by now. Waiting to feel like a real American. Or be treated like one someday. Waiting to feel safe again, someplace outside the ring.

In his heart he felt that there was no better trainer in the business. But if they didn't have a horse good enough to make it to Paris, Daniel's ability might not matter in the end.

Still, he could barely breathe as he watched, from the time the buzzer started as Becky approached the first jump until it sounded again, after she had pushed herself and the horse, pedal to the metal as she liked to say, past the timer set in the dirt, a few strides after the last jump.

Tonight while she was in the ring he did not need to call out to her a single time. Maybe he would tell her later that he had never seen her ride better.

But now there was still work to do. Emilio helped her down off Coronado and then Daniel and Becky watched his video of the jump-off course. He kept pausing it, showing her the places that he thought would make all the difference if she could go clean, particularly a rollback as tough and tight as he'd ever seen on a championship course.

"As good as you just were," he said, "you have to do even more now."

He saw her smile.

"Damn," she said, "I was afraid of that."

"You have to go inside on that turn," Daniel said.

"If I can," she said.

"There is no if," he said. "You do not play it safe. You go inside. Absolutely."

He put his phone away and looked at her. As nervous and scared and excited as he knew she was— all the things that he himself was feeling—her face was suddenly calm.

"Okay," she said.

Then he helped her back into the saddle, and she took Coronado around the schooling ring, once, then twice, then letting him rest on the side. From inside he heard the announcer saying the jump-off was about to begin.

Then Daniel saw Tyler Cullen walking his horse, Galahad, in Becky's direction. Cullen's back was to Daniel, so he didn't see him jogging to catch up and get ahead of the horse, putting himself between Tyler and Becky.

"You're in my way," Cullen said.

"I wouldn't," Daniel said.

He did not say it in a threatening way, or in a loud voice. This wasn't the playground and trying to show another boy how tough you were. Daniel knew he could do nothing to distract Becky in this moment. So he had kept his voice low. He had even forced a smile onto his face. Daniel was sure no one in the ring, not even Becky, had heard what he had just said to Tyler Cullen. He just stood there with his arms casually in front of him, staring at Cullen as Cullen stared back at him, hoping that things wouldn't escalate with the jump-off just moments away.

Unsure what would happen next if they did.

Then Cullen said, "I'll see you later, dude," turned his horse, and walked it away.

FORTY-THREE

THE TWO RIDERS ahead of her both got rails. First Jennifer Gates's horse. Then Georgina Bloomberg's. Becky couldn't believe that's the way the order fell. Both had tried to go inside on the killer rollback, both had gotten too close to the jump.

But they'd gone for it.

One a Gates, the other a Bloomberg.

Nothing for them to lose, as much as they wanted to win.

"Hey, maybe I won't need to go inside," I said to Daniel as we watched from the in-gate.

Daniel didn't even look up at me. Just slowly shook his head.

"Killeen and Cullen go after us," he said. "We go inside."

I kidded myself into thinking I could do some breathing exercises before I rode Coronado into the ring. Thinking maybe that would stop my heart from racing. Dad had talked about there being a big horse race here tonight. I felt like I had one running inside me. Tried to settle myself down by closing my eyes, imagining Daniel taking me through the jump-off course on his phone even though the course was in front of me, my ride a few seconds away.

Breathe, idiot.

Then we were out there.

No need to warm him up. Looked down and saw my hands shaking on the reins. *Three horses left,* I told myself. *And I had the best one.* I would happily have signed up for this three weeks ago when I was on my ass in this ring, even if I was going up against a course this hard, and against Matthew Killeen and Tyler Cullen.

Gave Coronado a little kick-start with my boots.

Seven jumps.

Eight if you counted the second jump in a wicked combination.

Now it felt like a horse race.

First jump clear.

And second.

One more before the rollback. Thought I was too close to it.

"Whoa!"

I'd laugh sometimes watching the video after, the weird noises I'd make out there, the things I'd say to my horse.

Not now.

Concentrate.

We weren't too close to the jump. Coronado almost seemed to buy himself some room on his own, veering slightly to the left.

Made the jump.

I was thinking about the rollback before I even landed the jump. *Damn, he is going fast.* He'd been fast before. Been fast at the end in the qualifier. A lot faster now. I never hesitated on the inside turn. Felt the horse leaning into it even without me asking him, leaning hard to his left, making me feel, just for a moment, like he was about to fall right over. Like a skier on a slalom run.

"Whoa!" I said again.

Squared him up.

Made the jump.

Hell, yeah.

All that was left was the combination, one more jump after that.

Get over clean, post a time, see what happened with Matthew and Tyler.

Crushed the combination.

Last jump.

Every rider's nightmare, no matter how good, no matter how many shows won. Knocking down the last rail after a kick-ass ride.

And this has been one banging, kick-ass ride.

Four.

Five.

Six.

Cleaned it, cleared it, nailed it, made sure to keep him going past the timer, the way I'd been taught, not wasting the couple of tenths of a second that could pass if you didn't ride like hell past that timer.

Didn't have to wait to hear my time, because there it was right in front of me on the screen.

38.4.

Even though Jennifer and Georgina had gotten rails, they'd been getting after it, too. Neither one had been under 40 seconds.

When I got back to Daniel, just as Matthew was entering the ring, he still hadn't changed expression. No shocker. Daniel being Daniel, even now.

"We watch from here," he said.

Somehow I was more crazytown with nerves now than I'd been all night. I'd been in control of Coronado out there, as much as an animal that big, going that fast, can be controlled. Now everything was totally out of my control. My gaze jumped up to the tent, into the stands. All I could do was watch.

Matthew was next into the ring. Tyler Cullen, going last, was in the in-gate. As I passed him, he said, "Don't spike the ball too soon."

I grinned.

"You talkin' to me?" I said.

Matthew went clean. But his horse, My Pirate, got away from him going into the rollback, and he had no choice but to go outside, and the lost time cost him. He came in at 39.9.

We were down to Tyler Cullen now.

"I can't lose to that bastard," I said to Daniel.

"You won't," he said.

It was as if time had stopped, even as I could see the clock going at the other end. Tyler had a lot of horse himself with Galahad, just one without quite as much size to him or speed as Coronado had. Or bloodlines nearly as good. And whatever I thought of Tyler Cullen, the guy could ride his ass off. Daniel knew in his head what my time had been after landing every jump. He said the splits out loud, and jump after jump, my time was better than his.

But not by much.

I stopped listening and focused on Tyler as he approached the rollback.

He went inside, looked as if he was about to cut it as well as I had.

But as he did, Galahad skidded slightly. I thought he might go right around the fence, but somehow Tyler got him under control, got him over the jump.

"He's a half second behind," Daniel said.

"Hush," I said.

I watched Tyler, then the clock, then Tyler.

Saw where he was after the combination.

Shit, it's like a dead heat.

36. 37.

I couldn't watch the clock anymore. Closed my eyes. Opened them and saw Galahad in the air over the last jump, saw him take it clean.

Saw Tyler raise his right hand in the air, like in triumph, as he landed.

Then he looked at the big screen at the same time I did.

FORTY-FOUR

MY TIME, THE previous best in the jump-off, was in the top right-hand corner: 38.4

His was 38.7.

Choke on it, Cullen.

Coronado and I had won the Grand Prix.

Only now Tyler Cullen whipped Galahad around, like he was making one more sharp turn, and the horse was galloping back toward the in-gate, Cullen only pulling him up at the last second, not waiting for his trainer, Mackey, to help him off, jumping down himself, nearly stumbling as he landed, as he handed Mackey the reins.

Then he was running for the judge's booth.

"No way!" he yelled at the judge. "No way. They skipped a second."

"What's he doing?" I said to Daniel.

"Challenging the time."

"Can you do that?"

"He thinks you can," Daniel said.

"What do *we* do?"

"We stay right here," he said.

We weren't close enough to hear what Cullen was saying once he was inside the booth and managed to lower his voice. We could see him leaning close to the judge, pointing a finger at him. Then he stepped outside, turned around, and yelled that he wanted to see a steward from the FEI. *Right now.* International Equestrian Federation. Our sport's ruling body. On a night like this, an event this big, the steward was as close as you could be to God.

"I'll tell him what I just told you," Tyler Cullen said now. "The clock was wrong. I saw exactly where I was when I landed."

I was off Coronado by now. Emilio had him. Daniel and I walked over and leaned against the first jump, waited for the steward to make his way from his perch at the other end.

"He's just a sore loser, right?" I said.

"The sorest I have ever seen," Daniel said.

"Can he get away with this?"

In a quiet voice Daniel said, "No."

"Why?"

"Because he is wrong," Daniel said.

The steward was Charles Kaiser, a tall, white-haired man in a royal-blue sport jacket and white pants. He walked slowly through the middle of the course. It only seemed to piss off Tyler Cullen more. He was standing in front of the judge's booth, hands on hips.

"Now what?" I said.

"I have only seen this happen a couple of other times," Daniel said. "They will connect to FarmTek, which supplies the timing device. Then they will sync up their system with the replay of his round. And then they will see that the clock did not skip anything."

"You don't know that," I said.

"I do," Daniel said.

Then we both watched the three of them, the judge and Mr. Kaiser and Tyler Cullen, all crouched over a laptop in the judge's booth. They were in there about five minutes, Daniel and I watching them as closely as we'd watched Cullen's round on Galahad.

Then Mr. Kaiser was outside the booth, walking slowly toward Daniel and me.

Shaking his head.

FORTY-FIVE

I REACHED OVER and squeezed Daniel's hand. I was afraid I might end up in the dirt again if I didn't have something to hold on to.

Or somebody.

"I'm so sorry," Mr. Kaiser said in an amazingly deep voice.

He even sounds a little bit like God.

Now I squeezed Daniel's hand even harder.

Daniel spoke first, because I couldn't.

"Sorry for what?" he said.

"For the delay," Mr. Kaiser said. "Mr. Cullen's time was correct. He slowed up at the end when he raised his arm in the air. He didn't ride the last few strides through the timer."

Now Daniel squeezed my hand. I saw him smile. I smiled, too, and in a quiet voice said to Daniel, "Somebody spiked the ball too soon."

Mr. Kaiser extended his hand to me then.

"You're a champion, Miss McCabe," he said. "Congratulations."

FORTY-SIX

I'D WATCHED CHAMPIONS honored on plenty of other Saturday nights. I'd watched Mom step up onto the medal stand and be handed the winner's check and have a special sash placed around her neck, before they handed her and the two runners-up bottles of champagne.

First time for me.

The check for $250,000, oversized for the photographers, was made out to me. When we got the real one, Grandmother and Steve Gorton would divide the money. I wasn't great at math. But I was good enough to know that our share was just over $100,000. Might have been pocket change to Gorton. Not to Atwood Farm. It didn't mean that we were in the clear. Just that we could keep on keeping on for the time being.

My place on the medal stand was slightly higher than Matthew Killeen's and Tyler Cullen's. Matthew had congratulated me. Tyler Cullen took his place and stared straight ahead, still caught up in his tantrum. After past ceremonies, the riders who'd finished second and third would pop the champagne and spray the champion with it.

Matthew looked over at Tyler's sullen face and told me, "Save it and drink it. You want mine, too?"

"I'm good," I said.

I saw Dad and Mom and Grandmother standing together off to the side. I couldn't remember the last time I'd seen them together like that. Maybe when I'd graduated high school. *One big happy family,* I thought. *One night only.*

I couldn't see Steve Gorton anywhere.

Dad waved. I smiled back at him. Tyler Cullen turned and apparently decided I was smiling at him. Or mocking him.

"Something you want to say to me?" he said.

First words he'd spoken to me since the jump-off ended.

"Nah," I said.

I walked over to my family.

"Everybody behaving here?" I said.

"Your grandmother is practically begging me to come back," Dad said.

Grandmother blew out some air. "Full of it to the end," she said.

"I think we need to go give that bottle of champagne the attention it deserves," Mom said.

Now I smiled at her. "What are the rest of you going to drink?"

Mom and Grandmother led the way out of the ring. Dad put an arm around my shoulders.

"I'm glad I didn't miss this one," he said.

As always, he'd cast himself as the cool dad and was playing his part before he took off again for New York or California and missed even more of my life.

"Can you stick around for a couple of days?" I said, pretty sure I already knew the answer to that one.

"Back to Gotham in the morning," he said.

I whispered, "How are you and Mom getting along?"

He grinned. "I'm fine as long as I don't make any sudden moves."

"Should have been with her tonight," I said.

"You know what?" he whispered in my ear, "I'm not so sure about that."

I looked around for Daniel now, but couldn't spot him. Knowing him the way I did, I figured he might already be back at the barn with Coronado.

Dad and I walked back through the in-gate and took a left, on our way to the tent.

"Ask you something?" I said to Dad.

"Your grandmother still hates me, if that's what you're wondering about," he said.

I poked him with an elbow.

"What did you say to Mr. Gorton at the tent?"

He grinned again.

"Well," he said, "I might have mentioned that if I saw him down there talking to you before you went into the ring, I was going to knock him on his ass."

"Still not a horse show guy," I said, then asked him to wait while I checked the schooling ring for Daniel. He wasn't waiting for me there, but Tyler Cullen was leaning against the fence and swigging from his champagne bottle.

Then he saw me.

"Looking for your boyfriend?" he said. "He left."

FORTY-SEVEN

Daniel

THE CEREMONY WAS over. Becky had invited Daniel over to the house for a family celebration.

"I did everything you told me to do," she said.

He smiled at her and said, "For once. I'll see you a little later."

The tent stayed open like a bar on championship nights and Becky had gone inside with her parents and grandmother. Daniel had passed the schooling ring on his walk to the barn when he heard a loud and familiar voice behind him.

Do not stop.

Just keep walking.

"Hey! Hey, Ortega!"

He stopped, turned, and saw Tyler Cullen, waving his champagne bottle in a mock toast. Directly above Cullen, on the pedestrian bridge, Daniel could see people streaming toward the parking lots. He wished he were with them.

Anywhere but here.

Cullen took a long swallow of champagne now, wiped his mouth with the back of his hand, then continued yelling.

"You know she was lucky to beat me."

Daniel was moving toward him and before he

realized it, he was climbing over the fence and into the ring.

"She had the better horse," he said to Cullen. "And she was the better rider, whether you want to admit that to yourself or not."

Cullen's hair was shaved close on the side, with longer hair on top. Daniel always wondered about men who worried that much about their appearance. It was well known around the sport how hard the married Cullen chased after younger women.

"Yeah, go with that," Cullen said.

He walked slowly toward Daniel.

Now it is the playground.

"You are just angry because you made an amateur mistake at the finish," Daniel said. "You didn't ride through the timer. That's not Becky's fault, or mine. It is yours. It is on you."

"You're going to explain riding to me, *señor*?" Cullen said, and took another drink. "Why don't you look up my record when you get home. You own a laptop, right?"

He laughed. It was not a pleasant sound.

"You got a little something going with her on the side?" Cullen said. "Everybody sees the way you look at her."

"Is it finishing second the way you did that is eating at you?" Daniel said. "Or something else?"

They were about ten feet from each other. The people were still walking across the bridge behind them. Daniel could not believe that Cullen would do something as stupid as starting a real fight with him. He had already embarrassed himself enough tonight. If he wasn't drunk, he was getting there.

"I'm the one who should be on that horse," Cullen

said. "I know it. You know it. She's the amateur, whether she did get lucky or not tonight."

"What really bothers you," Daniel said, trying as hard as he could to keep his voice even, "is that she is half your age and her best days are ahead of her."

"Veta a la mierda," Cullen said.

Telling Daniel in Spanish he must have picked up at his barn what he could do to himself.

"Look at me," Cullen said, "using your language." He shrugged. "Who knows, maybe before too long you'll be somewhere speaking your real language full time."

Daniel felt himself clenching and unclenching his fists. Telling himself that though Cullen may treat life as a video game, he was still one of the top riders in the world. The last thing he needed was for the police to show up and break up a fight. And have reason to believe that Daniel had started it.

"Before I went into the ring, you looked like you had something to say to me," Cullen said. "Nothing stopping you now. Just you and me."

Now turn and walk away.

"You know nothing about me," Daniel said.

"Maybe more than you think," he said.

"What is that supposed to mean?"

"I'd hate to see anything happen to you or any of your friends, is all," Cullen said. "Doesn't seem all that safe for you people these days. Seems like every time I turn on the news, one of you is going away. Like, for good."

You people.

There it was.

"The only place I am going right now is to a victory celebration," Daniel said.

"Hope you have proper ID in case you get pulled over," Cullen called after him. "You do have proper ID, right? I mean, I know you and your girl are thinking about Paris. But it'd be a shame if you ended up back in Guadalajara or someplace instead."

FORTY-EIGHT

MOM AND GRANDMOTHER and I had just finished a big breakfast of pancakes and turkey bacon and even Mom's homemade hash browns. Grandmother had gone off on her power walk. Mom said she was going to work out. Coronado was getting the week off. I was getting ready to ride Sky, let her know I hadn't forgotten her.

I was at the sink, handwashing Grandmother's china and silver. For a tough old horsewoman, she loved fine things, and decreed that none of those fine things would ever see the inside of a dishwasher. So the duty of washing and drying and storing the plates and cutlery usually fell to me.

But I nearly dropped one of the plates, one I knew had been a wedding gift, when I heard the familiar explosion of tires and gravel on the driveway, looked out the kitchen window, and saw Steve Gorton pulling up in an unfamiliar sleek blue car.

The window was open. I briefly imagined what had been such a nice morning flying out of it, down over the barn and away.

I snorted as loudly as one of the horses. Of course Gorton was talking on his phone as he walked across the driveway wearing a crimson cap printed HARVARD BUSINESS SCHOOL. As he got closer, I heard him say, loudly, "I'm telling you, I don't care what he says, he's lying out his ass."

Then he nodded and said, "How do I *know*? Because I do it all the time myself."

His disappearing act after the Grand Prix had stretched into a full week. The last person I knew who'd talked to him was Dad, when he'd whispered that heartfelt message in his ear.

Gorton put his phone away when he got to the ring.

I dried my hands and went out the kitchen door to meet him.

"Hey," he said.

"Good morning, Mr. Gorton," I said sweetly, all fake sincerity.

"Listen, I haven't had the chance to congratulate you since you won the thing," he said.

One way to do it without actually doing it, I thought.

"You saw the best part of the night," I said. "No need to stick around for the after-party."

"Including Tyler Cullen's little shit show," he said. "Heard about it, though."

"That *was* a little different," I said.

"I like Tyler," Gorton said. "Guy's a great rider. But he didn't do himself any favors with bullshit like that." He smirked. "You want a different result? Ride faster, am I right?"

"He still nearly beat me on a day our horse was perfect," I said.

Our horse. Smiling. Now I was Rebecca of Atwood Farm with him.

"Listen," he said, "I might not be the best loser in the world myself. But you won the thing, fair and square. Didn't just beat Cullen. Even beat my friend Mike Bloomberg's kid, too. Don't think I didn't call the former mayor of New York first thing the next morning." He paused. "Anyway, a deal is a deal."

He put out his hand to me. I hesitated at first, but then shook it.

"You stay on the horse," he said.

That was it. Meeting over. He walked away from me, got into his car, drove away, not pulling out like a lunatic for once. I watched the sleek blue car make the turn onto Stable Way, heading for Palm Beach Point.

I stood on the front lawn and watched him go.

"He *is* lying out his ass," I said to myself, and then went to ride Sky.

FORTY-NINE

Gorton

TYLER CULLEN'S VOICE over the speakerphone filled the interior of the new Maserati. Gorton had treated himself to it the previous Monday, using his share of the goddamn horse's winnings. Why not?

"Did they buy it?" Cullen asked.

"Who gives a shit?" Gorton said. "I actually kind of like Maggie. Might have tried to hit that under different circumstances. It's the kid and the old lady who piss me off. The kid especially. She looks at me like I'm some old loser trying to hit on *her*."

Gorton was taking his time driving back to the island. Blaine would probably just be getting up. He'd never seen anybody sleep like this girl. But the sooner he got back to the house, the sooner he'd have to talk to her.

"Tell me the truth," Gorton said. "Do I have the best horse?"

"We've gone over this."

"I want to hear it again."

"Yes, you do," Cullen said. "But that kid will never be as good as she was the other night. Just because she got hit by lightning doesn't mean she's still not over her goddamn skis. No chance in hell she's good enough to ride like that over the next three or four months and make it to Paris. But I am. One hundred percent."

"You screwed up the other night," Gorton said.

There was a pause at the other end of the call.

"Totally on me," he said. "Got ahead of myself because I wanted to beat her ass too much. Won't happen again."

"Better not."

"It won't."

"And the kid isn't good enough to get the points she needs?"

"No," Cullen said. "She's good. She is. She's got potential, if she doesn't let her arrogance get in the way. But she's not her mother."

His voice dropped for a couple of seconds and then Gorton heard him say, "And that kid sure as hell isn't me."

"Can you make the Olympics on your horse?" Gorton said.

"Probably," Cullen said. "But put me on yours and we don't just make it to Paris, we ride off into the sunset with a gold medal."

Gorton was only half-listening. He was picturing himself stopping at the Honor Bar for a Bloody Mary. He checked the dashboard clock. A little early, but they'd goddamn well open for him.

"So we're back where we were before she won the damn thing," Gorton said. "We've got to find a way to get her off the horse for good." He paused. Definitely the Honor Bar. He could already taste the first drink of the day. "You made any progress on what we talked about?"

Cullen was cautiously optimistic, saying he had to be careful.

"I like the way you think," Gorton said.

Cullen laughed.

"Only because it's the way *you* think," he said.

"Couple of sore losers," Gorton said.

They were both laughing when Gorton ended the call and headed for the Flagler Bridge.

Sometimes he screwed with people for the best reason in the world: because he could.

FIFTY

Maggie

MAGGIE WOULD HAVE gone to the gym instead of Gus's barn had Becky wanted to join her.

She told herself, when she finally made the decision to reach out to Gus, that it just hurt too much *not* to ride. Only now it was riding that hurt. Like hell. A lot. Every day. About an hour into this morning's ride, Maggie couldn't decide if she'd come back too soon. Or shouldn't have come back at all. Another way of looking at it.

She was being reminded right now how much riding taxed her legs. Her back was sore, too, and her neck, and even her forearms. And her butt. As she posted, the simple up-and-down of being in the saddle, every time she'd land, she'd feel a stab of pain that would shoot all the way up to her neck and shoulders, almost into her brain. At which point the ache in her upper body rivaled the pain in her legs. She'd get herself into a hot bath when she got home.

"Is there a problem?" Gus said from his chair. "You could always take up a new sport if this is too painful for you."

"Who said anything about pain?"

"You didn't have to," he said. "My legs don't work. But my eyes do just fine."

"If I wasn't ready for this, I wouldn't be here," she said.

"Don't tell me," he said. "Show me."

"Do your other riders get this kind of tough love?"

"Who said anything about love?" Gus said.

Dr. Garry had told her two months, absolute minimum, to get back on a horse. She'd done it in half that time, as much out of stubbornness as need.

She winced suddenly.

"What?" Gus said.

"Cramps," she said, through clenched teeth.

"Where?"

"Every…where."

They could come up on her that fast and cause her legs to seize up the way they were seizing up now. Gus yelled for Seamus, who came running. When her boots were on the ground, both legs gave out, and she sat down. Hard.

Gus reached into his chair's side pouch, grabbed a bottle of water, handed it to her, told her to drink all of it. She did. When the pain slowly began to subside and the muscles relaxed, she lay on her back and did some stretches that had helped her in the past.

Finally, slowly, she was able to get to her feet.

"You ready to get back to work?" he said.

"Now?"

"You know what they say," Gus said. "Don't tell me about the pain. Just show me the baby."

"You know who says that?" she said. "Guys."

It was when she had turned Paladin and put him back into motion that she saw Daniel Ortega staring at her from the other side of the fence.

FIFTY-ONE

Maggie

SHE TROTTED PALADIN one more time around the ring. When she finished, Daniel was the one coming out to help her down. Her legs were cramping again, though not as badly as before. But she wasn't going to let him see that.

"What are you doing here, Maggie?" he said.

"Isn't that obvious?" she said.

"What's obvious," he said, "is that it's too soon for you to be doing this."

"Probably so," she said. "But not your call." Then she snapped at him, "The one who has no right to be here is you."

She knew she had no right to be angry at him. But she wanted to be angry at somebody. Mostly because she'd been caught.

"We need to talk," she said. "Right now."

She ignored the pain in her legs, her knee really barking at her now, and led him out of the ring and over to the driveway where Daniel had parked his car next to hers. She resisted the powerful urge to sit down and she leaned against the side of her car instead.

"First things first," she said. "If you tell either one of them, you're fired."

They both knew she meant Becky and Caroline.

"You don't mean that," he said.

"Try me," she said.

Daniel suggested they have their talk over coffee.

"Right here is fine," Maggie said. "I'm not done riding yet."

"Gus seemed to be under the impression the horse was done for the day," Daniel said.

"Is he the one who told you?"

She just wanted to be sure.

Daniel shook his head.

"Are you certain of that?"

"Yes, Maggie, I am."

Don't sit down. Fight off the pain. Keep going.

"If you wanted to start riding again," Daniel said, "why here and not at home? Why aren't you training with me?"

"I don't need a trainer right now," she said. "I need a nanny."

"But why here?"

"Because I don't want them to know!" she said. *"Because I don't want them to see me like this."* She sighed and in a quieter voice said, "I didn't want you to see, either, if you want to know the truth."

"Maggie," he said, "as Dr. Garry told you, if you get hurt now, it won't be a month away from riding. It could be a whole year."

She could feel heat rising up in her, mostly because she knew he was right. She'd always told Becky: *When you're right, you're right.*

But she kept her voice calm.

"It's not your decision," she said. "Not Mother's, or Becky's, or even Dr. Garry's. It's mine. The same as it will be my decision when I want to tell my mom or Becky. And that is why you are going to promise me that you're not going to tell."

"You will have to tell them eventually," he said. "If they don't find out the way I did."

"Until I do," she said, "I don't want them looking at me like I'm a piece of my mother's precious china."

She looked at him.

"Okay?" she said.

She studied his face. Saw the hesitation before he answered, as if having a debate with himself Maggie could almost hear.

"Okay," he said finally.

"You promise to keep my secret for now," she said.

She knew it wasn't close to being a question.

"If that is what you wish."

"You've got your secrets, Daniel," she said. "Now you get to carry around one of mine. I've got this. I do. And until I tell them, I don't want you worrying about me."

That got a smile out of him.

"Now that," he said, "I cannot promise."

"And I will make a promise to you," she said. "I won't jump until I'm sure I'm ready. I promise."

They shook on it. At least her hands didn't hurt.

He told her he would see her back at the barn, got into his car, and drove away. Maggie watched until the car disappeared. Then she limped inside the barn and told Gus she wanted to spend just a little more time in the ring.

"Could you wait about fifteen minutes so I can watch you?" he said. "I've got a quick conference call in the house about this horse in Kentucky we've been looking at."

"I'm barely going to do more than walk," Maggie said. "I'll be fine."

"Okay," he said. "Because if I break you, your mother is going to be really mad at me."

Scamus got Paladin ready, walked him out, got Maggie up, then Gus wheeled around the corner of the barn toward his house. When Maggie was sure he was gone, she urged the horse into a trot.

But when she got to the far end and turned him back around toward the barn, she didn't hesitate.

Gave him one kick, and then another, telling him to pick up speed.

Then she was coming down the middle to where Gus had set up a small jump for his other riders, feeling as if she were flying, blocking out the fear now, oblivious to the pain she was still feeling, feeling herself smiling, even as she felt her breath coming as hard as the horse's.

She jumped Paladin then.

Felt the jolt in her legs as he landed, but kept going, circling like it was a tight rollback.

Coming back around.

Jumped him again.

FIFTY-TWO

I WAS GETTING READY to ride Sky in competition, for the first time since the fall.

Second Friday after the Grand Prix. In a side ring today, not the International Arena. Meter 30 today, less than what I'd jumped with Coronado. When I walked the course with Grandmother the top rail didn't look much higher than a curb after what I'd been jumping with Coronado.

Grandmother was training me today, not Daniel, who had driven to Fort Lauderdale to meet with an immigration lawyer, Mr. Connors.

"It is for a friend, not me," he had said.

"Is your friend in trouble?" I'd asked.

"Yes."

"Are you going to get into trouble helping him?"

"He is my friend," Daniel had said, and left it at that.

Normally Mom would have been the one to step in and act as my trainer. But this happened to be the day when Dr. Garry had scheduled an MRI and some other tests to see how she was healing.

"You don't need me anyway," she said at breakfast. "You've got the world's greatest trainer in your corner today." She nodded at Grandmother and said, "Just ask her."

"It's almost not fair to the other riders," Grandmother said.

She was chattering away as we walked the course, pointing out the hot spots in between bantering with other trainers and riders. Ever since we'd gotten Steve Gorton off her back and she wasn't worrying about money, at least for now, she seemed happier than she'd been since Mom's injuries. Clearly enjoying the hell out of the way things were going.

"God, it's good being back in the saddle," she said after we finished walking the jump-off course.

"Did you really just say that?" I said.

She winked and began singing. *"Back in the saddle again..."*

"I'll pay you to stop singing," I said.

"Out where a friend is a friend..."

"People are staring," I said. "You know that, right?"

"Just letting them know that the grandmother is back," she said.

There were sixty in the class today. Normally Tyler Cullen, one of the headliners for a four-star Grand Prix on Saturday night, wouldn't have bothered with a smaller event like this. But he'd decided to enter another one of his horses, Bandit. Grandmother and I were convinced he was doing it to mess with me, even though I wasn't riding Coronado today.

After we were finished in the ring, we sat on the grassy hill above it and waited for Emilio to walk Sky up from the barn. Suddenly, my grandmother threw back her head and laughed.

"What's so funny?" I said.

"I was just imagining that little twerp Tyler Cullen trying to smart-mouth me today," she said.

"He *is* kind of small, now that you mention it," I said.

"One of these days," Grandmother said, "I might ask him if he wants to sit on my shoulder."

When Emilio was back with Sky, Grandmother made a point of checking boots and saddle and bridle and spurs. *Totally* in charge today and loving every minute of it. Time for me to get up on Sky in the schooling ring. I put on the hairnet I wore under my helmet, put on my gloves. Walked down the hill. Emilio helped me up. Grandmother clapped her hands.

"Let's do this," she said.

She walked over and took her place next to the practice jumps. As I eased Sky into her first jump of the day, I heard Grandmother yell, "Eyes up. Heels down."

"I know," I said as we went past her.

"I heard that," she said.

We came back around.

"Hands up!" she barked.

"They *are* up," I said.

But I felt myself smiling.

"Not high enough," she said. "Different horse today."

"No shit," I said, my back to her.

"Heard that, too," she said.

Mom had always been her main focus, even after I'd started riding in competition and Grandmother told me I was wasting my talent, and my promise. But today was all about me.

Back in the saddle again.

After a few more jumps, getting closer to my place in the order, she waved me over.

"Remember," she said. "Coronado drifts left. Always. Into the jump, over it, through it. Sky does the opposite. She goes right. Go ahead and jump her again."

I turned Sky away from her, over to where Emilio was standing near the fence. As I did, I saw a flash of gray, and saw Tyler Cullen nearly cut me off with Bandit. No contact. But he had to have seen me. Which meant he'd done it on purpose. I was able to get Sky out of his way at the last second.

"Oops," Tyler said sarcastically. And loudly, as if for the benefit of everybody else in the ring.

I ignored him. I was five out by now. This was a big day for me, being back on Sky. I wasn't going to spoil any part of it by making a scene with Tyler Cullen.

So I was easing Sky away from him and his horse, and in the direction of the in-gate, when I heard my grandmother's voice, as loud as if she were using a megaphone.

"Cut the shit, Shorty!" Grandmother yelled.

FIFTY-THREE

TYLER CULLEN MADE the mistake of engaging her. Not all the other riders had stopped to watch the show. But most of them did.

"You have a problem, Grandma?" Tyler said.

"I saw what you did," Grandmother said. "Keep your horse away from hers."

"I'm just getting ready to go into the ring, same as her."

"No, you're not," Grandmother said.

I imagined the judges could hear her by now.

"Andrew in five," the announcer said behind us. *"Kyle four, then Becky, then Jennifer, then Tyler."*

"You better run along, Grandma," Tyler said. "Or you might miss the Early Bird Special."

Grandmother smiled wickedly.

"Oh, look," she said. "Tiny Tim got off a good one."

Now she walked me toward the ring. I leaned down and said, "I don't need you to fight my fights for me."

"I know that," she said. "But sometimes I can't help myself."

"Sometimes?" I said.

She looked, I thought, like a kid who'd just egged her enemy's house.

I expected Sky to be rusty. But once we were out

there, she wasn't. Not even close. It was as if I'd been riding her every weekend. She wasn't going as fast as I knew she could. It was like she was feeling her way, same as I was feeling my way now that I was riding her again, for real.

We killed it on the first combination, early in the round. No hesitation. Perfect line. Hit the first and the second. And just like that, we were into it.

"Eyes up!" my grandmother yelled.

I asked Sky to turn it up in the middle of the course. Chipped one rail. It stayed up. Maybe it was our day. One more combination, late, then a rollback. My girl made it look easy. We finished clear. For now, we had the best time in the class.

Today you didn't wait for the jump-off if you went clean, you went right into it.

"Stay ahead of your horse!" Grandmother shouted. *"Not the other way around!"*

We went clean in the jump-off, too, with a time of 33.8. There was a place near the end, a place where I could have gone inside. But Sky *was* leaning right and I didn't account for that enough. We were too wide and chose not to take a chance. I'd already asked enough for one day. Went outside instead. Not Sky's fault. Mine. It pissed me off, even though Grandmother had said the goal today was just to go double clean. I still felt as if I'd chickened out. But it was a solid time, and we still might have a chance to win.

But didn't. Tyler, going last, finally blew away my time in the jump-off, winning by nearly two full seconds. Jennifer Gates finished second. Sky and I were third.

Even as competitive as my grandmother was, she was thrilled as we walked Sky back to the barn, talking and talking about how she couldn't believe the horse had come that close to a first-place ribbon after not having shown in months.

"We found out one thing today," she said. "Somebody's still got it."

"Sky *was* pretty great," I said.

"I meant me," she said, and laughed.

"I still hate losing to that guy," I said.

Grandmother said, "You never will again when it matters."

She put a hand on my shoulder. "He rode like a crazy man today. And you know why? Because even though he's too mean and stubborn to admit it, he knows how good you are. You're in his head, not the other way around. And one of these days, kiddo, you're going to use that to your advantage."

I turned to look at her, saw her smiling still, squinting into the last of the afternoon sun. She was still walking in her stiff-legged way, going a lot slower than when we'd come up from the barn earlier, on our way to walking the course. But somehow, in the softness of the light, she looked young.

It was in the next moment that I heard her say "Becky?" in a small voice, right before she began to sway from side to side as if a strong wind had suddenly blown across the grounds.

Then her eyes rolled back and she dropped to her knees before pitching headfirst into the dirt.

FIFTY-FOUR

A COUPLE OF EVENTS were still going on, so there was a lot of horse traffic between the barns and the rings. I carefully rolled Grandmother onto her back, saw she hadn't bruised her face, took off my riding jacket, folded it and placed it as a pillow under her head.

I had no idea what had caused her to faint. Even though she was a diabetic, and I'd seen her get weak and shaky before, I'd never seen her faint until now. It was why I was so scared.

A rider I didn't recognize stopped her horse near where we were between a side ring and the food court and said, "Should I call 911?"

Before I could answer, Grandmother opened her eyes and said, "Don't even think about it."

She hadn't made any move to get up. But she was awake. And sounded pretty alert to me.

She looked up at me and said, "Now everybody in this family has ended up on the ground. I just joined the on-your-ass club."

"Is there something you want me to do, Miss Becky?" Emilio said.

He was still there, holding on to Sky's reins.

"Go see if you can find me some fruit or some yogurt or both," she said to Emilio. "It's the damn blood sugar again."

He handed me the reins, then ran toward one of the concession stands.

"That horse needs to get back to the barn," Grandmother said.

"The horse," I said, "is in better shape than you are right now."

"Wanna bet?" she said.

I was watching her get back into character, but when she tried to get up on her own, she made it only a few inches before putting her head back down.

"I need to call for the show doctor," I said, kneeling next to her.

"You need to do no such thing," she said.

Now she reached out a hand. I grabbed it and pulled her up into a sitting position.

"This is not going to be a thing," she said. "We have too much going on. I got so caught up in being a trainer again I forget to take my insulin shot this morning. Simple as that."

Somehow Emilio was already back, with an apple and some yogurt, and a bottle of water. She ate the yogurt first, then devoured the apple. Knowing her, she had probably forgotten to eat lunch, never a good idea for a diabetic, especially one over the age of seventy.

"All right, then," she said. "Feeling better already."

"All right, nothing," I said. "If you won't see the doctor here, we're going home right now and calling Dr. Garry."

"The hell we are," she said.

She reached up again with her hand and I got her standing. She still looked a little wobbly to me. But she stayed up.

"We're not calling anybody," she said. "This has happened to me before, just not in front of you. We've got way more important things to worry about than me having a little dizzy spell."

Then she grinned and brushed some dirt off her shirt and the front of her breeches. My grandmother, as much of a baseball fan as my dad, said, "Was I safe?"

I reached for her arm. She pulled it back. I handed the reins to Emilio. The three of us continued our walk toward the barn as if nothing had happened.

"We are not going to tell your mother about this," she said. "And if somebody tells her, we are simply going to tell her that I tripped, got it?"

"Got it," I said.

"We had another good day," she said. "That's what matters here."

We had to pass Tyler Cullen's owner's barn, which was much bigger, much fancier, than our own, with a lot more horses in it. As Emilio and Sky approached, Tyler came walking out, big smile on his face that signaled he already knew about Grandmother.

Shit.

"Down goes Grandma!" he said, and then barked out a laugh that I worried might scare all the horses in the area.

He looked as if he had more to say, but then Grandmother was slowly walking in his direction. Emilio stopped, but Grandmother put up a hand and said, "I got this."

Grandmother was about five nine. Maybe five ten in her riding boots. Nearly half a foot taller than Tyler Cullen. She got very close to him now.

She was smiling, but not speaking until finally, she said, "One more to put on my list."

"What list?" he said.

But she was already walking away.

FIFTY-FIVE

EVERYTHING WAS SETTING up perfectly for us, coming off a month of successes on both Coronado and Sky. I'd gotten a third-place ribbon on Coronado the previous weekend. Then a second on Sky this afternoon. Solid performances, by the horses and me, as we moved toward the big events in March and April that would determine whether I rode my way onto the Olympic short list.

Tyler Cullen was already on the short list. So was Jennifer Gates. But now I had started to think I had a legit shot at Paris. I could not only feel it, but I *wanted* it. Over the last month I'd started to perform like an elite rider. An awesome feeling. The way Mom had always felt.

We were having a family dinner: Mom and Grandmother and Daniel and me. Mom had been even more quiet than usual tonight, drifting into the background as was her way when Grandmother was holding court. Rarely would all of us have a meal together. Most days Mom left to work out before I got up, sometimes not returning until early afternoon.

Mom had even shocked the hell out of all of us by going on a couple of dinner dates with Gus Bennett, who had a barn not far from ours. It was just another sign that she was feeling better, mostly about herself. One subject practically off limits was her riding. She'd made it clear, a week or so after the accident, that she'd tell us all when she was ready to be in our ring again. I knew she had some kind of timetable in her head. But didn't ask.

We finished dinner, all of us helping clear the table, and then with the handwashing and drying of Grandmother's china and cutlery. Our dish-washer, Grandmother said, was "for the cheap stuff."

"You don't have any cheap stuff!" I said.

A few minutes later we were in the living room having coffee and chocolate chip cookies baked by Emilio's wife, talking a little more about the up-coming schedule for Coronado, and for Sky, all the way to what was essentially an Olympic qualifier in Kentucky in May.

All in all, a good, drama-free night.

Then Mom stood up suddenly, as if she was headed up to bed. But instead she walked to the front window, turning so she could face us all at once.

"There's no good time to say this," she said. "Or good way to say it. But I wanted to say it to all of you at once, so here goes."

She took a deep breath that I worried might have rocked her rib cage.

"I want to start riding again," she said.

"Mom," I said, "that's great! Why would there ever be a bad time for you to tell us that?"

She looked at me now and said, "You didn't let me finish."

She took another deep breath and said, "I want to start riding Coronado."

There was a long pause until Grandmother spoke.

"What are you saying, Maggie?"

Grandmother had asked the question, but Mom was still looking directly at me.

"I want my horse back," she said.

FIFTY-SIX

Maggie

ONCE MAGGIE HAD made her decision, there was no rationalizing the fallout: what this was going to do to Becky.

I want my horse back.

The words of a spoiled brat just hanging there, everybody staring at her, almost as if they hadn't heard her correctly.

It was Becky who spoke first.

"Wait," she said. "You're saying you want Coronado back *now*? You haven't even started riding yet."

"Yes," Daniel said, "she has."

"Where has she been riding?"

"At Gus Bennett's barn," Daniel said.

Becky's head whipped in his direction.

"You *knew* about this?" she said. "What the hell, Daniel?"

"I knew she had begun to ride again, with Gus," he said. "She made me promise not to tell, and I honored her wish. But I did not know about *this*."

"You told Daniel," Caroline Atwood said to Maggie. "And you didn't tell me, either?"

"Daniel found out on his own," Maggie said. "A week ago, before I started jumping."

Maggie took a deep breath.

No going back now.

"I looked like an idiot on the horse he had me riding," she said. "I didn't want to start here because I didn't want any of you to see me that way. I was tired of everybody looking at me like I was some kind of invalid. But then one day...I started to feel better. The day of my MRI, I finally told Dr. Garry what I was doing. When he looked at the pictures from all the tests, he basically told me it was my life."

Maggie turned to Becky.

"Honey," she said. "I am so sorry. I know it's not just my life. It's yours, too."

"No shit," I said.

"I want you to understand my decision."

"You chose your horse over me," Becky said. She gave a sarcastic thumbs-up. "Got it."

"That's not fair. You know how long this has been my dream," Maggie said.

She looked at Becky and saw both the hurt and anger on her face.

"What about my dreams?" Becky said, standing. "They don't matter?

"So what you're telling me," she continued, "is that you plan to go from Gus Bennett's ring all the way to a five-star Grand Prix, and then straight to Paris? I get off, you get on, is that it?"

She looked at her mother, face red, eyes red.

"Should we pass an effing baton?" she said.

"Honey," Maggie said, "it's a lot more complicated than that. I never dreamt I'd feel this good—this *ready*—this soon. But I finally decided that if I was going to try, it had to be now. And I mean, like, *right now.*"

"I'm glad you were able to work this out in your head, Mom, no kidding," Becky said. "Not only did you set the debate, nobody else got to join it." She nodded. "Very cool."

Maggie was breathing so hard, more deep breaths in and out, that her ribs were starting to feel sore all over again.

You've come this far.

No turning back now.

"I was going to wait another week," Maggie said. "Just to be sure that *I* was sure. But then at dinner you all got so excited talking about the calendar, and what's coming up, and what's at stake, and I decided my waiting any longer wasn't fair to anybody."

"Now we're talking *fair?*" Becky said. "To who?"

"You think me getting thrown from the horse was fair?" Maggie said.

Then she paused and said, "The Olympics was my dream first."

Maggie was waiting for her mom to weigh in. Or Daniel. Or both. But this was between Maggie and her daughter. The room crackled with silent tension. And the intensity of an electric storm.

"This is a lot to process," Maggie said. "Maybe we all need to sleep on it and talk in the morning."

"Coronado is your horse, Mom," Becky said. "You can do what you want with him. Next time, maybe think about giving me a heads-up."

Becky walked over to the front door, opened it, started out, stopped, stepped back inside.

"Have at it," she said to Maggie, and left.

FIFTY-SEVEN

Daniel

BECKY HAD GONE to Coral Gables for a couple of days to visit her old college roommate. According to Maggie and Caroline, they had found a note from Becky on the kitchen table. She needed a break and would be back on Wednesday to ride Sky. Until then, she wrote, *Don't miss me too much.*

Now it was Tuesday morning. Day two of Daniel being back in the ring with Maggie Atwood.

"Listen," Maggie said to him now. "I need to say this while Becky isn't around. We're all going to have to get used to the new normal."

Normal? Daniel thought. *This family?*

"Fair enough," he said.

"Don't sound so enthusiastic," Maggie said.

Maybe she'd always been this edgy, and he had forgotten. Today was starting out as awkwardly between them as yesterday had when Maggie had just been waiting for him in the ring, she and Emilio having already saddled Coronado. No request that Daniel continue to train her beyond "Let's do this," and they went right to work.

But *this,* Daniel knew, was about more than the horses and the women in this family riding them. So much more. Daniel, for all his misgivings and anger about the way she had pulled the rug—the horse, really—out from underneath her daughter, felt he owed her his best efforts.

He watched her do small jumps now, after having just trotted the horse the day before. She looked stiff in the saddle, as if afraid to even change her position slightly.

"You need to watch your posture, Maggie," he called out to her. "Shoulders back more, where they used to be."

"Small problem, Daniel," she yelled back to him. "A lot of things aren't *where* they used to be. You may have heard, some of my furniture got rearranged."

Tread carefully, he told himself.

She is still your boss.

"I told myself it would be like riding a bike," she said. "Guess what? It's not. My mind isn't fully connecting with my body."

"I'd like to see you press down harder into the stirrups," he said. "You're standing up more than you used to."

"I *know*," she said.

The edge again, the words brittle.

He'd set the rail at three feet, a height girls in the Hunters ring could clear with ease. Her distance was fine on the first jump she'd had on Coronado in a long time. The horse's form was perfect. Daniel closed his eyes briefly and tried to imagine her executing the same kind of jump at 1.6 meter in the International Arena.

Could not.

Maggie circled back around. Jumped the big horse again. As she landed him Daniel could see her wince, revealing the strain on her face, the tension in her whole body.

"Better," he said.

"Be honest, please," Maggie said, slowing the horse and coming in his direction.

"I have never been a good liar," he said. "You should know that by now."

Except when I need to be, especially with your daughter.

She said, "Do you honestly believe I can ride this horse in a Grand Prix in two weeks?"

He believed she *would* jump in that ring two weeks from now. But she was asking him how well he thought she would do.

"If you are going to be ready," he answered, "you need to ride as much as your body can stand. So even though you are finished with Coronado for today, I would now like you to ride Sky."

"Nope," she said. "Not happening. Not riding Becky's horse."

"She rode yours," Daniel said.

"This is different," she said.

"I'm not asking you to jump her if you'd rather not," Daniel said. "She needs a light workout, perhaps a half hour, tops. Or less."

She *was* the boss.

Finally, Maggie gave in.

Daniel went to the barn to get Sky ready, brought her back out, helped Maggie up. Her left leg went into the stirrup first, but as she swung her right leg over and settled herself into the saddle, Daniel heard her exhale sharply in pain.

"Enjoy the ride you are about to have," Daniel said, grinning. "I know that you will."

"Pretty sure of yourself."

"With this horse?" he said. "Yes. Very sure."

Right away Daniel could see Maggie's face light up with joy, as if in bright colors. Could see her posture suddenly improve and her attitude along with it. Saw her smiling for the first time in two days, as if abandoning for the moment she was not in competition with herself, and her own ambition, and expectations. Saw her effortlessly picking up speed. The joy Becky regained from riding Sky again full time had now passed to her mother.

"I'm going to jump her," Maggie called out to him from the other end of the ring.

She looked over at Daniel.

"You knew, didn't you?" she said.

He smiled and nodded.

After about ten minutes, she held up a finger. One more.

"Go for it," Daniel said.

"This is why I came back!" Maggie yelled from the far end of the ring. "This horse makes you feel like you're floating!"

As Daniel watched Maggie and Sky float one last time, landing the jump perfectly, he heard the sound of a slow, rhythmic clapping.

Becky was standing at the barn.

FIFTY-EIGHT

I STOPPED CLAPPING when I saw them both turn. Mom looked like a kid who'd been caught doing something wrong.

"Lucky I came back early," I said. "Or by tomorrow I might have no horse to ride."

I watched Daniel quickly help Mom down. She came walking over to where I was standing.

"Daniel asked me to ride her," she said, turning her back to him.

Daniel started walking Sky back to the barn, dropping the reins, palms down toward me in a calming gesture.

"Slight change of plans," I said. "Turns out I didn't miss college as much as I thought I did. I had to find out the hard way that you can only watch so many seasons of *Grey's Anatomy*."

"That seemed like pretty sarcastic applause right there," Mom said.

"What did you expect?" I said. "I sit in traffic on the turnpike for two hours then find you on my horse. I thought this was all about you being on *your* horse?"

Just Mom and me in the ring now. How many rounds had we gone like this? Hundreds? A thousand? But today's conflict was a totally different vibe.

All I wanted to do right now was walk away from her and all the weirdness between us and change into my riding clothes and ride my own damn horse.

Except that today Mom didn't just have her own horse. She had my horse, too.

"We really need to talk," she said.

"Mom," I said, "*you* might need to. I don't. Maybe it's a mom thing to believe that heart-to-heart chats fix everything except a broken leg. That's not me."

"Five minutes," she said. "To clear the air."

"The air's fine, Mom," I said. "It's the situation that kind of sucks."

"Five minutes, then," she said. "Up on the porch. We always did our best talking there."

That actually made me smile.

"Well, yeah," I said. "But as I recall, what I mostly did was listen."

I followed her up the hill to where the two of us had sat for so many talks. About Dad sometimes. Or about her and Dad, long after they'd gotten divorced. Or her wanting to know about a boy I'd just broken up with. Or was dating. Or a class I was failing. Or how I wasn't working hard enough at my riding.

I thought: *Now I'm working my ass off on my riding and it's doing me a hell of a lot of good.*

"Seriously, Mom?" I said. "You've made your decision. I accept it. Why are we here?"

"Because we need to handle being competitors going forward, that's why," she said, "even being from the same family and the same damn barn and being bossed all over the place by Caroline Atwood."

"We're only competing against each other if we enter the same events," I said. "This shit is difficult enough already and I'm not even up on my horse yet."

"But we've competed against each other in the past," she said.

"Things were a little different then," I said.

I noticed her absently rubbing her right knee. She was still in a lot of pain.

"You should ride in all the big events coming up, same as me," she said now. "You're ready for them."

"Not your call, Mom," I said.

"You're right," she said. "I've put everybody in a tough spot, but not by choice."

"There're always choices," I said.

"There was a lot of avoidance the other night," she said. "And that just ain't gonna cut it, not around here."

"Okay then," I said. "*Okay.* I heard what you had to say. You heard what I had to say. Now I really am gonna go change and ride my horse."

"Your horse is what I most wanted to talk to you about," she said.

"Now you're an expert on Sky?" I said.

"No," Mom said. "But I'm still enough of a horsewoman to know you should try to ride her to the Olympics."

FIFTY-NINE

WELL, I THOUGHT, *she's got my attention now.*

"You got that after one session in the ring?" I said. "Pro tip, Mom? You're the one with the Olympic horse, not me."

"Maybe not now," Maggie said. "But in a few months, I'm convinced Sky can be, too."

"You're wrong," I said.

"No, I'm not."

"Mom," I said. "I love you. I love Sky to death. But you really are talking some major shit here."

"No, I'm not," she said again, with more force this time. "You're the rider who's going to scare me the most once I'm back out there. *You.*"

"It's nice that you think so," I said.

"Tell you what," she said. "Why don't we go down the hill and ask Daniel?"

Maggie got out of her chair, looking the way Grandmother did sometimes when she'd been sitting awhile, flexed her right knee a couple of times, walked stiffly down the porch steps.

And she's going to ride in a five-star Grand Prix in two weeks?

But I followed her through the double doors of the barn.

"We may have some breaking news here," she said to Daniel, who was talking on his phone.

"I need to call you back," he said, then ended the call to listen to Maggie's theory on Sky and the Olympics.

Daniel looked at me.

"What do you say about this?" he said.

"You first," I said.

"Your mother is absolutely right," he said.

"Ha!" Mom said. "There you have it."

"Wait," Daniel said. "I have news of my own I want you both to hear. I was about to come up the hill and tell you."

Daniel was never easy to read, but whatever was on his mind was serious business.

"I have been doing a lot of thinking since the other night," he said. "And once Becky was back, I was going to wait a few days. But there is no longer any point in waiting."

He turned to Mom then.

"You are going to need to find another trainer," Daniel said.

"*Excuse* me?" Mom said. She tilted her head, and curiously raised an eyebrow. "I'm sorry, but have you suddenly inherited your own barn, Daniel?"

"I'm the one who is sorry," he said. "But I only want to train Becky."

"No," Mom said.

SIXTY

Gorton

STEVE GORTON AND Tyler Cullen were seated at Gorton's table in the tent at the International Arena. Before buying the top-tier table for the season, Gorton had checked its location, a little closer to the ring than Bloomberg's table and the one that belonged to Bill Gates.

It was a few minutes after twelve. The breakfast crowd had already cleared out. The waitstaff was setting up for lunch, which would be followed by some afternoon event in the arena. Gorton couldn't have said what kind if somebody stuck a gun in his ear.

"Wait," Cullen said. "Nobody told you that Maggie was back in the old saddle?"

"No one did," Gorton said. "You say it just happened yesterday?"

Cullen nodded.

"How did you find out so quickly?"

"I make it my business to know," Cullen grinned and said, "but maybe the owner of the horse is the last to know."

God, Gorton thought, *he is a cocky little bastard.* But maybe that's what made him such a good rider. He'd invested in a few movies and been around enough stars to know how much shit directors and studios were willing to put up with from them.

"This might actually help you get all three of those women out of your life," Cullen said.

"Why is that?"

"Because Maggie has no shot at winning on that horse, that's why," Cullen said.

Gorton sipped his Bloody Mary. Cullen had coffee in front of him. He was in his riding clothes, having told Gorton he was only schooling today—whatever the hell that meant—and due back to his ring in a few minutes.

"You're full of shit," Gorton said. "You don't know she can't win."

"Yeah, boss," Cullen said, "as a matter of fact I do. Maybe she's back in form by the fall, if she's lucky and doesn't break her ass again. But not before. Nobody comes back this fast. Don't ask me. Ask anybody. Trust me: The rider you thought you wanted in the first place isn't the rider you want now."

"Is that so?" Gorton said.

Cullen nodded. "You want to hear something funny?"

"Yeah, Cullen," Gorton said. "You can probably see how much I want you to amuse the living shit out of me."

"Not funny, actually," Cullen said. "More ironic. Because as much as it pains me to admit it, the kid is the better rider."

"Son of a bitch!" Gorton said, loud enough to turn heads at nearby tables. "I'd rather lose without that kid than win with her."

He finished his Bloody Mary.

"I could be boxed in here," he said. "And I effing hate being boxed in."

"Yeah," Cullen said. The smug grin again. "It's not like you're Steve Gorton or anything."

"Let me ask you something," Gorton said. "Say I *can* figure this out and get rid of them both once and for all and get you on the horse without looking like I threw brave little Maggie under the bus, what about the horse you're on now, and your owner, what's-his-name?"

"You give me a shot at Coronado," Cullen said, "and let me worry about the rest of it."

"You'd sell him out?"

"I'd sell my mother out," Cullen said.

Gorton said, "If everything else does turn to shit, and I'm with one or the other, we still need a Plan B."

"Still working on it," Cullen said.

"Work harder," Gorton said.

"I hear you."

"You better," Gorton said. "You've got a lot riding on this, too. So to speak."

"Hear that," Cullen said. "Some money might have to change hands."

Gorton smiled. "Now we're talking about my sport," he said.

Cullen stood up.

"Even you sometimes forget that you're the one who tells people how this shit is going to go," Tyler Cullen said. "Not the other way around."

When he was gone, Gorton picked up his phone, punched in a number, waited, drumming the fingers of his free hand on the table.

"I need to see you," he snapped. "Now."

"What about?"

"I thought I explained to you before that I don't like surprises," he said.

"Where are you?"

"At my table."

He put the phone back down.

He was working on his second Bloody, reading through some text messages, when he heard Caroline Atwood say, "What was so important that it couldn't wait?"

Then he told her how it was going to go.

"You wouldn't," she said when he finished.

"Watch me," Gorton said.

SIXTY-ONE

I WAS IN THE RING with Daniel in the late afternoon, just having schooled one of Grandmother's new
horses, when we saw Gus Bennett's trailer pull up the
driveway.

Mom walked toward us, announcing, "I'm moving
Coronado over to Gus's."

Just like that.

"Wait," I said. "Can we at least talk about this?"

"You're right about something," she said to me.
"We've done enough talking for one day."

She turned to Daniel.

"Gus is my trainer now," she said. "You're with
Becky. I was angry before. But no hard feelings. If you
don't want me, I don't want you."

Daniel didn't react except to offer his help. Mom
said they could handle it themselves. About half an
hour later, we watched the trailer pull away.

"Wasn't I winning a Grand Prix on that horse
about twenty minutes ago?" I said.

"Less," he said.

"But now there he goes."

Daniel and I had dinner that night at the Trophy
Room. We talked over my mom's suggestion from
every possible angle, some I hadn't even considered.

"I'm right," he said. "And so is your mother. In this case, you must trust both of us."

Now I was back from dinner, stopping in the kitchen to pour myself a white wine, hoping it might settle my nerves. And my brain. Still royally pissed off at my mother, as hard as she was trying to clean things up now. As much smoke as she was blowing at me.

If it was smoke, that is.

You hate to lose, Daniel had said over dinner. He was right. For all my newfound love of riding, how much did I want to win my way to the Olympics?

Maybe that was the real question, whatever Mom and Daniel thought: was Mom's dream now mine, too?

I drank some wine, starting to think that maybe I should have brought the bottle.

I heard a car in the driveway, then got up and parted my curtains and saw it was Mom's, finally back from Gus's. Briefly wondered if more than horse business had been going on over there. Left my glass and walked downstairs after I heard her close the front door.

"Everything okay with Coronado's new digs?" I asked.

She put a finger to her lips, motioned me to follow her into the kitchen.

"It was kind of crazy," Mom said, "seeing him in a stall at Gus's barn."

"The universe is crazy," I said. "You don't even have to leave our house to know that."

"We'll get through this," she said.

"Can I ask you one more question before you head up?"

"Please don't make it a hard one," she said. "It's

like we say about a horse that needs a cool-down, I feel like I've been rode hard and put away wet."

"Why do you really want me to do this on Sky?"

She didn't hesitate.

"Because in my heart I think it's the best thing for you," she said. "And I only want the best for you, even if you don't believe that right now."

"Best for me," I said. "Or for you?"

If she was insulted, she didn't show it. Instead she smiled.

"I can see how you might think that way," she said. "But all I keep thinking about is how unbelievable it would be if we both made it to Paris, on the same team."

Before I could answer, she said, "I assume you spoke more to Daniel at dinner."

"He's all in," I said. "Actually said a lot of the same things you did."

She looked very happy all of a sudden, as happy as she had been in days, like we'd been in an airplane and the clouds had parted and we'd finally cleared some turbulence. As if the worst was suddenly over.

"So you're going to do it then," she said.

"Not a chance in hell," I said.

SIXTY-TWO

SIX O'CLOCK SATURDAY night at the Winter Equestrian Festival, parking lots overflowing, the Fidelity Investments 5-Star Grand Prix set to start in an hour or so.

I was already in the field, having prequalified by winning a Grand Prix on Coronado, even though I was riding Sky tonight. Mom was riding Coronado. She'd qualified, barely, in her first competition since the accident. She'd gotten two rails, both early, managed to pull it together, just enough, over the second half of the course. Forty riders had made it. One more rail and she wouldn't have been one of them. But she was here. It meant she was back.

Daniel and I were on our way up from the barn to walk the course.

"You don't have to decide tonight," he said.

"I know I don't *have* to," I said. "But I've made up my mind. I'm going to give it this one shot. That's as much as I'm opening the door."

"Or," he said, grinning, "you could go out there tonight and kick the door in."

"You've always told me to ride my horse like I belong," I said. "I'll know by the end of tonight if Sky and I belong."

"At least you've stopped saying no."

"Not saying yes, either."

"Obstinada," he said.

Not the first time I'd heard that one.

Stubborn Becky McCabe. Obstinate Becky.

Or just Becky.

This would be the biggest event I'd ever had with my horse in this arena, this big a purse, this strong a field. I hadn't been bullshitting Daniel. I hadn't changed my mind on the Olympics. But after days of persuasion, I had promised him that I would at least try to keep an open mind. I'd told Mom and Grandmother the same. And then asked all of them to please drop the subject until after the Grand Prix.

Mom and Gus happened to arrive at the arena at the same time Daniel and I did. They were getting ready to walk the course, too. Gus, of course, riding his motorized wheelchair, bright yellow and black, thick, all-terrain tires rolling through the deep and soft dirt. *Everybody* could see Gus Bennett in that statement chair. *I'm here. Now what?*

Move along fast, or be prepared to get the hell out of his way or get run over.

"Hey," I said to Mom.

"Hey yourself," she said.

Over the past few days, Mom had spent most of her time at Gus's. I jokingly asked if they were finally dating, and she'd said, "I think of it more as boot camp. What he doesn't say to me in the ring, he says at dinner."

"Good luck," I said to her now, as we all started out on the course, Gus leading the way.

"Same," she said.

I thought: I could just as easily have been talking with Matthew or Jennifer or Tess or Georgina or any of the other heavy hitters in our sport. She hadn't known I was definitely entering the event until Friday, and only then because Daniel had told her.

She was going eighth in the order. In the past, she'd absolutely hated going early. When I mentioned that to Daniel he told me to focus on *my* place in the order—thirty-fourth—and not hers.

"You're riding your horse tonight," he said. "Not hers."

When we finished walking, I saw Steve Gorton up above us, as if the master of all he surveyed, leaning against a railing above the in-gate. Drink in one hand. Phone in the other. I knew he saw me. But he just looked away. Whatever. He was Mom's concern now. Her problem. Not mine.

Emilio wouldn't be taking the walk with Sky until the class had started. For now, Daniel and I made our way up through the bleachers to my usual perch: back row, corner.

"What do you expect from her, really?" I said when we got up there.

"Your mom or Sky?"

"You know who I mean."

"Seriously, I expect very little," he said. "But perhaps she will surprise us."

"She's world class at surprises lately," I said. "Now we're going to find out if she can still ride."

She then proceeded to ride like crap.

Not the horse's fault.

Hers.

She got too close to the third jump, on a terrible distance, and Coronado hit the rail so hard with his front legs that the sound was like a gunshot, even as far away from them as Daniel and I were.

"Don't give up," I said.

It was what she'd yell to me sometimes when I'd

catch an early rail, and she'd see my shoulders slump. Or my whole body. I looked down and saw Gus, usually the loudest trainer out there, sitting silent in his chair near the in-gate.

"She is way too forward on the horse," Daniel said quietly. "If he ever stops short, she will go flying right over his head."

Two jumps later, another bad distance, another rail.

"Her brain is going faster than her horse," Daniel said.

We were both leaning forward, watching her blow through another rail as she started the second half of the course.

Finally, second-to-last jump, Coronado refused. We could hear the loud, collective groans and gasps from the crowd. I could see the slump in *her* as she circled the horse. The death moment for any rider. The death move. She brought him around and this time he made the jump. They were done. Mercifully. I was vaguely aware of the announcer listing the faults and time faults. In the moment it sounded as long as a grocery list.

She walked Coronado slowly back toward the in-gate, her head down. As she did, Daniel said we should get down there.

"Not sure I want to talk to her right now," I said.

"No," he said, "I meant, Emilio is on his way with Sky."

As we passed underneath the stands, I could see Grandmother and Steve Gorton locked in heated conversation. When Grandmother laid a hand on his arm, Gorton jerked it away, nearly toppling her balance. Then he was moving away from her and down the stairs as if he'd been shot out of a cannon.

I wished that Gus were right here, right now, but

he was making his way toward the ring, slowly this time, navigating high-volume horse traffic with the wheelchair. Gorton was about to follow Gus when I managed to cut in front of him, nearly knocking him off balance.

"Hey," Gorton said.

"I got this," I said.

"Who do you think you're talking to?"

"Somebody I used to work for."

"There're some things I need to say to your mother," he said.

"Get in line," I said.

SIXTY-THREE

THERE WERE SO MANY horses in the ring, so much of the round incomplete, I couldn't spot her at first.

Then I saw her crouched in a far corner, taking deep breaths, her shoulders rising and falling, as Emilio passed behind her with Sky.

"I need to get down there," Gus said.

"Me first," I said.

"I'm the one training her now," he said.

"I'm her daughter."

I made my way along the outside of the ring and when I reached her I hopped the fence. She didn't see me at first.

"Hey," I said.

She looked up, as if startled. There were red blotches on her cheeks. Eyes a mess. She'd already taken off her hairnet and laid her helmet on the ground next to her.

"I just embarrassed myself out there in front of the whole world," she said.

I waited.

"I can't do this," she said. "I was crazy to think I still *could* do this." I wasn't worried about her crying, not here, in front of everybody. She looked more like she wanted to fight somebody. Maybe herself.

Finally she said, "You want the horse back, he's yours."

She pulled herself to her feet.

"Aren't you going to say anything?" she said finally.

"Yeah," I said. "Suck it up."

SIXTY-FOUR

IT WAS MORE THAN a year since I'd been in this ring with Sky. It had been a much smaller event, on a Wednesday afternoon. But I'd never been with her under the lights on a Saturday night. Never even considered it until now.

I kept telling Daniel that I needed to see how Sky could handle the stage. But the truth was, I wanted to see how *I* could handle the stage, riding her now and not Coronado.

I wasn't even going to start the Olympics process if I didn't think we were both up to it. She'd always been my wonderful little horse. My baby. But now, maybe for one night only, we were about to dial things up. And, being competitive as hell, I wanted to do well tonight. Maybe even shock the crowd and the rest of the field and win. But I promised myself from the first time Sky and I had started showing that I'd never make her do something that I honestly thought she couldn't.

Daniel and Emilio were with me in the gate. My mouth was suddenly as dry as the dirt on my boots. I could feel my hands shaking. Good nerves? Bad nerves? Who the hell knew, except that the horse ahead of us in the order had just finished its round. I took in the lights and the noise and the crowd and the atmosphere and even the excitement in the air, everything Daniel Ortega called "the moment."

Of truth, maybe.

Eric Glynn came past me on his horse, Valance, having just gone double clean.

Time.

I knew I was being introduced, heard my name, nothing after that. Trying to block out the noise, trying not to think too hard on the moment.

Truth or dare.

We took the first part of the course like breezing through low-height jumps in a side ring on a weekday afternoon. *I love this horse,* I thought. I could always feel how hard she was trying, how she wanted to do well. Tonight she was even more dialed in, almost as if she knew how much was riding on this, for both of us.

Don't tell me horses don't know.

Not thinking about the Olympics now. Just riding my horse. We were here. We might as well go for it.

We came up on the first rollback. Sky was usually great on even the tightest rollbacks, maybe because she *was* small, and closer to the ground than a horse as big as Coronado. Sometimes the hardest turns for the bigger horses were the easiest ones for her.

But I didn't rein her in enough, and she was suddenly drifting too far outside on an inside turn, Sky leaning so far to the left that I was afraid that we might go around the jump and not over it.

Pilot error.

Totally.

Sky nearly saved me. Tried her hardest to save me. Chipped up in time. Just not enough time. Took down the rail with one of her hind legs.

Shit.

I heard my voice inside my head: *Don't give up.*

Still good advice.

We came back around. Sky was still flying. Hit a combination like a champ. Forget about a ribbon. No reason not to finish strong. Maybe prove to me we did belong.

Then it happened, three jumps from the end. Nothing tricky, nothing complicated. Nothing fancy. Seven strides from the last jump to this one. Wide-open spaces.

But I misjudged the distance. Not by a lot. Just enough. Sky landed her last stride fine. But we were too far away from the jump. Not impossible to still *make* the jump. Just more difficult than it should have been.

"Come on!"

She tried again. She did. Tried to take one last small stride to get herself close enough. A horse with less heart would simply have refused. Either stopped or circled.

Sky tried her ass off.

Chipped up again.

Too late.

We were just too close, way too close, when she finally did elevate.

Then she didn't just take down one rail.

She crashed through the jump and took down all of them.

SIXTY-FIVE

DANIEL AND EMILIO got me off her as quickly as they could once we got to the schooling ring, Daniel crouching down immediately to inspect Sky's front legs.

I stood a few feet away, watching. Not angry at myself. Not embarrassed the way Mom had been.

Just scared for my horse.

After what felt like an hour, Daniel stood and said, "She seems to be fine. But I know Doc Howser is on the grounds somewhere. I am going to text him and have him meet us back at the barn so he can take a look." He paused. "Just to make sure."

He pulled out his phone, jabbing at it with his index finger.

"Okay," I said.

"She's not limping," Daniel said. "That's the good news."

"Okay," I said.

I heard the buzz from Daniel's phone. He looked down at his hand. "Doc is actually back near our barn. He can meet us there."

He spoke quickly to Emilio in Spanish.

In English he said, "I'll catch up."

Daniel turned to me and said, "Do you want to come with me?"

"I'll be as worried there as I am here," I said. "Let me know when he says she's okay."

He nodded.

"I need a few minutes alone," I said.

Emilio and Sky were already fifty yards in the distance. Daniel jogged after them. I climbed over the fence and crossed the narrow sidewalk to the ring across the way, sat down under the canopy on the small bleachers in there. I reached into a side pocket of my backpack, took out some warm Gatorade and drank it down.

I needed to think.

No, that wasn't quite right.

I'd *been* thinking since the moment we were out of the International and had pretty much made up my mind. I just needed some space now, some distance between what had happened, some time to start breathing normally again.

Twenty minutes later I felt my phone buzzing.

Text from Daniel.

our girl is fine.

takes more than a rail.

I responded:

or 9 . . .

Then he texted me again. He'd come meet me. When he made it to where I was sitting, he put a hand on my shoulder before sitting down next to me.

"I'm sorry," he said.

"About what?" I said.

"The way things turned out."

I stood up, took off my helmet, shook my hair loose.

"Yeah," I said. "I sucked big-time."

"So that's it? We're done with the Grand Prix?"

"Are you drunk?" I said to Daniel. "You think

we're done after I realized tonight my horse was even more awesome than I knew?"

"I am confused," he said.

"Lose the touchy-feely crap, Daniel," I said. "We are *so* doing this."

SIXTY-SIX

MOM DIDN'T RIDE AGAIN until Tuesday. I snuck over to Gus's, with his permission, to watch her, parking a half mile up the road, walking the rest of the way, hiding in the barn once Mom and Gus were in the ring with Coronado, not just watching Mom back up on her horse, but watching Gus zip around the ring in his Zinger like he was gunning a motorcycle.

When I'd talked to Gus on the phone he'd said, "She's talking about quitting."

"She can't," I'd said.

"No shit, kid," he'd said. "Not after practically stealing her horse back from her own goddamn daughter. She'd better make sure it was worth it."

"How's the vibe today?" I said now to Seamus, Gus's top groom.

"A little narky, as we say back home," he said.

"Which home?"

"Both," he said.

Gus and Seamus had set the rails at one meter. Six of them scattered around the ring. Like bunny jumps. On the third one, Mom pulled up Coronado, and we watched her circle him. Just Mom and Gus and the horse in the ring. A nothing height to clear. And they still circled.

"It's been like this near all morning," Seamus said.

"Any theories about why?" I said.

"It's like everything caught up with your mum," he said. "Perfect storm. The accident and the injuries and probably coming back too soon. Then Saturday night capped things off. And then she was like an empty sack trying to stand."

Mom put the horse in motion again. Pulled up on the fourth jump this time. Coronado just flat refusing. Circled again. I couldn't believe what I was seeing. Didn't know if I could handle seeing much more.

"She has no confidence," I said.

"Not to be contrary or nuthin'," Seamus said, "but I'm pretty certain people with no confidence at all have a wee bit more than her right now."

She didn't get down off her horse and walk out of the ring, I had to give her that. Wasn't quitting, at least for now.

Then Gus and Mom and Coronado began to move slowly along the fence line, Gus in his chair, Mom sometimes having to pick up the pace to keep up. Gus seemed to be doing most of the talking. For once, he wasn't using his bullhorn voice, so I couldn't hear their exchange.

But it all looked extremely animated.

They made two trips around the ring that way before Mom hopped out of her saddle and started to walk Coronado in the direction of the barn.

I got ready to make my getaway.

"Where do you think you're going?" Gus snapped at her. "We're not done here."

Mom stopped and turned to face him.

"I might be done in more ways than one," she said.

They were close enough to the barn that now I could hear them both quite clearly. But I would have been able to hear Gus Bennett where I'd parked my car.

"I'll never stop working with you because you're riding for shit," he said. "But I am the last person in this business that you want to feel sorry for yourself in front of. I thought that went without saying."

I could see her face, saw that the words had stung her. But she didn't answer.

"Now are you ready to get back to work?" he said.

"I'll call Seamus to help me back up," she said.

"We don't need Seamus," Gus said, and moved the chair closer to her and Coronado, extended his arms, and put his hands together.

Now his voice was very loud.

"Here," he said. "Let me give you a leg."

SIXTY-SEVEN

Daniel

THE TWO MEN SAT at the last table past the bar at the Trophy Room, each with a beer in front of him. The dimly lit restaurant was nearly empty at a little after six o'clock.

"Did somebody drive you?" Daniel said to Gus.

"I drive myself," Gus said. "I call it the van of the future. We can drag race later, if you want."

"Sorry," Daniel said.

"Don't be, not with me, anyway," Gus said. "I've had no use for sorry since I zigged when I should have zagged."

Zigged instead of zagged, Daniel thought. Like he'd given himself a bad line.

Gus had called Daniel for a talk without Maggie present, or Becky. Maggie mostly.

"About what, exactly?" Daniel had said.

"The women in our life," Gus had said. "What the hell else would we be talking about?"

They knew each other, not well, from the shows. As many times as they'd had horses in the same ring, Daniel would never have presumed to call them friends. Gus did limited traveling on the summer circuit, preferring to stay close to home. On a trip to Michigan, he observed to Daniel that flying was a royal pain in his ass, when he was still feeling pain in his ass.

But they had never spent time alone until now. And Daniel could not help feeling a tiny bit of hero worship. Maybe more than that. He had only heard what kind of rider Gus had been, had seen old footage of him before he'd been paralyzed. Everyone in their world, though, knew what kind of trainer he was now. The feeling was that Gus Bennett could have more riders than he did if he wanted them. But he only chose the riders he wanted.

In his second career, Daniel thought, he was still *leyendo*.

A legend.

"So how is it going with Maggie, really?" Daniel said.

"Really what I wanted to talk to you about," Gus said. "Her, not Becky. Because it's *not* going. If it is, it's going right over a cliff."

"There's still time for you two to get on the same page," Daniel said.

"Bullshit," Gus said. "If she rides in the next Grand Prix the way she rode the last one, we're out of luck and out of time. And screwed."

"If it's that bad," Daniel said, "I am not sure how I can help you."

Still not believing that the great Gus Bennett had come to him for advice.

"I usually don't need any help from anybody."

"So I have heard," Daniel said. He smiled.

"I've tried being nice, I've tried yelling at her, I've tried challenging her, I've tried backing off," Gus said. "Usually I don't give a rip about hurting somebody's feelings. If they want to work with me, I just assume they know the deal going in. But she's so goddamn fragile right now."

"We both know she was different before the horse threw her," Daniel said.

And was sorry all over again. As if Gus Bennett's whole world hadn't been different before he was the one thrown.

"I didn't mean that the way it came out," he said.

"Sure you did," Gus said.

"What I am trying to say is that Maggie was fearless before she was injured," Daniel said. "In so many ways, I had little to do because she trained herself." He pointed at Gus with his mug. "Is she not *allowing* you to train her?"

"Beats the shit out of me what she's thinking right now," Gus said. He grinned. "So tell you what. How about we switch riders?"

He said it casually, as if asking Daniel if he wanted another beer.

"You don't want that."

"Don't I?" Gus said. "Gonna tell you something right here: your Becky has a chance to be better than all of them if she stays with it and you don't screw it up."

"Not *my* Becky," Daniel said.

"Figure of speech," Gus said.

Daniel said, "I know how talented she is. I think I have always known."

"Does she know?"

"I am hoping she is in the process of finding out."

Gus checked his watch. Daniel asked if he had to be somewhere. "Not exactly," Gus said. Sipped some of his beer.

"But none of this helps you with Maggie," Daniel said.

"The goal is still that we all make it to the Olympics," Gus said. "Who the hell knows, this might be my last best shot."

"Maggie can still make it," Daniel said, "and so can you."

Gus shook his head.

"With what I'm seeing," Gus said, "she only makes it to Paris if she buys herself a ticket."

He leaned forward, the powerful forearms on the table between them, his huge hands clasped, not making any attempt, as usual, to lower his voice.

"Right now," he said, "she's not close to being the rider her kid is."

"Good to know," Maggie Atwood said.

Before he or Daniel could say anything, Maggie and Caroline were already heading for the door. Daniel started to get up, saying, "I need to go after her."

Gus Bennett clamped a hand on Daniel's arm. His grip felt like a vise.

"Let her go," he said.

SIXTY-EIGHT

I'D QUALIFIED ON SKY for Saturday night's Bank of America Grand Prix the day before. It had *not* been pretty. I felt as if we were out of sync even before two late, pretty careless rails. But I still made it to Saturday night. Barely.

I wanted to win, of course. But at the very least, I needed to make it to the jump-off. Needed to ribbon. Basically, I needed points on the board.

I'd been working hard over the past week, putting in countless hours in the ring. It wouldn't matter without results in the International Arena. As Grandmother had said at breakfast:

"This isn't travel soccer. Nobody's going to hand you a trophy for participating."

An hour later I was out in our ring for a practice session on Sky. Normally I wouldn't jump Sky, even over baby jumps, the day after any competition, serious or otherwise. But I was more on the clock than ever if I wanted to make it to Paris. Riding my own horse now.

When I did jump Sky two days in a row, I'd give her a longer warm-up than usual, like the one we were just finishing up. Then there would be a longer-than-usual cool-down after we left the ring.

In between, we were going after it hard today. So was my trainer. Especially my trainer.

"I'm sorry," Gus Bennett yelled at me now. "Are we going to trot the adorable little horse all goddamn morning, or we going to finally get to work?"

SIXTY-NINE

THINGS HAD HAPPENED FAST after Daniel told me how Gus had joked that they should switch riders. I'd laughed it off at first. He didn't, telling me that the more he'd thought about it, the more he didn't think it was such a crazy idea.

"Your mother is desperate for things to be the way they used to be," he said, "which means before her fall, which means when I was her trainer. And the more I think about the two of us, the more I think you might need someone to be tougher on you than I could ever be."

Before I could say anything, he said, "Talk about it with your mother. See what she thinks."

"What do you think?"

"Talk about it with her."

Mom made it easy, said she was willing to try anything at this point. She was the one who made the decision to leave Coronado at Gus's, at least for now, saying she didn't want us to get in each other's way, and that her horse was settled there. Daniel went over there every morning to work with her.

And Gus Bennett came to me, at the top of his voice from the time the driver's-side door to his van opened and the wheelchair platform would extend, before slowly lowering him to the ground.

"You're not riding Coronado anymore!" he yelled now. "Your horse drifts to the *right,* in case you forgot!"

He'd told me the same thing when I'd finished in the International Arena the day before. I *had* forgotten, just for an instant. It had still cost me a rail. After that, I had gotten a second rail and nearly missed qualifying.

All of it on me.

With Daniel, I used to answer back all the time— smart-mouthing was part of our deal.

Gus Bennett? No way in hell.

"Don't overcorrect! Keep her straight!"

I came back around. He'd set four jumps. I cleared them all this time.

"I thought you said today was going to be light jumping."

"Well, Becky," he said, "I lied."

As tough as he was, though, I could see why Mom had once had a crush on him. Maybe still did, for all I knew. He was still handsome as hell. But it was more than that. He was as real as anybody I'd ever known. Without an ounce of self-pity in him. And pity anyone who didn't see that.

Gus Bennett made you ignore the chair, is what he did.

"Again," he said to me.

I managed another clear round on the mini-course.

"Okay," he said.

"You mean okay as in, good job there, Becky?"

"Okay as in, we're done for today," he said.

I didn't wait for Emilio, hopped down off Sky myself, handed Emilio the reins. Gus gunned the Zinger to life then, spraying dirt in all directions, and headed straight for me.

"You're already tired of me," he said. "Admit it, you won't hurt my feelings."

"You have feelings?" I said, and was instantly sorry. Told him I was.

"I know what you meant," he said.

He paused.

"But anytime you want your old trainer back, all you have to do is say the word."

"I will," I said. "But I don't." I grinned. "Are *you* sure you want to train *me*?"

"Hell, yes," he said.

Gus Bennett actually smiled then. Didn't last for very long. The moment was there and gone. Like the sun peeking through the big cloud cover and then disappearing again. But I knew I'd seen it.

"I know you think this trainer swap was your call, Becky," he said. "Yours and your mom's. It wasn't. It was mine."

"But why?"

Then he told me why.

"Of course, if you ever tell anybody that," he said, "I might have to kill you."

"You know what?" I said. "I believe you."

"Maybe you *are* learning," Gus Bennett said.

SEVENTY

Daniel

DANIEL WAS NOW SEEING from Maggie what Gus had been seeing on a daily basis.

That she had lost her confidence.

She didn't need a full psychological work-up or a therapist to explain to her that she had come back too quickly from the accident. Maggie was smart enough to know why she was in this dark a place, this quickly. A perfect storm.

Perfect shitstorm.

Gus had seen it even before she'd gotten back into the International. He'd tried everything to get her past this, or through it. He'd even admitted that he'd invited her to the Trophy Room on purpose the night he'd been there with Daniel. He'd wanted to challenge her pride. Nothing had changed the next day in Gus's ring. She'd circled again. It's why he'd suggested to Daniel that they switch riders.

Gus said his thinking was simple enough:

Maybe Daniel could get through to her, because he sure as hell couldn't.

But she was still circling. No Gus, no audience, not even the grooms at Gus's barn, or other riders. Just her and Daniel. It should have been a pressure-free setting. The worst part was that she wouldn't know she was stopping the horse until it was happening again.

Somehow she hadn't stopped yesterday, as she'd made it through the qualifying on Wednesday. When Daniel asked her afterward what had been different, she said, "I...don't...know."

That night she'd even spent an hour on the phone with Dr. Bob Rotella, an old friend of Gus's who'd become the most famous sports psychologist in the country. He'd worked with other riders, some of them friends of Maggie's. And worked wonders with them. Everything he'd said made perfect sense to her. The hour flew by. It did feel like being with a great therapist.

She'd come out this morning and circled again.

She was taking a break when she said to Daniel, "I will not humiliate myself again on Saturday night. Nope. Not happening, Daniel. Can't do it to myself. Can't do it to this horse. Can't even do it to you."

They were in the middle of Gus's ring. Daniel said for her to remember that she had made it to Saturday night, that she'd made it through yesterday's round with no circling, even if she'd gotten two early rails. She'd fought through that. And, for one day, fought through her fears.

She just didn't know why.

"Maybe for once I didn't give the poor horse mixed messages," she said.

"The horse has never been the problem, Maggie," Daniel said. He made a sweeping gesture that took in the whole ring. "The problem is not even in here." He pointed to his head. "The problem is in here."

"So how do I fix it?" she said.

"I have an idea," he said.

"I'm all ears," she said.

"You need to take a trail ride," Daniel said.

SEVENTY-ONE

Maggie

THEY HAD BROUGHT Coronado back in Gus's trailer, had saddled him up at Atwood Farm. Then Maggie went out alone, the way she had the day of the accident. Breaking the rule about an unaccompanied trail ride one more time. Maybe one last time.

"I can follow if you want," Daniel said.

"No," Maggie said. "If I'm going to do this, I'm going to do it."

She left the barn behind her and made the left turn before she got to Stable Way, walking Coronado at first, slowly picking up speed, not pushing it.

Not yet.

She remembered every detail of her ride that day. She noticed all the familiar geography now. Imagining it was a course without jumps. But knowing exactly where the finish line was, past where the new barn was going up, past the barn owned by Tyler Cullen's owner, past another new construction site.

Feeling everything starting to happen fast now. Feeling a dryness in her throat. Feeling the tension in her back, legs, arms. Knowing it was probably just more of her craziness, knowing that the red fox wasn't coming out of the bushes this time.

Still afraid that he might.

Had Daniel been right?

Was that the fear driving all the others?

She slowed Coronado now, nearly to a full stop. Closed her eyes. Drank in some air. The inside of her mouth felt like sawdust.

The exact spot was right up ahead.

She didn't hesitate now, kicked her horse back into motion.

Started to pick up speed.

Coming up fast on the scrub and bushes to her left where she'd seen the fox that day, blowing past where she'd been thrown and where she knew Becky had found her, blowing past all of it like she'd cleared the last jump of a round and now was just making sure to clear the sensor and finish the course right.

Only then did she slow Coronado back down, feel herself smiling, then take a last look around and turn for home.

SEVENTY-TWO

Maggie

SIX HORSES MADE the jump-off on Saturday night. Coronado was one of them. Maggie had gotten around clean for the first time since last year. Now Seamus had Coronado in the schooling ring. Becky, going just six places after Maggie in the order, was on her way into the International on Sky.

Maggie and Daniel stood on the other side of the in-gate from where Gus was. But once Becky was into her round, Maggie also kept sneaking looks at Daniel. He was trying to act calm, detached from what was happening in the ring. But he kept betraying himself. It was there in his face, in the tension in his body. Everything about him revealed how much he wanted Becky to do well.

Maybe even beat her own mother.

"I sometimes forget what a beautiful rider she is," Maggie said.

Daniel's eyes stayed on Becky and Sky.

"Beautiful," he said. "Yes."

They heard Gus from across the way keeping up a steady stream of conversation, as if Becky could hear him even when she was at the far end. Maybe she could. Telling her to keep her hands up. Yelling *"Right!"* more than once as Sky began to drift to the right.

Yelling at her not to rush.

"Come on, kid," Maggie said to herself, in a quiet voice, only loud enough for Daniel to hear. *"Come on."*

Becky finished clean. Maggie let out a whoop that had people in the immediate area staring at her. She shrugged. "My kid," she said in explanation because, even after all the drama of the past few weeks between her and Becky, she *was* still her kid.

One who'd just finished with the best time of the class so far. For now, Maggie's time was second. It was where they finished and meant Maggie would go second-to-last in the jump-off order. Becky would go last.

"Can't make it up," Maggie said to Daniel.

"Not any of it," Daniel said.

By now she was back up on Coronado in the schooling ring. When Becky came back in on Sky, their eyes met, briefly. Becky didn't change expression. Maggie had to fight to keep herself from smiling at what they'd always called her daughter's resting bitch face.

Wouldn't have it any other way, Maggie thought. Then she gave Coronado a little kick. Letting the big boy know it was time.

And put on a bitch face of her own.

SEVENTY-THREE

Maggie

ONLY TWO RIDERS had gone clean in the jump-off. One was Tyler Cullen. Tyler had the best time at 36.14, relatively slow for this particular course. But he'd watched the others put rails on the ground and played it safe, going right before Maggie.

Down to Maggie and Becky now, Maggie next in on Coronado. Becky was right behind them in the in-gate. Maggie didn't turn around. She was studying the course one last time, replaying recent advice from Dr. Rotella by way of his old friend, a basketball coach. *When a game looked even, always bet the team that needed it more.*

Maggie knew how much *she* needed this.

The money was nice. They could always use the money at Atwood Farm. At least they hadn't been consumed lately by the subject of money once Becky had won on this horse. But Maggie knew it was more than that now. Way more.

"This is a good course for you," Daniel said. "It favors a horse with a longer stride."

Longer than Sky's, he meant, but didn't come right out and say it.

"Trust yourself," he said. Then added something, she thought, about the trail, but Maggie was no longer listening. She studied the first two jumps. All noise had dropped away now. Sometimes it was true. All you really could hear was the sound of your own heart.

Maybe she'd get scared again before the round was over.

But not now.

On the fourth jump, she used Coronado's length, knew she'd picked up time, shortening the line from seven strides to six. At the last moment, before he was in the air, she yelled *"Yeah!"* Knowing she'd been close to the rail with his front legs. Feeling it.

But they made it.

Came up on the rollback, a tight, dangerous one for a horse as big as Coronado. She still took the riskier lane, the inside one.

Made it.

Not overthinking things. Riding her horse. Letting this part of the course come to them.

Still not afraid.

One more jump. Seven strides to the finish. One last time, she asked Coronado to do it in six.

He did.

Cleared the last jump.

35.7.

Now Maggie was in first place.

She didn't celebrate, didn't pump a fist or change expression. Didn't show anything at all. Just patted the side of Coronado's head as she slowed him down and moved him back toward the in-gate as Becky went past her.

SEVENTY-FOUR

"LOOK AT ME," Gus said, jabbing his fingers at his eyes.

Mom had just finished. Crowd had gone wild. I was ready to get out there. But Gus had one last thing to say. He *always* had one last thing to say.

"You're not here to finish second," he said. "Got it?"

"Got it," I said.

"Make sure that you do," Gus said.

We'd discussed the course before leaving the schooling ring. It was built for bigger horses like Mom's. And Tyler's. They had longer strides. But their horses couldn't fly the way mine could.

I'd been taking my temperature, all the way into the International, the night coming down like this to Sky and me. I was nervous and excited. But I also knew I'd won here before.

We were halfway through the course, clean, in what felt like a blink. Coming up on the rollback. I'd seen Mom navigate it with Coronado, as big as he was. It would be a lot easier for Sky, if I got her squared up in time off the inside turn.

I did.

She cleaned it.

Halfway there.

Sky *was* flying now, into the double combination.

Cleaned that, too. Rattled a rail on the second jump. The people in the crowd would have told me if it went down. It didn't.

Three jumps left.

Then two.

Gus said when he was riding he swore he could *hear* his adrenaline in key moments. Like it was ringing in his ears. I could hear it now.

The second-to-last jump was an oxer, with uneven rails, that looked as wide as a barn. Even wider than the first two in the jump-off course. To me, it just looked like an easy target.

And a place to pick up time.

I'd seen Tyler cover this distance in six strides. So had Mom. Counted down both of them. I was sure my horse could do it, too.

Three strides away.

Kept my head down, and my hands high.

Told myself not to rush.

"Go!" I shouted at Sky. "Go…go…*go*!"

SEVENTY-FIVE

"YOU RUSHED," Gus said.

I'd stopped briefly at home, had half a glass of champagne to celebrate Mom's victory. Tyler had finished second. My time, even with a rail, had been good enough to get a fourth-place ribbon. But Gus was right, of course. I *had* rushed. My horse knew she was too far away, tried to correct with one more small stride at the end. She always tried. But she was too close to the jump. It was too late. Clipped the rail with her hind legs, as I'd seen in the video Gus took on his phone.

Now we sat in his ring, the only light coming from the moon. I'd brought out a chair from the barn. He sat in the Zinger, a glass of Scotch in his hand. He was wearing a hat that had BEIJING 2008 on the front, and the five Olympic rings.

He'd had his accident, I knew, on the way to Beijing.

"What did your mom and Daniel say?" Gus said. "Just curious."

"They thought I rode well, and that one mistake at the end cost me," I said. "But that's riding, right?"

"Is it?" he said.

"Listen, I know what I did wrong," I said. "And I'm more pissed off at myself than you could ever be. But I still got fourth. That counts for something, right?"

He drank some Scotch.

"You lost," he said.

"C'mon," I said. "You know me well enough to know I'm not satisfied with just making the jump-off. And *I* know I can ride better than that."

"Show me," he said.

He hit a button on the side of his wheelchair and suddenly the ring was illuminated in bright light.

"You want me to show you *now*?" I said. "You're joking, right?"

"Yeah," he said. "You know what a big kidder I am."

"But Sky is back at our barn and down for the night," I said.

"Go put a saddle on Infinity," Gus said, acting as if it were eleven in the morning and not eleven at night. "We call her Tiny. Small like your horse. Not as fast, or as good. But we think she's got a chance. She didn't get ridden today. You can do it now." He nodded at me. "You're still dressed for it."

"At this time of night."

"Do you have some sort of curfew?" He jerked a thumb at his barn now. "You'll find the girth and saddle and the rest of it, just inside the door when you walk in. Seamus was supposed to ride her today and didn't."

He took another sip of Scotch.

"You said you can get better," he said. "Show me."

"It won't be the same as riding Sky," I said.

Gus said, "No, it won't. But here's a heads-up for you, kid. This is about you. That magical, special horse of yours? She's not as good as your mom's. Or the one McGill's kid rides. Or the bazillion-dollar horse that Gates's kid rides. Or Bloomberg's."

He wasn't yelling now. Actually sounded quite calm.

"You need to get it through your head once and

for all that you're the underdog here," he said. "Yeah, your horse is a streak of light and full of heart. *But their horses are better.* So you've got to out-ride them. That's your shot. And it happens to be a long effing shot."

He pointed again at the barn. "Now go get the horse ready while I set a course. Tiny's in the fourth stall on the right."

Just Gus and Tiny and me in the night, for the next hour or so. The only sounds came from the horse, and Gus. He'd set six jumps. I don't know how he did it as quickly as he did. But he was Gus.

I'd finish a round and even if I was clear, this is what I'd hear:

"Again."

One time I knocked down the first rail. After I had finished, he raced the wheelchair over to me and said, "You acted like the rest of the round didn't matter."

"Is that what you think you saw?"

"What I know I saw," he said.

Spun the chair around and took off, spraying dirt on me this time.

"Now do it again," he said.

It was midnight when we finished. I hopped down off the horse, gave her an extra mint I had in my pocket. The horse seemed fine. I was exhausted. But wasn't going to show him that.

I walked the horse over to him as he shut the lights in the ring.

"Gotta ask you something," he said. "Do you really want this? Or does it just sound good when you say it?"

"Now you are joking," I said. "Of course I want it."

He stared at me.

"Are you sure?"

At which point I had heard enough from Gus

Bennett. Felt like I'd been riding all night—and yelled at just as long.

"*Yes!*" I yelled back now. "*Yes, I'm sure!*"

He smiled.

"See you in the morning," he said. "You can lock up."

And rode away.

SEVENTY-SIX

Gorton

THEY'D TAKEN THE first booth to the left of the entrance into the Palm Beach Grill, next door to the Honor Bar. Steve Gorton liked both places, chose between them depending on his mood. Both bars attracted equally good-looking women.

He was having Monday lunch with Tyler Cullen. Not as much an invitation as a direct order. Gorton liked making Cullen come to him every chance he got. Cullen wasn't technically one of Gorton's employees. But still treated him like one. Cullen let him. What choice did he have? Some things never changed. Gorton had something Cullen wanted.

Gorton's lunch today was a Bloody Bull, beef bouillon mixed in with his Bloody Mary. Cullen was having a salad, no dressing, with a Diet Coke. Little guy watched his weight like a jockey.

"I thought you told me she couldn't win," Gorton said.

"It's like an old trainer of mine says," Cullen said. "A lot of people have won one in a row."

"She looked pretty damn good on that horse to me," Gorton said.

"Obviously getting back with her old trainer made a difference," Cullen said. "You saw what she was like her first time out. Scared shitless. She was a different rider Saturday night."

Gorton leaned forward.

"The one who looks scared right now is you," Gorton said. "You have to know what usually happens to people who get shit wrong with me, right?"

"It won't happen again," Cullen said. "Trust me."

Gorton laughed so loud people at the other end of the bar turned around.

"Oh, wait," Gorton said to him. "You're serious."

"But you *can* trust me," Cullen said.

"A glorified jockey?" Gorton said.

Cullen just stared at him, almost as if seeing Gorton, really seeing him, for the first time. Gorton had seen the look plenty of times before. People swore up and down, all the time, about how they knew it was a mistake to underestimate him. Then they went ahead and underestimated him.

"You know how much I want to be in business with you."

"That actually brings me to the reason I got you over here today," Gorton said. "I need you to explain why I should still want to be in business with you."

He sipped his drink.

"Because for the life of me, I can't come up with a single good goddamn reason."

Cullen looked as if he'd been slapped.

"I've got some new intel on the whole situation," he said.

"I'll be the judge of that."

"Will you at least hear me out?" Cullen said.

Gorton did. Cullen talked for a long time, the words spilling out of him. Or maybe it just felt like a long time to Steve Gorton, who never had much of an attention span when hearing pitches. An idea.

A partnership. Themselves. It was what Cullen was doing now. Pitching himself all over again. Trying not to look desperate, or needy. But Gorton could always see it on people. Could *smell* it. It was like when he'd watch that show *Shark Tank* on television. Gorton had no use for the hosts. He had more money than they did. Even Mark Cuban. No, he just liked to watch some of the contestants beg.

"You're telling me this is about an effing *groom*?" Gorton said when Cullen finally shut up.

"My old groom," Cullen said. "And Daniel Ortega's best friend. Hector, the groom's name is. Got picked up about a few months ago and ended up in a detention center. Been there ever since."

"I weep for him," Gorton said.

Cullen told him the rest of it then.

When he finished this time, Gorton said, "You're telling me that this trainer is that big a threat to you?"

"Is now," Cullen said. "Whatever he said to her, he managed to get her mind right, at least for one night. And she did look like her old self. So, yeah, she needs him."

"A trainer can actually mean that much?" Gorton said.

"Not with me," Cullen said. "Obviously with her."

Cocky little bastard to the end, Gorton had to give him that. Making no apologies about having as much compassion as a vulture. Or venture capitalist.

"You want this horse that much?" Gorton said.

"More," Cullen said.

Gorton waved at the tall blond waiter who'd been covering their table. It was like a little competition he ran, here and next door, seeing who could get to him and get his drink back the fastest, all of them knowing the size of the tip usually depended on it.

The new Bloody Bull arrived at warp speed. He tasted the new drink while the kid was still standing there, slightly out of breath.

"Perfection," he said.

"Happy you're happy, Mr. Gorton," he said.

"I'm sorry," Gorton said. Screwing with everybody today. "Did you make the drink yourself?"

When the kid was gone, he leaned toward Cullen again.

"You're telling me this is the way it lays out," Gorton said.

"I am," Cullen said.

Gorton smiled. An old girlfriend once told him his smile was sharp enough to cut glass.

"Or maybe what you say is going to happen is something else that *doesn't*," he said. "At which point you've wasted my time and the mommy rides my horse all the way to Paris and I live happily ever after without you."

"Not if we get her trainer deported," Tyler Cullen said.

SEVENTY-SEVEN

GUS AND I WERE in the ring at eight o'clock, just the two of us, Seamus and the other groom working inside the barn. I'd just mentioned that while it wasn't a scientific study, I thought he did more yelling early in the morning.

"You want a hug?" he said. "Call your boyfriend."

"Daniel's not my boyfriend," I said.

"Yeah," Gus Bennett said. "Go with that."

We had settled into a solid routine now, as a way of not overworking Sky. There were days when I jumped her, days when I just hacked, not even looking at the jumps in the ring, just easy laps around the outside for half an hour or so. On the days when I didn't ride Sky, I rode Tiny over at his barn, just because it was clear by now that Gus didn't give a rip if he overworked me. And was never going to hear me complain about it ever again.

Today was one of those days when he had me saddle Sky myself, telling me it was all part of the process, being as hands-on as I possibly could with my horse.

"I'm surprised you don't have me muck her stall," I said.

"Who says I won't, princess?" he said.

Today was a jumping day. Serious jumping. I'd helped Gus set the rails. At 1.45. The National Grand Prix, what Gus called the beginning of the playoffs, was in ten days. He'd even entered us in an event before that, the following Thursday at WEF, telling me the reps would be good for me.

Gus, as usual, took his position near the last jump, wheelchair angled so he could see the whole course, a travel cup of coffee in the holder on one of the arms. He was wearing the Beijing cap. I wasn't sure whether it was supposed to be some kind of motivator for him, or me. He still had not discussed his accident with me. By now I'd seen the video of it, his horse coming to a dead stop in the huge observation event in Rome, the one he'd needed to win to officially qualify for the Olympics, in the spring of 2008. I'd read some of the articles about what happened that day, too. Nobody was sure what had spooked his horse and caused it to slam the brakes on the way it did. When they'd tried to ask Gus afterward, when he was finally out of the hospital, he'd refused to talk about it. As far as I could tell, he still never had.

The images were terrible enough to watch that only a couple of times could I bear the sight of him helicoptering through the air, the world so upside-down that he had no chance to get his arms out to break his fall, before his back landed squarely on the top rail. Everybody in riding knew how heavy those rails were. It was the same as falling on a rock.

"Hey," he said, "I said let's *go*. Where the hell was your brain at just now?"

I couldn't tell him Rome in 2008.

He'd had Emilio set a water jump today, Gus

telling me that there would probably be water in every one of the big events we had coming up over the next couple of months.

"Remember," he said. "We focus on process here. Every day. Every jump. Whether you're here or in competition. Treat them all the same and then you've got less chance to choke your brains out once the lights get turned up."

I saw him grinning at me.

"You know the real definition of choking, right?" he said.

"Help me out," I said.

"A cold rush of shit to the heart," he said.

"Have you ever considered motivational speaking?" I said.

He moved the Zinger closer to me.

"You want to hear my motivational speech?" he said. "Here it is, for the first and last time, and don't let it go to your head. You've got as much natural talent as anybody I've seen."

He'd never said anything like that to me before. Nothing close. I was so floored by what I'd just heard I wasn't sure how to respond, worried that he might take it back if I even tried to thank him.

So I didn't say anything, simply angled Sky toward the first jump.

He wasn't quite finished.

"But what you need to understand is that talent is *never* enough," he said. "The way having a fast little horse isn't enough."

"I know," I said.

"So know this, too," Gus said. "You never know how many chances you get in this sport." He paused and nodded and said, "Shit happens. Got it?"

"Got it," I said.

He squinted into the bright morning sun then, his face almost looking angry as he did, like he wanted to yell at the sun the way I knew he was about to yell at me.

"I hate light like this," he said.

SEVENTY-EIGHT

I'D STOPPED COMPARING his style of training, of coaching me, to Daniel's. It would have been like comparing an apple to a chocolate cake.

But I was starting to enjoy my time with Gus in the ring, even though I would never admit it to him if my life depended on it. The truth was, we seemed to have developed a mutual mind-reading ability. I was riding the way he wanted me to ride more and more, getting yelled at less and less. His style, if you could even call it that, wasn't for everybody. Wasn't sure I would have ever volunteered to work with Gus Bennett. But by now I'd figured out that his toughness was irrelevant.

My toughness was everything.

And there was something more:

Seeing his love for the sport was making me love it even more. One of these days, if I could screw up my courage, I might even ask him how much being a trainer filled the competitive void in him, accessed all the qualities that had made *him* a great rider in the first place.

"Sit up straight in that saddle, for chrissakes," he shouted at me now.

I turned my head so he couldn't see that I was smiling.

Six jumps ahead of me in the moment, in the high morning sun and heat. The water jump was second from the end. Gus was right. As usual. Sky did need more work on entry and exit: take off at the last possible moment, make sure not to land even one leg in the water. What we called dipping a toe. You did, you got a fault.

"Focus!" he yelled.

"I *am* focusing!" I yelled back.

I did that sometimes, just not too often.

Six strides to the water jump.

Then four.

Then two.

I could see the distance was going to be perfect. Could feel it.

Then in the very next moment the sun was in my eyes, reflecting off the water in the small pool, as if a spotlight was suddenly shining into my eyes.

And Sky's.

She came to a stop, turned her head, blinded the same as I was.

"Noooooo!" I heard Gus Bennett scream.

Then I was the one spinning through the air, staring straight up at the sky one last time before I came crashing down on one of my own fences.

SEVENTY-NINE

I WAS ON MY BACK when I opened my eyes. Sun still in my face.

I didn't think I had lost consciousness. But wasn't entirely sure of that. The last thing I remembered, other than the sound of Gus's voice, was hitting the top rail.

I lay there without moving. Feeling pain concentrated in my hip and lower back. No desire to move or try to move. This wasn't like the time on Coronado when I'd bailed before I went sailing over the horse's head. I'd been the one to decide how I ended up on the ground that night. Not today.

When I opened my eyes I could see Gus looking down at me. And Daniel.

Where did he come from?

Daniel started to reach down for me when Gus said, *"Don't touch her!"*

"Sorry," Daniel said.

"Becky?" Gus said now.

He almost never called me by my name.

"Here," I said.

My voice sounded as if it were coming from inside the barn.

"Do me a favor?" Gus said.

"Sure," I said, in the same weak voice.

"Lift one of your legs for me," he said.

Sounded like a simple enough task. Lift a leg. Anybody could do that. But when I tried to lift my right one, I felt like it had weights attached to it. Like the heavy ones we occasionally used in the gym.

Finally, I got the leg off the ground.

Gus said something I didn't hear right away.

"What?" I said.

"Now an arm, please," he said.

I did that.

"Good girl," he said.

"Becky," Daniel said. "Where does it hurt the most?"

"Everywhere," I said.

Daniel turned to Gus.

"Let's help her sit up," he said.

"Carefully," Gus said.

I reached up to them with both hands. Gus, leaning forward as far as he could in his chair, took one. Daniel took the other. Slowly they got me into a sitting position. I mostly felt the move in my upper back, not the hip area. I saw two rails next to me on the ground.

"We need to get you to the hospital," Daniel said.

"Where did you come from, by the way?" I said.

"Your mom beat me to Gus's today," he said. "There was something wrong with the strap on her helmet. She asked me to come over here and pick up her old one."

"I don't need to go to the hospital," I said. "I'm just sore and a little stiff."

"Daniel will take you," Gus said, as if that settled that.

Daniel started to take my hand again. I told him I could stand up on my own. And did. Wobbly at first. But upright. Telling myself I wasn't going down again. Screw that.

I asked where Sky was, and Gus told me Emilio had already taken her back inside the barn. We began to slow-walk out of the ring in that direction. Daniel was on one side of me. Gus rode alongside me on the other.

"It was the sun," I said, even though neither of them had asked what happened. "Got me and got my horse."

"Like I said," Gus said. "Shit happens."

He gave me a long look and said, "Happened to me that way once."

By the time Daniel and I got to the gate, after what felt like an hour and a half, I realized Gus wasn't with us. I turned and saw that he was back in the ring, near the jump where I'd crash-landed.

Staring back up into the sun.

EIGHTY

NO CONCUSSION, I FOUND out at Wellington Regional, first thing. No broken bones. No cracked ribs. Just some bruising, mostly where I'd landed on my hip. I hadn't been injured nearly as badly as Mom had been, even if I did feel as if Sky hadn't just tossed me but run me over.

Mom and Grandmother were in the waiting room when Dr. Garry was finished poking and prodding and X-raying and shining lights and asking questions.

"You were lucky, young lady," Grandmother said.

I grinned.

"I must get that from Dad's side of the family," I said.

"Not funny," she said.

"Kind of funny?" I said.

"You kind of need to take a couple of days off," Mom said.

"*You* wouldn't," I said.

"What did Dr. Garry say?" she said.

"That my body would tell me when it was okay to ride again," I said. "But for now I should go home and take a hot bath, then a shot of tequila before bedtime, and call him in the morning."

"Again with the jokes," Grandmother said.

"Well," I said, "I may have made up the part about the hot bath."

Most of the pain I was still feeling was in my upper back and neck area, almost like whiplash, which I knew happened to riders who'd gotten thrown the way I had.

I did take a hot bath when I got home, got into bed, alternated heat and ice to the back of my neck for the rest of the afternoon. I decided to wait until after dinner to medicate with a glass of the Patrón that Dad had bought me for Christmas. I was about to call him to tell him what had happened, then changed my mind. As cool as he was, he was going to tell me to take some time off, same as Mom had.

Or just retire.

We were finishing dinner when I told Mom and Grandmother I was heading down the hill.

"To check on Sky?" Mom said.

"To ride her," I said.

EIGHTY-ONE

"ARE YOU SURE the horse didn't drop you on your head?" Grandmother said. "You need to go to bed."

"I need to ride."

"No."

"Not your call," I said. "I'm not letting what happened be the last thing I see after I close my eyes."

I looked over at Mom.

"You got back up the first chance you got," I said.

"After a month!" Grandmother said.

"After surgery," I said to both of them.

Mom looked at me, then reached across the table and put a hand on Grandmother's arm.

"Let her go," she said.

I went upstairs to change into my breeches, then pull on my boots. It took longer than I thought it would. Bending over to put on the boots hurt way more than I thought it would. But I wasn't going to call downstairs and ask for a little help here. Emilio, I knew, had left my helmet in the tack room.

Mom and Grandmother waited for me in the kitchen. Grandmother reluctantly walked down the hill with us. She and Mom got Sky's saddle pads on her, saddle, girth, bridle.

"You guys really don't need to hang around," I said.

"Good one," Grandmother said.

We were walking Sky toward the ring when Gus's van showed up.

"You called him," I said to Mom, making no attempt to turn it into a question.

"I was too frightened to consider the consequences of *not* calling him," she said.

I stopped to watch his door open, the platform extend, then lower him to the ground. Wondering again what it must be like for him to go through what he had to go through daily. Glad in that moment that Mom had called him. Wanting him, more than anybody else, to see that I could play hurt.

Daniel's Kia showed up in the driveway a couple of minutes later.

Gang's all here.

Team Becky.

I hacked Sky slowly around the ring. The up-and-down, just the simple posting, caused me the most pain. Mom had told me the same thing had happened to her when she was back in the saddle. It was just something else my face wasn't going to show my audience. Every time I passed them, I smiled and gave them a thumbs-up.

The third time around Gus actually smiled back.

"You're so full of shit," he said. "Trying to act like you're not hurt."

"Now *that* hurts," I said.

"Shut up and ride your damn horse," he said.

When I finished, Daniel was the one to come into the ring and help me down. We walked her back to the barn together, got her saddle off her, found a carrot for her in the tack room refrigerator, hosed her down, let her have a big drink, put her in her stall.

She looked perfectly fine, despite doing double

duty today. I was ready for another hot bath, and that shot of tequila.

Grandmother had gone back to the house by the time Daniel and I were back outside. Gus and Mom were where we'd left them near the gate.

"I already knew you were a hard-ass," he said. "You didn't need to prove it tonight."

"Just trying to give you some much-needed positive reinforcement," I said.

"What I need is a drink," Gus said.

"Same," Mom said.

"I'm buying," Gus said.

He turned his chair around, pulled out a remote from the side pocket of his vest, pushed a button. The doors to the van opened. A minute later he was being lifted up behind the wheel as Mom got in on the passenger side.

"Date night?" I said to Daniel.

"Looks like," he said.

We watched Gus get the van turned around and head down the driveway and then out to Stable Way.

"You want to have a drink here?" I said.

"Thank you," he said. "But I have to be somewhere."

Then he got into his car and drove away. I went up to the house, got the bottle of Patrón, brought it back down the hill, sat down in the straw next to Sky.

"Cheers," I said.

She looked at me.

"Date night," I said.

EIGHTY-TWO

WHEN IT WAS TIME for the 3-Star the following Thursday, last tune-up before the National Grand Prix, I was still sore but hadn't missed a day of riding, on Sky or Tiny, since getting thrown. It was one of the reasons that Gus had started calling me Bad Ass Becky McCabe.

I told him it was probably the nicest thing he'd ever said to me.

Mom had even decided to enter the same event, right before the Wednesday four o'clock cutoff, after she saw how many of the other top riders were in the field.

Maybe they were angling to keep themselves and their horses sharp. I was there to win. Rode that way. Went clean in my first round, then straight into the jump-off.

"Ride like hell now," Gus said as I passed him at the gate. "Post a kick-ass time and let the rest of them chase you."

Gus didn't make a big deal out of the water jump when he'd looked over the course alongside me. Just talked about my line, and my distance, the way he did all the other jumps.

"We treat all jumps the same," he said, and left it at that.

Then Sky, bless her heart, handled it perfectly the first time through. I was nervous as we approached, even panicking a little as I saw the light reflecting off the pool, right before the sun, almost by magic, went behind a cloud.

Now we had to clear it again in the jump-off, where the water was on the other side of the second-to-last jump.

A lot of jumps before that. Sky took them all clean. The course wasn't built for long-striding horses. This one was built for speed. And my little horse had a ton of that.

The cloud was gone now as we came up on the water. We were going straight back into the sun. I heard Gus from behind me, yelling, "Get your head down!" I did. Thought at the last moment that I'd gotten Sky too close to the jump, and I *had*. Then my horse's big heart took over. And took care of it. When I looked at the video later, I was amazed at how high she'd gotten, how easily she'd cleared the top rail, how far past the water she'd landed.

Like she really was flying this time.

We sprinted to the finish from there. I jerked my head around to look at the big screen.

29.4.

We'd beaten thirty seconds on that tough, close-quarters course.

I couldn't help myself then, brought Sky back around to where Gus was sitting and threw a fist.

He didn't change expression.

"Bad ass," he said.

EIGHTY-THREE

THERE WERE FIFTY in the class. Tyler Cullen, going after me, got an early rail. He was out. Matthew Killeen in his first round had bested my time but couldn't beat thirty seconds in the jump-off. Nor could Georgina Bloomberg or Eric Glynn. Or Andrew Welles. Two rails for Tess McGill. Two for Jennifer Gates.

Six other horses had made it clean through the jump-off.

Nobody under thirty seconds by the time it was Mom's turn, going forty-eighth. Best rider left. Best horse. Gus and I were watching from up on the pedestrian bridge.

"Gotta be weird for you, right?" Gus said as Mom walked Coronado into the ring, Daniel beside her.

"Wouldn't be a problem if it was somebody like Tyler," I said. "But it's my mom."

Then we both watched in silence as Mom went clean. Not a particularly fast first round, but she was in control of herself and her horse, knowing exactly how to avoid a time fault.

Now the jump-off for her.

I want to win, I thought now, the feeling coming over me like one of those hot flashes Mom talked about from time to time.

I don't want her to beat me.

I wanted her to ride well. Wanted her to go clean. Just didn't want her under thirty seconds. I wasn't going to say that to Gus. I would never say it to her, no matter how things came out.

Nobody was making the Olympics today.

I still wanted to win. Wanted to beat her. Maybe to prove to myself that I could.

Prove to her that as competitive as she was, I was even more so.

Bad Ass Becky.

I watched her. Then watched the clock. She was riding like a dream today, even with her big horse, even on a tight course.

She was coming up on her only big choice, on the rollback, inside the two huge flower baskets, or outside.

Inside was where you picked up time.

She was sitting on *my* time. It was one of her many strengths as a rider, the clock she had inside her head when she couldn't see the screen.

She had Coronado set up perfectly as they made their turn. I thought she had him squared up in time. He might have drifted slightly to the left, the way he did. But it was a left-hand turn.

She still had room to make it.

But at the last moment she played it safe.

Went outside.

Cleared the jump fine. Handled the water like a champ. Finished strong.

Before her score was official, going into the last jump, Gus quietly said, "You got her."

"Yeah," I said. My voice sounded weird to me, thick.

She was 30.5.

Still two horses to go. Both got rails. My time had stood up.

Hell, yeah.

There was no ceremony today. The event wasn't big enough for that. The winners just went and collected their ribbons. I told Gus I'd get mine later. He told me to go get it now, he'd catch up with me, he had to take the wheelchair ramp back down to ring level.

"Go," he said again.

Mom was already off Coronado by the time I got there, walking out of the schooling ring with Daniel. I waved at them. Mom smiled and gave me a thumbs-up. But Tyler Cullen, beer can in his hand, somehow appeared out of nowhere and got to her first.

"You ought to give the kid your ribbon, too," he said, loud enough for everybody in the immediate area to hear.

Mom stopped. So did Daniel. So did I.

"And why would I do something like that?" Maggie Atwood said.

"You think everybody didn't see you let her win?" Tyler said.

Then he turned around and pointed the can at me.

"And you know who knows it better than anybody?" he said. *"Her."*

EIGHTY-FOUR

"SHUT UP, TYLER," Gus said.

I didn't know how Gus had gotten down to the ring as quickly as he had. But there he was. Breathing fire.

"Not your fight, Gus," Tyler said. "Not talking about your rider here. You need to stay out of this."

"Walk away," Gus said.

"You first," Tyler said.

He really did have a head full of rocks sometimes.

"Seriously?" I said.

"Didn't mean that the way it came out," Tyler said.

"No one cares," I said. "And no one let me win anything."

I started walking in his direction. Mom cut me off.

"I got this," she said.

When she was close to Tyler, she motioned for him to follow her to the other end of the ring, as if for a private conversation. When they'd made their way down there, Mom seemed to be doing most of the talking. She seemed calm, hands stuffed into the back pockets of her breeches. From a distance, I thought she might actually be smiling.

Then she leaned forward and said something into his ear. Tyler stared at her for a moment before replying. Mom spoke once more. Then Tyler turned, hopped the fence, and headed in the direction of the barn area, beer can still in his hand. Walking fast. Not looking back.

Mom came back to where the rest of us were waiting for her.

"Okay," I said. "What did you say to get him to shut his big mouth?"

"Well," she said, "the first thing I told him, sweet as you please, was that if he actually thought that about me, he doesn't know me nearly as well as he thought he did."

"C'mon, it *had* to be more than that," I said. "What did you say when you got up in his ear?"

Now she was really smiling.

"Just whispered 'Dick Gilbert,'" she said.

I smiled. It was the name of Tyler's owner.

"He asked what the hell that was supposed to mean," Mom said. "And I just asked what *he* thought Dick would think if he found out his top rider wanted to ride my horse and not his."

Gus Bennett nodded.

"Bad ass," he said.

Mom said, "At that point it was game, set, match."

Daniel said he was going to pick up Mom's ribbon. I asked if he'd pick up mine, too. Then Mom said they were headed to the tent to meet up with Grandmother, and invited Gus and me to meet them there.

"I hate that tent and just about all the people in it," Gus said. "Present company excluded, of course."

"Already knew that," Mom said. "Had to ask, anyway."

When she was gone, Gus said he needed a cold beer, and right now. I said I'd join him. We went up the wheelchair ramp together and made our way to the outdoor restaurant at the beginning of Vendor

Row. The tables were all high-tops. A no-go for Gus. So we took up a position at the end of the bar, plenty of room there, the crowd having thinned out now that the class was over and the show's afternoon events were winding down.

I ordered two beers, handed him one. We clinked bottles.

"Not bad out there today, kid," he said. "You might actually be getting the hang of this."

"Stop," I said. "You'll make me blush."

We drank, and went back over the class after that, jump by jump. When we finished, I asked Gus if he wanted another beer. He said he was done.

It was then that I noticed Mom and Daniel heading up the boardwalk deep in conversation.

When they stopped suddenly, I moved behind the open door to the kitchen.

"Where are you going?" Gus said.

"Eavesdropping," I said. "Something heavy going on out there between Mom and Daniel."

If they were afraid of being overheard, they weren't acting it.

"Maggie," Daniel said. "That is an answer, but not an explanation."

"Well, it will have to do," she said.

"Every other rider in the jump-off, every single one, went inside," Daniel said. He paused and said, "At least all the ones really trying to win."

"Drop this."

"I'm just trying to understand," Daniel said. "Because we both know the plan was to go inside."

"Plans change," she said.

EIGHTY-FIVE

GUS AND I HAD FINISHED our morning session, one that had started earlier than usual today, Gus having told me he had to be in Miami on business in a few hours.

We'd been talking again about what Tyler had said, and what Daniel had said to Mom on the boardwalk.

"You need to let this go," Gus said.

"I'm not a little girl she has to let win," I said.

"You said you asked her about it, and she said she *hadn't* let you win, correct?"

"I don't believe her," I said.

Sky was already back inside. Gus had moved his wheelchair out of the ring and into some shade near the front of the barn.

"Is she in the habit of lying to you?" he said.

"No."

"Then repeat: Let it go."

"But Cullen was right," I said. "There was no reason for her to take that jump the way she did."

He sighed, then looked at his watch.

"Do you need to get going," I said, "or are you tired of listening to me?"

"Little of both."

"I know it sounds like I'm whining."

"Only because you *are* whining!"

"But we're both reaching for the same goal," I said. "Mom and me. We're both trying to make the Olympics. And I've made it this far without her mama-bear-ing me. And you know who looks bad when she does something like this? *Me.*"

"If she did."

"Trust me," I said. "She did. Even if she won't admit it and neither will you."

I shook my head. "I mean, I've got enough going on without dealing with this shit."

"Got a lot on your plate, do you?"

He cursed. Loudly. As if he'd heard enough.

"Would you like to know who's really dealing with some shit today? Your boyfriend."

"Not my boyfriend."

"Hush and listen!" he said.

The words hit me so hard I was surprised they didn't knock me back. I saw Emilio poke his head out of the barn door.

"Daniel's appearing in immigration court today, trying to save his friend's ass," Gus said. "The guy was locked up in Fort Lauderdale. The hearing's in Miami."

"He didn't tell me."

"Probably because all *you're* dealing with," Gus said sarcastically.

"Is he in trouble?" I said.

"No," Gus said. "But he's about to be."

EIGHTY-SIX

GUS HAD INSISTED on driving and proceeded to do so like a maniac, taking the turnpike most of the way. On the way down he told me about Hector Suarez, who'd been a groom at Dick Gilbert's barn and worked with Tyler Cullen's horses until two ICE agents had arrested him at the Lake Worth home he and his wife shared with two other grooms. It was over an old arrest for assault, from a bar fight that, according to Gus, had started with a guy at the bar calling Hector a "spic."

At the time Hector had never appeared for his court date, afraid of being deported. Four months ago, he'd been caught in a big ICE sweep in our area, been thrown into a federal detention center in Fort Lauderdale, the closest detention center of its kind to Palm Beach County. The hearing about whether he would be permanently "removed" from the United States and sent back to Mexico was this morning.

"So that's where Daniel would disappear to," I said.

Daniel would be there to speak on Hector's behalf. They had been friends since their parents had come together from Mexico to the United States. As Dreamers, children of undocumented parents, Hector and Daniel had been free from government scrutiny. But now, as Gus said, nobody was safe while the Supreme

Court deliberated. Children of undocumented immigrants who *had* been born here, *they* were safe. Not Dreamers.

"But Daniel has done nothing wrong," I said. "Why would he be in trouble?"

"He's putting a target on his back by putting himself out there," Gus said. "The government will have all of his information after today. And even if the judge rules in Hector's favor, I know how this works, I've had my guys in the system before. The government will have eyes on Daniel going forward, especially if the judge *does* give Hector a pass on what sounds to me like a bullshit arrest. Trust me on this: the boys from ICE don't like being made to look bad."

I thought, *This was why Daniel had been so fearful of being deported himself.*

"Does Mom know?" I said to Gus.

"No," he said.

"You told me but not her," I said.

"Think of it as a reality check," Gus said.

The Florida Immigration Building was at Riverview Square. Gus parked the van in a lot about a block away.

"You must have a handicapped permit," I said.

Without thinking.

"Those are for handicapped people," he said.

I'd never seen him out of jeans and T-shirts and the Bennett Farm vest he wore on particularly cool mornings. Today he was wearing a blazer and gray pants and a white shirt.

The hearing had been scheduled for noon. But we found out once we were through security that it had been moved up to eleven o'clock. It was ten fifty when we walked into the hearing room. Daniel sat behind Hector and a man I assumed was Mr. Connors, the immigration lawyer Daniel had mentioned. At a small table about twenty feet to Mr. Connors's right, sat the man I assumed was the government prosecutor. Behind him were two men in dark suits who Gus whispered had to be ICE.

Judge Alexandra Ross reminded me of the actress who played Mrs. Maisel on TV. The prosecutor addressed her directly, acting as if Hector were some kind of terrorist for defending himself in a bar fight. He turned and nodded at the two men in the suits, identified them as Agent Dolan and Agent Josephs, and said they had no choice but to arrest Hector.

"No American, no matter where they're born, gets to decide which laws they want to follow," the prosecutor said. "Our legal system isn't a buffet table. Mr. Suarez originally broke the law with assault, and then broke it again by ignoring his court date."

Mr. Connors first presented some letters of support for Hector, then slowly laid out the case that if Hector hadn't been a scared kid without legal representation who would have gotten him to his court date the charges against him would likely have been dropped.

"Maybe the government sees Hector Suarez as a criminal," Mr. Connors said, shooting a glance at the ICE agents. "No other reasonable person should."

It was Daniel's turn to speak. There was no formal witness stand. He could have spoken to the judge from his seat. He chose to walk to the front of the room and stand in front of her, stating his name, age, address, occupation, employer.

When the judge asked for his immigration status, Daniel said, "DACA."

"For the record, Mr. Ortega is referring to Deferred Action for Childhood Arrivals," the judge said to the stenographer seated to her right.

I had never seen Daniel this nervous. About anything. He was wearing a gray suit, white shirt, tie. I didn't even know he owned a suit. One more thing, then, that I didn't know about Daniel Ortega. He answered a few questions from Mr. Connors about his friendship with Hector, before Mr. Connors asked him to explain to the judge, in his own words, why she should accept what the lawyer called Hector Suarez's "petition for cancellation of removal."

"Hector is as American as anybody I know, in all the right ways," is the way Daniel began.

He stood tall, hands clasped behind his back.

"They call people like us Dreamers," he said to the judge. "Do you want to know what my friend's dream is? To move out of the house where his wife watched him be arrested and own one of his own someday and start a family here and live the life he imagined for himself when he came to this country with his parents."

Gus reached over and squeezed my shoulder.

Daniel cleared his throat.

"Hector Suarez doesn't just conduct himself like he is a citizen of this country already," he said. "He is a *model* citizen. One who works hard. And pays his taxes. Who loves his wife and his friends and his job and horses. You don't ask someone like this to leave America. You beg him to stay."

Suddenly Daniel didn't sound nervous at all. His voice was sure and confident and had the complete attention of everyone in the room.

"Hector and I started out as grooms together at the same barn," Daniel said. "I told him he should be a trainer—he had a gift with horses. But he told me, no, I was the one who should be a trainer someday. He said that he knew how to care for horses and communicate with them. But I knew how to make great jumpers and great riders. It was Hector who found out about the assistant trainer's job at Atwood Farm. They wanted to interview him, but he told them to hire me before somebody else did. When I interviewed with Mrs. Atwood, my boss, I asked her how she knew about me. She said, 'Hector told me.' When I got back to the barn where we were still working, I asked him how I could possibly repay a kindness like that. He told me, 'Someday you will find a way.'"

He turned to look at Hector, and smiled, then looked back at the judge.

"With your help, Your Honor, maybe I have finally done that," Daniel said.

The judge thanked him. Daniel walked back to his seat. Even from a few rows back, I could hear him exhale, loudly, when he sat down.

The judge then stated that in chambers she would consider Mr. Connors's recommendations and the prosecutor's, read the letters and the original arrest report, and would then announce her decision.

When she was out of the room, Daniel came and sat with Gus and me. As cold as the air-conditioning was in the hearing room, he was still sweating slightly, as if he were still standing in front of Judge Ross.

She came back fifteen minutes later.

"First off, Mr. Suarez," she said, addressing Hector directly, "the next time somebody calls you a shitty name in a bar, go home to your wife."

I leaned over and said into Gus's ear, "Can she say that?"

"She just did," he said.

Judge Ross leaned forward slightly.

"But as for this proceeding, we have wasted too

much of your time in that detention center, Mr. Suarez, and too much government money," she said. "Your friend is right. You're not a criminal, unless being a victim of circumstances is now a federal offense in this country."

She shifted her gaze to the two ICE agents.

"Perhaps in the future, we should think about doing a little better job making that distinction," she said.

She banged her gavel.

"Your petition for cancellation is granted by this court, Mr. Suarez. As quickly as we can process you out, you will be released from custody." She smiled at Hector now. "Where's your wife?"

"Working," Hector said.

"Call her," the judge said, then announced that court was adjourned.

When we were all on the sidewalk, I took Daniel's hand and gave it a good squeeze.

"You're an even better friend than you are a trainer," I said to him.

"*Much* better," Gus said.

It got a laugh out of Daniel. Never, I knew from experience, an easy thing to do.

"You think this is funny?" we heard from behind us.

It was the shorter of the two ICE agents, showing us his badge, as if that were necessary.

"No, sir," Daniel said. "Please believe me, I don't think any of this is funny."

The taller one said, "We'd like a word with you, Mr. Ortega."

EIGHTY-SEVEN

THE COLOR DRAINED from Daniel's face, in a blink, as if he feared the judge had changed her mind while we were exiting the building. Daniel looked at both of the agents, then at me, then at Gus. I could see him trying hard to swallow. I remembered all the times he had spoken of the government. Now here the government was, in the form of these two guys, standing right in front of him, in front of a federal building.

But Daniel didn't get the chance to speak because Gus beat him to it.

"No," Gus said, "you may not have a word with him. But thanks for asking."

"Who the hell are you?" the taller agent said.

"Think of me as a concerned citizen," Gus said, then whipped around his wheelchair to face them both squarely, a quick move that bumped one of the wheels against the taller man's foot. I knew it hadn't been accidental. But what were they going to do, arrest a guy in a wheelchair for assault?

"Sorry," Gus said.

"I'll bet," the taller agent said.

"Got a question," Gus said to him. "Is it your intent to arrest Mr. Ortega?"

"Like we said," the shorter one said. "We just want a word."

"And like *I* said," Gus said, "if you're not going to arrest him, get the hell out of here."

The two agents looked at each other and shook their heads.

"Tough guy," the shorter one said.

"You have no idea," I said to them, smiling.

The shorter agent ignored Gus and me, turned his attention to Daniel.

"You need to know something, Mr. Ortega," he said. "Your buddy got lucky today, absolutely. Caught himself a dream judge. So he won, we lost, the judge gave us some shit. Happens. But not very often, does it, Eddie?"

"Hardly ever, Larry," Eddie said.

"And you know all that information about yourself that you gave the judge a few minutes ago?" Larry said to Daniel. "Now we've got it, too. We've actually had it since you went on the witness list. We know where you work, and who you work for. We know a lot."

"And now we're giving you a heads-up," Eddie said, "that one of these days you might get yourself on the wrong side of all this."

"You know what guys like us find out in our line of work?" he said. "That everybody has secrets." He smirked at Daniel. "You got any secrets, Mr. Ortega?"

I thought, *This started off badly and has gone downhill.*

"We should leave," I said to Gus.

Gus looked at the tall one, then the short one. Even dealing with a couple of federal agents, I knew how much he hated bullies.

"Them first," he said, his eyes still not leaving them.

No one said anything then.

"Screw it, the guy's been put on notice," the shorter one, Larry, said, before he and his partner walked back up the steps of the Immigration Building.

But when they got to the top, Larry turned around, shouted down at Daniel.

"Hey, Ortega?" he said.

Daniel looked up at him.

"Good luck with that horse of yours," the agent said, before he was following Eddie through the door.

I wasn't sure why that sounded like a threat.

But it did.

EIGHTY-EIGHT

—

WHEN GRANDMOTHER HEARD about the events in Miami she decided we needed to celebrate, and booked us a big table across from the bar at Duke's. The restaurant at the Wanderers Club overlooked the polo fields where they were setting up for a match the next night.

"Breaking news," she said when we'd all ordered food, "good guys win for a change. I should alert the media."

Mom was there, and Gus and Daniel and Hector and his wife, Maria. And me. Hector and Maria weren't saying much, just sitting next to each other and holding hands and mostly doing a lot of smiling.

Daniel clinked a fork against his bottle of beer to get everybody's attention, raised it and said, *"Mejores dias."*

Better days.

I looked at Maria Suarez and saw she couldn't stop herself from crying.

"No blubbering," Grandmother said from her side of the table, and everybody laughed.

Then Gus said he wanted to raise a glass to Daniel.

"Please, don't," Daniel said.

"Want to try and stop me?" Gus said.

"Obviously even the *federales* cannot do that," Daniel said.

"To Daniel," Gus said. "Who's what I call a fox-hole friend."

"Takes one to know one," I said.

"Zip it," Gus said.

It was as if everybody at the table was allowed to exhale tonight, for the first time in a long time and for a lot of different reasons. There was mostly show talk, once Gus finished his play-by-play of what had happened inside the Immigration Building and then outside later. Gus told Hector that he had a job at his barn starting in the morning. We all talked excitedly about the events coming up. It was a celebration tonight that had hardly anything to do with horses.

When we were all studying the dessert menu, Grandmother told a story I'd never heard about the time she'd ridden in Paris, at the Saint Hermes, and how she was chased from Notre Dame to the Louvre and back by a show jumper from Argentina.

"Too much information," I said.

"I was young once, too, missy," she said. "I had some horse that year, I don't mind telling you. But Juan Carlos, that was his name, he had a much better one. And had been winning all over Europe that year. But he *was* hot for me, which is why I think he might have slowed down just enough at the end to let me beat him out of a third-place ribbon. Knowing it meant a lot more to me than him."

I had my wineglass nearly to my lips, but slowly put it down now.

"Did he tell you he had?" I said. "Slowed up?"

Grandmother grinned. "I intuited it, especially after he invited me to an extremely romantic dinner at L'Ami Louis." She winked at me.

She was smiling. I wasn't.

"So riders *do* let other riders win from time to time?"

Maybe it was the wine.

"Becky," Mom said.

The tone meant *drop it.*

"You'd never do anything like that, right, Mom?" I said.

Gus was next to me.

"Everybody's having a good time," he said, almost under his breath.

"We've gone over this," Mom said to me. "I didn't let you win."

"I don't believe you," I said.

The whole table had gotten quiet.

"Every single rider in the jump-off made the inside turn," I said. "Except you."

"Good grief," Grandmother said, "you still haven't dropped this, Rebecca McCabe? You know the old expression about beating a dead horse? For the last time, this goddamn horse *died.*"

"And for the last time," Mom said to me, "why would I have let you win?"

"I know how much you want us both to make the Olympic team," I said. "Maybe you decided I needed the win more."

"Nobody wants to win more than I do," Mom said.

"Maybe *I* do now," I said. "It's why I don't want anybody giving me anything. Including you." Now I drank more wine. *"Especially* you."

"Enough," Grandmother said, trying to glare me into silence before waving theatrically for the check.

I *should* have dropped this by now. Or never opened the door in the first place. But I was still being carried along by adrenaline. The kind Gus said you could hear. Suddenly Mom was, too.

"I am going to tell you what I told that little shit Tyler Cullen that day," she said. "If you think I'd ever let anybody win, especially *you,* then maybe you don't know me as well as you think you do."

"Maybe I don't," I said.

I stood up, and pushed back my chair, nearly knocking it over in the process.

"Where are you going?" Mom said.

"I can get my own ride home," I said.

She caught up with me in the lobby, as I was calling my Uber.

"You're as stubborn as your father," she said. "You got stuck on things when you were a little girl, and you're still getting stuck."

"Pretty sure it runs on both sides of the family," I said.

She somehow forced a smile, and lowered her voice, so we didn't make a scene out here, too.

"Honey," she said. "No matter what happens, I'm still your mom."

"No," I said. "You're an opponent."

EIGHTY-NINE

IT WAS SUNDAY AFTERNOON, last day of the FEI World Cup finals, one of the biggest events left on the calendar, and not just because of the prize money. Three-day event. Speed course on Friday. A jump-off class on Saturday. They added up your points then. I'd always thought the scoring was way too complicated except for this:

If you were the leader by Sunday and then went clean, there was no jump-off. You won. Everybody else lost.

And by Sunday afternoon, I *was* the leader.

This after a second in Kentucky and a third in North Carolina over the past month in World Cup qualifiers. The best Mom had done was get a sixth in Carolina. It was as if we were headed in different directions right now. I wasn't sure how I felt about that. Just knew how I felt about my horse and me. And we were both bad ass right now.

Which felt good.

Very good.

Mom, Daniel, Gus, and I arrived at the schooling ring at the same time, with the final round about half over. Mom was in fifth place, which meant she'd go fifth from the end in the order. As the leader, I was going off last. I'd know what everybody else had done by then. I'd know exactly where I stood. And not just today. Because if I ended up winning today, I would move all the way up to fourth place in the Olympic standings. If the team were being selected today, I'd be going to Paris and Mom wouldn't.

But there were multiple events to ride before team selection. We still had the Rolex Grand Prix, back in Kentucky, and then the last big event before they did pick the team, up on the show grounds in Long Island where the Hampton Classic would be held later in the summer, after the Olympics were over.

As Gus liked to say, this shit was getting very real now.

"Good luck today, honey," Mom said before Emilio helped her up on Coronado.

"Back at you," I said, and walked over to where Sky was.

This was pretty much our relationship now. Sentence or two at a time. No overt hostility. No more angry words. The heat was gone. More an undercurrent of coolness now. Or iciness. It seemed like years ago that I had found her lying there on the trail.

Gus shook his head before getting his wheelchair out of the middle of the ring, and over near the gate, his usual position to watch me warm up.

"The two of you are still related, right?" he said.

He'd heard our brief exchange.

Seamus was tightening my girth one last time as I settled into the saddle. As he did, I leaned down so I didn't have to answer Gus in too loud a voice.

"We are," I said to him. "And we might know each other better than we ever have."

Then I got ready to ride my horse, try to do what Gus told me to do all the time, to the point where I could hear his voice in my sleep:

Act like I belonged.

And know that if I went clean, nobody could catch me.

I finally heard Mom's name called. Saw her walk Coronado slowly toward the big ring with Daniel alongside them. It was too soon for me to move Sky over to the in-gate. It meant I would have to listen to her round from here. Seasoned competitors in our sport, especially in the International Arena, could determine the strength of a round from the reaction of the crowd in the stands.

I heard a bad round for her now.

One collective groan early. Another one about twenty seconds later. Two rails down for her. Had to be. Knew the sound. If she made it to a jump-off now, she would be one of the last horses in. Maybe last one in.

I stayed away from Mom when she brought Coronado back inside the schooling ring. Tyler was going next, with Jennifer Gates to follow. Heard just one groan while Tyler was out there. Then another.

When Gus and I waited at the in-gate, Gus said, "Your mom is in the last spot if we have to go back out there for a jump-off."

"Ain't gonna be no jump-off," I said.

"You sound like Rocky Balboa," he said.

"Who?"

I knew he was just trying to relax me, because he always found different ways. I also knew from the walk what a long course this was, one with a little bit of everything. Two brutal rollbacks. Water. Big distances the second half.

"Act like you belong," Gus said finally.

I'd won against a field as deep and talented as this before. Had that muscle memory going for me.

But that was on Coronado. This time it was Sky and me. Maybe, on a stage like this, about to move out of Mom's shadow once and for all. Beating her and everybody else. Maybe trying to serve notice that this was my year now. My time.

Looking to show the Selection Committee that I really did belong.

I gave Sky a kick to put her in motion.

NINETY

THE ROUND WASN'T without drama. Not with the water jump this time, Sky clearing both the jump and the water with room to spare.

No, the problem was with the first rollback. When I got there, I knew I could easily shave time by going inside. But knew I didn't *need* to shave time. I was cruising by now. Sky had torn it up over the first half of the course, no chance of a time fault.

I made a sharp, clean turn coming into the rollback, my brain telling me not to take chances here, to go outside, I was in complete command as long as I didn't make a mistake. Outside was the safer route. My brain practically screaming at me to go outside.

But I was riding to win.

Screw it.

Went inside.

Nailed it.

Three jumps left.

Gave Sky perfect distances on the first two.

One more.

I could taste it now.

Then got Sky too close to the last jump.

Not by very much. Maybe half a stride off. But that was all it took sometimes to mean the difference between triumph and disaster.

Sky raised up just fine, did the best she could in that last second. It was when she was coming down that I heard the solid *thwack*—worst sound in the world for a show jumper—as she caught the top rail of the oxer with one of her hind legs.

No!

But it stayed up. The sucker stayed up. The cheer hit me then, a huge cheer that seemed to come from all directions. No jump-off. Just a first-place ribbon and trophy and another bottle of champagne.

And a ton of money and points.

We'd won the goddamn World Cup. Even Gus Bennett allowed himself to look happy as we came toward him from the last jump. I looked over my shoulder briefly, just to make sure the rail on the last oxer was still up there.

"That," he said, "is what I am talking about."

Only now was the crowd noise beginning to subside, and the force of that last moment when I was clean. I took one last look around, at the course and the crowd, the whole ring. It all looked sweet.

It was then that I heard a loud voice coming from the box seats above me and knew right away it was Mom's.

I brought Sky to a stop.

When I looked up, I realized that Mom wasn't yelling for me, or to get my attention.

She was standing next to Daniel, but really seemed to be yelling at herself.

"This is my own damn fault!" she said.

NINETY-ONE

Daniel

DANIEL COULD SEE PEOPLE in the immediate area looking at them.

"I know you're upset," Daniel said. "But your daughter just won."

"I'll tell her I'm happy for her later," Maggie said. "But right now I'm allowed to be *un*happy with myself."

He had seen her lose before, knew how she reacted, the way she would vent when it was just the two of them alone afterward. Today was different. Today she was completely defeated.

"I know you don't think this right now," he said. "But you keep telling me that part of your dream is for both you and Becky to make the Olympic team."

"She got closer today," Maggie said. "I got further away."

"You're still going to make it," he said.

"Not riding like this," she said.

The section of expensive seats next to them, one of the luxury boxes, was already empty. Daniel eased Maggie in that direction. In the middle of the ring, he could see them setting up for the awards presentation. Becky was down with Jennifer Gates, who had finished third, and Matthew Killeen, who'd finished second. Even from here, Daniel could see that

Becky was beaming, looking to him as if she might float away.

He felt himself smiling as he watched her, as excited for her in that moment as he could possibly be. He always wanted Maggie to win, of course. Just not as much as he wanted Becky to win. He wanted so badly to be with her. But knew it was better that she was down there and he was up here.

Maggie sat down. Daniel sat down next to her.

"Would you like something to drink?" he said. "You have not had anything since you finished your round."

"Got a bottle of vodka handy?"

She put her head back and closed her eyes and seemed to be talking to herself.

"If they had to pick the team today, I'm out," she said. She chuckled. "Ironic, isn't it? I took my horse back and she just passed me on hers."

"But that is the thing," he said. "They are *not* picking the team today. And you know better than anyone that there are more factors than just the final standings."

"Not if you're riding like crap at the worst possible time."

"So many of you are all just bunched together," he said. "First place down to sixth. And they all know your record before you got hurt. And if the Olympics had been last summer, you would have gone."

"These people have short *memories*!" Maggie said. "You think they didn't see what Becky just did?"

He was choosing his words carefully, as carefully as he ever had around her, not wanting to make her feel worse than she already did. Not wanting to make a bad day for her get any worse.

"It is not just her that you have to beat," Daniel said.

"But she *is* the one to beat right now!" Maggie said, the words rising out of her so hot they made Daniel think of steam.

Down in the ring they had set up the medal stand. A woman from FEI was placing Becky's ribbon around her neck, and then another woman stepped forward to hand her a bottle of champagne. When it was time for her to receive her trophy, Becky motioned for Gus to wheel his way out and Becky handed the trophy to him.

Maggie must have been watching Daniel watch Becky. In a quiet voice now she said, "Whose side are you on, Daniel? Really?"

"I want both of you to ride your best," he said.

"Not an answer."

"Let me put it another way," he said. "I am training you. I want you to get everything you want. But I would be lying if I didn't tell you that I want both of you to make it to Paris. And I believe that the Selection Committee will want that, too, if things are close in the end, just because it will make such a good story."

He turned to watch the ring again. Could not help himself. Saw Becky and Gus making their way out, the trophy nearly sliding off Gus's lap as he reached up to give her an enthusiastic high-five.

Gus's day, too, Daniel thought with more than a little regret.

Not mine.

When he turned back to Maggie, her eyes were on him.

"I'll talk to Becky later," she said. "But for now, could you please just take me home?"

They had come together today, his car. Maggie hung back as Becky and Gus passed underneath them.

Then she and Daniel walked in the opposite direction, toward the tent.

When they were outside, and making their way toward the barn, Daniel said, "What is making you like this today? You've lost before."

"Tyler was right that day," she said. "Becky was right. And you *knew* they were right whether you came right out and said it."

Daniel waited, maybe just to hear her say it. So at least he would know.

"I never should have let her win," Maggie said.

NINETY-TWO

I DIDN'T CELEBRATE with Grandmother that night, or with Mom. I celebrated with Mom's trainer. In our family, it made about as much sense as anything else these days.

"Just to be clear," I said to Daniel, "I did invite Gus to join us, so this isn't technically me asking you out on a date."

"What did he say?"

"He said he didn't need a third wheel," I said. I grinned. "Said he had enough wheels in his life on his Zinger."

We were out on the back deck at the Clubhouse, the restaurant at Palm Beach Polo. Dinner was over. Our waiter brought out my bottle of champagne, which he'd kept on ice for us.

The conversation during our meal had mostly been about my round, the whole weekend, what it meant to be going forward. Daniel had said it was the best he'd ever seen me ride. I told him I could still do better. He smiled and told me I was right.

Now we were back to talking about the scene with Mom and him in the stands, even though Daniel had announced when we sat down that he didn't want to talk about that on such a happy occasion. I'd told him that just off what I'd heard, they could have sold tickets to it. Being Daniel, he'd tried to deflect, saying again that it wasn't as heavy as it sounded, or might have looked from a distance.

"I honestly believe that it came down to how badly she felt about the way she rode," he said, "especially after she had put herself into position to win if you got one rail."

"She's always upset when she loses," I said. "Except when she's trying *not* to win."

An unreadable expression settled on his face. Not the first time.

"I thought we had made a deal to stop talking about that," he said.

I smiled. Smiling came easy tonight. Even now. There hadn't been all that many nights like this for us lately. When it was just the two of us.

"The only thing I really heard was saying something about it being her fault," I said. "What did she mean by that?"

"She was still upset about her round," he said.

"Why do I think it's more than that?"

"Becky," he said, his voice firm suddenly. "You have to be aware enough to know that anything she feels is making her dream slip away is going to make her angry right now."

He took a small sip of champagne. At the rate Daniel Ortega drank champagne, he'd finish his glass sometime late Tuesday afternoon.

"You have to know what a chip she has on her shoulder," he said, "despite the career she's had. It is something that drives her. As much as she has done, she feels she should have done much more. I have never known someone so talented and filled with regret. Now she has convinced herself that if she doesn't make the Olympics, she is a complete failure."

"And on top of everything else, I've passed her," I said. "For now, anyway."

"Yes," he said. "That is a part of this."

"Did she say that to you?"

"Not in so many words. But, yes."

He shifted his chair slightly so he could face me more fully.

"The two of you should be having this talk," he said.

"No," I said.

"Why not?"

"Because I'm only focused on one thing right now," I said. I drank some champagne. "Winning."

"This should be an adventure for the two of you, this journey," he said. "Not ultimate fighting."

"It is what it is," I said.

We sat in silence and looked out at the setting sun.

"Change of subject?" I said.

"Please."

"It's so weird, us not being a team," I said.

"Agreed," he said. "But it is best for everyone, even if your mother is not seeing it that way."

I finished my champagne. His glass was still half-full. I said, "Nice night for a walk?"

We went down the back steps, toward what used to be one of the two golf courses at Palm Beach Polo, now featuring walking trails and spots for bird-watching and bicycle paths and water hazards that had been turned into fishing holes. Daniel reached over and took my hand.

"I still think I could have gotten to exactly where I am with you still training me," I said.

"It doesn't matter," he said. "You're where you are supposed to be with things as they are."

We walked in silence for a few minutes, still holding hands, finally got to the top of a hill, saw a wooden bench there and sat down.

"Well," I said, "the good news is that we can still all make it to Paris together if things break right. Because I am announcing right now that even if I'm the one who makes it and Mom doesn't, you are still coming."

He leaned over then and kissed me lightly on the lips.

"I never thought I'd make it to Paris," he said.

NINETY-THREE

Gorton

GORTON HAD A LUNCH appointment in Wellington about buying the golf property at Palm Beach Polo, which used to have two golf courses but now only had one. A potential gold mine, if he could turn it into one of those high-end clubs. He didn't like golf, particularly. Too much of your day wasted if you played a full round.

He'd always heard about how much business got done on a golf course. Gorton had never seen the upside to spending four or five hours with people who'd worn your ass out after one.

At least you didn't have to waste the whole goddamn day at horse shows. Where he was right now.

"Coronado isn't jumping today," Caroline Atwood said to him. "Are you lost?"

They were standing outside the old lady's barn, at the far end of the property from the arena and the side rings and the shopping and the tent.

"We still need to have a chat about Coronado," he said.

"What about him?" she said.

Her riding pants were pretty tight for someone her age. She had an Atwood Farm ball cap pulled down over her eyes and a long-sleeved shirt despite the heat. Gorton had to admit, she still had a pretty decent figure. Probably was something to look at about a hundred years ago. He wondered if she used to give people as much shit when she was young. Men, especially.

"Not the horse so much as the rider," he said.

"Oh, for chrissakes," she said. "Are we back to that?"

He sipped some iced coffee. Starting to think about his first Bloody. Hell, it was already past noon.

"I'm thinking about making a change," he said. "And if I'm going to do it, sooner is better than later. It's late enough already."

"What, you just show up here and put that back on the table?" she said to him. "We dealt with this months ago. And besides, there's no issue with Maggie."

"She just got passed by her own kid," Gorton said, "and even I know the kid doesn't have nearly the horse that we do."

There were other people inside the barn. A groom. A girl rider. The old woman walked across the path to a fence and leaned against it. He followed her.

"Even if I would ever consider a switch, which I'm not," she said, "it's already too late."

She took off her hat and wiped the back of her hand across her forehead. Gorton took a close look at her face, tanned to the color of a saddle.

"Coronado is Maggie's horse, win or lose," she said. "You don't have to believe me. Maybe you don't want to believe me. But she's going to make this team."

"Or," Gorton said, "she could keep going one way while your granddaughter is going the other." He grinned at her. "I mean, how crazy is this shit? The granddaughter is the one I wanted to pull off the horse. Go figure."

She started to answer. Gorton held up a hand to stop her.

"Not finished," he said.

"But I am," she said. "I've got another horse going into the ring in about forty-five minutes."

Gorton looked over his shoulder. One of his go-to moves. "I'm sorry," he said. "Did you confuse me with somebody who gives a rat's ass about that?"

Then he said, "She slips one more spot, she's gone. I'm through screwing around here."

"You have no legal right to do that," Caroline Atwood said.

"Watch me," he said.

Gorton laughed then.

"When are you going to get it into your head that this isn't about her, and it isn't about you," he said. "It's about me."

"For the last time," she said. "We have a contract."

"And for the last time," he said, "I will do whatever I need to do to get this horse to the Olympics, including folding that goddamn contract into a paper airplane."

"My daughter will never give up that horse," Caroline said.

"Won't be up to her," Gorton said. "So we can do this the easy way or the hard way."

"There's an easy way?"

"Yeah," he said. "She quits now and saves all of us a lot of aggravation and I give the horse to Tyler Cullen."

The old lady told him what he could do with that idea, and where he could put it, and that it would happen over her dead body.

"Not the first to tell me that," he said. "Sure you won't be the last."

He turned and left her there, looking like a fighter hanging on the ropes. It was always the same, no matter what the business. They all thought they knew Gorton, how far he'd go to actually get what he wanted. They had no idea. He heard her curse him one more time. He just laughed even louder than before, waved without turning around, and kept walking. He had somebody else to screw with now on the other side of town.

NINETY-FOUR

Maggie

MAGGIE KNEW WHY she'd wanted Daniel back as her trainer, why it worked, having him back, until it didn't. But she had never understood, not really, why he had agreed to leave Becky. He didn't just love training Becky. He loved her, whether he admitted that to himself or not. And she loved him.

The other day when Gus was leaving Atwood Farm, she'd asked him whose idea it had been, really, to swap trainers.

"Mutual," he said. "Best for everyone to keep feelings out of it."

"Whose feelings?" she said.

"Like I just said," he told her. "Everyone's."

And it *had* worked, until it had stopped working.

It wasn't Daniel's fault. *No,* she told herself, *this one I have to own*. Daniel had been right today, of course. She *hadn't* ridden that badly. Just not well enough. Before she had got hurt just before the New Year she'd had six whole months to raise her level, with all the open ring in front of her. That time was gone. And was in the process of blowing an even better shot at the Olympics she'd had all those years ago on Lord Stanley. When she was a lot younger than she was now.

That was what had her scared now, not the fear

she'd been feeling before on Coronado. It was why she was angry so much of the time. Only when she was alone on Coronado, not even Daniel around, did she really feel any peace. Not jumping the horse. Just hacking. Making one leisurely trip after another around the ring at Gus's barn, usually when he was over at Atwood Farm working with Becky.

What if she did make it and I didn't?

What if everything had changed when I didn't make one inside turn because I thought Becky needed the win more than I did that day?

What if that had been a wrong turn in about a hundred different ways?

She cursed loudly as she slammed her hands down on the steering wheel, again and again, before getting out of the Range Rover and walking into the Trophy Room.

It was still early, so just a few people at the bar, and at a handful of the tables in the front room, one populated with riders she recognized from the show. Maggie gave a quick wave, not stopping to say hello, just grabbed a seat at the bar, the two next to it empty. She never went to bars alone. Or hadn't in a very long time. She was making an exception tonight. Becky was out to dinner with Daniel. Caroline had driven down to Coral Gables to spend the night with her oldest friend from high school.

Maggie had made a decision that left her feeling a sudden need to get out of the house. She'd officially entered herself and Coronado in a three-star event next weekend at Deeridge. The reason was simple: she needed points.

More than that, she needed to remember how to win before she lost everything.

The bartender was a big young guy in a crew

cut, weight-room muscles straining against his tight T-shirt, arms sleeved with tattoos. When he came over, she ordered a pinot grigio, after briefly considering something a lot stronger.

The bartender set the glass down on the coaster in front of her. Maggie took a sip then heard, "This seat taken?"

Tyler Cullen.

NINETY-FIVE

Maggie

HE SAT DOWN BEFORE she could say she was waiting for someone. Or make up some other lie. Cullen was already ordering a dirty vodka martini, some brand she'd never heard of, and four olives, and further instructions about exactly how little vermouth he wanted, as if he were telling the kid how to build a rocket ship.

Maggie thought, *The guy's a jerk even ordering a drink.*

"I don't mean to offend you, Tyler," she said. "But I just wanted to have one quiet drink here. Alone."

"No offense taken," he said.

But he didn't leave or change seats after the bartender brought him his martini. Maggie wished she could ping her own phone with a false emergency.

Tyler took a loud swallow, and sighed, almost blissfully.

"You know," he said to her, "I can remember a time when the two of us used to get along."

"I can't."

"Good one," he said.

"So how you doing, really?" he said, with his usual self-awareness of a fence post.

"Fine."

"Can't believe you're out of the top four," he said.

"I figured you'd have locked up your spot on the team already."

She turned to him.

"I don't want to talk about riding right now," she said. "Mine, yours, anybody's. I just want to finish my drink and head home."

"Ask you something before you do?"

She sighed. "Sure," she said. "Why not?"

"You ever worry that the parade might be passing you by?" he said. "When you're young and in a slump like yours, you're just in a slump. When you're old and in a slump, you're old."

"Thanks so much for that," she said.

"It's no crime to lose it," he said. "Have the parade pass you by."

Did he just say that?

"Never happen to you, I'm guessing," Maggie said.

Cullen snorted out a laugh.

"Hell, no," he said. "You might not like me. But you know how I can ride. I'm the guy who stays up there even without the million-dollar horses. You know that's what they say about me."

"And what are they saying about me?" she said. "I have a feeling you're dying to tell me."

"Can I be honest?"

"No," Maggie said. "Lie to me, Tyler."

Why am I still here?

"They're saying that you're not up to this anymore," he said.

"Is that so."

"You asked," he said. "It happens to everybody eventually. And it might happen to me someday." He plucked an olive out of his martini and ate it. "When I'm the one getting up there."

She had a sudden urge to slap him.

Then his phone pinged. He showed impressive speed getting it out of his pocket.

"Gotta run," he said. To the bartender he said, "Her drink's on me," before throwing down what Maggie saw was a fifty.

As he began to walk away, Maggie grabbed him by the arm, more roughly than she'd planned. It seemed to startle him.

"You're not getting my ride," she said.

Maybe it was the way she said it. Or what he saw in her face. Or both. But he shook his head, shook loose his arm, and kept going, never looking back.

She had come here to be alone. Mission accomplished, she thought, as she looked out the front window and saw Tyler get into his Mercedes convertible and pull out of the lot. Because she felt as alone as she ever had.

The bartender came over and said, "I couldn't help but hear some of your conversation with that guy. He was talking *some* shit."

"Only because he is one," Maggie said.

When she was back in the Range Rover, she pounded the wheel again, harder than before, as if trying to drive it through the dashboard.

In that moment, she knew where she was going. Where she needed to be. Drove over there fast. Pulled into the driveway, up the walk, rang the doorbell.

When Gus Bennett opened the door she looked down at him and said, "I don't want to go home tonight."

NINETY-SIX

Maggie

GUS WAS STILL SLEEPING when Maggie opened her eyes the next morning. Still on his back. Snoring slightly. She looked over at him and thought: Maybe what happened between them had been inevitable, had been happening for a long time without either of them acknowledging the depth of the feelings they had for each other. Until now.

Then she felt herself smiling as she suddenly remembered one of Becky's favorite books, one that Maggie used to read to her before they'd started reading it together.

Oh, the places you'll go.

She hadn't come here thinking she and Gus would sleep together. But after leaving the Trophy Room she just couldn't bear the thought of going back to the empty house, Tyler's words like some bad song she couldn't get out of her head. When she was inside the house, Gus had asked if she wanted a drink. She'd told him white wine would be just fine. He'd told her that her options were beer or whiskey. She'd said whiskey. He'd poured them both a glass. She had told him about Tyler showing up at the bar and what he'd said to her. Gus had responded that he wasn't worth the time or trouble, they already knew what kind of weasel he was, they didn't need more proof.

Then they had both been quiet, staring at each other until Maggie had gotten up from his couch and walked over to him and kissed him. Had gotten her arms around him and then they were kissing again.

When she'd pulled back, he'd said, "You sure about this?"

She'd laughed.

"Hell, no," she'd said.

He had always been great looking and, she'd always thought, sexy as hell. He still was. When he was in his bed, on his back, head on the pillows, he'd turned so that their faces were nearly touching.

Grinning again.

"Don't worry," he'd said. "Nobody's broken me yet."

"Stop talking now," she'd said.

They both did.

NINETY-SEVEN

Maggie

WHEN HE WAS FINALLY AWAKE, she told him her plan, what she planned to do this week, and why.

"You okay with it?" she said.

"Ballplayers go down to the minor leagues all the time to get themselves straightened out, no reason why riders can't do the same," he said. "I did it myself once or twice. Helps you remember shit you forget when you're going good."

"I just need to get around," she said.

Now, late Wednesday afternoon, she was trying to do just that. She felt as if she'd traveled back in time to pony camp as she prepared for an event at Ring 9, Level 1 jumps, just over three feet. She was as far away from the International Ring as she'd ever been and close to being all the way off the property. But it had to be done, she was more certain of that than ever.

One round, a speed class, nothing more. The only other top riders anywhere near Ring 9 were on their way to their barns across the way, or to the parking lot. Most of the riders had entered her class to try out young horses.

She hadn't even told Daniel what she planned to do until the previous afternoon. Now they were talking it over again as they finished the course walk.

"I really should have thought of this myself," he said.

"Can't think of everything."

"It's still the right thing to do."

"Better be," she said, pacing off the distance to the final jump.

There were other familiar trainers in the ring. Occasionally she had to raise her voice to be heard over the sound of the tractor dragging a nearby practice ring, and all the golf carts racing past them, like they were the ones in a speed class.

They had finished dragging the practice ring. Seamus was there with Coronado, having walked him over from Gus's barn. Seamus helped Maggie up and then she was doing some practice jumping before they got to her place in the order. Doing what Daniel had told her to do today. Riding her horse.

When she was at the in-gate, Maggie looked to the other side of Ring 9, the small viewing area over there behind the taco stand. Gus was there, and Becky. Maggie and Becky had been talking the past few days, the way they used to. Maggie had asked her what had melted the ice. Becky had grinned and said, "I just can't watch you suck."

"That bad?"

"Worse."

"Because I'm your mom?" she'd said.

"Because you're too damn good to suck this badly," Becky had said.

Maggie was two out. Looked at a scoreboard about half the size of the one in the International Ring and saw that the time allowed was 72 seconds.

Not for me, Maggie thought. All the times in her life when she'd wanted to go fast. Just not today. Today she didn't care if it looked like she was pulling a carriage up in Central Park if she got around clean.

She did. Two full seconds over the time allowed. Nearly five seconds behind the winner. Not even close to winning the class. And could not have cared less.

Because she'd gone clean.

"I found what I was looking for," she said to Daniel when she hopped off Coronado herself, not waiting for Seamus, and was on her way over to Becky and Caroline and Gus Bennett.

"You just needed to slow things down," he said.

"Well, I sure did that," she said.

"You know you sound like Becky, right?"

"Don't tell her I said this," Maggie told him, "but maybe I need to be a little more like my daughter."

"In what way?"

"Attitude," she said.

Daniel smiled.

"Ask her," he said. "I'm sure she'd be happy to loan you some."

Maggie smiled then. It was not something she had done lately, especially when leaving the ring.

"I got my groove back," she said.

NINETY-EIGHT

Daniel

DANIEL MADE THE SHORT WALK with Coronado to their barn, the shortest walk he had ever made there after a class. Thinking as he did what a crazy sport this was, how complicated the act of riding a horse and jumping it could be, losing making Maggie feel as good about herself as she had in weeks.

It wasn't how much she had wanted to go clean today. She had needed to go clean, even over what looked like baby jumps. Needed to get around without putting a rail on the ground. She didn't care how low the bar had been set. In all ways. She didn't care about the level of competition. Daniel, being from Mexico, was a huge soccer fan. Football, they called it in his country. There were three tiers of football in the Mexican league. Maggie had to feel today as if she had competed in Liga Premier. The lowest tier.

But she had done what she needed to do. What she had set out to do. Just as Daniel's sports psychology books explained, process over result. And this: sometimes doing more is accomplished by caring less. Really today she had only been competing against herself, not the clock.

When he had Coronado back in his stall, Seamus having fed him a carrot before washing and cooling the horse down, Daniel took the long walk back to the front entrance of the show grounds to avoid the traffic crawling out to Pierson Road after the last event of the day. But he had driven Maggie over here and used her VIP pass to park so that she would have a much shorter walk to the tent for lunch with Caroline.

Even on a weekday, cars were backed up to make the left out to Pierson.

Daniel sighed as he saw that Steve Gorton was in one of the cars, an obviously expensive convertible.

Gorton pulled over to the side, into a handicapped space, allowing the cars behind him to pass.

He waved Daniel over.

"Hey," Gorton said. "Come here."

As if Daniel were a parking attendant.

Daniel stopped. Technically, though he and Gorton had exchanged barely more than a few sentences, Daniel knew he worked for him. As mean and obnoxious as he was, Gorton was still the majority owner of Maggie's horse.

In that way, she worked for him, too. Daniel had to show respect even if he did not feel respect.

Gorton got out of the car, leaned against the driver's-side door, and crossed his arms in front of him.

"So now she loses to losers?" he said.

Maggie had made it around the course in 74 seconds. Two seconds over the time allowed. Two time faults. But she had gone clean. Daniel tried to explain the reasoning to Gorton.

"Today's round was really just a glorified workout," he said finally.

"Were they keeping score?" Gorton said.

"Excuse me?"

"Were they keeping *score*?" Gorton said.

"Well, yes."

"There were fans at that ring in East Cupcake, right?"

"I saw you there," Daniel said. "You know some people were watching."

"Then it wasn't a workout," Gorton said.

"She rode well," Daniel said. "That is the most important thing."

"She rode like crap," Gorton said.

"I tried to explain," Daniel said patiently. "She wasn't here to go fast."

You'd know that if you knew anything about the sport.

"Stop making excuses for her!" Gorton said. "I know what I saw."

Daniel did not want to be here, trapped into talking with this man.

"She was nearly five seconds slower than the goddamn winner!" Gorton said.

"She rode today the way she needed to ride," Daniel said, stubbornly refusing to be lectured by someone who wouldn't know how to saddle a horse if his miserable rich-man life depended on it.

Feeling as if he were talking to a child.

"You know as well as I do," Gorton said, "the way the bitch is dropping like a rock in the rankings."

Daniel took a deep breath, then another, trying to calm himself.

Bitch.

Could not stop what came out of his mouth next.

"She deserves more respect than your name-calling, Mr. Gorton," he said. "She is a great rider still. And a better person."

"Says who?" he said. *"You?"*

Daniel thought, *I have to get out of here before I say something that gets me fired.*

"We're all supposed to be on the same team,"

Daniel said, "that is all I am trying to say to you. And please lower your voice."

"She's running out of time, and I'm running out of patience," Gorton said. "For a month, she's ridden no better than average. Everybody can see it. Maybe the only one who won't admit it is you, *chico*."

Daniel felt the heat rise up in him, as if a switch had been thrown, feeling it in his face, the back of his neck, everywhere. Wondering if Gorton could see it.

Chico.

Boy.

It took all of his will not to respond.

"Got anything else to say?" Gorton said.

You have no idea.

Daniel forced himself not to challenge this man, not to take irreversible action. But as much as he wanted to smash a fist into the man's face, he knew a rash move could ruin everything.

So he kept breathing slowly. Telling himself he was not a violent man. No matter how much he felt like one now.

"Didn't think so," Gorton said, and got back into his fancy car, putting it in gear and cranking up the music.

Daniel walked over to his own car and started the engine, turned on the air-conditioning as high as it would go and just sat there for a few moments, forehead pressed against the steering wheel. The heat drained out of him. He felt his whole body unclenching, releasing the fierce restraint that had kept him from hitting the last man in the world he could afford to hit.

NINETY-NINE

THREE EVENTS REMAINED that would shape the United States Olympic team. One was playing out in front of me at the Rolex Ring, Kentucky Invitational.

Mom was one rider out, Tyler Cullen set to go into the ring ahead of her on Galahad. Then Eric Glynn and Matthew Killeen.

Then me.

I'd gotten a second in the three-star event back in Wellington. Mom had gotten a fourth and ridden well, ultimately losing in the jump-off by a second and a half. More important, it moved her back up into fourth place in the Olympic rankings. I was third.

Even people who didn't follow show jumping had started to take notice of what Mom and I were trying to do, make the same Olympic team. The Lexington newspaper ran a feature when we'd arrived in town, the writer calling us the Kris and Kim Kardashian of our sport.

"Fake news," Grandmother said that morning at breakfast. "Neither one of you has grown up yet."

Tyler went clean in the jump-off, a beautiful round, even I had to admit, a time of 35.6. Mom was better with 34.8. Three riders left. I was one of them. I was happy that Mom had done well. No BS. I honestly was. I still wanted to beat her. I wanted like hell to win.

"Use your head today," Gus said. "And go out there and kick some ass."

It was time. Nobody was beating Sky and me today.

I looked around the ring from the in-gate and realized all over again how much I loved this. *This.* The moment. Nobody else mattered now. Not Mom and me or Daniel and me. Not Grandmother or Gus. Not even Steve Gorton. None of the drama we'd all had outside the ring. Not even everything that was on the line today.

Just Sky and me.

I heard the announcer call my name, then Sky's. Knowing we might be a little more than a half minute from walking away with one of the biggest weekends of the year. By now, after the way things had gone for us lately, it wouldn't shock anyone if we did. Certainly not me.

Didn't think Coronado was the best horse now. I thought mine was.

The buzzer sounded. Everything got quiet before what Gus liked to call bat-out-of-hell time. I took one last look around. What I was feeling right now, it was why riders did this, young or old. Man or woman. Million-dollar ride. Or a horse your dad gave you.

The toughest combination came early, a tight one, hardly any time to react after the first jump. Sky treated it all like a speed bump, clearing both jumps so easily it was like they stood half their actual height. Like the ones Mom had jumped at Ring 9 that day.

Just like that we were into it. Big-time. Feeling a strong wind at my back, even though there was no breeze to speak of.

We took a killer inside turn on the rollback two

jumps later. No choice but to go inside if I was here to win. And I sure as shit wasn't here to finish second.

How could anybody have gone faster than this?

Three jumps to the finish. Clock on the huge Rolex scoreboard behind me. But I didn't need a clock. I knew.

Go.

Next jump clean.

Then the next.

Still flying.

I told myself not to leave anything to chance.

Bat out of hell.

I was going for it all now, deciding, on the fly, to shorten the distance before the last jump, taking out a stride like I had in the middle of the round, with no problem. Sky had done everything I asked. Sometimes the moments of the day all fell into place between horse and rider.

It was at the last second, very last, I knew I'd asked too much.

She didn't have the length.

Was too far away.

And refused.

ONE HUNDRED

MOM'S TIME STOOD UP. This time I watched her get the ribbon and medal and champagne and pose for the pictures and hear the cheers from a crowd that looked twice as big as we got in Wellington. In our intensely private competition, she was the one on top today. She was champion. Because of the way I'd finished—Sky refusing and circling and then refusing again before I was buzzed out of the ring—I felt as if I'd finished last.

I'd done the thing that Gus preached to me about all the time:

Gotten ahead of myself. Had gotten fixed on the result and not the process. It had only been for one stride. But it had cost me.

Before Mom was out of the ring, I told her how happy I was for her, because I genuinely was. Hugged her for the first time in a long time. Now we were back at the rented house, getting ready to drive to Cincinnati for a late flight back to Florida, and I was back to being pissed off at myself.

Just not as pissed off as Gus Bennett was.

The rest of us were flying back to Palm Beach International. Gus was driving home in his van. Though he'd left Florida at dawn, the drive to Lexington had taken him fourteen hours. He'd decided to drive home overnight, telling me that he could do it with one stop, be back in Wellington in time for breakfast, and wanted me in the ring by nine o'clock, even if only to ride Tiny.

"I don't get a day off?" I said.

"You didn't earn it," he said.

Mom had offered to make the drive with him. He said he wanted to be alone.

"Mom was the better rider today," I said. "Is that some kind of crime?"

"Bullshit," he said.

Mom and Grandmother and Daniel were inside. Emilio was already gone, my horse inside our trailer. Seamus had Coronado in Gus's trailer.

I'd offered to throw Gus's suitcase into the back of the van. He said he could do it himself. It was nearly two hours from when the Invitational had ended. He was still mad as hell. At me.

"You need to let up on me," I said. "I made a mistake. I *know* I made a mistake. But it was one jump—the *last* jump—in an event I was about to win."

"Hey," he said, "that gives me an idea." Making no attempt to hide the sarcasm in his voice. "Let's call over there and get the stewards on the line and tell them that since you were about to win, we'd like them to not count the last jump. I'm sure they'll understand."

"I made a mistake!"

"Yeah," he said. "You did. The kind of mistake that can be the difference between making the team and not making it. You had a chance to win the goddamn Kentucky Invitational. You think that chance comes around all the time? And you blew it."

He'd been angry at me before. Not like this. He

slammed the back door of the van and said that as soon as he said his good-byes, he was ready to take off.

But when he was halfway up the front walk, he stopped suddenly, whipped the chair around, glared at me one more time, still on fire.

"You know when you get over an important loss in this sport?" he snapped. *"Never."*

"I know that," I said.

"No," he said, "you don't."

ONE HUNDRED ONE

Gorton

GORTON WAS ORDERING another vodka when Tyler Cullen found him in the owners' tent. Cullen had finished second today, a second behind Maggie Atwood in the jump-off.

Cullen told the bartender he'd have what Gorton was having.

"Thought you might already be gone," Cullen said.

"Well, Tyler," Gorton said, "that's one of several advantages of having your own plane. It's wheels up when you say it's wheels up."

Gorton looked across the room now and toasted a tall redhead he'd been eyeballing since he got here, wondering how she'd like to see the inside of a Gulfstream IV. Hell, if they left right now, they could be at Honor Bar by ten o'clock. He'd finally managed to get rid of Blaine.

"You mentioned something about maybe getting a ride back to Palm Beach with you," Cullen said.

"Full up," Gorton said. "Sorry."

"You filled up a plane as big as yours?" Cullen said.

"I'm just a boy who can't say no," Gorton said.

Gorton held Cullen's look now, smiling at him, keeping his eyes on him, long enough to make him thoroughly uncomfortable.

Finally, Gorton said, "Congratulations on finishing

second, by the way. Puts you one behind the kid and two behind the mother if I'm not mistaken."

"I've got time," he said. "You don't have to worry about me."

"But see, that's the thing, I do worry," Gorton said. "Mostly because you've turned out to be completely full of shit about them every step of the way."

"Wait a second," Cullen said.

"No, *you* wait a second," Gorton said. "You know what kind of people last with me, Tyler? People who give me good information."

He pointed at his glass for a refill. Not Cullen's.

"First you told me the kid couldn't ride," he said. "Then you told me the mother had no shot, and that you were going to get the trainer deported, all *that* before you told me the sainted Maggie couldn't do anything without the trainer. Finally, you told me Maggie had lost it." Then he paused and said, "You ever get tired of being right all the time, Tyler?"

"I'm telling you," Cullen said, "I'm still your best shot at gold."

Gorton smiled again.

"I don't think so," he said.

He looked across the room. The redhead was gone. The bartender was coming over with his drink, but Gorton waved him off, before throwing a hundred-dollar bill on the table.

"Know what I've decided to do?" Gorton said to him. "Quit listening to you—quit *you*—while I'm ahead."

"You're shitting me."

"I don't think so."

"I'm telling you, I'm still a better rider than either one of them," Cullen said, starting to sound desperate now.

And starting to bore Gorton, even more than usual. Gorton was already second-guessing himself for standing next to him at the bar. He should have moved on the redhead before, given Cullen the bad news another time.

"Not feeling you on that one," Gorton said.

"I thought we had a deal!" Cullen said.

His voice had gone up at least an octave, maybe more, by Gorton's measure.

"You probably thought the deal was set, too," Gorton said. "Maybe you never heard the old Hollywood line." Patting Cullen dismissively on the head. "Turned out it wasn't *set*-set."

Gorton pulled his phone out of his pocket, called his pilot and told him he was on his way.

"Hey," he said to Cullen. "Safe flight."

ONE HUNDRED TWO

Gus

BECKY WAS IN THE RING, Atwood Farm, late morning, finally having turned the page after Kentucky. Gus watched her ride Sky the way she was supposed to, glad they'd had a fair amount of time before the five-star Mercedes Grand Prix coming up at WEF. She needed to be at her very best now, the stakes were too high not to be, because of where the event fell in an Olympic year.

This morning Gus had even gotten her to make a couple of jumps with her hands off the reins, his way of reminding her that sometimes the best thing to do, especially when you had a horse with this much talent and this much heart, was to get the hell out of her way and just let her run, and jump, the way she was born to do both.

Now Becky did it again, letting go after the first jump of a combination, just two quick strides between the fences, hardly any room at all, taking the jump clean, whooping when Sky landed.

Caroline Atwood had arrived at the ring by then.

"Hands-free riding?" she said. "I don't believe I've ever seen that one before."

"It's an exercise an old trainer taught me," he said. "Worked for me, works for her."

"Would you have her drive a car that way?"

"Horses are way smarter than cars," he said. "And most people I know, as a matter of fact."

Gus turned away from her and yelled at Becky, "Again."

They both watched Becky do it again, as if she'd been doing it her whole life. Gus videoed it this time. Watched the replay as soon as she and Sky were over the second jump. Felt himself smiling. A beautiful thing, he told himself. All part of her getting her confidence all the way back after that refusal in Kentucky.

When Becky came over, he handed her the phone. She watched the round and smiled.

"Niiiice," she said, dragging the word out as far as it would go.

"Go cool down your horse," he said. "And give her an extra carrot, on me."

Becky hopped off before Emilio could get to her and walked Sky toward the barn.

Just Gus and Caroline now, watching her go.

"God, she's a natural," Caroline said. "Maggie made herself into a great rider. But the things Becky can do, she does instinctively. The rest of it anybody can teach."

"Well," Gus said. "Almost anybody."

From inside the barn, they heard a shout of laughter from Becky.

"My daughter and granddaughter might actually do this," Caroline said. "How crazy is that?"

"Getting less crazy by the day," he said, "from where I sit."

"They wouldn't just be making the team," Caroline said. "They'd be making history."

Gus motioned for her to follow him out into the ring, farther away from the barn.

"I've been meaning to ask you," he said. "If they both do make it, who will you root for to win the gold medal?"

"Not fair."

"Won't hold you to it," he said. "And whatever you say will stay between us."

"Maggie," she said, without hesitation. "She wanted it longer. End of story."

She looked at him.

"What about you?" she said.

Neither one of them had heard Becky coming into the ring behind them.

"What about him?" Becky said.

ONE HUNDRED THREE

BEFORE A BIG SUNDAY event like the Mercedes, Mom and I would spend Thursday doing light hacking on Coronado and Sky. Maybe a half hour in the ring, tops. Gus had scheduled mine for eleven o'clock.

A little after eight on an uncommonly cool morning for South Florida, I was headed out for a run when I saw one of Gus's small trailers pull into our driveway. Mom was behind the wheel. She'd spent another night at Gus's house. It was happening more and more often.

When she got out, she said, "Glad I caught you. Let's take a walk."

She was in her riding clothes.

"Going for a run here," I said.

"I meant a trail walk," Mom said. "Give us a chance to talk."

Uh-oh.

"About anything in particular?"

"How about everything?"

"Oh," I said. "One of *those* talks."

"Go change," she said. "Quickly."

When we were on our horses and out on the trail, it occurred to me that this trail was where our story had really begun. Mom's. Mine. Everybody's. Because we weren't out here together that day.

"I worry that I never gave you a choice about being a rider," she said.

I shook my head.

"Nope," I said. "My choice all the way, Mom. It just took me a while to understand how *much* I wanted it."

We rode in silence for a few minutes, out past the barns and the construction sites, unhurried in the morning quiet.

"We have one point to resolve," she said. "I'm not going to apologize for how much I want this, and that means even if I make it and you don't."

"Clear on my end," I said. "But just because you've wanted it longer doesn't mean you want it more. Because you don't."

The trail narrowed again. Mom gave Coronado a kick and got him into a trot. I did the same to Sky, right behind her.

Thinking, *I've been following her my whole life*.

Maybe until now.

"Good talk," she said.

"You know something?" I said. "It was, even though it doesn't change the fact that I'm still going to be looking to kick your ass."

"Wait," she said. "That's my line."

Close to the end of the trail, Mom asked if I was ready to head back. I said I was. The last time we'd been together out here was the day I'd found her.

Just then I heard a rustling in the bushes.

The horses didn't react. But Mom had heard the same thing. We brought our horses to a halt and at the same moment turned to see the red fox stare at us before running in the other direction.

Mom turned to face me.

"Maybe it's an omen," she said.

"Or that fox just didn't want to take us both on."

Mom was smiling now.

"I missed you, kid," she said.

"Missed you, too, Mom," I said.

We put our horses back in motion and headed for home.

ONE HUNDRED FOUR

WE WERE AT OUR TABLE in the tent, all of us lamenting in the middle of the Friday night Mercedes cocktail reception how much we hated cocktail parties, especially ones for horse people.

"Call off the contest line," Grandmother said. "I hate them more."

The event wasn't officially a command performance for the owners and riders and trainers and various family members. But it was close enough. The owners of WEF were there, representatives of the sport's ruling bodies, stewards I recognized, local TV personalities, and politicians. And TV camera people. And photographers. I'd never seen the tent this crowded, this hot, this loud.

"Pay the ransom," I said to Mom, "and get me out of here."

"You know, honey," she said, "it wouldn't be the worst thing in the world for you to mingle."

"Oh, wait," I said. "You're serious."

She turned to scope out the room. I looked at her in profile, thinking there was no better-looking woman in the place. Knowing how little effort it had taken, or prep work. A blue dress on her I couldn't remember her wearing in a long time. Jimmy Choo suede pumps. Pearls. She hadn't even had her hair done, just let it hang down her back. She was standing next to Gus, hand on his shoulder.

"Yeah," Gus said. "Go talk to people you normally wouldn't talk to on a bet."

"What about you, tough guy?" I said. "You going to work the room?"

"I go where she goes," he said, grinning at Mom.

He was wearing the same blue blazer he'd worn to the courtroom. Daniel was in the same suit he'd worn that day. They both looked handsome as hell. When Mom and I were dressed and ready to come over here I'd said, "How is it that you ended up with more of a love life than me?"

"Patience," she said.

"Easy for you to say," I said.

We looked across the tent and saw Steve Gorton standing at his table, surrounded by a crowd of men and women, all of whom suddenly burst into laughter at something he'd just said.

"Nobody is that funny," Daniel whispered to me.

"Certainly not him," I said.

Against all odds, Gorton had been acting more decently to Mom, really to all of us, lately, even though I realized it was a low bar. He'd even found a way to be civil to Grandmother, who said that even though weeks had passed since he'd discussed making a change on Coronado, that he would always be one of those loudmouth jerks, insecure no matter how much money he had. But also obsessed enough with appearances to know how he'd look if he pulled Maggie Atwood off Coronado this close to the Olympics.

I asked Grandmother if she was going to say hello.

"Let a sleeping dog lie," she said. "And I do mean dog."

"More like a dog who lies," Mom said.

Mom and Gus went to talk to Jennifer Gates. Daniel and I headed in the direction of the bar.

"Are we really going to mingle?" he asked.

"Ish," I said.

Then I said, "Am I allowed to ask how things are going with you and the United States government?"

"Slower than an old horse," he said. "It's complicated, but things might not get resolved before I'm supposed to go to Paris."

"There's still a chance, though, right?" I said.

"There is always a chance," he said. "But for tonight, let's just try to enjoy ourselves."

We did our best, chatting with some of the big shots from FEI, then Tess McGill, who I genuinely liked and who was now in first place in the rankings. And Kevin Seth, who'd been the best rider in the country before major back surgery had ended his career. That was four years ago.

"Kevin was such a champion," Daniel said. "He just finally had too many falls."

"That could have been Mom," I said to Daniel. "Not coming back, I mean."

"Or you," Daniel said, "landing on that rail the way you did."

When we turned to make our way back to the table, Steve Gorton was standing right in front of us.

"What is it with you trainers," he said to Daniel, voice as loud as a bullhorn, "ending up with the hottest women?"

He didn't seem drunk. Maybe the simple fact of things was that he was simply being Steve Gorton.

"No shit," he said, "you guys are killing it in more ways than one these days, am I right?"

"Which guys would that be?" I said.

He nodded in the direction of Gus and Mom, talking now with Matthew Killeen.

"Maggie and the wheelchair guy," Gorton said. "Or so I hear."

"His name is Gus Bennett," Daniel said quietly.

Maybe there was something in his tone. Or in Daniel's eyes.

"Hey," Gorton said. "I'm just having some fun here."

At least you *are.*

"Like when I was just messing with you the other week in the parking lot," he added. "You gotta learn to let shit go."

"What other day?" I said to Daniel.

"Very nice to see you, Mr. Gorton," Daniel said, trying to end the conversation right there. "Good luck with Coronado on Sunday."

Daniel took my hand now as we stepped around Gorton and headed back toward our table. But from behind us we heard Gorton's voice, even louder than before.

"Hey," he said, "I wasn't done talking to you."

"Yes, you were," Daniel said, softly enough that only I could hear.

We left Gorton where he was, alone in the middle of the crowded tent. I turned to see him staring at us.

We kept walking.

ONE HUNDRED FIVE

Daniel

BECKY AND MAGGIE had to stay around to take pictures with some of the Mercedes people, with the other riders, with each other for the *Palm Beach Post,* to go with the story the newspaper was running about them on Sunday.

Before Daniel left, Becky said to him, "What happened between you and Gorton the other day?"

"Nothing," he said.

"Something," she said.

"We can talk about it later," Daniel said, before saying good-bye to the others, telling Maggie he would see her in the morning.

Then he was walking toward the door.

"Don't let that guy get to you," Gus said to him. "He freely admits that he screws with people because he can."

"Thank the Good Lord that he only has a piece of one of our horses," Caroline said.

"Still the biggest piece, Mother," Maggie said.

"Don't remind me," she said.

Daniel was finally outside then, happy to be breathing fresh air. Happy to be out of that tent. But he had once again kept himself and his temper under control. Now he just wanted to get home. As usual for sponsor events, there were golf carts lined up to drive the patrons back down the hill to the VIP parking lot. But it was still early, so Daniel was the only one leaving right now. He was happy this part of his night was over and that he could be alone. He breathed deeply, looked up at the stars, and started walking toward the parking lot. He looked over his shoulder and saw the lights from the back of the tent, and heard the voices from inside, as the party continued without him.

He saw Gorton coming right at him.

"You don't walk away from me like that, especially not with people watching," Steve Gorton said.

Even in a tent full of people, Daniel thought, *Gorton had probably imagined that everyone was looking and that all of the cameras were trained on him.*

"I thought we were finished after I wished you luck on Sunday," Daniel said.

"We're done talking when I say we're done talking," Gorton said. "That's the way it works for guys like me and guys like you."

Guys like you.

Gorton smiled. It was, to Daniel, a particularly ugly sight. As if he had put on a clown mask.

"I was not comfortable with you talking about Becky that way in front of her," Daniel said.

"Get over it," Gorton said. "I was paying you a compliment. Don't think I haven't thought about what she might be like in the sack."

Breathe in, breathe out.

"You need to stop talking about Becky now," he said.

Gorton still had the ugly smile on his face. He hadn't moved any closer to Daniel. Still, Daniel felt the distinct sensation that Gorton was crowding him.

For now, it was just the two of them out here.

"What, you gonna marry her?" Gorton said. "Do

one of those green card things? Way to go, dude. Win-win."

"Shut up," Daniel said.

Gorton's smile disappeared.

"Excuse me?"

"I told you to stop talking about Becky," Daniel said.

"I don't think so," Gorton said.

Daniel hadn't gotten into a fistfight since he was a boy. Once they got here from Mexico his father had told him that he must walk away, no matter how much he was provoked, no matter how much the other man wanted to fight.

Walk away.

He turned to leave and Gorton spun him around.

"No shit," he said. "If I was the one hitting that I'd be telling everybody."

"I won't tell you to shut up again," Daniel said.

"Or what, *chico?*" Gorton said. "You gonna defend your girlfriend's honor by kicking my ass? Well, here I am, you dumb bastard."

He was like the drunkest man in the bar, Daniel thought. Only he wasn't drunk. Just being himself. Mean as a rattlesnake. Just much louder.

"Please lower your voice," Daniel said.

Gorton, taller and heavier than Daniel, shoved him then.

The move surprised Daniel, staggered him back a couple of steps. He nearly went down.

Suddenly Gorton was completely out of control, throwing a wild punch, one Daniel could see coming from a mile away, giving him plenty of time to snap his head back and out of the way. Gorton hadn't come close to connecting.

Suficiente.

Thinking in Spanish in that moment.

Enough, he told himself.

Enough.

When Gorton stepped in to throw a second punch, Daniel stepped slightly to the side and set himself and threw a punch of his own, hitting him in the middle of his face with a straight right hand, heard the crack of Gorton's nose and felt it at the same time as Gorton went down.

Daniel watched now as Gorton got himself to a sitting position, put his hand to his face, pulled it away, stared at the blood on his hand, then looked down and saw the splash of blood on his white dress shirt.

"You broke my nose!" he screamed.

His voice had risen a couple of octaves.

"Yes," Daniel said. "I did."

Gorton sat there, seeming to be in no hurry to stand up. Or come at Daniel again.

"Do you realize who you just hit?" Gorton screamed, at an even higher pitch than before, even more volume, the blood still streaming from his nose, down across his chin and back onto the shirt.

Daniel leaned forward and looked Gorton in the face. Gorton recoiled, as if Daniel were about to hit him again.

"Yes," he said. "I realize exactly who I just hit."

He turned and walked away.

Daniel was nearly to the parking lot when Becky, out of breath, caught up with him.

"What happened back there?" she said.

"I finally had enough," Daniel said.

ONE HUNDRED SIX

DANIEL WAS ARRESTED after Gorton called the police, charged with assault, taken to the county jail in West Palm Beach. There was no way for him to get a court appearance until Monday morning. It meant he would spend the weekend in jail.

If Daniel were an American citizen we could have gotten him released on his own recognizance over a bullshit charge like this, for a fight he didn't start. But he wasn't a citizen.

Early the next afternoon, Grandmother and Mom and Gus and I gathered in our living room to figure out our next move. Grandmother's lawyer, Paul Gellis, had gone to see Daniel, first thing in the morning, but said he really couldn't do anything until Daniel's arraignment. He also relayed a message from Daniel that he didn't want any of us to visit him at the jail.

Grandmother had put me on the phone with Mr. Gellis. I asked how much trouble Daniel might be in with the government now that he'd been arrested.

"He's DACA," Paul Gellis said. "So unless he's got priors he's not telling me about, this shouldn't affect his status. He should be fine."

"This whole thing is totally bogus," I said.

"Steve Gorton doesn't think so," Gellis said. "And not gonna lie: his lawyers are bigger than your lawyer."

We had already decided that Gus would train both Mom and me tomorrow at the Mercedes. None of us much wanted to talk about riding right now. But they weren't going to cancel the event just because Mom's trainer was locked up.

When I'd gotten home, I'd called the office of Mr. Connors, Daniel's immigration lawyer, gotten his out-of-office. I left one message, then another, told him it was about Daniel Ortega, and it was important. Hadn't heard back yet. But it was a Saturday.

"I'm starting to get that you should never break a rich guy's nose on a weekend," I said.

"Never break a rich guy's nose *ever*," Gus said. "Even though this guy has been begging for a good smack since you all went into business with him."

"Or his whole life," Mom said. She closed her eyes, shook her head. "Of all the owners in all the world…"

"Forget about the government," Gus said. "Just wait. It's Gorton who's gonna try to make a federal case of this now that the picture of him holding that bloody handkerchief to his nose has gone viral."

People had heard him screaming out curses and had come running down from the tent, snapping away with their cell phones when they saw Gorton's face and shirt full of blood.

"Is he too thick to understand that by pressing charges and taking Daniel away from Maggie he's only hurting himself in the end?" Grandmother said.

"Sure he does," Gus said. "He just doesn't care. He's not gonna let somebody pop him and get away with it."

"He's the one always talking about doing anything to win," Mom said.

"The only thing he cares about more is not looking bad," Gus said. "Or getting laughed at."

Gus looked at Mom.

"You ready to do a little work in the ring?" he said.

"No," she said. Forced a smile. "But I will."

"I'll come back here after and watch you," Gus said to me. "This situation sucks. But you both gotta find a way to turn the page tomorrow."

He looked at Mom, then me, then back at Mom.

"The only thing you can do for Daniel right now, both of you, is ride your damn horses," Gus said.

"Don't say it's what Daniel would want us to do," I said.

"Wasn't going to," he said.

I felt my phone buzzing then. Pulled it out of my back pocket and felt myself smiling for the first time since Daniel had put Steve Gorton on the ground.

Heard the car pulling into the driveway then. Heard the knock on the front door. Said I'd get it.

I opened the door and my dad walked in.

"Heard somebody might need a lawyer," he said.

ONE HUNDRED SEVEN

AFTER I'D LEFT the message for Mr. Connors, I'd called Dad, trying to explain everything that had happened, and what I was afraid might happen to Daniel. My words were flowing like a faucet I couldn't turn off.

Dad had let me babble for about a minute.

"Tell me the rest when I get there," he'd said.

"You're coming?" I'd said.

"In the afternoon," he'd said. "Just to even up the sides."

Now he hugged Mom and did the same with Grandmother before she could pull back.

He walked across the room then and shook Gus's hand.

"Heard a lot about you," he said. Grinning, he continued, "Unfortunately, you've probably heard a lot more about me."

Mom smiled.

"Don't flatter yourself, Jack," she said.

I made him a cup of coffee and then took him, step by step, through every detail.

When I finished, Dad said, "Let me guess: Nobody outside the tent saw anything."

"It was down the hill and around the corner from

where the golf carts are parked," I said. "Daniel said that he didn't see anybody else around."

"So for now it's his word against that asshat Gorton's," Dad said.

"Daniel's not going to get deported because of this, is he?" I asked.

"Oh, hell, no," he said. "The assault charge is bull-shit. If it had been Gorton who popped Daniel and not the other way around the closest he would have come to jail is if he'd taken a wrong turn on the way back to Palm Beach."

He got up now.

"Nice to see all of you," he said.

Grinned at Gus.

"You're even braver than I heard," Dad said.

Mom made a sound that was half-sigh, half-groan.

I walked Dad to the door. He gave me another hug, and whispered "I got this" in my ear.

"Gorton's a bad guy," I said.

"Kind of my thing," he said.

I walked him to the car, then hugged him again, just because it made me feel better about things every time I did. He said he was dropping his bag at the Hampton Inn and then heading over to the jail. Then I watched him gun the rental car out of the driveway, spraying rocks everywhere, mostly for Grandmother's benefit, I was certain.

He called me two hours later, after I'd ridden Sky.

"There's a problem," he said.

ONE HUNDRED EIGHT

MOM AND I WERE WALKING the course early Sunday afternoon, Gus alongside us. As we counted our distances, he was talking to us, nonstop. Just not about distances.

"I'm gonna say this for the last time," he said.

"I wish," I said.

"Very funny," he said. "But this isn't about Daniel today. It's about the two of you. You help yourselves today. Not him. There. Now I'm done."

"It's not going to be easy," Mom said.

"Well, you need to figure it out fast," Gus said. "If you don't, you're both going to get knocked out of this ring with all those points sitting there for the taking. And an awful lot of money."

We finished the walk. Seamus and Emilio still hadn't brought our horses up from their stalls. Mom was going twelfth in the order. I was going twenty spots later. Still plenty of time for both of us to start getting our minds as right as Gus wanted them to be.

Mom and Gus and I stopped to take one last look at the Grand Prix show grounds, starting to fill up with spectators, and also fill up with the electricity that always crackled inside and outside the ring this close to a big event. I looked up at the flags flying, heard the music from the live band, even saw Grandmother waving at me from the grassy area between the ring fence and the tent. This was supposed to be a great day for all of us.

But Daniel wasn't here.

Somehow in that moment it was as if Gus were reading my mind.

"Focus," he said. "Good's not good enough today, for either one of you. You both need to be great. And you can't do that worrying about what's going down with Daniel tomorrow."

I knew he was only talking to me in that moment.

Then he went over the course one more time, for both of us. Distances and combinations and opportunities to slash some time and rollbacks and how the water jump, where it was positioned, might be the greatest challenge of all. We could make mistakes, but not there. A bad landing, he said, and good-bye.

"Fourteen jumps," he said. "Go clean. Get to the jump-off. Go clean there and go fast. Both of you get pretty ribbons. Go home."

Now I grinned at him.

"You're going too fast for *me,*" I joked.

"Yeah, yeah, yeah," Gus said.

"Anything else?" Maggie Atwood said to him.

"As a matter of fact, there is," he said. "Think how good I'll look if the two of you look good." Then he spun his chair around and headed for the schooling ring. I watched him and wondered what was really going through his head today, training the woman he was involved with and probably in love with, and training me. With the stakes the same for both of us.

Mom went to get her horse, saying she'd decided to walk him up to the ring today. Gus watched her go. Smiling. I saw him do that sometimes when he didn't know I was watching him, looking at her as if it were the first time he'd ever seen her here, when they were both in their twenties.

Then he turned to me.

"You want to know the truth about all the shit that's going on?" he said. "That ring behind us will be the best possible place in the world for you to be today. Maybe the easiest."

"And why is that?"

"Because it's the only place where you're in charge of things," he said.

I went up to the pedestrian bridge to watch Mom's round, her first in weeks without Daniel, thinking that maybe what was happening this weekend, and then tomorrow with Daniel's arraignment, had brought Mom and me even closer together. The Atwood women against the world.

But once she was in the ring, she didn't need me, or Daniel, or Gus. She rode Coronado like a dream. There was one close call, almost not putting enough air underneath him on the water jump, clearing the water by less than a foot. No hesitation today on the rollback. She took the inside turn, even with that big horse, like a champ. Finished strong. Still early in the class, of course. But for now, she had the best time. More important, she was in the jump-off.

So far, so good.

I walked down from the bridge and got on my horse in the schooling ring. Only rooting for me now, and Sky. And from the time the buzzer sounded, it seemed as if *both* of us were in charge.

We didn't need to break any records. Just needed to go clean. When we finished, we were a half second behind Mom's time of 71.6. Didn't matter. What mattered was that we were in the jump-off, too. By the time the round was over, there were five riders who'd gone clean. Tess, Jennifer, Matthew, Mom, and me.

Back in the schooling ring, there was no conversation between Mom and me as we leisurely flatted our horses to keep them warm. Tess McGill pulled up alongside me at one point and said, "You and your mom riding like this in the same event and the same ring? Crazy."

"You have no idea," I said.

Tess was beautiful, talented, rich, never big-timed anybody because of who her dad was. Always had great horses. As great as *she* was, she still hadn't made the Olympics yet. It meant she wanted it as badly as Mom and I did.

Maybe more, if that was even possible.

Mom went first in the jump-off, went clean, came in at 35.5. Sky and I went next. She was fast, but somehow Coronado had found an extra gear today. We came in at 36.2. Mom was still in second by the time Tess McGill was in the ring. I was fourth.

Then Tess proceeded to blow everybody away. Her ride, Volàge du Val Henry, pretty name for a pretty horse, went around the jump-off course at what looked like the speed of light, finishing clean in 34 flat.

Still not a bad Sunday for the women of Atwood Farm, all in all.

Monday wasn't anything like that at the Palm Beach County Courthouse in West Palm Beach. As soon as the judge in Daniel's assault case had released him on his own recognizance, ICE was waiting for him outside the courtroom.

ONE HUNDRED NINE

DAD HAD TOLD ALL OF US—me, Mom, Grandmother, Gus—to say our good-byes before Dad walked Daniel out of the courtroom and into federal custody.

"Trust me," Dad had said, "what happens next happens fast."

"How did the feds even know about the fight?" Gus had said.

"As soon as our friend Daniel got arrested," Dad had said, "he went right into the system."

"All because he screwed up some paperwork?" I'd said.

"Our tax dollars at work, kid," Dad had said. "We all know the late filing for the DACA renewal was an honest mistake. But the fact is, he *was* late. Once he *was* late, he technically lost his Dreamer status. Which means that for now our friends in the government don't care whether the assault charge is total crap. They've got him."

"By the balls," Gus had said.

"Now I've got to try to make things happen fast for our side," Dad had said. "Get the charges dropped. Get a new DACA renewal filed. Get this kid's feet back on solid ground. Goddamn, immigration law is a bear. The lawyers who do this full-time ought to get a medal."

I'd seen the two ICE agents from Miami, short and tall—I'd blocked out their names—sitting in the back of the courtroom. They'd left before Mom and Grandmother had hugged Daniel and Gus shook his hand. I'd waited and then kissed him and put my arms around him and held on until Dad said, "Honey, let's get this done."

Then we were on the sidewalk watching the ICE agents walk Daniel toward the black town car parked out front, having cuffed him for no apparent reason other than they could. The shorter one opened the back door and Daniel got inside. The taller agent was making a phone call, maybe informing their boss that they'd apprehended a dangerous outlaw like Daniel Ortega, horse trainer.

"You have to make this go away, Dad," I said.

"We've got to get rid of the assault charge," he said. "Then we have a chance to stop any removal proceedings before they really get started. At least in theory."

Removal. Deportation.

"But he still has to go into detention," I said.

"Unfortunately," Dad said.

"This sucks," I said.

"That ought to be the legal definition of bullshit like this, for guys like Daniel," Dad said.

We all watched as the taller ICE agent finished his call, took out his keys, and walked around to the driver's side. The shorter one—Dolan was his name, I now remembered—opened the door and started to get in on the passenger side, but not before taking one last look at where we were all standing on the sidewalk.

For some reason, I felt as if he were looking directly at me. I wondered if the smirk were permanently frozen on his face. I wanted to give him the finger, thought better of that. I stared back at him until he shut the door and the car pulled away, wondering when I might see Daniel again.

ONE HUNDRED TEN

THE HAMPTON INVITATIONAL was the second week of June on eastern Long Island. By the time we arrived, Daniel was still in the federal detention center in Fort Lauderdale.

"Dad, when are you going to get him out?" I asked daily, to which he always replied, "Working on it."

"When we get back I want to see him," I said.

"He doesn't want you to see him there, kid," Dad said. "That's still set in cement."

Tess McGill was solidly in first place in the latest Olympic rankings. Then came Mom and Tyler and me, close enough to cover the three of us with Sky's fancy horse blanket.

The last chance to move up, or down, or influence the selectors, would be on Sunday in Bridgehampton. As obsessed as Tyler had been about Coronado, he would end up top-ranked with Galahad if he won on Sunday and likely make the team for sure with a decent finish. Mom and I were right there behind him. Three of us would make the team. One would be an alternate.

Gus and Mom had arrived that afternoon at the house we'd rented a few miles north of the show grounds. The drive from Florida had taken them two days, having overnighted in Raleigh. I asked Mom if they'd booked the honeymoon suite at the Raleigh Hyatt. She told me to zip it. Grandmother and I had flown up and arrived on Saturday, when the horses did. So we were all in the Hamptons now. Dad was still in Florida, working Daniel's case.

I had finished flatting Sky in a practice ring about twenty minutes before. Now while Mom and Gus checked out the stalls, I was taking a walk around the place, amazed at how much bigger it had gotten and how much it had changed since Mom used to bring me up as a teenager when she'd ride in the late-summer Hampton Classic. My first time competing here would be on Sunday at one. The main event. Money on the table. Gus training both Mom and me.

Our lives were overlapping. Gus was her former trainer, current boyfriend. He was my current trainer. Daniel was Mom's trainer, or had been until he ended up in jail. My dad, Mom's ex-husband, was now Daniel's lawyer. And there were more layers than that. Mom had a horse that had come up lame when she was on her way to the London Olympics. Gus had been injured, permanently, when he was on his way to Beijing.

Here we all were, anyway, a long way from home.

All of us except Daniel.

In the late afternoon I walked all the way to the Grand Prix ring at the east end of the property. It was empty, except for me.

I climbed up to the last row of the bleachers and surveyed the whole scene, from the distant railroad tracks to the grade school across the street to the fences and rails stacked against side walls covered with sponsor names. Imagined how it would look and feel on Sunday when the bleachers were full.

What if it somehow did come down to Mom or me for the last spot on the team?

How would I feel if I got it and not her?

Or she did?

And not me.

I made my way back down the stairs then, hopped the fence, walked to the middle of the ring, imagining myself down here, *in* here, on Sunday afternoon. What the view would be like then. What I would be feeling like *then*.

Walked back over to the fence, hopped it again, sat down in the first row of bleachers this time. Leaned back, closed my eyes, tried to see Sky and me here, late in the jump-off, imagining what Sunday afternoon would look like and feel like—and sound like—if we made it that far.

I felt myself smiling.

"Long time no see."

I looked up to find Steve Gorton standing over me.

ONE HUNDRED ELEVEN

GORTON WAS RIGHT. I hadn't seen or talked to him since the night Daniel had punched him in the face. Until now.

Mom hadn't had any contact with him, either, nor had Grandmother, even though they both had plenty they wanted to say to him. Coronado hadn't competed since the Mercedes, so there had been no real reason for him to show his face—and what I could see was a still swollen nose—around WEF. But now he was standing right in front of me. I had read somewhere that he had an oceanfront home in East Hampton. And he had his horse going Sunday.

Lucky me.

"Mr. Gorton," I said.

"I came up here about a week ago," he told me without being asked. "So I'm a little behind the news. How's your boyfriend doing in prison?"

I felt the sudden urge to hit him in the same spot Daniel had. I took a nice, slow, deep breath instead. Somehow managing to smile at him as I did.

"Listen," I said. "I am respectful of the fact that you're the majority owner of Mom's horse. And

I know how close we all might be to making it to the Olympics. So I'm not looking to mess with you or have you mess with me. But I hope *you'll* respect that I'm not talking about Daniel with you."

Gorton had a plastic cup in his hand. He took a healthy sip of whatever was in it, then acted as if he hadn't heard a single word I'd said.

"Guy's a hothead," he said. "Must be that Latin blood. Probably gets your engine running, am I right?"

I told myself to get the hell away from him and do it *right now*. Nothing good could come of me staying here, not for Mom, not for me. Certainly not for Daniel. I'd already seen how little it took to set Gorton off. The real hothead, I knew by now, was him. But I didn't walk away. Stayed where I was instead. Bad Becky. Don't give an inch.

"He's not a hothead," I said. "You're the one who provoked him."

"Is that what he told you?" he said. He put his index finger to the side of his head, as if suddenly curious. "But if I did, how come he's in the slammer and I'm on my way to Bloomberg's house in Southampton for a party he's throwing for his kid?"

"You know you provoked him," I said.

"Says him," Gorton said. "It's like Jack Nicholson said in that movie with my friend Tom Cruise. Your boy messed with the wrong Marine."

"I saw that movie, too," I said. "Wasn't the colonel the one who got locked up in the end?"

He raised his glass and toasted me.

"Touché," he said.

And drank.

"I need to go find my mom and Gus," I said.

"The other two lovebirds," he said. "The odd couple."

I sighed.

"She's lucky he's here to train her now that Daniel isn't," I said, "at least if you're still interested in your horse winning on Sunday."

"She'll be fine," Gorton said. "If there's one thing I've learned watching this sport, it's this: In the end, it's not about either one of us, honey. It's about the goddamn horse. You don't have that, you have shit. And not just horseshit."

"I'm not your honey."

I felt incredibly tired all of a sudden.

"You got that right," he said. "Not my type. Too mouthy."

"At the risk of getting even mouthier," I said, "I am curious about something. If all that matters is the horse, how come you were so fixated on getting me off Coronado after Mom got hurt? And then getting *her* off Coronado when Mom was back on him?"

"Rookie mistake," he said. "Bought into Cullen's bullshit for a little while, is all." He shrugged and finished his drink. "Live and learn. But want to know my biggest mistake when I got into this business? I should have gone after McGill's kid."

"Wouldn't she be the lucky girl," I said.

I walked away then, the way Daniel should have. If somebody was watching us, I didn't want them to get the idea that I was the jackass.

But Gorton couldn't resist shouting after me, as a way of getting the last word.

"It must kill you," he said, "knowing that if your mom wins on Sunday, I do, too."

I waved without looking back and kept walking, picking up the pace as I made the turn at the end of the bleachers.

The truth was, I had nothing.

Even Steve Gorton was right once in a while.

ONE HUNDRED TWELVE

Maggie

BY THE TIME MAGGIE heard her name called by the in-gate announcer, Becky had just gone clean, and was on her way out of the ring as Maggie was on her way in.

Becky smiled at her mother and nodded. Maggie smiled back. Nothing left to be said, by either one of them. This was as close to the Olympics as Maggie had been since Lord Stanley. She didn't want to think about that now, or Daniel, or how much might be on the line today. Tried to clear her mind, but couldn't, couldn't stop it from racing as she walked her horse out, and heard the public address announcer formally introducing her and Coronado.

All she had to do then was wait for the buzzer to sound.

When they were out there, Coronado was nearly perfect, fast and clean, running as well as he had all spring, no worries for Maggie, none, about the possibility of a time fault. Not today. No, this already felt like one of those dream days when everything was in sync between her and her horse, when Coronado knew what to do before Maggie even had to ask him.

They were four fences from the end when her left foot came out of its stirrup.

It happened out of nowhere, Coronado landing

awkwardly after clearing the rollback fence. It had happened to her before. Happened to all riders from time to time. The last time for Maggie was her first time in Gus's ring, when she'd first gotten back on her horse. Now she jammed the foot back in, same as she had that day. It was what you did. Remembered it hurting like hell at the time.

Today the pain felt as if the knee had exploded, as if she'd done something to the ligaments all over again.

Like stitches popping.

The pain shot up her leg, intense enough to momentarily blur her vision. Maggie bit down on her lip so hard she thought it might be bleeding.

But she rode through the pain. Had to. Pretended it was a bad muscle cramp. Three jumps left. Two a combination.

Keep going.

"*Come on!*" she yelled.

Not yelling at the big horse. At herself. The power in her riding came from her legs. She just couldn't do it now, at least not with both of them. It was all Coronado now.

No problems on the combination. Just seven strides now to the last jump. Maggie told herself not to rush him. He had this. *They* had this.

Goddamn, her knee hurt.

One last long stride to the fence.

Coronado did all the work from there, even though Maggie's heart briefly dropped a couple of floors when she felt one of his hind legs brush the rail.

It stayed up.

They'd made it around clean.

Maggie whipped her head around, saw her time, saw that she was a second under the time allowed.

She was into the jump-off. The knee wasn't hurting any less. But in that moment, it wasn't hurting any more, either.

As she passed Gus, he looked up at her and said, "What happened there at the rollback? You looked like you seized up for a second or something?"

She forced a smile.

"Or something," she said.

"You want to get off and walk around a little before you go back out there?"

"Not so much," she said.

ONE HUNDRED THIRTEEN

BECAUSE OF OUR TIMES, Mom and I were in the middle of the pack for the jump-off. She was going fourth, I was going fifth. Tyler, with the best time in the round, would go last. Matthew Killeen got an early rail. So did Eric Glynn.

Tess McGill had just rocked everybody on the grounds by announcing that her horse, Volage, had come up lame and couldn't go in the jump-off. No one knew the extent of the injury, at least not yet, and what that would do to her Olympic chances. But I couldn't worry about that right now, as much as I liked Tess. There was work to be done, first with Mom, who seemed to be grimacing slightly when we left the schooling ring. I asked if she was okay.

"Fine," she said. "Just tweaked my knee a little."

She moved ahead of me to the in-gate. One more time I felt almost as nervous for her as I did for myself.

But just almost.

Felt as if I were holding my breath the whole time she was out there, until she'd gone clean, with a time of 36.1. Flawless round. Maggie Atwood at her very best.

My turn.

Following Mom again, trying to get ahead of her at the same time.

We got this, I told myself as Sky flew around the first half of the course.

We got this.

But just like that, after she'd cleared the water jump with ease, no small feat for a small horse, I could feel her tiring. It happened sometimes, happened to all horses. One more thing they knew and couldn't tell us. When she started to make a wide turn going into the rollback, I had no choice but to take her outside, knowing that the time it cost us would probably make all the difference. It did.

We came in at 36.7.

One rider left. Our dear friend Tyler. With as much on the line today as anybody. If he could beat Mom's time and win, he would jump past both of us in the Olympic rankings. I liked to joke with Gus that I'd leave the numbers to him. The fact was, I knew all the numbers, down to decimal points, even knowing that sometimes the numbers weren't the only determining factor with the ones on the Selection Committee, that they'd also apply an eye test in the run-up to the Summer Games, and decide who they thought the hottest riders were near the top of the list.

It turned out to be his day, simple as that. Not Mom's. Not mine. By the time he finished he had blown both of us away, with a time of 35 flat. First place today. First place in the rankings. Just like that.

Tyler, waving to the crowd as if he'd already won an Olympic gold medal, was first to walk out to the center of the ring for the awards ceremony, right after telling Mom and me that Steve Gorton could come down here and kiss his skinny ass in front of everybody.

Mom watched him and said, "A charm school dropout until the end."

She followed Tyler out after the PA announcer called her name. Then I followed her one last time. She sometimes limped slightly after her rounds, because of her knee surgery. It seemed more noticeable today.

"Hey, you sure you're okay?" I said.

"Never better," she said over her shoulder.

ONE HUNDRED FOURTEEN

I WAS HAVING BREAKFAST with Dad at Too-Jays, a Wellington deli he liked because it reminded him of New York. He wanted to bring me up to speed on Daniel. It had been a week since he'd gotten arrested.

"Finally, some good news," he said. "Later today I'm going to get the assault charge tossed."

"Shut up!" I said. "That fast?"

"I needed help from a decent assistant DA and an even more decent judge," he said. "But yeah."

"This is *way* cool," I said.

He held up a hand.

"But I need to explain why it's not *all* the news," he said.

"Will this explaining make my head hurt?"

"Immigration law for dummies coming right up," he said.

"Hey."

He took me through it as quickly as he could, reviewing how Daniel's late DACA renewal application had started him down an immigration rabbit hole even before he threw his punch at Steve Gorton and enabled ICE to slap what Dad called a "detainer" on Daniel and throw him into custody. But now with him confident the assault rap was about to go away, they could eventually restore Daniel's DACA status and, with a little help from some friends, get the immigration case against him dropped, and get Daniel released.

"What kind of help?" I said. "And what kind of friends?"

"Working on that," he said. "Lots of moving pieces still."

"How long is all that going to take?" I said.

"That's the bad news to go along with the good news," he said. "It can take up to six months."

"Shit!" I said, too loudly, getting the attention of the old people at the closest tables, and maybe those in line at the cash register. "Even if you get him off, he's still screwed in terms of making it to Paris."

"But getting him out of that hellhole is job one," Dad said, "and two, and three. Then the line can really get moving. And as much as you want him to get to Paris, I just want to get him back to Wellington, Florida."

"How *are* you vaporizing the assault charge?" I said.

He grinned.

"I persuaded Gorton to drop it," he said.

"You must be joking," I said.

"I joke about a lot of things," he said. "But not about something as important as your boyfriend."

"Told you before," I said. "Not my boyfriend."

"This is me you're talking to," Dad said. "I see the way you look when you talk about him. He looks the same way when he talks about you. I don't need to be a lawyer to figure that one out. Just your father."

Then he slid his phone across the table. He said the

video was ready to go, just to make sure the volume was low before I hit Play.

"Got this from one of the waiters who was working the tent that night," he said. "He'd gone out back to have a smoke. Heard some loud voices from the road leading down to the parking lot. Recognized our friend Gorton and decided to shoot some video for his own amusement."

"How'd you find him?" I said.

Dad shrugged. "When you're good," he said, "you're good."

And there were all the good parts: Gorton calling Daniel *"chico"* and objectifying me for all the world to hear. Gorton putting his hands on Daniel and throwing the first punch. Finally, there was Steve Gorton nearly bursting into tears when he saw all the blood on his clothes.

"What did he say?" I asked. "Gorton, I mean. When you showed this to him."

"Tried to be a tough guy," Dad said. "Told me he had lawyers to make things like that go away. I had to tell him at that point that Daniel's lawyer was better."

"You."

"Me."

"My hero," I said.

"Many people might say superhero," he said.

He dipped some toast into what was left of his eggs over easy, drank his coffee before waving at the waitress that we needed more.

"Anyway," he said, "that's pretty much all of it, at least for now. Still a long way to go."

There was something about the way he said it.

"Pretty much all of it?" I said.

"Well, I might have mentioned something to

Gorton about the video, just in case I needed him to do us a favor someday," he said.

"Don't make me beg," I said.

"Actually, it was just three letters," Dad said. "TMZ."

ONE HUNDRED FIFTEEN

MOM HAD GOTTEN HER MRI results back that afternoon, Dr. Garry informing her that she'd suffered an "incomplete" tear of the ligament he'd repaired when she first got hurt. He told her that in a non-Olympic year, he'd recommend arthroscopic surgery, and she'd be as good as new in a month.

"Not good enough," she said.

Then she asked if she could hurt it more by continuing to ride. He said that he wouldn't recommend it but he couldn't stop her.

"But he warned me there were going to be days when it hurt like hell," Mom said. "I told him not going to Paris would hurt a hell of a lot more."

We'd just finished dinner at the house and had brought our drinks into the living room. Wine for Mom and me. Whiskey for Gus. Before her fainting spell, Grandmother had never been much for drinking, maybe an occasional glass of wine. Since the fainting spell she'd stopped completely. Mostly her drink of choice was strong black tea.

"Then he told me not to get into any ass-kicking contests for a while," Mom continued. "I told him that's what the Olympics were."

We were getting ready to watch the announcement show on NBCSN for show jumping, the sport's first time presenting it this way. By now, I'd had nearly a full week to convince myself that I was going to be the alternate and that Mom and Tess and Tyler would be the ones riding in Paris, in both events, individual and team.

"I'm prepared for it, I really am," I said, not speaking to anyone in particular, more stream of consciousness. "Mom and Tyler have done it longer. They've got results going back years, not a couple of months. It's going to be them. Totally. I get it. I do."

"Who are you," Grandmother said, "and what have you done with Becky McCabe?"

"Consider yourself lucky," Gus said to her. "I've been listening to this crap all week in the ring."

"Then we get it when she gets home," Maggie said, "on what feels like a continuous loop."

"You guys know I'm right," I said. "Especially you, Mom. Both you and Tyler were already short-listed coming into the year. And the last thing the selectors saw was Tyler dusting me in the Hamptons when I had a great chance to win. If I'd done that, we wouldn't be having this conversation, I'd already have punched my ticket to Paris."

"*We* aren't having this conversation," Grandmother said. "*You* are."

"The show's coming on," Gus said. "Can we turn up the volume on the set and mute Becky at the same time?"

I sipped some wine, still working on my first glass. I'd briefly considered walking down to the barn after we finished dinner and not coming back until the announcement had been made. But in the end, I knew I couldn't *not* watch, as Mike Tirico welcomed everybody to the show. His cohost was Bitsy Morrissey, one of the all-time great American riders, who'd competed until last year before finally retiring from competition at the age of sixty-five.

Right away they started to drag things out, milk the drama for all it was worth. Mike Tirico let Bitsy explain the selection process to the audience, and how some of the best riders wouldn't be going to Paris, starting with Tess McGill, whose horse had been diagnosed with cellulitis after the Hampton Invitational, Bitsy pointing out how it was the same thing that had stopped Lord Stanley when Maggie Atwood was sure she was on her way to the Olympics in London.

And Bitsy talked about how it was about more than just numbers, and how that made it much more difficult for the people picking the team, especially in a year like this when the top riders were grouped so closely at the top of the rankings.

"Blah blah blah," I said.

"Hush," Grandmother said.

On the television screen Bitsy Morrissey then said, "And Mike, it's worth reminding the viewers, especially on a night like this, that the enduring beauty of our sport never changes: Men competing against women, men and women my age competing against riders a third of our ages, men or women. Nick Skelton, from England, won the gold in Rio at the age of fifty-eight. If Becky McCabe makes the team tonight, she'll get her chance at the gold medal at the age of twenty-one."

"Big if," I said.

"And she might get a chance to do it alongside her mother, Maggie Atwood," said Mike.

"*Hush!*" Grandmother said, even louder than before.

They took everybody through the rankings then, right before showing some of the interview NBC had done with Mom and me a few days ago at the barn, on the chance that we both did make the team for Paris.

"In truth, Mike," Bitsy Morrissey said, "it's Becky McCabe who's the outlier. Her and her horse, Sky. At the start of the year, neither one of them was supposed to be here."

"Becky McCabe the alternate, she means," I said.

Gus said to my mom, "Can you send her to her room?"

"It never worked," Mom said sadly.

Ten minutes from the end of the half-hour show, after they'd tortured those of us in the room that long, they finally got to it, Mike Tirico actually holding up an envelope as they did at the Academy Awards. The riders' names would be read in the order they'd been chosen, first to fourth, including the alternate.

"But first," he said, "one more message from our sponsors."

"Kill me now!" I yelled.

At least they didn't kill more time when they came back from commercial.

"First is Tyler Cullen," Tirico said. "No surprise there. He's been at the top of the rankings for the past three years, and now qualifies for his first Olympic team."

When Gus and I would watch videos of my rides, he'd sometimes point out that I wasn't breathing. I wasn't breathing now.

"The second name on the list, and we've just told you about her inspiring comeback story, is veteran Maggie Atwood," Tirico said.

A cheer exploded in the living room. Roof raiser. Everybody shouting except Mom. I looked over at her. She just sat quietly in the chair she'd moved over next to Gus, still staring at the TV set motionless. I started across the room from the couch to give her a hug. She held up a hand.

"Let him finish," Mom said. She smiled now. "And by the way? Veteran just means old."

Mike Tirico turned to Bitsy Morrissey now.

"Any prediction on who's next?" he said.

"It has to be Rich Grayson and Becky McCabe," she said. "It's just the question of who's the alternate."

"Out with it!" Grandmother yelled.

I hid my face behind a pillow, knees up to my chest, the way I would when I was watching a scary movie in this room when I was a kid.

One more pause from Mike Tirico.

Then he smiled and said, "The third rider on the team is...Becky McCabe." He smiled. "The young woman Bitsy called the outlier is *in*. And she's going to compete alongside her mother!"

More cheering in the room, even louder than before. We never heard Mike Tirico announce that Rich was the alternate.

Now I got off the couch and went over and hugged my mother.

"Damn," I said, "we did it."

"Didn't we, though?" she said.

Paris

ONE HUNDRED SIXTEEN

MOM AND I scored a two-bedroom apartment at the Olympic Village, which had been built in the Seine-Saint-Denis area outside of Paris. Mom had said that at her age, she was too old for dorm life. But the place was new, clean, spacious, even quiet, despite the fact that there were fifteen thousand athletes from all over the world living in the Village. And when we weren't riding, we were hanging out at the Hotel Pont Royal downtown, where Grandmother had booked rooms for her and Gus.

We'd been in Paris a full week before marching with the United States team in the Opening Ceremonies. Me and Mom, along with the NBA players and tennis players and America's best golfers, swimmers, and track and field stars filed into the Stade de France, which became the selfie capital of the world.

When we weren't riding, we'd all eaten well and seen as many of the obligatory tourist sights as we could. Mom had occasionally gotten Gus to go along with her and Grandmother and me, even though he kept saying that the only tourist attraction he cared about was the inside of the ring where our competition would be held, about twelve miles outside of central Paris, at the Chateau de Versailles. That's where they'd built the horse park for equestrian events. The ring, the far end of the property near the Grand Canal, had officially been named Etoile Royale. Gus just called it "The Royal."

As much as he liked to be a professional grump, though, he was clearly enjoying himself. He was even working well with an old competitor of his, Charlie Benedict, the official show-jumping boss for the US team. His title was "Chef d'Equipe." Gus said that made him sound like he should be cooking at one of the fancy restaurants where we'd been eating. Charlie and Gus were the same age and had come up through the ranks together. Everybody had figured Charlie as an alternate on the team that went to Beijing in 2008. That was before Gus got hurt. But now they'd made it to Paris together, with our team, enduring the wait for the first day of competition.

Which had now blessedly arrived. There were still two hours before the competition would begin. But we were all out walking the course. You got out there a lot earlier at the Olympics.

"Long way from Wellington, right?" Charlie said to me.

"I keep looking around for Marie Antoinette's horse," I said.

Mom said, "Here's hoping things work out better for us in the end than they did for her."

Seventy-five riders today, from all over the world, in the qualifying round. By the end of the afternoon, that number would be cut down to the thirty who'd compete for the individual gold medal two days from now, on Friday night. After that there would be a two-round competition for the team gold medal, beginning Sunday. It meant that after everything that had happened over the past few months, it all came down to these six days and nights. Yeah.

Charlie Benedict was right, I thought. *We are one hell of a long way from Wellington.*

If there was any kind of favorite here, it was the Irish team, just because both Matthew Killeen and Eric Glynn had had such tremendous years, not just in the States but all over the world. But the draw for the qualifying was random. I was going forty-eighth in the order. Mom was going tenth.

We had moved over to the schooling ring, waiting for Seamus to arrive with Coronado. Gus was with Mom and me.

"Listen," he said, "I'm not going to tell you that this is just another ring. You're not idiots and neither am I. But once you get out there, then this does become every qualifier you've ever ridden in. You've got one job: Get to the next round. Today that means getting into the top thirty and living to fight another day."

"Sounds easy when you put it that way," I said. "Piece of cake, really."

"French pastry," Mom said.

"But you need to know something else," Gus said. "Everything is going to feel bigger when you get out there. Look bigger. The jumps will probably look higher. Just the way it is, for you and the horses. So you gotta be ready for anything. And everything. It's the Olympics. Shit happens."

Seamus came walking into the ring with Coronado. Gus spun his chair around, heading over to where the ring announcer sat. When he was out of earshot Mom said, "I want this for him."

"Not as much as he wants it for you," I said.

"Hey," she said. "He's your trainer, too."

"He likes me," I said. "He's in love with you."

"As somebody I know likes to say," she said, "blah blah blah," before Seamus helped her up.

Gus was out in the middle of the ring by then, next to one of the practice jumps, his focus on her so intense as she began to canter Coronado, I was surprised she wasn't bursting into flames. I knew how excited and scared she was. Probably more scared than excited. I felt the same way. But she looked happy that the waiting was almost over, and she was up on her horse. For once, she was probably thrilled that she was going early in the class.

Before long, they were calling out the names of the first six riders in the ring. I knew by now that Gus wanted to watch alone, from his usual spot to the right of the gate. I had my competitor's badge around my neck—at the Olympics the badge only came off when it was time to compete. Or went to bed. And maybe not even then. I knew I had plenty of time before Emilio brought Sky up here. So I made my way down to the opposite end of the ring, in the grassy area between the outside fence and the stands. Struck one more time by the size of the place, and how everything inside seemed to be perfect, from the different-colored rails to the fresh white paint on the oxers and skinnies to the shrubbery, which looked as if it had been planted that morning. Even the footing, which had just been dragged in anticipation of the first horses and riders, looked brand new.

I kept taking in the whole scene in front of me, thinking, *It isn't just the stakes that are as high as they've ever been and might ever be for Mom and me. Gus was right: even the damn jumps look higher*. My heart suddenly made me feel as if I'd run all the way here from the Village.

I'd been in college eight months ago. Now we were both here. I found the small, roped-off area where competitors could watch, past where the photographers were set up. I heard someone shouting my name from the stands, realized it could only be the voice of Steve Gorton, with whom we'd had to endure one drink a few nights ago at the Hemingway Bar at the Ritz. I ignored him. Maybe he thought we were about to have a moment. We weren't. In the end, he didn't know anything about us, or what was about to happen in the Royal.

About twenty minutes later, having watched the first riders into the ring, I looked down at the in-gate and saw Mom and Coronado. The PA announcer told the crowd who she was and where she was from and who owned her horse. There was a polite cheer for them. Then it was briefly as if the sound had been turned off. I stared at Mom. For one last moment, she and Coronado were completely still, before she moved the big horse away from the gate and out into the middle of the ring.

She'd finally made it to the Olympics.

Then, as she waited for the buzzer to sound, Coronado suddenly spooked and reared up.

ONE HUNDRED SEVENTEEN

Maggie

MAGGIE DIDN'T PANIC, even as she was holding on for dear life, managing to stay on her horse the way she hadn't been able to hold on that day on the trail when it had been a fox spooking her horse.

The good news was that she wasn't on the clock yet. She knew she had time to get Coronado under control, if she could, before the buzzer finally did sound. She still couldn't believe this was happening, when it was happening. Gus had told her there shouldn't be any surprises over the first part of the course.

What about before her course even began?

Only one thing to do. Lean forward and hope like hell he stopped. If you leaned the other way all you were doing is pulling the horse back, maybe on top of you.

But Coronado stopped rearing as suddenly as he'd started. Maggie circled him back toward the in-gate. She had no idea what had spooked him. But it didn't matter what. Something had.

She made a wide turn around, moving him back into position. As much as her mind was racing, she did manage this one fleeting thought:

Better now than when we're out there.

Then he started to shake his head.

It was as if whatever had bothered him a few moments before was bothering him all over again. She knew she was out of time. The buzzer was about to sound. If she couldn't get him under control, she would be eliminated before she ever got to the first jump.

Maggie kicked him then.

She'd never needed to really kick this horse. She did now. The buzzer sounded as she did. If she wasn't in total control of Coronado, they were at least on course. They were in the game.

Get one fence underneath us.

After all the plans she and Gus had made for this course and this round, that was the only plan now.

Coronado got over the first jump. Then the next. Then came a combination. Then a rollback.

All clear.

So far so good. Still such a long way to go. Maggie wasn't getting ahead of herself. But then they were through the first half of the course clear. Another rollback coming up, much tighter than before, a bitch of a turn. The big horse got his head turned around, though, in a good way this time, and then they were coming up on the water jump now, the pool behind the fence looking wide enough today as if it needed one of those Paris bridges over it.

Coronado got over the rail, over the water.

She had her horse under control. Finally had her breathing under control. She went clean over an oxer on the right side, was heading along the fence at the opposite end of the ring from where the in-gate was, toward some photographers, when one of them wearing a bright red vest got up and ran to another position.

He was right there in Maggie's sight line.

And Coronado's.

The photographer should have known enough to wait, with a horse coming straight for him. He didn't. And that was all it took to spook her horse. Again. His head was all over the place.

Maggie kicked him harder this time. Telling herself she'd apologize to him later. It worked. Again. But he wasn't entirely squared up yet, was drifting to the right just enough. Maggie was glad the oxer coming up on them was wide. If it was a skinny, half as wide, just one rail, she might have missed the fence entirely. But in that moment the oxer looked wide as a four-lane highway. Coronado cleared it. Made it through the combination. Up, down, up again.

Yes.

One more rollback. Two more fences after that. The last *was* a skinny. For a horse as big as hers, Maggie sometimes imagined trying to fit him through a doorway. But she gave him a perfect distance. His head was screwed on straight now.

With all that, she still felt him catch the rail with one of his hind legs.

Felt herself holding her breath as she waited for the crowd to tell her if the rail had come down. One of those moments in riding, less than a second, that always felt like an eternity, especially this close to the end.

The cheer she heard told her she'd gone clear.

She didn't need to go clean today. But she wanted to. She wanted to post a time this early in the round, set a tone, for everything that would come after this. And give herself confidence in the process. Mission accomplished. Nightmare beginning today. Pretty much a dream finish.

As she rode past Gus, he grinned at her.

"Interesting ride," he said.

"Yeah," Maggie said, "if you like roller coasters."

ONE HUNDRED EIGHTEEN

MAYBE IT WAS WATCHING Mom's near calamity with Coronado. Or maybe all the waiting for this round had finally gotten to me, on a night when I actually wished I had been able to go early the way Mom had, post what was still the best time, then be sitting around watching everybody chase me.

But suddenly all the doubts I'd had about myself in the run-up to the selection show—all the self-doubt that was still in my DNA despite the year I'd had, despite being *here*—was hitting me like this huge wave, one I didn't see coming, like I was standing on the beach and had turned my back on the ocean.

How many times had Gus drilled it into my head that I needed to act like I belonged?

But what if I didn't?

There was a screen in the schooling ring that listed the next riders in the order. I wasn't on it yet. The round seemed to be taking forever. Sky still hadn't left her stall. I went and grabbed a folding chair from the viewing area some of the trainers used back here and carried it out of the ring and behind the scoreboard and sat alone and tried to convince myself that I wasn't having a panic attack.

I'd had them occasionally as a teenager, when I first started competing. The last one had been at Tryon, in

Carolina, the first time I competed outside of Florida. I didn't tell anybody about it. I hadn't told anybody about the previous ones. Just got my shit together and told myself I was being an idiot and got on my horse and finished third. And told myself I was never going to feel that way again. And hadn't.

Until now.

It wasn't a case of nerves I was feeling now. This was beyond that, as irrational as it all felt. This was fear. Like that universal dream about getting ready to take a final exam without having been to class all semester.

Only the whole world was going to watch me start to take this final exam, and soon.

My dad told me one time about a famous basketball player, I forget which one, some great old-time player, who used to get sick before every single game.

I felt that way now.

Bad Becky, my ass. All of a sudden, I was back to feeling like a frightened little girl. It made no sense. There it was, anyway.

I saw Gus come around the corner.

"Been looking for you," he said.

"Well," I said, "you found me."

"You okay?"

"No."

I put my hands to my face and rubbed hard. When I pulled them away, I said, "I'm scared shitless, if you want to know the truth."

He made a snorting noise.

"Is that all?" he said.

"Is that all?"

It was still just the two of us back here. It was as if we'd found the only quiet place at the Olympics.

"Are you kidding me?" he said. "Everybody with

a *horse* is scared here. And not just riders, in case you were wondering. When your mother's horse lost his shit out there, you know what I did? I covered my goddamn eyes, that's how scared *I* was. *Me.*"

"But what if this is the day when Sky refuses again?" I said. "What if she spooks the way she did on me that day when it was just us in the ring?" The words just spilled out of me now, my voice sounding way too loud. "You heard Bitsy on that show. She said I'm the one who wasn't supposed to be here. Well, what if I'm really not?"

He moved the chair closer to me and took my hands. I couldn't ever remember him doing that. Behind him I could see that Emilio and Sky were here.

"We are going to get back inside this ring now, and you are going to ride your horse like a goddamn champion," he said.

I started to say something. He still had my hands and gave them a squeeze.

"Shut up and listen," he said.

I waited.

"In your life you have never heard me talk about what happened to me when I got thrown, or what I lost that day," he said. "So I'm gonna tell you this just one time: I want you to think about what I would give to get the kind of chance you have today."

"Okay," I said finally, just because I couldn't think of what else to say.

"We're never having this conversation again," he said.

"Okay," I said.

He let go of my hands.

"Now go ride your ride," he said.

ONE HUNDRED NINETEEN

SKY AND I WERE in the ring twenty minutes later and they were introducing me as her rider and her owner. Rebecca Atwood McCabe. Wellington, Florida. United States of America.

Gus hadn't said another word to me, not while I was warming Sky up, not as we made our way into Etoile Royale. Mom had totally kept her distance. Forty-seven riders had been in this ring by now. Mom *still* had the best time, at 75.5.

I knew I didn't have to beat her time. Didn't need to even go clean to make it to Friday. You could make it to Friday, give yourself a chance at the gold medal jump-off, with a rail down today. Or even two, depending what happened after I finished my round.

I didn't intend to find out if I might be one of them.

Screw that.

I still wasn't convinced I'd rewired my brain, even after the talking-to that Gus had given me. There were still a lot of crazy thoughts spinning around inside my head. But I had made up my mind about this, now that I was out here:

I wasn't going to ride scared.

Screw that, too.

I didn't look around, didn't try to take in the moment. I just focused all of my concentration on the first jump. Tried to swallow. Felt as if my mouth was full of the footing underneath me.

The buzzer sounded.

I put Sky in motion.

And from that moment on, it was as if we were being chased by the other horses. Or daring them to chase us. My horse was fearless enough for both of us. If she was scared of anything, it was going slow. Nothing else. Not the size of the ring. Not the sound of the place. She went full tilt into every fence and turn, the first half of the course flying past us, making me feel as if I was looking out the window of a speeding car.

We were past the first rollback, then the first combination, then easing into the turn along the fence where Coronado had spooked again. I just let Sky run. It was one of those times when the real truth of what was happening came by doing as little thinking as possible about the process. Just letting it happen.

Finally, we were coming up on the water jump.

And the light off the water was blinding me.

Not sunlight reflecting off the pool, the way it had in our ring at Atwood Farm that day. Not at nine o'clock at night. It was all the lights that ringed the top of Etoile Royale, making night in here as bright as day. Like all the lights of the Olympics were smacking me in the face at once, high beams hitting Sky and me when she was four strides from the fence.

When it had happened back home, the light had stopped Sky dead in her tracks, and then I was the one flying through the air before landing on a fence.

I had no idea if that might happen here. Or what was about to happen here. No idea whether Sky would come to a dead stop again. Or keep going. Just put my head down and squeezed my eyes shut and held on and trusted my horse.

No time to even pray that Sky could see better than I could right now. I didn't open my eyes until I felt her go into her jump. I still couldn't see very well. But I could hear just fine.

And what I didn't hear was a splash.

"Hell, yeah!"

Finally, it was green light time with the last skinny fence dead ahead. Then she was over that one. When I looked at the replay later, looked at some of the photographs of that one jump, Sky looked as if she were higher in the air than she'd ever been in her life.

As soon as I could I got her turned around, like we had one last turn to make, I looked for our time, eyes very much back to being wide open.

74.5.

Up there in lights.

Just in a good way.

ONE HUNDRED TWENTY

BITSY MORRISSEY CAME OVER to the practice ring on Thursday morning with a TV crew to interview Mom and Tyler and me. Tyler had also gone clear on Wednesday, just with a time a full second behind Mom. He'd still be going right before her in the first round on Friday afternoon. The US team had the three best times. The three of us were last in the order. Simon LaRouche, born in Paris and the hometown favorite, would go before Tyler. Matthew Killeen and Eric Glynn before him.

"What's it like being on the same team with this mother–daughter act?" Bitsy asked Tyler. "I'm told there might have been some tension between you and them in the past."

Tyler grinned.

"Let's put it this way," he said. "I've grown since then."

"Well," Mom said, "not *literally,* Tyler."

He managed a laugh, whether he meant it or not, before Bitsy asked me what Tyler was like as a teammate.

"Your basic annoying older brother," I said.

Tyler laughed at that, too. We were at least getting along. It didn't mean I'd forgotten all the crap things he'd tried to do, and the things he'd said to Mom and Grandmother. But he'd been tolerable since we'd all gotten to Paris, if not likable. And whatever happened tomorrow, the three of us would be trying to win a team gold medal together next week.

Mom had brought a change of clothes with her from the Village. When we'd finished hacking our horses, she and Gus were off to meet Grandmother in the city. It was a good thing, for them, and for me. Even living together, I wanted to put some distance between Mom and me until we were the last two riders into the ring tomorrow, not just for the first round because we'd had the best times yesterday, but maybe even for the jump-off that would decide who would win the gold medal.

I still had to wait a whole day to find all that out.

I took a long walk around the Village, listening to music. Then made another lap. When I was finally back in the apartment, around dinnertime, I put on the television and tried to watch gymnastics. It did absolutely nothing to calm my nerves. Actually, made things worse. I made it through fifteen minutes, feeling as if I were making every move with them, knowing that any slip on the balance beam, or on the dismount, could cost them a chance at a medal. All it took was one bad moment, one false step, to cost them everything they'd trained for, and dreamed about themselves.

One mistake.

Like the kind you could make in the ring, on your way up to the next fence.

After I'd made myself a salad and managed to eat some of it, I got back on the bus and went over to the equestrian park and went down to the stall to be with Sky. She seemed as happy to see me as I was to see her, and not just because I'd brought my girl extra carrots, and even thrown in a couple of mints.

I stayed with her for about an hour, went back to the apartment, and watched yesterday's round a few times, feeling myself get nervous all over again as we approached the water jump, even knowing that we made it. Blinded by the light? Who sang that?

Every time I watched, I saw how perfect Sky had been, how cool she'd been running when I was the one blinded by the light. But it was only the preliminary, Gus had reminded me that morning. Tomorrow, he said, tomorrow was the main event.

I tried to watch a movie in English, couldn't remember a thing that had happened or a thing anybody had said before I turned off the set and went to bed and somehow managed to fall asleep. Then didn't stir until I heard Mom coming in. Checked my phone and saw that it was still just ten thirty.

I saw my door open slightly and Mom put her head in.

"You awake?" she said.

"Kind of," I said.

I sat up. She walked over and sat at the end of my bed the way she used to when I was little.

"How was your night?" I asked.

"Snootiest restaurant yet," she said.

"Low bar," I said.

"Go back to sleep," she said. "I heard somewhere we've both got a big day tomorrow."

When she got to the door I said, "Mom?"

She stopped and turned around.

"Wish there was a way we could both win tomorrow," I said.

"Get over it," she said.

ONE HUNDRED TWENTY-ONE

THERE WAS A PRETTY DECENT cloud cover over the ring when we were walking it the next morning. I told Gus and Mom it could stay there all afternoon as far as I was concerned.

"I don't need no sunlight reflecting off that pool today," I said.

As soon as I said it, as soon as I heard the words, I turned to Gus.

"Sorry," I said.

"Don't be," he said. And grinned. "I don't need no sun in anybody's eyes today, either."

Then he said, "What do you think of the course?"

"I'll tell you in my bad French accent," I said. "It *eez,* how we say, bru-*tal.*"

One rollback in the first part of the course and a combination. A double. Then another rollback in the second half, followed by a triple. Then the water. Then one more turn, and a spring to the last fence.

Yeah.

Bru-*tal.*

By the time Tyler was at the in-gate, Simon LaRouche had just made the crowd go wild by going clean. He was in the jump-off along with Matthew and Eric. Mom and I had come over from the schooling ring to watch Tyler. Both of us up on our horses.

"Good luck," I said to him, and actually meant it. Still wasn't giving him a pass on the things he'd done or tried to do. But he had been trying to get here as long as Mom had.

He gave me a quick, surprised, sideways glance and then said, "Thanks."

His mistake, his false step, came at the water jump. It wasn't the glare off the water. The afternoon had gotten a little darker, if anything.

It was rider error all the way.

I could see halfway to the fence that he'd given Galahad a bad distance, after what had been a flawless round until then. He was going to be short. For all of Tyler's obsession with Coronado, Galahad was a pretty terrific horse himself, or they wouldn't be here.

But when they got to the jump, Galahad was just too far away, and there wasn't a damn thing Tyler Cullen could do about it. He tried to get his horse closer at the last second. Not even a second.

Just too late.

Galahad stopped.

This time it was Tyler Cullen coming out of the saddle and off his horse, going over Galahad's head.

The horse didn't clear the fence.

Tyler did.

And belly-flopped into the pool.

ONE HUNDRED TWENTY-TWO

Maggie

MAGGIE COULD BARELY WATCH from the in-gate as Tyler made the long walk of shame out of the ring, soaking wet, after his trainer had collected Galahad.

It had been a long time since Maggie and Tyler had thought of themselves as friends, or anything close. She still remembered the night at the Trophy Room when he'd basically told her she was washed up. But they were teammates now. This was the Olympics. More than anything, he was a fellow rider. She felt terrible about what had happened to him and happened here. At least he'd landed on his stomach and not his back. Or arm. Or shoulder. At least he hadn't come down on the fence.

It reminded her of what had happened with Coronado on the trail that day, at the worst possible time.

They'd given her a few extra minutes while Tyler and his horse had left the ring, to warm applause from the crowd. All in attendance were show-jumping fans who understood how much Tyler had lost, even with the team competition still to come.

But Maggie needed to forget that, and forget him, unsee what had just happened and do that *right now*. She had to get her mind right, and quickly, and stop thinking about what could go wrong, and just *go*.

Ride *your* ride, she told herself.

Barely heard her introduction. Just the buzzer. Then she and Coronado were moving, into the course, no problem with the first jumps, no problem with the first rollback. Quickly she was into the first combination, feeling a slight chip on the second fence, on the way up, nothing more.

She felt as if she were through the first half of the course in a blink, coming up on the water jump, telling herself Coronado had never had trouble with a water jump. And didn't now. Landed clear out of the water, by what felt like a country mile.

They were coming up on the triple now.

Even at this pace, Maggie's vision once more registered in slow motion. A good thing. The line. The distance. Don't think. Just react.

We've got this.

Easy as one, two, three.

Two jumps to go. They made the turn, she squared him up.

One fence left.

The skinny.

Trying to keep her breathing and her emotion under control. Feeling her excitement rise, wondering if her horse could feel it, too. They were over the last fence and finishing clear then. Even then she couldn't make herself slow Coronado down right away, made one more turn before she allowed herself to look at her time, 77.1, as she heard the ring announcer say, *"Premier place."*

Four riders in the jump-off for the gold medal now, Matthew and Eric and Simon. And Maggie.

Her kid trying to make it five.

By the time Maggie came out of the ring, Becky was already out there.

ONE HUNDRED TWENTY-THREE

I WAS OUT THERE as soon as Mom looked up at her time.

I didn't want to say anything to her, not right now. Didn't even want to make eye contact. She'd ridden her horse. I needed to ride mine. I was happy for her, no doubt. When she had been asked to deliver, she had produced, at least for now, the ride of her life. I knew how much she wanted this.

But more than ever, I knew how much I did.

I had shocked everybody, including myself, by making it this far. It didn't matter if I didn't make it to the jump-off, if Matthew and Eric and Mom were the ones competing for the gold medal and not me.

Now I was the one being asked to deliver. Me and my horse. You never knew until you were out there. You always had to wait to find out. And what I found out, quickly, was that Sky had saved her best for today.

These weren't 1.6 m jumps; today felt half that high, as if we were covering speed bumps. By the time we got to the water jump, she was in the zone and so was I.

We cleared the water, breezed through the triple. I didn't have to ask for anything. She just nailed it like a champ.

Two fences left. The hardest jumps behind us, the hardest turns. Made the last soft turn. Cleared the oxer.

One to go. To go clean and keep going to the real main event.

"Let's go!" I heard myself yelling.

Yelling at myself by then.

But three strides before the fence I felt her stumble slightly.

It was almost as if she'd stepped in a hole. Her first wrong step all day. As she made it, she started to turn her head to the right. The rest of her started to follow.

Shit.

I gave her a kick and it got her head squared up. She still took off late, managing to get her forelegs up and over the bright green rail.

But one of her hind legs hit it hard.

Not just hit it, but rattled the living shit out of it.

I felt all the air come out of me at once. Knew it had to be going down. I'd heard it and felt it. Waited to hear it from the crowd, one way or another. Up or down.

And then the crowd cheered.

Only then was I able to exhale, get Sky and me turned around, and allow myself a look at the scoreboard. Knowing I didn't need to be first. But still wanting to be first, wanting to beat them all, all day long.

76.8.

I'd gone faster than Mom, faster than the Irish guys, faster than everybody, at least for now. It wouldn't help me in the jump-off. But Mom and I would be the last two riders out there in the jump-off.

I thought: *Maybe this is the way the story is supposed to end*.

ONE HUNDRED TWENTY-FOUR

THEY DIDN'T WASTE any time starting the jump-off. The cloud cover had broken into rain and the day was getting very dark, very fast. I'd been too busy to notice that they'd put the lights on at the top of Etoile Royale.

Matthew Killeen went clean. Eric Glynn didn't. Then Simon LaRouche beat Matthew's time and he was in first place and the home crowd pretty much lost its shit.

In the steady downpour, I hadn't noticed Simon having any problem with the footing, didn't see the rain affecting his horse.

Mom and I were in the gate.

Gus said to Mom, "You'll be fine. You're gonna beat the rain. But even if you don't, the drainage for this ring is fantastic."

"You know this how?" Mom said.

"Because it's the Olympics, that's why," he said.

Mom was off the moment the buzzer sounded, trying to beat not only Simon's time, but the rain. Sometimes she liked to take one more look around. Not today.

I knew Simon's time was beatable, one hundred percent. Matthew had come in with 40.1. Simon was at 39.8. When we'd walked the jump-off course, I thought the winning time might be two seconds better than that. Simon had a really nice horse. He was a very good rider, especially in Europe. But he wasn't the rider Mom was. And didn't have the horse she had.

She had good pace from the start. In the early part of the course, nothing was slowing Mom and her horse. I hadn't paid any attention to Simon's splits, but my gut told me that neither he nor Matthew had attacked the course the way Mom was attacking it.

By now Coronado soared over the top rail, then cleared the water.

I closed my eyes as she came up on the second rollback. To me, this was her last real challenge, even more than the triple. If Coronado had a weakness, it was the way his size impacted sharp turns.

This time he lost just enough traction as he made his left turn, and she had no choice but to go outside instead of inside. Maybe cost her half a second. It wasn't because she was afraid. She just couldn't take a chance. And she knew that Simon *still* had a beatable time.

The triple now. I thought she had him too close to the second jump. But Coronado got over it. And the next one. And the next. If the rollback hadn't been the last trouble for her on this course, the triple should have been. Wasn't.

Just about everybody saw Mom's time before she got Coronado turned around, still being careful with him as she slowed him to a walk.

39 flat. Nearly a second faster than Simon LaRouche. Going outside hadn't cost her. As she was coming out

of the ring, I was going in. I could see how happy she was. She smiled at me. I smiled back, and nodded, and then was past her.

The skies opened then.

ONE HUNDRED TWENTY-FIVE

IT HAPPENED THAT FAST. Within a half minute the rain was blowing sideways, and I could barely see the fences. An end-of-the-world storm in Etoile Royale.

Maybe if this were a Grand Prix in Wellington, in the middle of April, they would have stopped things right here and waited it out, waited for the storm to pass, even this late in the round. But it was the Olympics. The judges were one rider away—me—from awarding gold.

I needed to get around this course. It didn't matter that the other riders, including Mom, had gone in better conditions. A storm like this would blow in and it didn't matter that some of the riders had already gotten around a dry course and others were now going to ride in the rain. It was part of the deal in our sport.

The idea of the first rollback, that first sharp turn, was scaring me to death. Not Sky. She got over the jump, breezing.

By now the water was pouring into my eyes off my helmet. The course was becoming more wet with every jump. Puddles were already forming. The rain was coming that hard.

I kept tight reins on Sky through the double. Then

we were clearing the pool. No splash there, before we started splashing our way toward the next fence. I knew I couldn't get reckless or go full throttle. But if I slowed down too much, I had no chance to win. And hadn't come this far to lose.

I put my head down.

Rode my ride.

We got over the jump on the last rollback. She slid a little, but I got her squared up. She got over. No time to celebrate. I slowed her down, just slightly, coming into the triple.

But she went clean there.

We made our last turn and didn't slide and got over the second-to-last jump and now it was just a sprint to the end of the course.

Or so I thought.

Sky's hind legs slipped and came out from under her then.

She didn't stop. But it was the same as her rearing up, even while still going forward between jumps. Just like that, the back of her was lower than her front and she started to go down.

ONE HUNDRED TWENTY-SIX

I HAD SEEN IT HAPPEN to riders before, their horse going backward and going down when their legs came out from under them that way, sometimes with the rider still in the saddle, sometimes with disastrous results.

It was happening to Sky now.

At least she was still going forward. If she could keep doing that, if she could stay up, we still had a chance. But whatever I was going to do to help her, I had to do right now.

And there wasn't much I could do to stabilize her. I lifted my hands up, squeezed her harder with my legs. But it was all up to Sky now, and the instinct she shared with all horses: not to go down.

She didn't.

One of those Olympic miracles.

Somehow she got her hind legs underneath her, and kept moving. Somehow I managed to keep her in line. Got her a good distance into the last jump. The skinny. They were known as verticals, too. Made them look higher than they actually were. Right now this one looked as tall as the Eiffel Tower.

Sky didn't care. She'd come this far, too. One more time she flew, and we'd gone clear. She skidded when she landed. It didn't matter now.

Then I heard the loudest cheers I'd ever heard, at least cheers for me. I turned and with my left glove did my best to rub water out of my eyes and squinted through the rain one last time.

I still couldn't see much in the ring, but I could see our number:

38.4.

I'd won the gold medal.

Mom had gotten silver. I yelled my head off then, knowing only Sky could hear me, the sound of the crowd combined with the sound of the storm. I walked Sky over to where Mom and Gus were.

"You were great!" Mom shouted up at me.

"So were you!"

"You're better!" she said.

"How did you keep that horse from going down?" Mom said.

I leaned down and shouted back at her.

"Way I was brought up."

I wasn't sure where to go then, what to do. Neither Gus nor Mom nor I had allowed ourselves to discuss what would happen if one of us won. So I didn't know when the medal ceremony would start, or even where. All I knew was that I needed a moment alone with my horse.

So I walked her back to the schooling ring, the footing in there nearly underwater by now. Emilio helped me down, then hugged me. I felt like a stupidly wet swamp thing and didn't care. I was stupidly happy. I walked over and leaned against the fence, put my head back as far as it would go and let the rain hit me in the face, not knowing whether to laugh or cry.

Then I walked back over to Sky and got close to her ear and told her, Bad Becky style, that holy shit, we just beat them all.

ONE HUNDRED TWENTY-SEVEN

Four days later

I WALKED ACROSS the schooling ring toward Tyler Cullen, about to do something I could never have imagined. But knowing I had to do it.

Tyler was roughly fifteen minutes away from being part of the jump-off that would decide who won the team gold medal. Five riders had qualified for the jump-off, and Tyler was one of them.

I wasn't.

Sky had finally gotten her first Olympic rail, on the last day of the team competition. But that was all it took to keep us from continuing. After everything my horse had done, she finally got tired. It was a cheap rail, at the third fence. It had shocked the hell out of me, just because of the way she'd performed every time we'd been in that ring, even in the rain. Didn't matter. She still had enough in her, and enough heart, to finish strong. We had come that close to going clean for the Olympics, giving ourselves a chance to throw what Gus called a perfect game. And had put more pressure on Mom and Tyler.

They were our team now. We'd all still win gold if their combined score took first in the jump-off. But all I could do now was watch, which wasn't how this part of the story was supposed to end:

Mom needed Tyler to get a gold medal.

And Tyler needed her to get one of his own.

I needed both of them.

The team competition had started out with twenty countries, cut to ten after the first round on Sunday afternoon. And after the final qualifying round tonight, only the five riders who'd gone clear remained. All of them would start even in the jump-off.

Teddy Milestone, from England, took the ring first. His horse knocked down two rails, one early, one late. Matthew was next in. He got one. But Eric had just gone clear. Now for the US—*us*—to win the gold medal, both Tyler and Mom had to go clean. Or, if one of them did get a rail, the other one had to beat Eric's time of 38.8.

That was the margin for error.

By now they were extending the time between horses entering the ring, maximizing the drama on the last night of the show-jumping competition. Tyler had complained after his first round that his back was seizing up, and he was worried about spasms. The slowdown allowed him a few extra minutes after Eric's round to get down and do some stretching.

It was right before he was ready to get back up on Galahad that I went over and gave him a hug, thinking it might be the craziest thing to happen in this whole crazy year.

"Not too hard!" he said.

"Sorry."

"Kidding."

I waved off Tyler's trainer then and helped him up myself.

"Sure," he said, "now you love me."

I grinned. "Love is kind of strong, frankly."

"Is this some insane shit or what?" he said. "It coming down to me and your mom, I mean."

The announcer in the schooling ring told him it was time.

Tyler winked at me.

"Don't worry, kid," he said. "I'm gonna kill it. Then tell your mom to do the same."

I gave him a fist bump, like he was my best friend. And for the next couple of minutes, he was going to be, if Mom was going to get one last shot at a gold medal, and I was going to get another. Insane shit indeed.

I gave Mom her space as she was getting ready for the jump-off. A good look at her revealed the nearly visible force field she put around herself in big moments. Even Gus gave her room. Now it was her turn to be the one who hadn't come this far to finish second.

Gus watched from the in-gate. I walked outside the fence, maybe twenty yards from him, and got ready to watch from there. Tyler Cullen. The guy with the rep for being better than his horses. But we didn't need that today. We just needed for him to be as good as his horse, on this day when he needed Mom and she needed him, after everything that had happened between them for months.

Couldn't make it up.

At breakfast Grandmother had said, "I can't believe that I have to root this hard for that little bastard."

"Get over it," Mom had said.

I'd laughed.

"What's so funny?" Grandmother had said.

"Inside joke," I'd said.

While Tyler waited for the buzzer in the middle of the ring, I heard a familiar voice calling my name from the stands. *Steve Gorton.*

Tyler had told us the other day about how he felt Gorton had strung him along just to mess with him, until he'd finally screwed him over. Tyler, being Tyler, had no sense of irony about the fact that they'd both tried to screw over Mom.

I turned around and found where Gorton was standing, saw him pointing at Tyler.

"My guy!" he shouted.

I just nodded and thought: *We finally have something in common.*

The two rollbacks on the short course were the places where you could win or lose. Rails could go down anywhere on the course. But to me, those were the two biggest trouble spots.

The weather was perfect today. The footing looked absolutely perfect after they dragged the course following the first round. Some sun, but not too much.

And then Tyler was out there riding a seamless course, with good pace, but not a reckless one. His technique, I thought, was pretty damn impressive considering what was on the line, all the way through the first combination. Then the second. With three fences left, I knew he was faster than Eric had been at this same point in the course. If he could stay clear and beat Eric's time, then Mom wouldn't need for Coronado to break the land speed record. She could even get a rail and still win.

Second rollback coming up now for Tyler, the tighter of the two. He went inside. Everybody before him had. His Olympics were over in three jumps. No reason to leave anything out there. Had his horse perfectly lined up after he came out of the turn, flying.

Galahad touched the rail with his left hind leg. I could see the fence clearly from where I was standing not more than twenty yards away. I could barely *hear* him touch it. All I saw was this ripple, like it had been hit by a strong breeze.

The rail ended up on the ground.

Now Mom didn't just have to go clean, she also had to be faster than Eric Glynn, or Ireland would win the team gold medal.

Our team would end up with silver.

And Mom would walk away with a second silver.

ONE HUNDRED TWENTY-EIGHT

Maggie

MAGGIE'S LEFT KNEE, the bad one, the one she was going to get fixed when she got home, had been killing her all afternoon.

Nobody to blame but herself. She'd walked too much since she'd gotten to Paris, the past couple of days walking the city alone, getting herself ready for this moment, for the whole thing coming down to her, in case it actually did. She'd spent hardly any time with Becky. Or Gus. Even her mother. Just walked. Even lit a candle at Cathedrale Notre-Dame. Now she was paying a physical price, at the worst possible moment. It wasn't just her knee hurting. It was her neck and back, too. If her horse wasn't slowing down this close to the finish, Maggie Atwood sure as hell was.

And now the whole thing *had* come down to her, and this ride. Tyler came out of the ring, head down, cursing loudly at himself. Maggie ignored him. She wasn't just thinking about going clean. She was clearing her mind. If she thought any more about what was on the line, how much this all meant to her, she might feel as sick as Becky said she had before her first round in the individual.

In all ways, she wanted this so much that it hurt. Becky had her gold medal. Now Maggie wanted her own. She didn't think she was owed one, or deserved one, because of her own crazy journey, and everything she'd gone through to get here.

She just wanted to nail this one last ride.

No issue with speed at the start. None with the rollback. Her knee was killing her now, even worse than it had in the schooling ring. How much time did she have left at the Olympics? Twenty seconds?

But as they came out of the combination, next fence, Coronado over-jumped, landed harder than he should have, and jarred her enough that her left foot came out of the stirrup.

Again.

Seriously?

This time there was no surprise or hesitation. After everything that had happened in this ring, to her and to Becky, Maggie was ready for anything and everything by now. She jammed the foot right back in. But as she did, she felt as if it sent a shock wave all the way up her left leg.

Focus.

Last rollback now. She went inside, no hesitation, she hadn't come this far to finish second again. She knew this was the fence that had just gotten Tyler. Such a cheap rail. Just a touch.

Now Coronado touched it with a hind leg. No idea which one. But Maggie heard it, felt it, and for one split-second felt herself die a little.

Waited one final time to hear it from the crowd. Up or down?

It had stayed up. Then Coronado was over the next jump, coming up on the last vertical.

He was over that, and clear.

Maggie didn't even wait to slow him down, just whipped her head around as soon as they were through the timers. It only made her neck and back hurt even more.

Maggie didn't care.

Her time was 38.3. Half a second better than Eric.

Feeling no pain now.

She'd won her gold medal.

Last week at the individual medal ceremony, when Becky had gotten her gold, it was her daughter who had stood a little higher on the platform. There was a bigger platform today, room enough for her and Becky and Tyler, all three of them standing higher than the other two teams.

The woman from FEI placed one gold medal around each of their necks. Maggie got hers last, right before the national anthem began to play. She was fine, totally fine, with sharing the gold medal. She knew what she'd just done, with what felt like her career on the line.

She wasn't just sharing the gold medal. She was sharing the Olympic ceremony moment with all the athletes, in all the sports, when the camera came in close to show them mouthing the words to the anthem.

She felt Becky reach over and take her hand. She looked over and saw their faces on the huge screen, saw the tears on her cheeks and the smile shining through them.

Once and for all:

For this one day, she'd been the best horsewoman in the world.

ONE HUNDRED TWENTY-NINE

GRANDMOTHER WAS NEVER ONE to invite a jinx but had booked a private room at L'Atelier de Joël Robuchon, the restaurant connected to her hotel. After we'd done our interviews, we'd gone straight there, changing in her room.

Gus was there, too. And the grooms. Tyler Cullen and his trainer. Charlie Benedict. And Rich Grayson, our alternate, and his trainer. The private room, though, was just off the main room and it didn't take long for us to get very loud, almost ugly American for a classy room like this. Champagne toasts preceded wine flowing in waves as our party turned up the volume. Even Grandmother allowed herself a glass of champagne.

About an hour in, the maître d' asked us to please keep it down, citing complaints from other customers. At this point Charlie Benedict, who spoke fluent French, had a word with the guy.

When Charlie came back to the table, I asked what he'd said.

"Tu peux redevenir calme demain soir," he said.

"I hope that means go screw yourself," Gus said.

"I told him he could have quiet again tomorrow night," Charlie said.

Then Gus was clinking his fork against his glass

and telling everybody to quiet down for one second. When we did, he raised his glass of whiskey and said, "To the Atwood women, for giving me the greatest goddamn week of my whole goddamn life." Right before Mom leaned over and kissed him.

It was about the time when we thought we should at least think about ordering some food to go with the wine that I saw Grandmother smile as she picked her phone up off the table and walked out the door toward the front room.

She came back a couple of minutes later and stopped in the doorway, wearing a much bigger smile now as she was the one asking for everybody's attention.

"These *are* the Olympics, right?" she said.

"Last time I checked," Gus said.

"Well," she said, "I think we might be taking part in the best miracle since that hockey team in Lake Placid."

I thought she was talking about all the medals we'd won and the way we'd won them, and how it might be her turn to make a toast. But she wasn't.

She stepped aside to make way for Dad and Daniel.

ONE HUNDRED THIRTY

WHEN ALL THE YELLING and hugging had subsided and we'd made even more of a spectacle of ourselves, Dad apologized for being late, then asked if somebody could go get him a real drink.

"We finally caught a cab after the medal ceremony," he said.

I turned to Daniel and said, "How did this happen?"

"Your dad should explain," he said. "But your grandmother is right. It is a bit of a miracle."

He looked much thinner than the last time I'd seen him, and tired, and more than a little overwhelmed. But he was Daniel. And was here. All that mattered.

"But you got to see us ride?" I said.

"We barely got there in time," he said. "But, yes. Both of you."

He turned to Mom then.

"See," he said. "You didn't need me after all."

"Now you tell me," she said, and hugged him again.

"You are aware," I said to him, "that you saw me knock down the only rail I knocked down all week."

He shrugged and smiled.

"What do I always tell you?" he said. "Don't get ahead of your horse."

"So I'm still not perfect," I said.

He smiled again. "There's still time."

One of the waiters produced two more chairs. Grandmother walked across the room and told the maître d' that dinner would have to wait. He was not pleased. By now it was his permanent state. The two of them then seemed to go at each other pretty hard until Dad walked over there. As he was talking and smiling, I saw him discreetly hand the guy a fistful of cash.

He came back, still smiling, and sat down next to Daniel and me.

"Money," he said, "the international language of love."

"If *I* pay *you* will you now tell us how you two got here?" I said.

"How we got here," he said, "is that the system finally worked the way it should for guys like Daniel, and not the way it usually does when somebody like me doesn't come over the hill like the First Army."

"He said modestly," Mom said.

"Tell your mother she doesn't need to give me a gold medal," Dad said to me.

Then Dad took us through it. The room got quiet for the first time. He told us he couldn't have done it without the immigration lawyer, Gleason Connors. Said he'd actually tried to hire him when it was all over, but Connors had told him that the Daniels of the world needed him more than Dad's firm did.

"Goddamn, the system really is messed up," Dad said, and drank.

By the time we'd arrived in Paris, Daniel's DACA application had been renewed, even though he was still in detention. Then Dad, being Dad, fast-tracked his way to a meeting with an immigration judge who realized pretty quickly that the whole case, including ICE putting a detainer on Daniel, was total bullshit, including the original criminal case. By then Daniel's new paperwork, minus the criminal case, had been moved along to another judge.

"The second judge was with the United States Something and Something," Dad said.

"Customs and Immigration Service," Daniel said.

Everything happened quickly after that. The removal proceedings on Daniel really were stopped before they began, and Daniel got released.

"That was Friday," he said, "when my baby girl was winning her first gold medal. By then he'd refiled his DACA renewal, adding the part about getting arrested but the charges being dismissed. Which we did. Then the last piece to the puzzle was getting his parole application approved, the one that allowed him to leave the country now that his Dreamer rights had been restored, so he could watch the fabulous Atwood women become the darlings of the Paris Olympics."

He sighed so loudly it sounded like a jet engine.

"Everybody got all that?" he said.

"Barely," Mom said.

"You told me the parole application was the biggest long shot of all," I said.

"Well, it should have been, even for your brilliant father," he said. "Which is why I had to call in a favor, from somebody who's practically besties with the governor of Florida."

"Wait for it," he said.

He paused for dramatic effect.

"Mr. Steve Gorton himself," he said.

"What!" Grandmother yelled, loud enough I was afraid the artwork was going to fall off the wall behind her.

"There is no way you got that jerk to help you!" Mom said, and even slapped Dad on the arm.

I laughed.

"TMZ," I said to him.

"What the hell does that mean?" Grandmother said.

"My daughter will explain it later," Dad said. "Right now, it's time to really get this party started."

Mom said, "He means because *he's* here."

The night only got louder after that. Dinner eventually was served, not that anyone had much interest in it by that time. Daniel wanted to know all about the jump-off for the individual, and about the storm, and about how Sky had managed at the last second not to fall down.

It was near midnight by then. There was one last raucous conversation about whether we might need to have a few more bottles of wine when the door to our room opened and someone shouted, "Hey, is this the gold medal party I heard about?"

Steve Gorton.

Dad leaned over and whispered, "I might have told him where we'd be, just for my own twisted amusement."

"Thanks so much," I whispered back.

Gorton stood there in the middle of the room as if just by showing up he'd immediately turned into our host.

"Well," he said, "it wasn't easy, but we all managed to end up with gold medals in the end."

"We?" Tyler Cullen said to Gus.

Gus lowered his voice for once and said, "A horse's ass to the end."

Mom sighed, breaking a silence that was beyond awkward. Gorton stared at us. We all stared back at him, until the smile had completely disappeared from his face.

Finally, after what felt like an hour had passed,

he said, "I get it, okay? I get it," and turned and walked out.

The noise level shot right back up to where it was before, and maybe beyond, before more bottles of wine appeared, as if by magic. Grandmother then stood up one last time, raised her water glass, and announced that she wanted to make one more toast, which was why nobody noticed Daniel and me as we slipped out.

ONE HUNDRED THIRTY-ONE

DANIEL AND I WALKED over the bridge known as Pont des Arts. We held hands. I had already asked if he wanted to talk about the detention center.

"Not tonight," he said.

He asked if I knew where we were headed.

"Right now," I asked, "or in general?"

"Either one," he said.

"Not a clue," I said.

Then I told him that I knew the damn Louvre was over on this side of the river somewhere. I looked over at him and saw that he was smiling.

"I should have left the party earlier," he said, smiling, "and walked this particular course myself."

"You know they call Paris the City of Lights, right?" I said.

"I believe I might have heard that."

I giggled. I wasn't drunk. The night air had helped out with that. But I was just light-headed enough. In a good way. Knowing it wasn't just the wine.

"Well, I didn't think the lights of Paris were so great when I was coming up on that water jump in a monsoon," I said.

"You got over it," Daniel said.

"My horse got over," I said.

"You two are a good pair," he said. "You take care of each other."

We walked in silence for a few minutes, still holding hands. He was as comfortable with it as he'd ever been. Daniel being Daniel.

"You know," I said finally, "I was thinking that if Dad had gotten you out a few days earlier, you could have been here in time to help train Mom."

"It is like I told her, she didn't need me," he said. "What I really wanted was to make it here in time to watch you."

"Get a rail," I said.

"Get another gold medal," he said.

"Oh," I said, "that old thing."

"By the way?" Daniel said. "Gus thinks it's time for you and Maggie to switch trainers again."

"He might have mentioned that to me, too," I said. "But I couldn't tell if it was the whiskey talking."

"How do you feel about that?"

Now I smiled. "I'll have to think about it," I said. "But you definitely show promise."

He asked if I was getting tired. I told him Sky was the one who ought to be tired after the way she'd carried me, and not just in Paris. Then he asked what I wanted to do when we got back to Florida. I said it was time for me to get back to school.

"But I had one hell of a semester abroad," I said, "just over the last two weeks."

"As I recall," Daniel said, "your original plan was to do that for your mother."

I lifted my shoulders and dropped them.

"Merde arrive," I said. "I learned that one while I was over here."

"Now you are the one who must translate for me," he said.

"Shit happens," I said.

We walked over the Pont Neuf, the old stone bridge that was my favorite by now, the lights of Paris reflecting off the water in a spectacular way this time. We were halfway across when he stopped and kissed me. And if I was going to get kissed like that, I decided pretty quickly, this was the place for it to happen.

"So what do you want to do tomorrow?" Daniel said.

"Ride my horse," I said.

About the Authors

James Patterson is the world's bestselling author. Among his creations are Alex Cross, the Women's Murder Club, Michael Bennett, and Maximum Ride. His #1 bestselling nonfiction includes *Walk in My Combat Boots*, *Filthy Rich*, and his autobiography, *James Patterson by James Patterson*. He has collaborated on novels with Bill Clinton and Dolly Parton and has won an Edgar Award, nine Emmy Awards, and the National Humanities Medal.

Mike Lupica is a veteran sports columnist—spending most of his career with the *New York Daily News*—who is now a member of the National Sports Media Association Hall of Fame. For three decades he was a panelist on ESPN's *The Sports Reporters*. As a novelist, he has written sixteen *New York Times* bestsellers. His daughter has been a competitive rider since the age of ten.

READING GROUP GUIDE
DISCUSSION QUESTIONS

1. Do you think that Becky would've been a stronger rider if her mother and grandmother were less focused on winning and more focused on their relationship as a family?

2. Was it fair to expect Becky to qualify for the Olympics with only a few months of training? How do you think she handled the pressure?

3. Do you think it was wise for Becky to begin a relationship with Daniel?

4. How are the characters' motivations different from one another? What do the motivations tell you about the characters as people?

5. Becky was willing to sell her own horse in order to have another shot at making it to the Olympics. Have you ever wanted something so bad that you were willing to give up everything for it?

6. Maggie's dream to ride in the Olympics was threatened by an accident. Do you think she handled her injury well?

7. What's the most important thing that Becky and Maggie learned from each other? Why?

8. Gorton comes across as very aggressive when it comes to having his horse win in competition. Do you think he's ultimately the bad guy in the story? Or is he a businessman looking out for his investments?

9. Did you root for Becky or Maggie to win the gold?

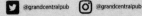

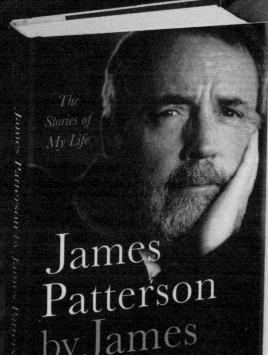

JAMES
PATTERSON
RECOMMENDS

JAMES PATTERSON

THE FIRST LADY

BRENDAN DUBOIS

THE FIRST LADY

The US government is at the forefront of everyone's mind these days and I've become incredibly fascinated by the idea that one secret can bring it all down. What if that secret is a US President's affair that results in a nightmarish outcome?

Sally Grissom, leader of the Presidential Protection Division, is summoned to a private meeting with the President and his chief of staff to discuss the disappearance of the First Lady. What at first seemed an escape to a safe haven turns into a kidnapping when a ransom note arrives along with what could be the First Lady's finger.

It's a race against the clock to collect the evidence that all leads to one troubling question: Could the kidnappers be from inside the White House?

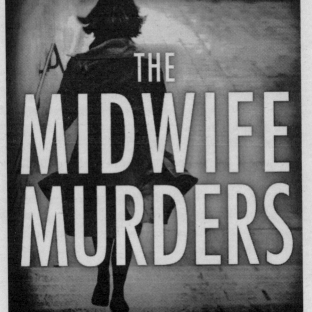

JAMES PATTERSON

THE MIDWIFE MURDERS

and RICHARD DiLALLO

THE MIDWIFE MURDERS

I can't imagine a worse crime than one done against a child. When two kidnappings and a vicious stabbing happen on Lucy Ryuan's watch in a university hospital in Manhattan, her focus abruptly changes. Something has to be done, and senior midwife Lucy is fearless enough to try.

Rumors begin to swirl, with blame falling on everyone from the Russian mafia to an underground adoption network. Fierce single mom Lucy teams up with a skeptical NYPD detective, but I've given her a case where the truth is far more twisted than Lucy could ever have imagined.

JAMES PATTERSON
J.D. BARKER
ONE KISS
AND
YOU'RE DEAD
DEATH OF THE
BLACK WIDOW

DEATH OF THE BLACK WIDOW

A twenty-year-old woman murders her kidnapper with a competence so impeccable that Detroit PD officer Walter O'Brien is taken aback. What Officer O'Brien doesn't know is that this young woman has a knack for ending the lives of her lovers—and getting away with it. Time after time, she navigates her way out of police custody, forcing the authorities to throw up their hands. When Officer O'Brien is later promoted to detective, he becomes even more fixated on uncovering the truth behind that young woman's carnivorous ways. Soon he realizes that murder does not stand alone as a peculiar case.

JAMES PATTERSON

JUROR #3

and NANCY ALLEN

JUROR #3

In the deep south of Mississippi, Ruby Bozarth is a newcomer, both to Rosedale and to the bar. And now she's tapped as a defense counsel in a racially charged felony. The murder of a woman from an old family has Rosedale's upper crust howling for blood, and the prosecutor is counting on Ruby's inexperience to help him deliver a swift conviction.

Ruby is determined to build a defense that sticks for her college football star client. Looking for help in unexpected quarters, her case is rattled as news of a second murder breaks. As intertwining investigations unfold, no one can be trusted, especially the twelve men and women on the jury. They may be hiding the most incendiary secret of all.

For a complete list of books by

JAMES PATTERSON

VISIT
JamesPatterson.com

 Follow James Patterson on Facebook
@JamesPatterson

 Follow James Patterson on Twitter
@JP_Books

 Follow James Patterson on Instagram
@jamespattersonbooks